# Edna AND John

*In loving memory*

# Irene Mazer Shein

(October 15, 1925–June 19, 1977)

*Many women have done valorously,*
*but you excel them all.*

Proverbs 31:29

# Edna AND John

## A Romance of Idaho Flat

### ABIGAIL SCOTT DUNIWAY

#### EDITED WITH AN AFTERWORD BY DEBRA SHEIN

Washington State University Press
Pullman, Washington

## Washington
## State University

Washington State University Press
P.O. Box 645910
Pullman, Washington 99164-5910
phone: 800-354-7360
fax: 509-335-8568
e-mail: wsupress@wsu.edu
website: www.publications.wsu.edu/wsupress
© 2000 by the Board of Regents of Washington State University
All rights reserved
First printing 2000

*Library of Congress Cataloging-in-Publication Data*

Duniway, Abigail Scott, 1834–1915.
    Edna and John : a romance of Idaho Flat / Abigail Scott Duniway ; edited
with an afterword by Debra Shein.
        p. cm.
    Includes bibliographical references.
    ISBN 0-87422-188-9 (paperback)
    1. Women's rights—Idaho—Fiction. 2. Women pioneers—Idaho—
Fiction. 3. Married women—Idaho—Fiction. I. Shein, Debra, date II. Title

PS1558.D5 E36 2000
813'.4—dc21

                                                                99-053703

# TABLE & CONTENTS

*Woman's degraded, helpless position is the weak point of our institutions today—a disturbing force everywhere, severing family ties, filling our asylums with the deaf, the dumb, the blind, our prisons with criminals, our cities with drunkenness and prostitution, our homes with disease and death.*

—National Centennial Equal Rights Protest, 1876

ABOUT

# ABIGAIL SCOTT DUNIWAY

*The following overview of the life of Abigail Scott Duniway has been distilled from an intensive study of her writings, including letters, scrapbooks, the newspapers she edited, and other published works. It is particularly indebted to her autobiography,* Path Breaking. *Ruth Moynihan's excellent biography,* Rebel for Rights, *has provided further insight. For additional sources on Abigail Scott Duniway, and a list of her published works, please refer to the "Selected Bibliography" at the back of this volume.*

I N AN ERA WHEN WOMEN WERE, in the words of Susan B. Anthony, "political slaves," Abigail Scott Duniway (1834–1915) accomplished what others dared not even dream. Her simple beginnings as an Illinois farm girl would seem to place her in a league with other American heroes, such as fellow Illinoisan Abraham Lincoln, until we realize that Lincoln's quest was by far the less remarkable; the apparatus of the American Dream has long included the expectation that men could and would rise above their humble origins while placing enslaving obstacles in the paths of women with similar hopes. But despite deterrents her male counterparts never faced, 17-year-old Abigail Jane ("Jenny") Scott joined her family on their 1852 trek overland to Oregon, embarking on a course that would eventually establish her as one of the best-known women in the Pacific Northwest: a noted author and publisher, and a nationally famed champion of women's rights.

As the journey began, Jenny was appointed family scribe by her father, John Tucker Scott (1809–80), and recorded the history of their migration—made on foot, by horseback, and in an ox-drawn wagon—in what she titled her "Journal of a Trip to Oregon." It is an often-eloquent diary filled with joy and wonder at the magnificent landscapes traversed, and with heartfelt sorrow. The hardships endured on the trail by the Scott party were proverbial. There were deaths from disease and drowning. Cholera was epidemic that year. Before the Scotts could reach Oregon, Abigail's mother (Anne Roelofson Scott, 1811–52), and her youngest brother, Willie, perished.

After their arrival in Oregon, John Tucker Scott became the manager of a temperance house (a restaurant/hotel of sorts that did not sell hard liquor), and Abigail and her siblings—Mary Frances, Margaret Ann, Harvey Whitefield, Catherine Amanda, Harriet Louisa, John Henry, and Sarah Maria—pitched in to help.[1] Her early experience as restaurateur/hotelier adds realism to and is reflected in the entrepreneurial pursuits of several of Duniway's fictional heroines, including Edna of *Edna and John.*

After a short while in the family business, Abigail decided to set out on her own, securing a position teaching school, though she had very little formal education. She  taught until the following year (1853), when she married a prospective farmer, Benjamin Charles Duniway (1830–96). The Oregon Donation Land Act of 1850 allowed each married partner to claim 320 acres (later reduced to 160 acres apiece), and for a time it was rumored that the wife's portion could only be obtained if the couple married before the end of 1853. As a result, the Scott girls were fairly inundated with suitors. Abigail's older sister, Mary Frances (Fanny), married Amos Cook in 1853, shortly after Abigail's marriage to Ben. Margaret married George Fearnside in April of 1854 at the age of 17. Harriet became the youngest Scott girl to marry when she wed William McCord in 1856 at the age of 15. Catherine (Kate) was married in 1857 at 17, and Sarah Maria, much younger (born in 1847), did not marry until 1869.

The Duniways occupied two homesteads. The first was in an area in Clackamas County, south of Oregon City, that Abigail nicknamed Hardscrabble, and the second, located in Yamhill County, was dubbed Sunny Hillside. By 1859 three children had been born—Clara Belle (1854–86), Willis Scott (1856–1913), and Hubert Ray (1859–1938).

Abigail's farm life was full of drudgery. She labored long and hard to keep up with the never-ceasing tasks of a farm wife in an era with little mechanization. She later contended that such arduous work led many women to early graves, but somehow, in the interval in which she was preparing for Hubert's birth, she managed to find time to complete her first novel, *Captain Gray's Company, or Crossing the Plains and Living in Oregon.* Published in April 1859, it was the first commercially printed novel in Oregon and one of Oregon's first five literary books.[2] It was  Duniway's first fictionalized version of the Scotts' 1852 migration to Oregon, though by no means her best work. Her later serialized novels are stylistically superior and so much more sophisticated, they almost seem to have come from a different pen.

Despite the author being twenty-five at the time it was published, it would be kindest to look at *Captain Gray's Company* as a work of juvenilia. And yet it was a story that the author felt compelled to write, and it marks her entry into the larger world of affairs beyond that circumscribed by hearthstone and barn. Duniway's experiences along the Oregon Trail were formative ones that would surface time and again in her many serialized novels and would receive a final treatment in 1905 in another published novel, *From the West to the West* (i.e., from Illinois to Oregon).

The Duniways did not prosper as farmers, and in the spring of 1862, Ben left to try his luck in the Idaho mines. Abigail returned to teaching school, continuing to manage the farm and raise her children at the same time. But Ben was less successful as a miner than as a farmer, and returned in the fall. Because of debts that he had incurred—principally from cosigning on a loan for a friend, against Abigail's advice—Sunny Hillside was sold, and the Duniways moved to a house in Lafayette. Abigail pursued her career as a teacher, and Ben took a job as a teamster. However, soon thereafter Ben was run over by a wagon pulled by a team of runaway horses, resulting in a severe back injury that permanently disabled him. Although he would work as he was able and contribute to the family's support, Abigail later claimed in her autobiography, *Path Breaking,* that the accident threw "the financial, as well as domestic, responsibility of our family upon my almost unaided self."[3]

In 1865 the Duniway family moved to Albany, Oregon, where they hoped to recoup their fortunes. Abigail opened a school, but soon chose to try her hand at business instead. In 1866 she established a millinery store that "flourished reasonably well in a financial way."[4] According to her own account, Abigail's business dealings brought her into contact with so many women suffering from the effects of unjust laws and customary degradation that she felt compelled to begin her public campaign for equal rights. In 1871 she volunteered to represent Oregon at a woman's suffrage convention in San Francisco. There she met some of the most passionate leaders of the woman's movement, and underwent a radical transformation.

After arriving home, Duniway decided to move to Portland, Oregon, where she began her career as a publisher. By this time, her family included its final complement of six children; Wilkie Collins (1861–1927), Clyde Augustus (1866–1944), and Ralph Roelofson (1869–1920) had been born after Hubert's birth in 1859. However, motherhood did not dissuade her from establishing the *New Northwest*, a weekly newspaper that proclaimed on its masthead to be "devoted to the interests of humanity, independent in politics and religion, alive to all live issues and thoroughly radical in opposing and exposing the wrongs of the masses." Her career as a vocal and indomitable proponent of equal rights had begun in earnest.

The *New Northwest* remained in publication until 1887. During its sixteen years, the paper's editor-in-chief rose to prominence as one of the best-known women in America. She crisscrossed the continent many times to lecture and attend woman's congresses in far-away cities, retracing quickly by railroad the route she had arduously traversed on foot and by wagon in 1852. Her fiery oratory made her a much-sought-after speaker in meetings coast to coast, and she served as one of the several national vice-presidents of the NWSA (National Woman Suffrage Association), headed by her close friend and admired associate, Susan B. Anthony. Duniway also spent many weeks and months on the road closer to home, travelling the Pacific Northwest (predominantly Oregon, Washington, and Idaho, the states of the old Oregon Country, which she termed her "chosen bailiwick") by "river, rail,

Abigail Scott Duniway, editor of the *New Northwest,*
holding first edition —May 5, 1871.

stage, and buckboard," while she canvassed for the *New Northwest*, addressed public meetings, and raised support for women's rights.

The *New Northwest* was a family affair. At home in Portland, Abigail's children assisted in publishing the periodical, learning skills that would help in their later careers. For a time, her sister Kate (Catherine Coburn Scott) served as associate editor. She later became an editor with the Portland *Oregonian,* whose chief was brother Harvey Scott. Over the years, Abigail's relationship with Harvey was tempestuous. At times, he adamantly opposed the equal suffrage initiatives she advocated. He was very influential in the delay of woman's suffrage legislation because of his enormous clout as director of Oregon's biggest newspaper.[5]

The pages of the *New Northwest* were home to many columns written by Duniway. Seventeen of Abigail's serialized novels were published in this weekly, as was a serialized version of the earlier-published *Captain Gray's Company*. When Abigail was away from home, she regularly sent in her "Editorial Correspondence." These columns consisted of an ongoing narrative of her travels campaigning for equal rights and comprise some of her finest literary work.

Duniway's novels, which are entertaining, highly melodramatic fare in the spirit of the times, can perhaps best be termed Women's Westerns. These action-packed narratives, which could play quite well upon the stage, form a vital record of what life in the old West was like from the perspective of an ardent feminist. They contrast sharply with the many male-authored Westerns that typically depict women of the West as clinging vines in need of rescue by men. Although her stories employ many of the same melodramatic conventions, the situations are reversed—strong women rescue their menfolk from trouble and law enforcers are generally villains because they enforce legislation that robs women of their rights.

Duniway's Westerns are more intellectual and realistic than most, providing a broader view of the many elements that constituted the new society being formed in the West—elements that combined to make these states a haven for equal rights activists. Woman suffrage can rightly be said to be a Western institution; all of the states in which women won full voting rights in advance of the Nineteenth Amendment to the U.S. Constitution, enacted in 1920, are located in this region. Eastern states lagged far behind. Abigail Scott Duniway's novels, which depicted the actual conditions that plagued women and suggested new courses of action that would remedy the injustices she described, were instrumental in bringing about many of the early victories in the West.[6]

In 1886 Duniway suffered a sharp blow when her only daughter, Clara, died from tuberculosis. At this time, Abigail had fallen out with a number of the leaders of the woman's movement because of her protemperance, antiprohibition stance regarding alcohol. The Women's Christian Temperance Union (WCTU) was a rising force, gathering support for the nationwide prohibition of alcohol (eventually leading to the passage of the Twentieth Amendment). Duniway foresaw that prohibition would be ineffectual, but, more importantly, she was keenly aware that agitation by women for prohibition would delay gaining voting rights, which had to be granted by men. Many powerful men had vested interests in alcohol-related businesses, or did not desire any infringement on their own rights to drink.

Duniway was vociferous in her denouncement of the prohibitionist element among woman's movement activists. Her detractors claimed that she had "sold out to alcohol" and they made it difficult for her to continue operating in the usual way. These circumstances, as well as her bereavement over Clara's early death, seem to have made Abigail amenable to a decision to sell out of the newspaper business and invest in ranch property in Idaho's Lost River Valley, where mining interest was high and irrigation was bringing agriculture to lands formerly thought of as unsuitable for such pursuits.

In 1887 Abigail moved to their new property, but soon realized that she could not remain there. Not only were the prospects for prosperity slim, but she felt out of her element on a remote ranch, accustomed as she was to being in the public and political limelight. Also, she was unhappy in her marriage. For years she had regretted her early, hasty marriage to Ben, realizing they were mismated. She might have considered divorce, but since it was considered scandalous, she knew that any such action would be used by her detractors to destroy her credibility and influence in the woman's movement. With her sons Willis and Wilkie choosing to remain in Idaho with Ben, and her younger sons Clyde and Ralph soon leaving for Eastern universities, Abigail chose to separate from her husband and return to Oregon. This estrangement would last, except for occasional visits back and forth between Oregon and Idaho, until Ben returned to Portland shortly before his death in 1896.

In the early 1890s, Duniway began publishing another periodical, the *Coming Century*, but was unable to obtain sufficient financial backing to continue. Then, in 1895 she undertook the editorship of a new weekly, the *Pacific Empire*, published by Portland entrepreneur Frances Gotshall. It was influential but never assumed anywhere near the proportions of the *New Northwest*. However, in the short time she was associated with the *Pacific Empire*, Duniway published the last three of her serialized novels, including her final vision, a utopian dream (*'Bijah's Surprises*, revised in 1912 as *Margaret Rudson*). In 1897, frustrated because the publisher did not have the resources to turn the paper into the expansive journal Duniway wanted it to become, Abigail resigned.

After this last venture in journalism, Duniway, by then 63, was in a sense retired, although by no means inactive. She continued to lecture, head the Oregon State Equal Suffrage Association, campaign for equal rights, and write. She revised several of her serialized novels and submitted them to book publishers in the East, but with no resulting success. There has long been an East-West schism on the American literary scene, and Western writing, as well as women's writing, has been devalued by those considering themselves the elite. In addition, literary tastes were changing. Duniway's style belonged more to the era just past than to the modernist whirlwind that scoured the beginning of the twentieth century.

And yet, Abigail did achieve remarkable success in the tasks to which she most ardently devoted herself. By the time of her death at eighty in 1915, this Mother of Woman Suffrage in the Pacific Northwest had seen women win full voting rights in all the states of her "bailiwick"—in Idaho (1896), in Washington (1910), and in Oregon (1912). Duniway wrote Oregon's Equal Suffrage Proclamation in her own hand at the behest of governor Oswald West, and was the first woman in the state to register to vote.

In 1905, when Portland celebrated the Lewis and Clark Centennial, Duniway was hailed as the quintessential "pioneer mother."[7] Today this expression summons a picture of a tired woman in a sunbonnet with children on her knees and oxen and wagon in the background. But for Abigail Scott Duniway, such a scene only marked the beginning of a much broader career. The term "pioneer mother" takes on new meaning when we realize that it was Duniway who was once reputed to best fulfill the role.

The lives of Abigail Scott Duniway and her relentless, visionary co-workers in the equal suffrage movement bridged the gap between the oppressed, often meek-and-mild women of their mothers' generation, and the bold and modern "New Woman" of the turn of the twentieth century. Fueled by their wrath at a government that classed all women with "idiots, insane persons and criminals" in denying them the vote, women like Duniway dared to break the mold and fight for their rights. Their contributions should not be forgotten nor underrated.

At the time Abigail began her career, women's civil disabilities extended far beyond mere lack of the vote. The situation was terrible for those who were single, yet even crueler for married women, who had no legal existence apart from their husbands. They could not sign contracts, had no title to their own earnings, no right to property, nor any claim to their children in case of separation or divorce. From the perspective of these disadvantages, the accomplishments of leaders in the vanguard of the woman's movement— including Susan B. Anthony, Elizabeth Cady Stanton, and Abigail Scott Duniway—are even more remarkable.

By 1912, when Oregon issued its Equal Suffrage Proclamation, Duniway had spent over forty years directing her efforts towards alleviating women's civil disabilities. She had demanded the right to engage in any and all occupations, the right to receive equal pay for equal work, and the right to live free from abuse. Finally, in 1920, the Nineteenth Amendment was ratified, and women across the nation won the right to vote. However, this was only a partial victory. After this momentous event, the woman's rights movement lost momentum and was not revived in force until the 1960s. Nearly a century later American women are still confronting some of the same inequities that Duniway strove to eradicate. Women in other parts of the globe fare much worse. In remembering Abigail Scott Duniway, we celebrate her triumphs, but also note the issues yet unresolved. As we enter the next *Coming Century*, we can give this pioneer mother no more fitting memorial than to read the lively stories she wrote—and reflect.

# NOTES

1. Ruth Barnes Moynihan, *Rebel for Rights: Abigail Scott Duniway* (New Haven: Yale University Press, 1983), 44–45.
2. Alfred Powers, *History of Oregon Literature* (Portland: Metropolitan Press, 1935), 192–220.
3. Abigail Scott Duniway, *Path Breaking: An Autobiographical History of the Equal Suffrage Movement in Pacific Coast States,* 2d ed. (Portland: James, Kerns, & Abbot, 1914; Reprint, New York: Shocken, 1971), 16.
4. Ibid., 21.
5. Lauren Kessler, "A Siege of the Citadels: The Search for a Public Forum for the Ideas of Oregon Woman Suffrage," *Oregon Historical Quarterly* 84 (1983): 117–50.
6. T.A. Larson, "Dolls, Vassals, and Drudges—Pioneer Women in the West," *Western Historical Quarterly* 3 (1972): 1–16.
7. *Woman's Tribune* (Portland; Washington, DC), October 28, 1905, "Abigail Scott Duniway Day," 1. The epithet "pioneer mother" was presented by the president of the exposition held in Portland to commemorate the Lewis and Clark centennial. Abigail was the only woman honored with her own day at the celebration.

# PREFACE

## ABIGAIL SCOTT DUNIWAY'S IDAHO TRILOGY

Abigail Scott Duniway's trilogy of Idaho novels—*Edna and John* (1876), *Blanche LeClerq* (1886), and *Margaret Rudson* (1896)—compose an exciting part of the state's literary record, and add a unique dimension to the understanding of the development of the Pacific Northwest as a region. Specifically, they chronicle how the women of Idaho achieved increasing political and social equity in degrees corresponding to other historical events in the development of the state. Also, using the circumstances particular to Idaho as a model, insight can be gained into similar processes experienced in adjoining states that led to the enactment of women's rights legislation in this region much earlier than in the rest of the nation. Although Duniway resided chiefly in Portland, Oregon, her far-reaching influence, extensive subject matter, and the varied settings of her novels (which take place in many locales throughout the Northwest) dictate that her writings be viewed as major contributions to the canons of Oregon, Washington, and Idaho.

The rediscovery of the Duniway trilogy, a major addition to the somewhat slim ranks of early Idaho literature, adds significantly to our understanding of Idaho in its formative years, particularly with respect to its importance as one of the earliest locations in which women won the right to vote. When equal suffrage legislation passed in Idaho in 1896, only three other states—Wyoming, Colorado, and Utah, all located in the Rocky Mountain West—had already enacted such laws. This region figured powerfully in the move to legislate equal rights for women. Duniway's novels not only chronicled the significant progress achieved in the West, but helped shape that progress. In their own time, her stories depicted the injustice and hardships faced by women living under the old laws imported from the East, and also generated enthusiasm for change. It is reasonable to believe that Duniway's writings played a meaningful role in the efforts to transform the West into a bastion of hope for women all over the nation.

The most notable woman writer to have made Idaho her home in the nineteenth century, and heretofore included in the state's canon, was Mary Hallock Foote (1847–1938), who spent her early years in New York and her later life in California. Her novels, short stories, and drawings reveal key facts about women's presence in the mining West, but they are written from the perspective of a woman who associated mainly with society's upper classes, and do far less to reveal issues affecting the lives of most women than do Abigail Scott Duniway's. The novels authored by Duniway examine life in territorial Idaho from the perspective of a devoted equal rights activist; her heroines are all working women fulfilling often unexpected roles, and serve well to counterbalance images of the nineteenth-century West created by Frederick Remington, Owen Wister, Zane Grey, etc. Such male myths, or fantasies, never did exist in reality; life in this region was far more complex than they portrayed. Duniway's narratives include many elements that the previously better-known Westerns omit.

Collectively, *Edna and John, Blanche LeClerq,* and *Margaret Rudson* present the several phases of Idaho's history in the territorial era. They reveal how the successive stages of this history can be related to the stages in the transformation of the proverbial, sunbonneted pioneer woman to the pioneer New Woman of the turn of the twentieth century.

*Edna and John*, set in the Boise Basin in the early 1860s, depicts Idaho's early gold rush days, the placer mining era that led to Idaho becoming a territory. The heroine, Edna, migrates West from Missouri by covered wagon. Her experiences of life-in-the-raw in Idaho's mining camps destroy her delusions regarding women's "honored" status, and open her eyes to opportunities for economic success. In the newly established territory of Idaho, her services as a fledgling restaurateur and hotel owner are in high demand. Nevertheless, her hopes are repeatedly dashed by a restrictive legal system that allows her indigent husband, John, to steal her profits. Even after his death, and her remarriage to Shields, equity is not completely achieved. The epilogue explains that he, a lawyer, has become "a shining light in the political firmament." However, Edna, with no professional education and without a vote, must struggle to the best of her ability (much like Duniway) as a zealous worker for "woman's emancipation from her degraded and helpless political and financial condition," without equivalent distinction.

In *Blanche LeClerq*, set in the 1880s in the Wood River district (near present-day Sun Valley), the author illustrates the later lead-silver-gold lode mining (or hard rock mining) boom that led to statehood. Presented here is a second stage of development, a transitional phase in both heroines and territorial conditions. Mining has become industrialized, and transportation networks have linked Idaho to the East; the booming economy has readied the territory for statehood in the near future.

Although the novel is named for its heroine, Blanche, arguably her foster-mother, Madam La Fontaine, an actress turned mining magnate, is the real heroine of the story. Forsaken after a youthful marriage to a man who later denied they had ever been truly married, La Fontaine makes the most of her natural resources and, like Edna, finds her niche (here, as the organizing force of a troupe of actors) in a developing area desperate for diversions. However, just as the territorial opportunities had been expanded by the introduction of modern mining technology in recent years, making the "Mother Mine" of La Fontaine a large-scale operation the like of which

Idaho Flat had never seen, she found that she was able to take advantage of prevailing conditions to amass a personal fortune much larger than Edna's. Indeed, her wealth becomes great enough to allow her to become a venture capitalist and finance a large-scale mining operation of her own. When she marries a titled count in the denouement, she does so boldly because she is a self-fashioned woman whose very American-style entrepreneurship has allowed her to meet him on equal terms, despite his hereditary fortune and titled line—just as, with the endowment of statehood, Idaho will meet the older states with longer membership in the union.

Although *Blanche LeClerq* has a happy resolution, Duniway clearly portrays Madam La Fontaine as having endured much hardship in life. Because of biased laws favoring men over women and the added encumbrance of a double standard branding "discarded" women such as herself, she overcame obstacles greater than a man would find in a similar situation. For example, she was humiliated because of prevailing assumptions held about women in the theatrical profession, and was obligated to live apart from her cherished only son.

Finally, in *Margaret Rudson*, which takes place in the 1890s near Mackay in the Lost River Valley, emerges the "New Woman of the New West" (Duniway's title for her heroine Margaret Rudson). Margaret is an enfranchised woman, directing an irrigation project designed to pave the way to a flourishing agricultural future. Here Duniway presents a new phenomenon indeed. Although as a young child Margaret experienced brutal conditions because her mother was entrapped by an abusive man who took advantage of all the prerogatives that sexist laws and double standards offered him, she was miraculously freed from these circumstances early in life. (This circumstance allegorically parallels the boon given to all girls of Idaho in that era because of progressively changing laws and attitudes). With the acquisition of an inherited fortune and the opportunity to live in a decade affording greater educational opportunities for women, Margaret grew to maturity fully equipped to take her place as a "mover and shaker" in the world formerly reserved for men. She does not even consider getting married until equal suffrage legislation is passed to ensure that, by marriage, she will not lose all her rights.

The passage of the Idaho state constitutional amendment granting women the right to vote, occurring six years after its entrance into the Union, celebrates women's true emancipation from ancient custom and enslaving laws. This emancipation, however, is portrayed more as a joining than as a severing of bonds. As Idaho has been inducted into the union, so Margaret is joined to her Silas, and women come to share in the rights held by men from which they were earlier excluded. Together, they look forward to a future whose brightness is limited only by their willingness to work toward their common goals. And, just as Idaho is moving from a mining economy toward an agricultural one, the New Woman and New Man of the New West, at the head of the new utopian community of Utilitaria, will unite to "find something more useful than gold awaiting their future operations in agriculture." Nevertheless, the novel emphasizes that the new state's proudest claim to fame will *not* be its agriculture. Rather, it is the "fiat" that, in 1896, went forth, "proclaiming that the women of all the mighty Rocky Mountain states would soon be clothed with the insignia of freedom," which is the real reason that on the day of Idaho's statehood "on the mountaintops of the broad, free, breezy west . . . the sun was shining."

## READING *EDNA AND JOHN*

Dating the events in *Edna and John* poses something of a problem. No actual dates are given at any time in the story, and the author is purposefully vague in establishing exact place, claiming the need "to prevent the unpleasant results of the possible identification of the real actors," and warning the reader "to studiously avoid being too inquisitive or critical about localities, identities, or even facts" on the basis that her aim in writing is to "lay facts before you; facts as parables; facts as lessons; facts as they are in the every-day life of more than one woman who pursues the allotted rounds of a life of heroic effort, combining the heroism of a general with the wisdom of a statesman, the toil of a bondwoman with the self-abnegation of a martyr, and the conscientiousness of a Christian with the lie-living existence of a hypocrite" (Chapter IX).

However, we do know that in 1876 Duniway embarked on an extended journey to the East, to meet with other woman's movement leaders who were protesting the celebration of the national centennial on the basis that only "one-half the people" were free. At the special invitation of Susan B. Anthony, she left Oregon in June, and did not return until ten months later. Funding was still insufficient at the outset of the trip, so Duniway scheduled lecture stops along the way to help finance her expedition. These events are covered in greater detail in the *Afterword* following the novel.

While thus engaged en route, Duniway visited the towns of Idaho City and Placerville in the Boise Basin area (to the north of the city of Boise), as well as Silver City in the Owyhees (to the south). As she describes these regions in her "Editorial Correspondence," they sound suspiciously like the environs of "Idaho Flat."[1] In fact, on July 28 the *New Northwest* reported that "A New Serial Story" would commence shortly, "the principal incidents of which she [Duniway] doubtless collected during her recent visit to Idaho." In *Edna and John*, she writes that "A recent mining excitement had broken out among the men who were digging for gold in myriads in another part of the Territory, and the crowd was now assembled" at the location where the story takes place (Chapter IX). If this is indeed the Boise Basin area, then the year must be 1863, because gold had been discovered in that region in late summer of 1862, and miners thronged there from the earlier Florence and Clearwater strikes further north.[2] Evidence for this geographic location is further substantiated by the description of the land traversed and the length of time taken for John Smith and Jim Young to reach Lewiston in Chapter XIX, as well as by the suggested proximity of the LaSelles' later home in Boise.

Idaho gold fields, early 1860s.

There is some evidence to suggest that Idaho Flat might in fact be Idaho City (or should be, if this were not a parable). At the beginning of Chapter XXIII, we read that "The Territory of Idaho had recently been judicially districted, and Circuit Court was now to hold its opening session in Idaho Flat." This division in actuality took place in 1863, and court was first held in the various districts in February through March of 1864 (Hailey 293). In the second judicial district, comprised of the County of Boise, court was scheduled to be held at Idaho City on the second Monday of February, but from an entry in the *Boise News* on February 27, 1864, we learn that "The first term of the district court in and for Boise County convened here last Tuesday, the 23rd inst., Hon. Samuel C. Parks presiding. This county having more population at that time than the balance of the territory, and never having had a term of court held in the county, there was a large number of civil and criminal cases on the docket."[3] Twenty-three attorneys previously admitted in other states and territories were enrolled as members of the bar. This would place Edna's divorce trial less than one year after her taking up residence in Idaho (if she arrived during the summer of 1863), even though the events of the story suggest that two, or possibly even three years have transpired.

Even though historical facts suggest a relationship between Idaho City and Idaho Flat, it should be noted that the terrain described in *Edna and John* makes a complete correspondence impossible. Idaho City is *not* the "rocky gulch" described in Chapter IX; it is *really* built on a flat. Actually, it has the flattest town site of any of the Idahoan mining camps of this era, and, ironically, this argues for identifying Idaho Flat with Idaho City, despite the fact that the author describes an entirely different sort of terrain. However, the geographical features of the fictional, steep-sided Idaho Flat are much closer to those of Silver City in the Owyhee mountains on the south side of the Snake River plain, belonging to a region that experienced a brief flurry of placer mining beginning in 1863 followed by a longer era of quartz mining, which (despite boom/bust cycles) sustained Silver City as a thriving community many years into the twentieth century. It was not one of the towns designated as a site for Circuit Court in 1863, nor could it have been, for Owyhee County in which it is situated was not created until 1864, and Silver City was not named county seat until 1866. Today it is a ghost town, frequented by weekenders and summer residents who maintain the antique cabins that still dot the hillsides, many of which have been handed down in families for several generations.

The topography of Duniway's Idaho Flat may also have been suggested by the terrain traversed by her stagecoach trip over the narrow switchback road between Idaho City and Placerville (which has a somewhat more gulch-like setting). In any case, Duniway desired that her readers not investigate facts too closely, not only because accuracy was irrelevant to her purposes, but because she was writing a romance and not an historical novel. She obviously felt entitled to artistic license.

The dates of the narrative cannot be exactly pinpointed and are open to conjecture. Duniway might have imagined Edna and John arriving in Idaho in 1862 because her own husband, Ben, had left to seek his fortune in the Salmon River mines of Idaho that year. Ben returned home, unsuccessful, from Florence (then a boom town but now vanished) and probably detailed his experiences to Abigail. This would have informed her about mining conditions in that era, because she herself didn't visit the region until years later.

There are at least two major chronological inconsistencies in *Edna and John*. One may be explained by surmising that Duniway wove into her narrative conditions she remembered from her own overland journey in 1852 (when for the first time she witnessed slavery practiced as they passed through Missouri). If the early 1860s dating is correct, the events take place during the Civil War, and yet, the description of conditions in Edna and John's Missouri homeland suggests this to be a pre-Civil War narrative. When Aunt Judy connives with Sambo in Chapter IV to deliver to Edna certain items belonging to her (but denied her by her father because of her elopement), it is implied that Sambo is a slave. This might indeed have been the case if the events occurred any time before September 22, 1862, when the Emancipation Proclamation was issued, or even before the enactment of the Thirteenth Amendment prohibiting slavery; nevertheless we are given no hint of the turmoil of the Civil War.

Sambo[4] is portrayed as "one of the farm servants that before the late 'unpleasantness' abounded as chattel property throughout the South," and Aunt Judy laments that "Like married women they are servants without wages" (Chapter IV). The discrepancy in chronology can be overlooked, however, if Duniway is allowed the generous license normally granted to the romancer, or if her exhortation not to be too inquisitive is followed and if one reads "facts as parables; facts as lessons" (Chapter IX). In light of the latter, Sambo's inclusion in the narrative is used by Duniway to juxtapose the character of the typical slave against the character of the typical married woman in order to emphasize the slave-like condition of married women: they were subject to labor without compensation, to degrading subjugation, and often resorted to stealthy opportunism as a means of self-protection.

The other primary chronological inconsistency in the novel lies in the apparent fact that Sue Randolph's daughter, Blossom, after being restored to her mother in Chapter XX, remembers events previous to her parents' separation. This would be impossible without a lengthy lapse in time not accounted for in the story, because Blossom would have been a mere infant when parted from her mother. Perhaps the author meant to imply that several seasons had passed in Idaho Flat beyond those detailed, during which Edna continues to suffer and John continues his descent into depravity. This would also explain the comment in Chapter XXII that the cross-country journey taken by Edna's mother, Susan, was "very different" than the one taken by Edna "years before."

However, as these issues are relatively minor to an understanding of the novel, there should be no hesitation to date its events to the early 1860s. This would also be consistent with the status of the situation described in the epilogue (Chapter XXVI). If the concluding paragraphs can be said to depict life in what was then the present—i.e., 1877—then a little over ten years would have elapsed since Edna's second marriage to Mr. Shields in 1865 (a year after John's suicide, which was the year of the trial in, assumedly, 1864). In this time, "sons and daughters" could have been born to the Shields, and Idaho and her brother (Edna's children from her marriage to John) might still be in the process of "being educated under their mother's personal supervision."

It should be noted that the inconsistencies discussed above that complicate the reader's task are typical of nineteenth-century serialized novels, whether authored by Duniway or Dickens. When subsequent chapters of a story are written and published either weekly or monthly, the complicated plots that sometimes seem too full of action or else poorly connected, result from evolution over time. As Julia Prewitt Brown states in *A Reader's Guide to the Nineteenth-Century English Novel,* "Serialized novels are a little like long-cooking stews; all the ingredients (or all the main characters and conflicts) are there in the beginning, but they thicken and change in consistency over time, or over the extended length of the serial."[5] In the case of *Edna and John,* it is remarkable that the novel is as consistent as it is, considering the hasty composition of its chapters amidst Duniway's ten-month-long, harum-scarum trip across the continent and back. At times, she even wrote chapters without having previous ones on hand (having sent them to Oregon for publication without retaining copies).

To fully appreciate any novel originally published in serialized form, one must attempt to imagine it from the point of view of its contemporary readers. Each chapter constitutes its own mini-story. The plethora of exciting events found in successive chapters seem implausible if read one after the other, but appear more realistic when read at intervals. The advantages of building a long-standing relationship between readers and her novel and its characters worked to further Duniway's aim of raising the collective consciousness of her audience regarding the true nature of women's oppressed situation, and inciting them to action. According to Brown, when readers engaged such novels simultaneously, they "created a common culture."[6] Forging such a bond was a necessary precondition for uniting residents of sparsely populated Idaho behind a drive for women's rights.

According to Linda K. Hughes and Michael Lund in *The Victorian Serial,* reading novels chapter by chapter over a period of many months was a course that "was intertwined with a vision of life no longer shared by the dominant literary culture of the twentieth century."[7] The medium *was* the message, and showed how life was a continuous process. One could see how characters were built and progressed over time, and thereby more easily imagine that such fictional changes for the better could be instituted in real life. Readers had time to become intimately acquainted with the lives of the characters in the serials they were reading, little by little, just like becoming acquainted with people in real life. They were drawn more closely into the characters' joys and sorrows, much like present-day soap opera aficionados. However, because Duniway's novels are exemplary, intended to teach lessons like parables, the empathy generated in the reader was designed to induce them to action. Hughes and Lund note that at the beginning of the twentieth century a new modernist aesthetic in literature, which elevated "the whole over the part," and created "doubts about the integrity or identity of the individual," arose and supplanted the serialized form.[8] They discuss that without the "localized framework" showing that humans are "individuals cooperating to build over time a larger whole," literature in the modernist tradition is very ineffectual at creating community, or spurring readers to action. The literary tradition that Duniway worked within was eminently suitable for her purposes.

The modern reader will no doubt read *Edna and John* in a far shorter period than the original nine months of its publication. Nevertheless, to preserve a sense of the experience of its earliest readers, each chapter is headed by its publication date. Nine times, while Duniway was on her sojourn to the East, the promised installment did not arrive in Portland in time for publication, and readers' expectations were held in abeyance until the following week(s). These occasions are marked by the inclusion of the notices that appeared in the *New Northwest* concerning the story's absence. In addition, each chapter begins with an excerpt from the "National Centennial Equal Rights Protest," a document presented by Susan B. Anthony and others to Ulysses S. Grant, President of the United States, on July 4, 1876, at the key event of the United States Centennial Celebration in Philadelphia. This document boldly impeached the entire United States government on the grounds that the rights of "one-half the people" were ignored. It is reproduced in its entirety in the *Appendix*. A more detailed discussion of its relationship to the events in *Edna and John,* as well as a more thorough treatment of other aspects of the novel, can be found in the *Afterword*.

But before reading that, I encourage you to relax, allow yourself to drift back to the days of Idaho's gold rush, and enjoy Duniway's artfully constructed story.

Debra Shein
January 1999

## NOTES

1. Abigail Scott Duniway, "Editorial Correspondence," *New Northwest,* July 21, 28, and August 11, 1876.
2. For more details, see Leonard J. Arrington, "The Gold Rush in the Early 1860s," in *History of Idaho,* vol. 1 (Moscow: University of Idaho Press, 1994).
3. John Hailey, *The History of Idaho* (Boise: Syms-York, 1910), 296.
4. It should be noted that Duniway's characterization of Sambo is lamentably stereotypical and evidences racism. However, there is some explanation for this depiction. The name "Sambo" is highly offensive today because it has so often been used in conjunction with the stereotypical, falsely viewed, happy-go-lucky slave, or used synonymously with the denigrating "boy." However, originally it was an African name and not a pejorative, as explained by Peter H. Wood in *Black Majority: Negroes in Colonial South Carolina from 1670 through the Stono Rebellion* (New York: Norton, 1974), 185. Although by Duniway's time it had taken on negative connotations, Duniway did not consciously intend offense,

even if such usage reveals that at a deeper level she lacked sensitivity and understanding. In this instance, the author gives her character a name that reveals him to be a representative type (here, a representative slave), according to the practice derived from allegory, and used also to denote "Solon" Rutherford, Mr. "Shields," and even "John Smith."

5. Julia Prewitt Brown, *A Reader's Guide to the Nineteenth-Century English Novel* (New York: Macmillan, 1985), 110.
6. Ibid., 109.
7. Linda K. Hughes and Michael Lund, *The Victorian Serial* (Charlottesville: University Press of Virginia, 1991), 2.
8. Ibid., 274.

# ACKNOWLEDGMENTS

**F**IRST AND FOREMOST, I would like to acknowledge my debt to Abigail Scott Duniway herself, whose vibrant personality, wit and wisdom, have reached across time and touched my heart. The longer I have worked with these materials, the more I have come to admire their author, and appreciate the fact that without her and other such valiant souls of a generation not so far removed from our own, we women of the present might very well have remained chained by the shackles of the past. However, I might never have become so intimately acquainted with Duniway's writings if it hadn't been for the University of Oregon's Special Collections staff, who first brought me into direct contact with her work by allowing me the privilege of cataloging her papers when they were received. All of them have been very enthusiastic about this project, and have aided me in countless ways.

My sincerest appreciation is extended to Jean Ward for her earlier work on Abigail Scott Duniway, particularly her fine synopses of Duniway's novels, and to Ruth Moynihan, for her insightful biography, *Rebel for Rights*. I also thank those at the Oregon Historical Society Library for providing me with microfilms of the *New Northwest*, and for allowing me to photocopy the *Pacific Empire*. I am deeply indebted to the entire faculty and staff of the University of Oregon Department of English, as well as to many others in the university community, and to my colleagues at Idaho State University in Pocatello. Special thanks go to Glen Love, whose wide-ranging knowledge of Western American literature has been an inspiration. My most sincere appreciation is also extended to Louise Bishop and James Earl, who supplied me with a microfilm reader to complete this work, and to Suzanne Clark, Martha Ravits, and Mary Wood.

The research on Duniway's Idaho novels was assisted immeasurably by the presence of my friend, Fred Wilbur, who accompanied me on an adventurous trek across the state, which included an unavoidable car crash outside of Horseshoe Bend. Without his support and encouragement, it is unlikely that I ever would have embarked upon, let alone finished, this project. The trip to Idaho, the beautiful state in which I am now privileged to reside, was made delightful by the many warm and friendly souls we encountered who were willing to share their knowledge of local events and history. I thank them all.

This volume is dedicated to my mother, Irene Mazer Shein, to whom I owe all that is finest in my life. She was a true woman of valor—deeply compassionate, a supremely empathetic listener, and wise beyond mere mortal proportions. In the hearts of those who loved her, she lives on. Finally, I would like to thank my two sons (in order of their entry into the world), Francois Godfrey and David Joseph Boulanger, my most remarkable accomplishments, whose shining spirits have made me grateful to be alive, even in my darkest hours. A mother could ask for no finer recompense than to have two such excellent children.

from
*The New Northwest*
Friday, September 29, 1876.

# EDNA AND JOHN:
## A ROMANCE OF IDAHO FLAT.

### BY Mrs. A. J. DUNIWAY,[1]
AUTHOR OF "JUDITH REID," "ELLEN DOWD," "AMIE AND HENRY LEE,"
" THE HAPPY HOME," "ONE WOMAN'S SPHERE," "MADGE MORRISON,"
ETC., ETC., ETC.

*Woman's degraded, helpless position is the weak point of our institutions today—a disturbing force everywhere, severing family ties, filling our asylums with the deaf, the dumb, the blind, our prisons with criminals, our cities with drunkenness and prostitution, our homes with disease and death.*—National Centennial Equal Rights Protest.

## CHAPTER I.

THERE WAS MOURNING in the home of Solon[2] and Susan Rutherford—mourning that far exceeded the great grief that had wrung the hearts of the husband and wife fifteen years before, when three-year-old baby Ethel, twin companion to the now grown and married Edna Rutherford, had closed her blue eyes beneath the shadows of the great maples and folded her tiny hands under the mysterious influence of the death-sleep.

"I thought my heart was broken when Ethel was taken," said the sorrowing mother; "but I had the comforting assurance that God took her, and that, somewhere in the illimitable vastness of the filmy hereafter, she would blossom into a more perfect angelhood than could be reached in the earth-life. So I trusted in the Lord and was comforted. But now—"

Great sobs choked her further utterance, and she leaned languidly upon the sofa pillow—the pillow that Edna had so often shaken up and arranged for the comfort of her aching head—and the blessed tears fell like summer rain.

Solon Rutherford was stupefied with an overpowering loneliness. Seven children had been born to the household, of whom four sons had grown to manhood and settled themselves upon farms adjacent to their parents in the valley of the Missouri. The eldest child was a daughter who had married young, and had also always lived, since marriage, in the neighborhood adjacent to the old homestead. The early ambition of this daughter's parents, who had marked out for her—as what young parents have not—a career of brilliancy, having its root in a fortunate matrimonial alliance, had so long been thwarted that their fond anticipations in relation to her were well nigh forgotten. Not but that the eldest born had married reasonably well; her husband, plain, unpretending Thomas Jones, having proved a plodding, well-to-do farmer, who looked upon a wife as something handy to have in the house, and as being his own, by law and gospel, without any sentiment of love or any sense of obligation to cherish and protect her further than to keep her in good working order through the busiest seasons; so her father and mother had long ago laid away their early parental dream, but had cherished a new and intensified longing for Edna's matrimonial success—a longing which had spared them neither pains nor expense in providing her with many accomplishments.

Four years at a fashionable school for young ladies had "finished" Edna's education. At least, as was very unusual in the great West among farmer's daughters at the time of which our story opens, she could play superbly, sing divinely, and talk like an educated parrot or an animated dictionary. If she had learned aught of the practical lessons of life at school, her mother failed to discover it; if she had imbibed knowledge combined with understanding, relative to the duties of wifehood, motherhood, and above all, of womanhood, nobody was able to discern her progress; but she was pretty, witty, and brilliant, and had emerged from school thoroughly imbued with the ideal extravagances respecting the divinity of the other sex, which are the bane of all the pupils in any one-sexed school. Why parents will not see the folly of bringing up their children in schools where the sexes are wholly represented, in order to unfit them for a life wherein the sexes are to live together in the most intimate relations ever afterward, is one of the anomalies of human inconsistency, which, while deprecating its existence, we will not here attempt to account for.

For a brief season after Edna's return from school she had reigned in the rustic vicinity in which she had been cradled as a star of the first magnitude. True, the young ladies disliked her, and their mammas unanimously dubbed her "a forward minx," but she was queen of hearts among the gentlemen, and swayed her scepter with a royal hand. Why she had fancied John Smith, nobody could imagine. She had had scores of other suitors, far better looking than he, and certainly quite as intellectual; but Cupid is a capricious marksman, and there is little certainty in the aim of his arrows.

It was enough for Edna that her parents disliked him. While in boarding school she had slyly read many a novel wherein the heroine had figured as a much-persecuted maiden, and the lover as a noble-hearted suitor, and a perfect Adonis in form and feature, with whom, after much tribulation, the enraptured girl had escaped through a window, in a single suit of cheap attire, to be ever after shielded, protected, loved, cherished and provided for, as none but wives and mothers are.

Nobody else could see anything prepossessing about John Smith. Solon Rutherford fancied that the name, of itself, was sufficient to satisfy any woman with common sense, without accepting the man that bore it as an additional incumbrance, but there is no accounting for taste. The name of Smith was grand enough, if only the man who bore it possessed sufficient moral, mental, and physical stamina to make it honored and respected.

Their courtship had been carried on mostly by letter.

Edna Rutherford was a girl for whom nature had fully done her share. Possessed of more than ordinary physical beauty, of neither the brunette type nor blonde, you would not have thought, to look at her, that she was in any degree capable of emotions, much less would you have supposed that an irresistible, impetuous will held a fiery temper constantly in abeyance, and dominated over the will of her associates in all things. But appearances are often deceiving, and Edna's was no unusual exception. It was against the rules of the seminary where she was utterly unfitted for the self-abnegation of ordinary wifehood for the young ladies to associate in any manner with gentlemen.

They were often deprived for months together of all associations with the opposite sex, except that which was necessarily accorded them by the squeaky-voiced president and his spindle-shanked assistant, who parted their hair in the middle and acted the constant spy over the "proprieties," so the girls hated them while they learned and harbored extravagant admiration of other men in an accelerated ratio, which might have been, and doubtless was, duly reprehensible, but it was none the less ardent on that account. Contraband love letters regularly found their clandestine way to a ledge in the great stone wall beside the iron gate, where sundry romantic young gentlemen readily exchanged them for their own garden fancies; and Edna Rutherford was through this medium rendered desperately in love with John Smith before she was at all acquainted with him in any other way; and from the vows thus plighted she was far too conscientious to recede.

She had never met her adored but once before leaving school, and then but for a moment, and the interview had been a stolen one, under the lee of the great wall, where the dark shadows cast by the moonlight had heightened his beauty and magnified his diminutive proportions.

How their correspondence began, she never could exactly remember; but the arrangement had been brought about by a mischief-loving sprite who was the pedagogue's favorite, and who, consequently, had her own way in all things.

Edna distinctly recollected that John had for an instant pressed her hand in the shadows; that he had begged permission to marry her, and that her ready assent had been followed by a hasty and passionate embrace, accompanied by a few thrilling words of endearment, sealed by a kiss, which let all other memories fade, and would ever be to her the most sacred experience in her store-house of retrospection.

From that day Edna Rutherford had considered herself, before God, as engaged. Her red lips became fully ripe under the inspiration of love, her chest expanded, her eyes grew strangely luminous, and her mind passing clear.

John Smith's letters were models of propriety, intensity, sentiment, eloquence and poetry.

Well had it been for Edna could she have known that they were copied bodily from a model guide to love-letter writing,[3] which the pale youth in whom her existence was becoming absorbed had learned to imitate, even in punctuation and paragraphing. But Edna knew nothing of the world, and cooped as she was behind the high walls of a stately edifice devoted to making fashionable fools of women, how was she to know anything about men?

On commencement day (why so named is another human anomaly), when Edna's school days were ended, and she stood before the world ready to pronounce her valedictory in a trembling, fluttering voice (and why she should be expected to do such a thing, when ever after she was to consider public speaking unladylike, was another fashionable anomaly), and she stood, as we have said, before an expectant public, to make the last speech ever expected by the aforesaid public from a full-fledged woman, John Smith sent her a bouquet, and her glad heart was filled with a blissful state of quiet exultation, not unmixed with sincere sympathy for the other graduating girls, not one of whom, to her certain knowledge, was yet "engaged."

If she sometimes wished that John's surname had been "Rutherford" and her own maiden synonym "Smith," that the marriage rite might thereby fix upon the new alliance a more pretentious cognomen, she choked back the aspiration, and whispered the objectionable "Smith" to herself so often that she gradually grew accustomed to it, though, in truth, she was always a little ashamed of the title because it was "so common." "De Smythe" would have suited her exactly, and she made many secret resolves concerning special acts of possible legislatures, wherein the name might be legally altered to suit her fastidious imaginings.

School was over, and she was not only of age, but "engaged," blessed thought, and John's bouquet was in her hand and his *billet doux*[4] in her bosom. Her father and mother were foolishly proud of her, as though every daughter in the land who thus graduates isn't a paragon; and when John Smith formally proposed for Edna's hand in marriage, doing up his proposition in another faultless letter, copied *verbatim* from the same "guide" that had aided him in winning his bride—to be—and Edna's father fumed and swore, and Edna's mother wept and scolded, the work was done; for hadn't all the cruel parents of whom she had ever read, in the stolen novels upon which school-girls feed, treated their persecuted daughters just so? And could any girl in the land become the subject and object of ecstatic bliss, in the ever rapturous marriage relation, unless she would break away from parental restraints and step right out into marriage and freedom?

So reasoned Edna Rutherford, and upon this reasoning she hastily acted, thereby beginning our story, good reader, just where every other story ends. It was idle to say that she thus renounced her home and its old associations without regret. True, her four years' alienation from home life, during the period of probation spent at school, had so far weaned her from her mother that she had been robbed of the most necessary teachings of a daughter's experience; and the mother-love which should have crowned her womanhood with a halo of abiding glory, was to her a shadowy myth, an intangible dream of olden memories, scarcely ever recalled, and never prized as it should have been.

"It's useless for us to fret, wife," said philosophic Solon Rutherford. "Edna's made her bed, and if it proves a couch of nettles, she it is must lie upon it. I've discharged my duty."

"God knows I've tried to discharge mine," was the heart-broken response; "but I can't find any consolation in the reflection that her bed of nettles is of her own choosing. I wish we hadn't sent her away to school. I wish she had always remained where I might have watched and tended and loved her. Then I'm sure she wouldn't have been disobedient. Solon, do you have any idea of their intentions?"

"In what way, mother?"

"I mean, where do you think they'll go and what do you think they'll do?"

"I don't know, and I don't care! I wash my hands of further responsibility in the premises," said the indignant father.

"But *I* care, Solon," was the sad reply; "and if I had my way, I'd give them a start in life and a parental blessing and let them go."

"And make a fool of yourself, dear."

"And make a mother of myself, you'd better say. Solon, do you see these worn hands? I've toiled and suffered for you forty years without recompense. Mainly off of the fruit of these hands you have grown rich. I have never been a burden to you in any way. Even the doctor bills that my periodic confinements have incurred have been paid by my own toil, and now I have a request to make. You won't be angry, dear?"

The voice of Mrs. Rutherford trembled and her whole frame quivered with ill-suppressed expectancy.

"What the mischief do you mean, Susan?" said her husband, in an injured tone. "One would think, to hear you talk, that I had been a very tyrant, exacting from you such constant sacrifices as would shame a Blue Beard. I'm astonished at you."

The eyes of the bereaved mother were filled afresh with tears.

"I thought," she said, diffidently, "that if I might have control of a thousand dollars or so, that I'd like to make Edna a present and help her on in life."

"Woman! do you think I'm made of money, that I could give you a thousand dollars to throw away on that disobedient hussy—"

"Stop, Solon!" pleaded the wife. "She was my baby, and all I had left. I can't bear to hear you call her names."

"Whether she was all you had or not, you haven't got her now," replied the father. "You know I threw away thousands upon her education. Much good it'll do her! She'll spend her life at the cradle, cook-stove, and wash-tub. Better have kept her in the kitchen all her life."

"I objected to a boarding-school education, as you know, Solon; but you had it your way, and this is what's come of it. There is no kind of sense in our being unreasonable. All our obstinacy will only make the matter worse. Let me draw a thousand from the bank. I've earned it, Solon. I'd get it as my dower if you should die. *Please,* dear."

But Solon Rutherford was not to be mollified. The idea that any inherent, inalienable property right was vested in his wife, the mother of his children, and for nearly half a century the uncomplaining servant of his needs, desires, passions, and caprices, had never for an instant found lodging in his brain. And now, when he was smarting under the lash of bereavement and the double sting of wounded pride, for this silent partner in his great possessions to demand a fraction of the patrimony which he had always considered entirely his own, was but adding insult to his injured dignity.

"They may go their way for all o' me!" he said, decidedly. "I wish the puny, soft-headed popinjay all the joy he'll find in his new possession."

Mrs. Rutherford saw that further entreaty and remonstrance were alike useless. There was no law in all this land of free men to compel any one of the law-makers to give to any bond-woman "of the fruit of her hands," and thereby fulfill the Scriptural injunction to "let her own works praise her in the gates,"[5] so the mother of rash Edna Rutherford took up again her daily duties, crushed back the longings of her soul, and hid away her deep sorrow behind butter firkins[6] and wash-tubs, while her bereaved lord and master jogged leisurely over the neighboring highways behind a gentle roadster, and daily sought to soothe his ruffled senses with the perfumes of an old-fashioned pipe.

John Smith had married Edna Rutherford under the implicit belief that her parents would in a very little while so far relent as to give them a fine setting up in the world; but it took a very few days of wedded waiting to convince him that for once he had reckoned without his host.

The honeymoon was spent at a fashionable hotel in the same aristocratic town in which Edna had attended school, and for a brief period, until John's very light exchequer was exhausted, the couple were the admiration of the inmates of the school, who envied Edna, and thenceforth laid many additional snares wherewith to entrap unsuspecting swains into the meshes of promissory matrimony.

The third week of conjugal bliss was over, and John could not pay the accruing board bill. This was Edna's first great humiliation. She had learned from her stand-point of inexperience to look upon marriage as the open road to plenty of spending money, though what reason she had for this expectation she could not have told. Certainly, if she had looked at home, she would have discovered the very opposite fact, but who ever knew a modern-educated girl of eighteen endowed with a modicum of practical business sense?

Edna pawned her wedding ring to pay the offending bill, laying many injunctions of secrecy upon the old man who carried on a second-hand brokerage behind a sign of three gold balls—injunctions which were industriously disobeyed as soon as redemption day came and brought no owner to re-claim the property.

John Smith was happy as the day. He had never learned to struggle for a livelihood, the moderate monthly allowance from an estate of great expec-tations having thus far sufficed for his own needs and luxuries, though la-mentably inadequate for the maintenance of two. The possession of a wife as well connected as was Edna Rutherford was glory enough for him. He could not see that she had any further use for the wedding ring now the marriage was consummated, and his indifference to their financial wants aroused a feeling of indignation in Edna, that ere the honeymoon was over had settled into the barest toleration of his presence.

But something had to be done. Some change must be made in their mode of life, and what that change could be, or would be, was an anxious problem to Edna, and after a while became a matter of decided interest to John.

[To be continued.]

from
*The New Northwest*
Friday, October 6, 1876.

# EDNA AND JOHN:
## A ROMANCE OF IDAHO FLAT.

### BY MRS. A. J. DUNIWAY,
AUTHOR OF "JUDITH REID," "ELLEN DOWD," "AMIE AND HENRY LEE,"
"THE HAPPY HOME," "ONE WOMAN'S SPHERE," "MADGE MORRISON,"
ETC., ETC., ETC.

*Woman's degraded, helpless position is the weak point of our institutions today—a disturbing force everywhere, severing family ties, filling our asylums with the deaf, the dumb, the blind, our prisons with criminals, our cities with drunkenness and prostitution, our homes with disease and death.*—National Centennial Equal Rights Protest.

## CHAPTER II.

"**WHAT'S THE MATTER, JOHN?**" queried Edna, as her liege lord came sauntering into the dainty suite of rooms which a young couple in their circumstances would not have thought of engaging at the price, had they been brought up with the remotest idea of the value of money.

John was pale and careworn and cross.

"I wish I hadn't married!" he exclaimed, bitterly.

Edna had not before seen him in such a mood; but, in truth, she had been wishing ever since they had been twenty-four hours married the very same thing, yet she would not, for the world, have wounded his feelings by saying so.

"Why, John, what's the matter?" and her heart gave a great painful throb of dread and expectation.

"Matter enough, Ed. I'm dead broke! The ole man's cut off my 'llowance, and left me without a shilling. It would have been hard enough if I'd been a bachelor, but with a wife on my hands to support, it's deuced tough."

Edna turned deathly pale. Was this the same adorable John who had courted her so faithfully? Who had written scores of model love-letters, any one of which abounded in enough of protestations of eternal fealty to have stocked a lifetime, had they been ratified by conscientiousness?

"Are you tired of me, John?"

The question came as though wrenched from her with a spasmodic pang.

"Much good it'll do me if I *am* tired!" said John. "I'm in for it, and I'd just as well submit to fate."

"I'll be a burden on your hands no longer, John," replied Edna, her lips white and her eyes flashing.

John laughed, impudently.

"What now?" he asked, in a constrained attempt to appear playful.

"Just what I mean, John Smith! God knows I'd be free from you from this time forward if wishing would free me; but the fiat has gone forth. I've become your lawful wife and must abide the consequences; but a burden on your hands I never will be."

John attempted a facetious whistle.

"One would think you belonged to the short-haired tribe of the strong-minded,[1] to see you put on airs!" he said, after a painful silence on Edna's part.

The dinner bell rang.

"Are you going down?" asked John.

"No, Mr. Smith. You've enough to do, according to your own statement, to support yourself. I'm going to my mother."

This was a turn in the tide of John's affairs which was wholly unanticipated.

"What new crochet are you nursing now?" he asked, in alarm.

"The crochet of a new and unlooked-for necessity," was the calm reply.

Edna had left her father and mother to cleave unto John,[2] accompanied with but a single change of wardrobe. This meager allowance had been liberally replenished by the enraptured Benedict,[3] upon the occasion of their marriage; but now that he was taunting her with being burdensome, she would not touch an article that he had bought.

"Mr. Smith," said Edna, for the second time in her life addressing her husband by the name of which she was ashamed, "we must rigidly observe the proprieties. You go down to dinner and tell the inquisitive boarders that I've been invited out. It's half true, you know, for you've given me an unmistakable invitation to go out. After I'm gone, you can pretend you've concluded to go and join me. You can go where you like. I'll go to my mother."

"And get a fool's luck for your pains."

"What do you mean?"

"I mean that you'll find the home of Edna Smith a very different establishment from the home of Edna Rutherford."

"It can't be any worse than the home of my husband, when he not only has none to offer me, but accuses me of being burdensome, even in the honeymoon," sobbed Edna.

One by one the little trinkets her husband had bestowed upon her in their short-lived period of happiness were laid aside.

"If you had only told me your circumstances, John, I wouldn't have encouraged you to buy these," she said, holding up a glittering pair of gold bracelets, with claspings set in amethysts.

"It goes in a life-time," answered John.

How Edna did wish that John would urge her to remain; how she longed for him to say: "Never mind poverty. We'll live and love and toil together."

It did not occur to her that she ought herself to make such a suggestion. She only realized that John was weary of her. Her pride did the rest.

The single change of clothing she had brought to the new copartnership was away at the wash, and she would not attempt to wait for it.

With a great load of suppressed emotion tugging at her heart strings, and a deep sense of unutterable humiliation overpowering her whole being, the young wife turned her footsteps from the fleeting, unrealized dream of her marriage into the aching void of another rash endeavor, which, let Fortune's wheel turn as it might, could but add to her present perplexity.

John did not believe that she would go. Edna did not mean to go when she had first threatened. She thought he would have said something by way of urging her to remain and bear with his bad humors, or give him opportunity to amend them, while he fancied that she would break down and weep and beg to be reinstated.

Both reckoned without their host, as we have seen.

With a firm step Edna descended the broad stairs and directed herself toward the consummation of the second great folly of her young life.

A few hours' ride and she beheld herself in the little mirror of her mother's great farm kitchen, as pale as a corpse, and panting like a frightened hare.

Mrs. Rutherford dropped the roll of butter she was moulding and instinctively wiped her hands.

"Oh, Edna!"

"Mother, may I come home to stay?"

Mrs. Rutherford was almost as badly shocked as she had been over her daughter's elopement.

"You don't mean to say you've left your husband, Edna?"

"Yes, mother."

"Why?"

"He says he can't support me."

"My child, you should have taken that part into consideration long ago. But come into the parlor, dear. I want to talk to you. As Mrs. Smith, I am willing to do what I can for you, though God knows that's very little; but I cannot harbor you as a fugitive wife, daughter; not even if my heart-strings break with a longing to do it."

"Why, mother?"

"Because, child, you have taken upon yourself the marriage vows. If your husband casts you off, and refuses to allow you to remain in his custody, you may come to me, of course with your father's permission. I have no rights of my own in the premises. But, if he will not harbor you, there is no alternative. You must look out for your own support."

"Mother, were you always of this opinion?"

"Yes, my child."

"Then, why in the name of common humanity did you not keep me out of a boarding school and bring me up in the kitchen?"

"Alas, child! I had great anticipations for you. I thought your accomplishments would enable you to marry a rich and honored and titled gentleman. You spoiled my dream and thwarted my hopes by a runaway and inferior match. It would not do for your father to see you here. There is no telling what he might do or say."

Before her marriage Edna would have willingly risked her own influence over her father in any common emergency. Now she was afraid to meet him, and not without reason.

"Mother," she said, sternly, for she seemed suddenly to have launched, full-fledged, into experienced womanhood, "you can help me, and you must."

"How, child?"

"You must loan me some money."

"*I,* Edna? You must be crazy. Why, I've never had control of a dollar in all my married life!"

"Do you think father would help me?"

"He swears he will not. Oh, Edna, if you had only remained at home!"

"My mother dear, I'll not reproach you; but I cannot forbear declaring that you and my father are more to blame for my life-mistakes than I. You brought me up a hot-house plant, when you knew I would some day be transplanted to the weather-beach. You secluded me from the society and acquaintance of men, though you knew that such associations were natural and that through all my after life I'd be thrown into the power of a husband. If I have made a mistake, my parents should help me bear it."

Solon Rutherford had entered unperceived and had heard his daughter's truthful speech.

"What now?" he asked, merely as a matter of form, for the news of John Smith's disinheritance had already reached him.

Edna approached him in tears.

"Go to the devil!" stormed the excited father.

"All right!" said Edna. "Mother, farewell! And now, *mark my word,* you'll be proud of me some day. You'll never see me again till I have conquered life and brought fate to my feet."

In a moment Edna was gone, and the unhappy parents were glaring upon each other like tigers.

"You curse her, Solon, and she's your own flesh and blood!" said the mother, bitterly.

"She's no Rutherford!" was the excited response.

From that day henceforward, for many years, the name of Edna was not breathed in Solon Rutherford's presence. The good wife grew strangely reticent, and a queer gleam of cunning sometimes lit up her mysterious eyes; but Solon noted no change, or if he saw, appeared purposely indifferent.

Twilight was coming. Edna passed out through the hall of the old house and down the back steps, out into a waving cornfield.

"Where can I go, or whither flee?" she asked herself; but no answer came to solve the fearful problem. "I can't go back to John; I can't seek refuge at the homes of my brothers and sisters after my parents have cast me off. I'm too conscientiously proud of their standing in society to seek service in the neighborhood and cause a nine days' scandal[4] and make them ashamed of me. In all the wide world I have nowhere to lay my head."

In the far edge of the waving cornfield dwelt an old lady in a rude hut, surrounded by a kitchen garden with sun-flowers guarding the entrance, and at the humble door a festoon of morning-glories.

"Aunt Judy will not drive me away," she said, half audibly, as she climbed the stile and walked timidly up the narrow path leading to the humble entrance.

For many years "Aunt Judy" had inhabited this rude hut alone. She was a distant relative of Edna's father, and had sometime seen better days, though nobody could break through the icy reticence of her demeanor to learn why it was that she had come to poverty, loneliness, and grief.

"Aunt Judy," said Edna, with an air of abandonment that to the lonely individual thus addressed, who had only known her in her brilliant moods, was perfectly bewildering, "will you let me share your home? I need a friend, and in all the wide world I have no other to whom I can go for protection."

"What, my child! So soon?" and Aunt Judy offered her an old-fashioned easy chair, and when the weary child was seated, stood over her smoothing her brow and patting her pale cheeks with her soft, cool palm. "Have your Sodom apples[5] turned to ashes already, pet?"

Edna had been nerved to apparent stony-heartedness under censure; but the sympathy of Aunt Judy broke up the fountain of her tears.

"Yes, auntie. I've reaped the bitter fruit of rashness, ignorance, and disobedience much sooner, it seems, than you imagined."

"Has your husband discarded you?"

"No, auntie; not that, exactly; but he taunted me with being a burden on his hands to support, and I couldn't bear it."

"Is that *all,* child? Why, bless your simple heart, there's millions of women bearing that taunt every day in meekness and submission."

"No, auntie, it isn't all; but it's enough, goodness knows. Yet there's a greater trouble. There's nothing for a support—nothing at all. John has always lived on an annuity, from which his friends have cut him off, now he's married, and my father won't help us, and neither of us knows how to do anything."

"The more shame for you both, if you don't, Edna."

"I know it, auntie. But what can I do? You know how it would humiliate my friends[6] if I should create scandal here by going out to service or to teach, now I'm married. And it would humiliate me so I couldn't hold my head up, to have the world say my husband couldn't support me."

"Why, bless you, child, there isn't one man in hundreds who has the name of supporting a wife that does it. Look at your father, for instance, and your married brothers. The nucleus of their riches is in their farm-houses, where the wife holds the helm. There was old man Case, down in the Missouri bottom. He was rich, you know. Well, his wife died a few years ago, and he was like a watch with a main-spring broken. He ran down and remained down. He came here a-courting me one day," Aunt Judy blushed and hesitated, "and he said there was no such thing as prospering without a woman."

"What did you tell him, auntie?" and Edna smiled through her tears.

"Told him I was sorry for him, but not quite sorry enough to walk in the track of the dead Mrs. Case," replied the old lady, with a mellow chuckle.

"Well, auntie, what shall I do? I've resolved that I will not endure the taunts of John about my helplessness. When women were uneducated and kept in utter ignorance of their own dormant powers, maybe they didn't mind it; but it's different now-a-days."

"My child, if you intend to do as you please, don't mock me by asking my advice, I beg you."

"But, auntie, I only want your advice about making a living."

"Edna, dear, you married your husband and took the vows upon you for better or for worse, you know."

"I never thought of the worse, auntie. There wasn't any 'worse' considered in any book on love and marriage that I ever read. I wish I had the framing of text books for schools."

"Would you improve them?"

"Indeed I would. I'd teach both boys and girls the ethics of matrimony, financially considered. I'd keep them together during school hours, too, and give them opportunity to get mutually acquainted. Then I'd see that each candidate for wedded experience had mastered some particular business and had learned to apply it practically before legal marriage was possible."

"You're learning lessons rapidly, my dear," said Aunt Judy, as she left her visitor to prepare a cup of tea.

"Alas, I've learned too late!" sighed Edna, as she closed her eyes to think and plan.

By and by the frugal meal was ready, but Edna could not eat. Aunt Judy purred about her like a motherly house cat, but encouraged and soothed her to little purpose.

"There's one thing certain, child," she declared, earnestly; "you've made your bargain and you must abide by it. I'll gladly harbor you for the present, but only with the understanding that you'll return to your duty as soon as your plans are made. If only somebody had harbored, advised, and encouraged me in the long ago—but that's all past—"

"Have you a history, auntie?" cried Edna, with a show of the old girlish interest.

"Yes, child—a buried, and not-to-be-resurrected one," was the apathetic answer, while a far-away look beamed in her faded eyes, and a fluttering, half-stifled sigh escaped her.

"You cannot leave your husband, Edna," she continued, after a dreamy pause. "You have crossed the gulf between yourself and girlhood. Grass widows[7] are not to be tolerated in our family."

"But my husband is utterly incapable as a business man, auntie," protested the inexperienced girl-wife.

"Then, dear, you must be doubly intelligent, firm and strong. You have formed a legal, indissoluble tie between yourself and him. You have done this deed deliberately, and must abide the consequences. It's the old adage, 'Marry in haste and repent at leisure.'"

"But repentance without restitution is fruitless, auntie."

"So the rich man Dives[8] discovered to his sorrow, but 'twas all the good it did him," was the hopeless answer.

[To be continued.]

from
*The New Northwest*
Friday, October 13, 1876.

# NO PAPER NEXT WEEK.

The State Fair commences next Monday, and, in accordance with our usual custom, there will be no paper issued from the NEW NORTHWEST office next week. As before, our subscribers will lose nothing, as the regular number of papers will be sent to each patron. Observe that the present issue is No. 5, and the next, under date of October 20th, will be No. 6. In the interim, we hope to visit the fair, and will be prepared to take subscriptions, renewals and arrears, and furnish receipts therefor, and we hope and expect to do a lively business in that line. Let subscribers, delinquents, and friends come prepared to renew, liquidate, or subscribe.

from
*The New Northwest*
Friday, October 20, 1876.

# EDNA AND JOHN:
## A ROMANCE OF IDAHO FLAT.

### BY Mrs. A. J. DUNIWAY,
AUTHOR OF "JUDITH REID," "ELLEN DOWD," "AMIE AND HENRY LEE,"
" THE HAPPY HOME," "ONE WOMAN'S SPHERE," "MADGE MORRISON,"
ETC., ETC., ETC.

*Woman's degraded, helpless position is the weak point of our institutions today—a disturbing force everywhere, severing family ties, filling our asylums with the deaf, the dumb, the blind, our prisons with criminals, our cities with drunkenness and prostitution, our homes with disease and death.*—National Centennial Equal Rights Protest.

## CHAPTER III.

JOHN SMITH FAILED to partake of his solitary dinner with the accustomed relish. He had not imagined that Edna would dare to put her threat into execution, and his taunts had been given only because of the impunity with which, as her husband, he felt it possible to assail her defenseless position.

To the questions from chatty friends as to whether or not Edna was indisposed, he returned the answer that she had gone out for an hour or two, and to the rallying replies upon the rapid waning of the honeymoon that followed, he merely responded in monosyllables.

"I'll never trouble her again!" he exclaimed bravely to himself, but the resolution choked him, and his appetite vanished before the meal was half over. Returning to the room where his dream of happiness had been so sweet and yet so evanescent, the miserable husband threw himself upon the bed and wept in helpless agony.

He felt, too, a depth of bitterness in thinking of his wife, that was natural enough to be excusable under the circumstances.

Wasn't she *his* property, to have and to hold for better or for worse? and couldn't a man do what he pleased with his own?

Then came another query. If she was *his,* and *his only,* why might he not compel her to remain in his custody?

Had John possessed only a moderate income, he would have immediately planned to compel her to return; but the problem of how to obtain food, lodging, and raiment for *one* was now demanding solution, and the poor Benedict, being unfitted for any other avocation than the idle one of great expectations, was baffled at every turn.

Morning came, and brought with it a determination to assert his rights, and with John Smith, to resolve was to execute.

"I'll go to my respected father-in-law as a repenting prodigal, and throw myself upon his mercy!" he declared, humbly.

So he walked bravely enough over the lonely way till he came within the environs of the Rutherford farm, and then his courage failed.

"They'll only insult me!" he said, in despair, "and I'll not go there to be humiliated. I've heard of old Aunt Judy. They say she's eccentric, but kind. Maybe she'll harbor a fellow till something can be done."

John looked long and wistfully at the great farm-house.

Would Edna allow him to go away without one kindly word if she only knew he was there? Had she forgotten the old gushing tenderness that had filled her soul and his with joy unspeakable? And was she indeed lost to him forever?

Thus musing, he walked rapidly across the field in the direction of Aunt Judy's cottage. As he neared the door, he paused and listened, and his heart rose in his throat. Edna was singing. A low, plaintive melody that reminded him of the wild *miserere*[1] of an Eolian harp rose upon the air.

> "Nothing on earth is tender and true, Nothing on earth;
> Love-light is fleeting, and fades from the view,
> Leaving ashes o'erspread with the damp of Death's dew,
> Leaving desolate hearts to bewail the untrue
> And to sing of the soul's save dearth."

"We might be happy yet, if we would only try!" said John, while a lump in his throat clogged his breath.

"Who's *you?*" asked Aunt Judy, peering over her glasses through the little window that struggled to admit what light it could through the interstices of overhanging morning glories.

"*As I live! It's John!*" cried Edna, in consternation. "Hide me quick, Aunt Judy, for he shall not see me!"

"You are very foolish, child," said Aunt Judy.

But the admonition was lost upon Edna. There was a "loft" or attic over the cabin, accessible only by a ladder. To mount the ladder and draw it up after her and close the trap door, was the work of a moment.

John entered, and Edna was gone.

"Good-morning, ma'am."

"*Morning, sir!* Anything wanting?" and Aunt Judy eyed his diminutive proportions with a motherly gaze of mingled surprise and pity.

"I'm John Smith, madam, and I wish to see my wife."

"I've seen John Smith before, sir, and I can't say that you resemble him," said Aunt Judy, with a mellow chuckle.

"None o' your nonsense, old woman! I'm not the only John Smith!" exclaimed John, unhappily losing control of his temper.

"What?"

Aunt Judy's surprise was exhibited as much in face and manner as in exclamation.

"Just this, ma'am. You're harboring my wife, and I'll let you know it's a thing you can't do with impunity."

"And so you're the man that coaxed Edna Rutherford to leave an elegant home and a mother that idolized her, and then, when she'd married you, and thereby given up everything else on earth for your sake, you taunted her with being a burden, eh?"

Aunt Judy was surprised at her own audacity. Edna, from her perch overhead, could hear every word.

"I'm sorry," said John, humbly.

"And would you ask her pardon? And would you promise on your bended knees, before Edna Rutherford, that you would never *dare* to taunt the wife of your bosom, who gave up everything in life worth living for and accepted as a paltry compensation your own pigmy and impudent self— would you *swear* that you'd fit yourself for some useful occupation, and adapt yourself to life's circumstances, as a sensible man ought, if I should introduce you to Edna Smith?"

John looked at Aunt Judy in complete bewilderment.

"You don't speak," said the old lady, earnestly.

"I'll never kneel to any woman," said John, sullenly.

"It isn't a month since he knelt at my feet to beg for the privilege of kissing my hand!" cried Edna, *sotto voce.*

"Very well, then. Good-morning!" replied Aunt Judy, as she adjusted her spinning-wheel and sat down beside her distaff.[2]

"But I'm not gone, yet; neither am I going till I find my wife!" answered John.

> "Hey diddle-diddle,
> The cat's in the fiddle,
> The cow jumped over the moon."

Sang Aunt Judy, keeping time with her foot on the treadle, while the wheel purred a brisk accompaniment to Mother Goose.

"*Say! Aunt Judy!*" cried John, desperately.

> "Old Mother Hubbard
> Went to the cupboard
> To get her poor dog a bone."

"I'll Mother Hubbard *you,* if you don't talk to me!" interrupted the angry Benedict.

"Sir?"

"I demand civil treatment, ma'am. You're harboring my lawful wife against my expressed wishes; and, if you don't show me her hiding-place, I'll try what virtue there is in law."

Aunt Judy chuckled, and Edna came near fainting. John Smith strutted up and down the room, inflated with imaginary importance.

Aunt Judy kept on with her spinning, and did not seem to hear.

"Come, old woman, none o' your nonsense! I don't want any trouble, but I assure you that you'll have it if this thing's kept up. A pretty spectacle you'll cut, figuring in the courts as one who parted husband and wife!"

Aunt Judy seemed suddenly to have regained consciousness. Pausing in both work and ditty, she rose in her chair, and, confronting the irate husband of her charge, exclaimed coldly,

"Young man, you're cracking on too much steam—quite too much. You seem to forget that I did not meet Edna at all during your courtship or after your marriage. How I could have parted you is, therefore, a mystery which I should be pleased to have you make clear. I do not believe at all in separations between husband and wife. I believe, rather, that if men and women take upon themselves the marriage vows, they should at all times be ready to sacrifice their personal comfort for each others' benefit. But, in order that these sacrifices be beneficial, they must be mutual, sir. I am an old lady, and an old-fashioned one. I have seen much of life, and known much of its sorrows. And now, let Aunt Judy give you a little advice. Are you too angry to listen? Tell me, for I will not allow you to sauce me. No man ever did but *one,* and he got enough of it, and so did I, too, for that matter. No man ever dares to taunt a woman, or expects to taunt her with impunity, except she is bound to him by a marriage law that gives him all the advantage in everything but a divorce court; and the man who taunts a woman under such circumstances is a very chivalrous man, John Smith—a very chivalrous man."

"What would you have me to do, Aunt Judy?" asked John, falteringly.

"Now you're talking sensibly!" and the old lady offered him a chair.

John dropped into the proffered seat and fidgeted uneasily.

"I'd have you go to Edna and in all humility make what amends you can for the great wrong you have inflicted upon her. You have wronged her in more ways than one. You lured her from her parental home, where luxury and freedom were her portion, and took her, without any adequate provision for her needs, to share your lot in poverty. Then, when financial troubles came, which you might have foreseen if you had not been an idiot, you called her a *burden,* and assumed the air of a martyr, as though you, and you only, were to bear the humiliations and privations of poverty."

"I always had a good support till I got married."

"Yes; but it was a temporary support, and dependent wholly upon the changing whims of a rheumatic uncle."

"You seem to know a great deal about my affairs, madam."

"And why shouldn't I? If I'm to be the only protector to yourself and wife, I'd better know, hadn't I?"

John Smith smiled, in spite of himself.

"You'd better learn not to despise the day of small things," continued Aunt Judy. "It is very evident that neither of you are able to be your own protector, and, as to protecting each other, that bubble has burst already."

"Are you willing, then, to be my friend, Aunt Judy? And will you try to reconcile Edna to me if I will be guided by your counsels?"

"I will, most certainly."

"But you don't tell me what you would have me to do."

"I have told you more than once, if I know myself, and I rather think I do."

"Well?"

"Are you ready to make proper acknowledgments to Edna, apologizing, like a gentleman, for having insulted her?"

"Yes," tremulously.

"Edna! O, Edna!"

Poor child! Her heart beat hard for dread.

"I think you'd better give John another chance, dear. We're all human, and liable to err, you know," cried Aunt Judy, loudly.

"Is she in the cellar?" asked John.

Aunt Judy gave a mellow laugh. She was in her element when acting as a go-between in cases like this.

"Are you quite *sure* you'll respect and honor her in the future, even as you would feel compelled to do if you were not married to her, John Smith?"

"Quite sure, Aunt Judy."

Indeed, John was getting anxious enough for almost anything now.

"Then, Edna, if I were you, I'd come in and talk it all over, and kiss and make it up," cried the old lady, while her ample chin shook with satisfaction, and her motherly face rippled all over with smiles.

"All right! I'll try!" sang out a silvery voice, and Aunt Judy suddenly remembered that a brood of chickens needed her immediate attention in a neighboring barn-yard.

Edna descended from her novel hiding-place, and stood before her husband pale and resolute.

John eyed her as a martyr might gaze upon the faggots that were to form his funeral pyre.

"I hear that you desire an interview, Mr. Smith. May I inquire concerning the nature of your demands?"

"I simply want you to return to my bed and board, and be to me a loyal and obedient wife, madam."

"And whither would your highness convene?" Edna arched her neck as a princess might, and asked the question in a tone of bitterness.

"Oh, Edna!" cried John, pleadingly, and the poor fellow's humiliation was pitiable. "You only care for me for a home's sake. And when poverty comes, and we are both cast out penniless, do you feel satisfied to throw away my love as a cast-off garment, not caring what is to become of me in the future?"

"If I go with you, where can you take me?"

The question was a practical one, certainly, and, under the circumstances, as excusable as John's indignation had been in the outset.

"I don't know, darling. I only know I cannot live without you," and tears glistened in his eyes.

The bride of a few weeks blushed, and burst into tears. One stronghold was gained already.

"I don't know, Edna. I haven't had time to think of that. Only let me know that you still care for me, and I can go away, content to struggle for your sake—for your sake forever."

Edna sobbed outright.

"I was a brute!" continued John. "I might have known better than to treat you as I did. Will you forgive me?"

Edna did not imagine the humiliation which this concession cost her husband.

"I'll forgive you, John, on one condition."

"Name it."

"Will you promise what I demand?"

"Yes, Edna. Anything you ask."

"Promise me that you will never hereafter forget the courtesy that is due to Edna Rutherford as a lady."

"I do."

"Now promise me that you will at once go to work, as a poor man should to provide for your maintenance. I assure you in advance that I shall do my part."

"It shall be as you say."

"And will you always hereafter remember the vows you made before heaven to love, respect, and cherish your wife, John Smith?"

"I promise, most solemnly. And now, will you promise, while we are about it, to bear with my short-comings, and help me to grow strong in manhood and honor?"

"Yes, dear; I promise willingly."

Aunt Judy was struck with a sudden blindness when she came blustering in. John and Edna were seated together upon the lounge, under the morning glories that reached their tendrils to caress them through the open window.

"Edna, where are my spectacles?" she exclaimed, nervously.

"On your wheel, auntie. Here they are," rising, and placing them in her hand.

"Have you made it up, children?" There were tears in the good old lady's voice.

"Yes, Aunt Judy. It's all right now between us—that is, as to each other," said John, "and the next thing is to look out for a living."

"My potatoes want hoeing badly, and I don't mind giving you a job that will board you for a spell," suggested Aunt Judy, speaking as though half certain that her proffer would receive a contemptuous refusal.

"All right," said John, promptly. "Where's your hoe?"

The implement was procured, and, for the first time since John Smith had reached his teens, the young man used it vigorously.

"Now, child," said Aunt Judy, "you must learn to work, too. As the wife of a poor man, yourself penniless, you must neither be afraid or ashamed to turn your hands to useful occupations. You'll find a woman's work no child's play, I assure you, especially if you raise a family, and that's more than likely, for you remember the old adage, 'A fool for luck and a poor man for children.'"

"Teach me to spin, won't you, auntie?"

"No, child; that won't pay. I only spin for amusement, and to keep myself busy. You must learn to cook and wash and make and mend and starch and iron and economize and manage. In raising a family for a poor man, you'll find your hands full of such labor, and you can only save—at least, till you get cows and chickens and pigs to make your pin money."

"I wish I had talked this all over with you before I was married, auntie," and Edna heaved a sigh. "But then, your allusions won't fit my case, for I don't intend to have a family."

Aunt Judy laughed immoderately.

"That was just the way your mother talked before you, dear. Never was there a higher spirited young woman than she. No matter what examples had been set by others, *she* was going to show the world how to get along sensibly. And she *did,* with a vengeance. Seven children in single file, and one pair o' twins. I'm not trying to discourage you, but it's well enough to warn you that you may be prepared to encounter squalls and breakers."

"I wish I were dead!" cried Edna, in despair.

"If that wish would kill married women, there wouldn't be many left," replied Aunt Judy. "And now, dear, I've a plan in my head that I propose to carry out for your especial benefit. I'm going South to make a visit, and will leave you and John to harvest my corn, milk my cow, feed my pigs and chickens, gather in and secure the vegetables and cook your own food. I shall be absent one month, and if you do your work well and let nothing go to waste, I'll give you a hundred dollars to begin house-keeping with on my return. It's a better setting out than your parents had, by great odds."

[To be continued.]

from
*The New Northwest*
Friday, October 27, 1876.

# EDNA AND JOHN:
## A ROMANCE OF IDAHO FLAT.

### BY MRS. A. J. DUNIWAY,
AUTHOR OF "JUDITH REID," "ELLEN DOWD," "AMIE AND HENRY LEE,"
" THE HAPPY HOME," "ONE WOMAN'S SPHERE," "MADGE MORRISON,"
ETC., ETC., ETC.

*Woman's degraded, helpless position is the weak point of our institutions today—a disturbing force everywhere, severing family ties, filling our asylums with the deaf, the dumb, the blind, our prisons with criminals, our cities with drunkenness and prostitution, our homes with disease and death.*—National Centennial Equal Rights Protest.

## CHAPTER IV.

A UNT JUDY TOOK ESPECIAL PAINS to instruct her wards in their several lines of business.

"You see it's the only alternative," she would say, decidedly. "John might teach, if qualified, which he isn't, or might practice at the bar, if a lawyer, which he couldn't be under a year's close application to study; Edna might teach, only there's other work for *her,* and so you must learn to farm. I'm giving you a splendid chance."

And so, after a few days of diligent fussiness on Aunt Judy's part, and passive yet diligent obedience on the part of her charges, the kind lady was ready for her journey; and the young couple, who had embarked upon the matrimonial voyage with visions of future splendor before them, found themselves glad to get possession, as temporary tenants, of a lop-sided log cabin with a puncheon[1] floor, furnished with blue-edged tableware and unvarnished chairs, with seats of braided hickory bark.

There was plenty of work to do, indoors and out. Good Aunt Judy resolved to start Edna right in all the paths of industry, so she ordained that her spare time should be occupied in quilting at a great maze of patch-work that hung overhead in the frames at night and at meal time, and was lowered to suit her convenience when there was nothing else to occupy her hours. Edna would sometimes cry, and John would often curse his stars, but neither crying nor cursing proved of any avail.

"They were *in* for it," as Aunt Judy had wisely observed, and now they must both endeavor to make the best of a bad bargain.

Aunt Judy's benevolent face was flushed with satisfaction as she bade them adieu; and she started on her journey with a happier feeling at her heart than she had realized since that never-to-be-forgotten day, ever so long before, when the light and joy of her life went out through a mystery that her friends had never been able to unravel.

"I guess I'll call on Susan on my way to the steamer landing," she said to herself. "No doubt she'll be able to make some wise suggestions about the young people. She'll be glad, too, to hear from Edna, for mothers will be mothers. I know mighty well that my poor mother's heart was broken because of her truant—*there!* There's no use in worrying. She went to her long home years ago, and I'm still spared. What for's always been a mystery, but doubtless for some wise purpose."

"How d'ye do, Susan?" she cried, stepping briskly in spite of the redundancy of her avoirdupois,[2] as she entered the great farm kitchen of Solon Rutherford.

"Poorly, Judy, poorly," was the sad reply of the weary wife of the wealthy farmer, who lifted a heavy cheese and turned it nether side up as she spoke. "Sometimes, Judy, I get to wondering what life's for, anyway. It seems so barren of anything lasting or real that's worth having! It's toil, toil, scrimp, scrimp, save, save, to the end of the chapter. Twenty-five or thirty years ago I stood it first rate, for I thought we'd be able to live comfortable in our old days; but the more property Solon accumulates the harder I must work to pay taxes. You know the hundred-acre lot that Will Caples owned down below the big meadow?"

"Yes, Susan; I've gone a strawberrying through it many a time," said Aunt Judy, wondering much that her friend had nothing to say upon the all-absorbing theme of which she was herself so full.

"Well, Solon sold the cheese last week," continued Mrs. Rutherford. "There was a prime lot of it, too—two thousand pounds at 20 cents—and it netted four hundred dollars. I've never asked him for any money till lately, except for necessaries, you know."

"I know," said Aunt Judy, still wondering what all this preliminary was about.

"I've worked hard," continued the good woman, "and well nigh worn myself out, soul and body, in serving the owner of all the real estate belonging to this plantation; and when Edna went away," here the old lady broke down, and dropping upon a chair, wiped her tearful eyes with her checked apron, "I know she didn't do just right, but she was the last I had, and she was *so* dear to me, and I wanted to make her a present. She married a poor stick of a fellow who might get along if he had a start, for Edna's no shirk when she's aroused, and she'd help him; but Solon flared up when I asked him for a thousand dollars he had in bank that I knew he'd no earthly need for, and he acted like I meant to rob him. Then, when he sold the cheese, he took that money which I couldn't help hoping he'd give to me, seeing I'd served him for thirty years for nothing, and the thousand I'd asked him for besides, and put the sums together and bought that hundred acre lot. And now he says he won't be able to buy a new carpet for the sitting-room, no new paper nor curtains, for it will take all the fall yield of cheese to pay the taxes. So I've begun to wonder what it's all for, and to wish I could have a little more that's my own, even if I had to put up with a little less that's Solon's. What's to become of Edna, is more than I know. Penniless, without clothes, books, or parents' blessing, I feel like I could die to help her, and yet I am powerless."

"Do you know where she is, Susan?"

"No. But would to God I could know."

"Would you help her if you could, whether Solon knew it or not?"

"I don't know as I'd dare to try that. I never disobeyed him in my life."

"Have you always done just what your conscience approved in carrying out your implicit obedience?"

"No, I can't say that I have."

"Then you've stultified your womanhood and let the will and conscience of another hold your own in abeyance, Susan. Is that right?"

"I don't believe it is."

"Then, take a friend's advice and never do it again."

"I don't think I understand you."

"Do you know where Edna is, did you say?" asked Aunt Judy again.

"Alas, no."

"She's at my house."

Mrs. Rutherford turned deadly pale.

"And John?"

"Is with her, and they've made it up."

"And what do you intend to do with them, pray?"

"I've set them to work and I'm going on a visit to my relatives in the South. I mean to let 'em try house-keeping on a small scale till they get able to do better."

"O, Judy! If Solon would *only* help 'em, or let *me!* There's no kind of use in our holding out against them. If he'd minded me in the first place, I'd a kept Edna out of the boarding school, and then she wouldn't have run off and been disobedient. She told me once in vacation that the beaux were all the girls thought of or cared for in that school."

"Do you know what I'd do if I were you, Susan?" and Aunt Judy laughed melodiously as she fidgeted to another chair, planting her ample proportions in very close proximity to her friend.

"Not being you, Judith, how should I know?" was the quick reply.

"Would you like to know?"

"I'd like for somebody, or anybody, to light me through this trouble," and Mrs. Rutherford's checked apron again sought her eyes to hide the falling tears.

"If Edna was my daughter, and I the wife of a rich man, whose riches I had mainly earned myself, as you have, I'd teach him a trick worth a dozen of what he's up to, Susan."

"How?"

Mrs. Rutherford could not even see, as through a glass, darkly.[3]

"I'd go to the bank and get the money," said Aunt Judy.

"Where? What bank?"

"The St. Louis National. Solon has cords of money there, gorging itself to repletion on compound interest and doing nobody any good."

"But how would you get it?"

"Go and demand it as the wife of Solon Rutherford. They won't imagine but it's all right, and they'll be afraid of offending your rich husband if they refuse it; so, as a bird in the hand's worth two in the bush, you'd better go while you're in the notion and secure your cash."

"But how can I leave home?" asked Mrs. Rutherford, in a fright.

"I'll stay here till you return," said her friend. "I'm in no hurry. There's the boat, now, and you'll be compelled to hurry up. The dress you have on is all right. A clean, well-starched gingham is good enough for any farmer's wife. Here's a clean collar, and here's your cap, and you may wear my silk mantilla. Now you're ready, and here's money to pay your fare and hotel bills. You'd better stop at the American Exchange. They're used to farmers there. And don't you come back without that thousand dollars."

"But Solon—what'll he say?"

"Just nothing at all. Or, if he does fume, it won't hurt him, or you, either. Just leave him to me. I'll manage him."

Before Mrs. Rutherford had time to reflect, she found herself on the steamer and going rapidly down the river. Then, after it was too late to retract her resolve and its consequences, she began to grow timid and regret her course.

Aunt Judy had no sooner gained temporary control over the home of Solon Rutherford than she began collecting the various articles of wearing apparel that belonged to Edna.

"I'll see that the silly child has the rags, at all events," she said, looking wise and smiling to herself in perfect complacency. "Dresses enough to stock a second-hand clothing store, and all going to waste unless Edna gets 'em," she continued, while she fairly hugged herself with delight. "And here's sheets and pillows-cases and patch-work quilts and table-linen by the bale, and it all smacks of the good old days when girls were kept out of boarding school and taught house-keeping. I'll see that Edna gets her share of all this, if she does her duty while she's on trial."

The afternoon was waning rapidly. Supper must be ready for Mr. Rutherford and the farm hands, and Aunt Judy was quite exhausted as she finished cooking the meal, and dropped into a chair at the head of the table and wielded the fly brush while waiting for the head of the household in nervous expectancy.

"Where's Susan, and how are you, cousin Judy?" asked that dignitary, as he gazed at the unexpected yet plump apparition in genuine surprise. "Is anybody sick?"

"A friend of Susan's is in great trouble, and she was obliged to go away on the steamer to see about the matter, and hadn't time to tell you good-bye. She left me to keep house and keep things a-going while she's away. Maybe she won't be gone but a day or two."

Solon Rutherford was thunderstruck. The possibility that the patient wife who had uncomplainingly drudged for him for a third of a century, and, during all that time, had never dared to think and act for herself, would ever do such a thing, had never before occurred to him, even for an instant. He was both grieved and angry.

"Indeed, she couldn't help it, cousin Solon," said Aunt Judy, soothingly. "She didn't know as you'd be at home for a day or two—you so often go away like that, you know—and the boat was coming and I was here, and I just bustled her off. If you feel angry with anybody, I'm your customer."

The ruler of the Rutherford realm ate his food in sullen silence. The farm hands partook of his moodiness, and Aunt Judy, who was accustomed at home to the purring companionship of her harmonious kitten, felt gloomy and wretched. But she kept her own counsel and toiled diligently. She was an adept in all the intricacies of house-keeping, not even excepting the drudging of making butter and cheese for market.

"Solon's like a hen with its head off," she exclaimed to herself. "Wish I had the training of him for a while! I'd show him whether or not my soul was my own."

But she didn't have the training of the husband of Susan Rutherford, and there was no use in speculating upon it.

The head of the household lost interest in his habitual buggy rides, lost regard for his hundred acres of recently purchased real estate, and lost concern for even the constantly accruing taxes, about which he had for years had a chronic habit of annoying his uncomplaining wife. What to him was the world without Susan, now that she was gone? What to him his vast possessions if she were not there to guide and direct their management? Not that he was in the habit of allowing her any control over the business; as head of the firm, such a possibility was not to be harbored by him for an instant. But he missed her as his body servant; missed her, as the unresisting recipient of his gloomy moods; missed her, in short, upon general principles, chief among which was the fact that he considered it her duty to be at home.

He had heard of strong-minded women, so-called, who had managed affairs in some degree according to their own liking. When other men had sometimes complained that their wives did not always obey them implicitly, it had been the boast of Solon Rutherford that *his* wife knew her place and kept it; and now she was gone—gone without so much as saying "by your

leave," compelling him to remain in uncertainty as to her exact whereabouts. Was a man ever abused like this before?

Do what he would, however, he could not complain that the machinery
of home was being neglected during her absence. Aunt Judy took good care
that he should have nothing of that kind to worry over. Had he known the
overhauling for Edna's benefit that was going on over the house when he
was out of sight, he would have been insufferably angry; but there was
quite as good care taken that he should not know as there was to keep the
work about the house and poultry-yard well up to the accustomed scratch.
So Solon had nothing to do but be miserable, and he enjoyed the opportunity to his heart's content.

"Are you good at keeping secrets, Sambo?" asked Aunt Judy of one of
the farm servants that before the late "unpleasantness" abounded as chattel
property throughout the South.

"Yes, missus. Any orders?" and the darkey crossed his feet, cocked one
eye, and grinned expectantly.

"Yes, Sambo, I have orders, and I want you to promise that you'll try to
execute them promptly and keep my secret faithfully."

"Any pay in it, missus? Ye see, dis nigger's been runnin' on sh't
'lowance for nigh onto forty yeah, an' if dar's cash in the job, I nevah stan' on
scruples."

"Here's a handful of coppers, Sambo, and you shall have them every
one if you'll come to-night after you're sure your master is sound asleep and
get a two-bushel grain sack from my chamber window and carry it over to
my cabin for my late mistress, Edna Rutherford. And mind you, not a
word of this is to get out. Edna, poor child, has married a poor man, and is
destitute. Her father won't assist her, her mother can't, and Aunt Judy must.
Do you understand?"

"Law, yes, missus! We niggers have that very way o' managing, an' it
works prime."

"Poor things," sighed Aunt Judy as she turned away. "Like married
women they are servants without wages, and like the most of them, they'll
appropriate whatever they can gather surreptitiously if they can't do any
better."

Sambo was ready at the appointed time.

The great watch dog was silenced in obedience to his command, and
nobody being astir to discover him, he readily got possession of the booty
and disappeared in the waving corn.

Depositing the burden upon the humble door-step of Aunt Judy's home
and departing as noiselessly as he came, the inmates of the cabin did not
know till morning that he had visited them and the much-needed prize had
come.

Edna laughed and cried by turns. The very things needed most were in
the selection, and she laid many plans for their completest utilization as she
unfolded them one by one.

"What has come over my mother that she has dared to do this?" she
asked herself over and over again.

"I'm glad you've got your duds, Edna; but let *my* wife even try to deceive me in any way, and I'll see if she don't rue it."

"And who made *you* the custodian of *your* wife's will and conscience, pray, that she is to be compelled to live, breathe, and have her being only as you shall dictate?" cried Edna, her eyes flashing with mingled anger and contempt.

[To be continued.]

from
*The New Northwest*
Friday, November 3, 1876.

# NO STORY THIS WEEK.

Owing to circumstances which are doubtless unavoidable, and to us at present unaccountable, Chapter V, of "Edna and John" has not yet come to hand. We regret this exceedingly, and ask our friends to be patient, as all will be made right in due time.

from
*The New Northwest*
Friday, November 10, 1876.

# NO STORY YET.

A letter from Mrs. Duniway, under date of October 21$^{st}$, informs us that she mailed the story at that date at New York City, but it has not yet arrived, and, much to our regret, we are again compelled to go to press without it. The vexatious delay is doubtless owing to the careless handling of the mails.

from
*The New Northwest*
Friday, November 17, 1876.

# EDNA AND JOHN:
## A ROMANCE OF IDAHO FLAT.

### BY Mrs. A. J. DUNIWAY,
AUTHOR OF "JUDITH REID," "ELLEN DOWD," "AMIE AND HENRY LEE,"
" THE HAPPY HOME," "ONE WOMAN'S SPHERE," "MADGE MORRISON,"
ETC., ETC., ETC.

*Woman's degraded, helpless position is the weak point of our institutions today—a disturbing force everywhere, severing family ties, filling our asylums with the deaf, the dumb, the blind, our prisons with criminals, our cities with drunkenness and prostitution, our homes with disease and death.*—National Centennial Equal Rights Protest.

## CHAPTER V.

WHEN SUSAN RUTHERFORD found herself alone upon the busy docks bordering a great city, where, among all the thousands who were hurrying to and fro, as though each individual life depended upon individual dispatch, her heart gave a great flutter and her brain grew clouded with confusion. Hackmen offered all sorts of civilities which she was afraid to accept, lest the drivers should attempt to rob or insult her; street-car men looked unconsciously at their dash-boards and failed to answer her very faint halloo; policemen gave terse, unsatisfactory replies to her uncertain questions, and her head swam with bewildering sensations.

"How I wish Solon was here!" she exclaimed, repressing her hot tears with much effort. "Yet, if he were, I couldn't accomplish my errand," she added, as an afterthought. "Let me see! I've got to depend upon myself, so I'd just as well keep cool. Aunt Judy said I must go to the American Exchange. Dear me! I didn't know I did depend so much on Solon! When we came down here once to a barbecue, ever so many years ago, I just hung to his arm and paid no attention to streets or squares or numbers."

Thus soliloquizing, Mrs. Rutherford felt for her pocket-book to assure herself that nobody in the crowd had stolen it, clutched nervously at her great reticule, and ventured across the street.

A dapper little man stood behind an elegant counter in a profusely ornamented drug store, abounding in nauseating redolence.

"Can you direct me to a good, first-class hotel, sir? I'm a stranger in the city, and want to go to a respectable place."

The obliging vender of drugs directed the wanderer to an elegant uptown palace, where, had she known the prices for entertainment, she would not have thought to enter.

A woman whose three-score years of life has been spent in constant toil and strict economy upon a farm, where scarcely a dollar comes into her own hands in a quarter of a century, is illy prepared for the extravagance of a modern city hotel.

"If wives would only learn a little self-dependence!" sighed Mrs. Rutherford again. "But *there!* That's just what I am learning now. I love Solon— God bless him—and I want him always to be near me; but, when I know I'm right in wanting to do or not to do a thing, and he has all the power and all the say, and I've no alternative but to deceive or defy him, and I hate to do the first and won't do the last; and as I'm as determined as he is to have my own way a little, there's nothing else left to do but to go my way and attend to my own business. I will assist Edna! That's settled. But I feel like a sheep thief! I wish mothers either hadn't hearts and souls, or else that they had legal power to acquiesce in the dictates of their own consciences."

The colored porter stared impudently at the lone woman who dared to seek protection for the night in a first-class hotel without the fostering care of a man to guide her; and as Mrs. Rutherford sat waiting in a little reception-room while her name was being registered, she became so nervous that she would have gladly retraced her steps had she known how to do so. But the winding corridors bewildered her, and, with her plain shoes patting restlessly upon the cold stone floor, she waited, waited, waited.

She could never remember just how it was, but after a long while, in obeying the directions of another servant, she found herself within an elevator—a rarity in Western cities in those days—and ascending heavenward through a square tunnel with a velocity that was frightful, was soon landed at the door of her room. The good woman gave a little shriek, the ebony conductor chuckled, and as they reached the sixth floor, gave her the key and number of her apartment, indicated its direction, and shot down again, leaving her in utter trepidation. She would have escaped, but to her unsophisticated mind escape was impossible. Hurriedly disrobing, she laid her weary form upon the bed in that dingy chamber, and composing her anxious brain as best she could, fell into a restless sleep. As she slept, it seemed to her that in a far-off city a vast concourse of human beings had assembled to consult upon some very important public measure. Distant as they were, it yet seemed that they were nearer; or, rather, it seemed that she could span the intervening space with thought and place herself *en rapport* with the great assembly. Soon she saw that the gathering was of women;

and behold! they had drawn up petitions, protests, and resolutions, in which grievances many and various were ably presented and calmly discussed, each woman speaker proclaiming her belief in the inalienable right of every sentient being to life, liberty, and the pursuit of happiness.

"Is it possible," she thought, "that I have lived so long and never considered these things, as applied to womanhood, before?"

Then she bethought herself of the great world outside, and wherever she willed to go she went without further effort. And here she heard the comments of men; met the rude jeers and coarse, unfeeling laughter of the drunken loafers in bells and bagino's, who make laws to govern women. She floated through brick walls, into the private sanctums of the public press, and noted the glee with which the champions of freedom for men seized hold of each shaft of ridicule and misrepresentation which their ingenuity could devise to thwart the progress of freedom for women, and sent them forth as barbed arrows to fester in the flesh of timid, clinging, and conservative, though secretly discontented, wives and mothers, frightening them for a long time into silence, and often even forcing them into bitter denunciation of their best friends—those who had dared to brave the storms of public opprobrium in their own interests. Then she saw, too, that the barbed arrows struck sometimes into the quivering flesh of some woman less timid and more combative, and rankled there until the frantic sufferer gave vent to unseemly expressions of bitterness, whereupon the men who had sped the arrows, noting their effect, exclaimed, "Behold! The mothers who are discontented with the mastery of their sons over them are unreasonable, tyrannical women. Let us grasp our power still more tightly, lest we lose it altogether."

In her dream Mrs. Rutherford marveled much at all this. Then an angel approached her in shining raiment. His face was as the face of the sun, and as he advanced he held in his hand a mighty balance.

"Who art thou?" asked the dreamer, marveling that she was not afraid.

"I am Justice," said the angel; "and in this balance I am ready to weigh the motives of mortals. Let thine aim be for liberty, equity, responsibility and honor for man and woman, and in due time the oppressed shall receive of the fruit of her hands, that her own works may praise her in the gates."

"And I am Liberty!" cried a voice from an unseen source, while ringing tones of exultation reverberated through and through her being.

Looking eagerly, and it seemed strange that she could with her closed eyes see clearly, she beheld the feminine emblem of masculine freedom, the Goddess of Liberty, coming toward her, her classic face aglow with holy joy, a wreath of amaranth upon her brow, and the floating folds of the star spangled banner falling in billowy waves from her shoulders to her feet.

"How beautiful!" exclaimed the dreamer, involuntarily.

The Goddess shook her left hand deprecatingly, and a chain clanked in response.

Looking whence the sound proceeded, Mrs. Rutherford beheld the chain; and lo! it was riveted tightly around the wrist of Liberty, and descending, clasped her foot and held it as in a vise. Wondering as to what it all might mean, she looked again at the shapely wrists, and behold! with her right hand the Goddess was busily engaged in plucking at the massive chain, and one by one its many links were falling to the ground. Glancing toward the feet of the apparition, she saw, as though it had been a plank for Liberty's footsteps, a jeweled slab, and upon it was written, in letters of living light, the golden words, "Columbia[1] shall yet be free!"

The angel of Justice smiled radiantly as he noted the illumined thoughts of the speaker, and taking Liberty by the hand, held aloft the balance and gracefully assisted her upon its massive plate.

To the surprise of Mrs. Rutherford, instead of coming down with the weight of her body and the massive chain, the scale upon which she stood ascended till it kicked the beam with violence.

Again she looked and marveled much. But gazing earnestly with her closed eyes, she saw a dark form crouched heavily upon the lower plate, half hidden by his gloomy robes.

"And who art thou?" she asked in wonder.

The monster scowled and made no answer.

"His name is Tyranny!" said Liberty, as with a nervous twitch she sought to undo another link of the massive chain that bound her. But while the eyes of tyranny were fastened upon her, the attempt was vain.

"Dear mortal," cried Justice, holding aloft the scale, "when human law shall work in harmony with Justice, Liberty shall be no longer bound, but free. Appropriate, though galling, are the chains that Freedom weareth now. But, as one by one, when Tyranny sleepeth, Liberty picketh off the links of her bondage, so one by one shall the claims of Justice be established, and then Columbia shall be free indeed."

Mrs. Rutherford was not a literary woman, and was illy prepared to interpret her dream. She awoke in a confused state of bewilderment that was doubly enhanced by the sudden recollection of the terrifying elevator, the ebony conductor, the great hotel, and the fact that she was at the mercy of those who might keep her a prisoner at their own discretion if they should be so disposed.

"I don't much believe in dreams," she soliloquized, "but it does seem as if that one meant something."

She had cause, long after, to remember her vision and wonder much why its portent had been so hidden during all the intervening years.

She got on better in finding her way through the city than she had dared to hope. A few kindly directions gave her needed assurance, and at ten o'clock she presented herself at the bank, where her husband's name was good for any reasonable amount, and here she demanded a thousand dollars in his name.

"Have you an order from your husband, ma'am?"

"What should I want of an order?" was the amazed reply. "You know me. Solon introduced me to you the last time we visited the city together."

"Don't remember it, ma'am. Could you get anybody to identify you?"

Now, this was the very thing Mrs. Rutherford did not want to do, and which she had shunned her relatives in the city in order to avoid.

"No!" she said, indignantly, her womanly tact taking the place of her want of freedom, and, for the nonce, serving her exceedingly well. "I'll go back to my home and inform my husband that you refused, though you knew me well, to grant me the control of a few hundreds of the many thousands he has on deposit. You'll hear from him, gentlemen! Good-day, sir!" bowing to the teller with an indignant air.

"Wait one moment!" was the quick response, and Mrs. Rutherford sat down.

A private conference was held, which resulted in offering her a receipt for one thousand dollars, plus prepaid interest for one year, which the lady signed, clutching the bills in a nervous manner, and bowing herself out with a consequence that can only come to the possessor of, at least, pocket change.

To return to her hotel, settle her bill, and embark for home, was her next thought. Excitement kept her up till she found herself aboard the steamer, where she was seized with a nervous fear lest she should be robbed. Although for thirty years her dairy products alone had netted her lord an annual sum greater than the amount she now carried, to say nothing of her other multitudinous avocations, of which nobody took account, she had all her life been so utterly impoverished that a little money seemed like a mountain; and she caught herself wondering if everybody on board couldn't guess how rich she was. Thus the day wore on, and night came, bringing her near her home.

"I cannot face Solon with this money in my pocket," she thought. "He always knows all about everything I think, say, or do. I feel as guilty as a sheep thief. I'll just go on, up the river, to Aunt Judy's landing, and pay a surreptitious visit to Edna and John."

Her resolve thus taken was not hard to execute, as the obliging river steamers will generally stop at any possible landing-place for the least favor to a traveler. When the boat touched at the wharf near her home to deposit a few pounds of carpet-warp, and Solon came hobbling down to the river to get it, his wife hid herself in a state-room, as a fugitive might hide from the arm of justice.

Once on their way up the stream, she breathed more freely, and ordered herself landed under the hill, hard by Aunt Judy's home, without a perceptible tremor in voice, or manner. It was dark now, and her way was very uncertain; but mother love groped through and over every obstacle, and Mrs. Rutherford knocked at the rickety front door of the little cabin, her heart beating in audible thumps, as she awaited the tramp of dear, familiar feet.

"O, mother!" cried Edna, bursting into tears and falling upon her neck in a hysterical sort of way, "I am so very unhappy."

"Why, darling? A bride should never be unhappy! What does this mean?" and her mother caressed her tenderly.

"John!" was all that Edna could say.

"Why, pet? Isn't John kind to you?"

"Yes, mother; kind enough in his way; but he doesn't seem to have an atom of financial ability. I don't see how we're to make a living! He's perfectly contented if he has plenty to eat and some place to sleep, no matter at whose expense, and he has no thought at all for the future. I wish I were dead!"

"Child! child!" cried Mrs. Rutherford, "this won't do. Don't you know it's an unpardonable sin to speak ill of your husband? How do you expect to live with him through a lifetime if you are to begin like this, at this stage of the game?"

"O, mother, don't mention a lifetime! I hate the word! I can't bear the thought of it!"

"Alas, child, it's the old adage verified. 'Marry in haste and repent at leisure.'"

"I know it; and I've heard it till I'm ready to die."

"Where's John?"

"I neither know nor care."

"Why, Edna!"

"I don't!"

"Worse and worse!"

"Maybe I did wrong, mother; but, as you know, for this contemptible old hut of Aunt Judy's, we wouldn't have even a temporary roof over our heads; and, but for her bounty, we'd have no food. She left us here for a while to give us an opportunity to learn to work—to form our own nucleus, as she terms it. I'm doing my best, I'm sure. I've experimented till I can cook anything there is here. I can make butter and wash, and you know I always could sew. Well, I'm trying to do my part, but John doesn't see the necessity of doing his. I want him to spend some of his spare hours in fixing up things comfortably for Aunt Judy. Winter is coming, and she needs some kindly offices that he could as readily as not perform for her, when he's doing nothing but live upon her bounty. He turns up his nose at our surroundings, but I think beggars shouldn't be choosers. What do you think?"

"I think it's very naughty for my daughter to be talking thus about her husband," said Mrs. Rutherford dryly.

"But, mother, you know that I never was a member of the angelic sisterhood. If I had been, I shouldn't have married John Smith. That's certain!"

In spite of herself Mrs. Rutherford mentally agreed with her daughter.

"Where is John, did you say?"

"I didn't say."

"But do you know where he is?"

"No. We had a tilt at the supper-table, and he left the house pouting. He'll be back before morning, though, for he hasn't a cent to buy him a bed or a breakfast, and never will have, unless I can contrive some way to earn it for him."

"How did he live before you were married, Edna?"

"He had an allowance; but that was cut off as soon as old Rutherford cut *me* off penniless."

"Why, Edna! How *dare* you speak thus disrespectfully of your father?"

"He's no father of mine!"

"Have you a mother, child?"

"Yes; since she's visited me. I thought an hour ago I hadn't."

"What are your plans, child?"

"I haven't any."

"What!"

"I haven't any! I want to go to the Pacific Coast, but we've no money nor outfit, nor prospect of any. If I only had a wealthy father, I might borrow a thousand dollars; but I've only a mother and mothers never have any money."

"Would John take care of money if he had it?"

"He'd mean to, but he wouldn't know how. I don't want money; that is, not much. I want a wagon and team, and a complete outfit across the plains. That's all. And I want to winter here, if John will work enough for Aunt Judy to pay our expenses. It isn't much like your home, but it's better than none; only I don't want to sponge it."

"Do you think you could be happy if you should go to California?"

"I don't know and I don't care. Life is nothing but husks."

Mrs. Rutherford resolved to say nothing to Edna concerning the crisp roll of bank notes in her pocket until after another conference with Aunt Judy.

To place thousands of miles between herself and Edna was a terrible thing to think of; but, with a mother's usual self-abnegation, she was ready for any sacrifice for her child's happiness, and she heroically resolved to endure the separation at whatever cost to herself.

John came home, moody and silent. Like all incompetent husbands or wives, he considered himself a badly injured individual.

Mrs. Rutherford was frigid and calm; Edna was tearful and cross, and, taken altogether, a more unpromising prospect for connubial happiness could not well be imagined.

[To be continued.]

from
*The New Northwest*
Friday, November 24, 1876.

# EDNA AND JOHN:
## A ROMANCE OF IDAHO FLAT.

### BY Mrs. A. J. DUNIWAY,
AUTHOR OF "JUDITH REID," "ELLEN DOWD," "AMIE AND HENRY LEE,"
" THE HAPPY HOME," "ONE WOMAN'S SPHERE," "MADGE MORRISON,"
ETC., ETC., ETC.

*Woman's degraded, helpless position is the weak point of our institutions today—a disturbing force everywhere, severing family ties, filling our asylums with the deaf, the dumb, the blind, our prisons with criminals, our cities with drunkenness and prostitution, our homes with disease and death.*—National Centennial Equal Rights Protest.

## CHAPTER VI.

**M**R. RUTHERFORD met his wife with an injured air. He had been *lonesome!* She hadn't asked his permission to leave home, and so on.

"I know it all, dear," was the good woman's kindly reply. "I've been lonesome and uneasy about you many a time, and I knew how you'd feel, but duty called me away from you, and I really couldn't help it."

"No duty ever calls a woman away from her husband!" said Solon, angrily. "I provide this home for you, and furnish it with every needed comfort, and it's as little as you can do to be contented with your lot, and remain in it, madam!"

"Am I complaining, Solon?" asked the wife, kindly.

"You'd better be!" was the sulky answer.

Mrs. Rutherford did not care to prolong the controversy. But she could not help remembering the long and anxious years of weary trials of motherhood through which she had passed in her younger years of wifehood, when an infinitesimal fraction of her husband's present professed solicitude about her personal safety and comfort would have been to her weary body and tired spirit like refreshing rain drops to the thirsty earth; neither could she avoid recognition of the fact that in departing from her home on her own business, and at her own discretion for once, she had only followed the example set by her protecting liege in the beginning of their matrimonial career—an example to which he had adhered, whenever the occasion suited him, ever since.

It was also impossible for her to help knowing, woman though she was, that the "every comfort" her husband boasted of having so liberally provided for her to "stay at home and enjoy," had been the product of her own domestic industry.

But argument, where right is all upon one side, and usurped power all upon the other, is utterly useless, and no one is better aware of the fact than the powerless party in any controversy.

Finding that his wife so skillfully avoided further conversation upon the subject that so seriously annoyed him that its further pursuit was useless, Mr. Rutherford ordered his horse and buggy and drove away through the fields, leaving Aunt Judy and Mrs. Rutherford to talk over their business in unmolested security.

"Such a time as I've had!" said the latter. "I really didn't know how much I did depend upon Solon about some things till I went to the city alone. Accustomed as I am at home to taking the lead in everything that's disagreeable, giving him opportunity whenever he's in the house to read the newspapers and smoke to his heart's content, while I build fires and churn, and scrub floors and press cheese, and do everything else unaided, I was not prepared to find myself such a baby as I proved to be without him, when alone in St. Louis. Yet I couldn't help asking myself if it wasn't all in use, after all. And, Judy, I believe it is. The places of responsibility that require little exhibition of physical strength are all monopolized by the stronger half of humanity. Solon rides over the country in a buggy and speculates in land, using the money I've earned at the cheese press to complete his bargains, and puts the surplus in bank—"

"There, Susan!" interrupted Aunt Judy. "I'm glad you're coming to the bank business. Did you get the money?"

"Yes, I got it; but only by a little tact. I said something that led them to believe Solon would withdraw all his funds if they failed to honor his wife's demand. Men have a certain pride in impressing other men with the idea that they hold their wives' orders as honorable, and altogether above question. But I may make much of what I've got this time. I'll never dare to repeat the experiment. Yet, after all, why haven't I as good right to control the accumulated funds of our marriage copartnership as Solon? I felt like a thief when I took the money, although I knew that in God's eyes it was mine, if anybody's. When Solon discovers it he'll scold and act injured, and nearly break my heart by his coldness," and Mrs. Rutherford wept bitterly.

"Women don't deserve to be free, because they're such precious fools!" said Aunt Judy, contemptuously.

"I hope you speak from personal experience," replied her friend, laughing in spite of her tears.

"Yes, I do!" was the decided reply. "Women are slaves to their own hearts—slaves to the love they bear their fathers, husbands, brothers and children. They give men all the advantage, all the power, and then complain because the men accept it."

"I think you're wrong there, Judy. Men take the power, take the property, make the laws to protect themselves from each other, and then depend upon the chivalry which they cannot trust among themselves for justice to womanhood. Woman accepts the situation, first, out of her great love for her husband, and secondly, because she cannot help herself."

"But what of Edna and John?" asked Aunt Judy.

"Indeed, you've asked a question I cannot answer. Edna is already so sick of her foolish and hasty bargain that she is making both herself and husband miserable. He, poor fellow, means well enough, but he isn't a Solomon or an Atlas. He hasn't the wisdom to build a temple or rule a realm, nor the energy and perseverance to bear a world on his shoulders. Edna feels his incapacity, and, what is more, admits it. Wives generally stimulate their pride to enable them to endure their burdens by denying that their husbands can do wrong."

"Did you give them the thousand dollars?"

"No, Judy."

"You were wise in that. Those children must be taught from the beginning, as though they were babies. They don't know anything about the value of money."

"I don't know about that, Judy. Edna has suddenly developed a wonderful business acumen. She lays plans for the future, or tries to, rather, for you know she has no power to carry them out, but she tries to lay them with as much forethought as though she had all her life been accustomed to considering the ways and means of livelihood. But it won't do to trust John with money. Should I give them the roll of bills I have procured at such a sacrifice to my own peace of mind, he'd simply board and dress and ride in buggies and play billiards till it was all gone."

"What, then, do you propose to do?"

"It breaks my heart, Judy; but Edna wants to go with her husband to the borders of the far Pacific. She fancies that a new beginning away out in a new country will stimulate him to effort. I didn't tell her about the money, but I've made up my mind, if you'll give 'em shelter till spring, to provide them a team and traveling outfit and send them away with my blessing."

"But if Solon discovers that you have drawn the money from bank, what then? It's his, you know, in the eyes of the law, and he can seize the team you purchase, or anything else you get for them, if he so wills, and you cannot help yourself."

"I've thought that all out, Judy. You are to take the money, keep it through the winter, and do the buying in the spring. It will be quite a tax upon you to feed them through the winter, but I can slip you a little provision now and then, and will save some butter, and occasionally a cheese, for your pin money. If Solon only would let me, I should be so glad to open this great house to them, that I might enjoy Edna's society for the last time!"

The good woman could bear no more. Breaking into uncontrollable sobs, she stole away to commune in solitude with her own bitter thoughts. She remembered Edna in her babyhood. All the sweet, endearing recollections that clustered around the bright young life that had budded and blossomed in the old house were dead now, and she did not even have the sympathy of her husband in the dearth of her bereavement. Her heart ached for Solon, too. She knew how many fond hopes he had builded through all the years of Edna's childhood upon her brilliant future; how his every aspiration had centered upon the possibility of a brilliant match for her, the thought that she should ever excel upon her own account never having crossed his brain; she knew that, in spite of his stern exterior, he secretly loved his daughter still, and she longed, with an irrepressible loneliness, for his cordial acquiescence in her desire to make the best of circumstances from their present unsatisfactory standpoint. But Solon Rutherford was not to be approached upon the subject. His will was law, and his wife would have approached the Sultan of Turkey upon a forbidden theme with quite as much assurance as she could have mustered for the ordeal of approach to him.

Being a wife, and therefore incapacitated for doing business on her own account, except that business was fully understood and sanctioned by her protector and head, Mrs. Rutherford wisely gave the entire responsibility of her plans into the hands of Aunt Judy, who, being unsupported and unprotected, was in a measure free to follow the dictates of her own conscience.

Law books were procured for John, by Edna's contrivance, but the effort to make a lawyer of him only succeeded when she was by his side, reading with him, and absorbing legal lore for him. Besides, she could learn and retain knowledge so much faster than he, that his simple recitations became exceedingly distasteful to her. But she heroically nerved herself to endure his slower progress, and thus the winter wore away, bringing early spring-time, but, to Edna's great concern, no visible change in their prospects.

John was as contented as a pet kitten. He had plenty to eat, a warm fire to toast his toes before, a wife who belonged to him, and what more did he need? An ambitious man would have been uneasy as to the future, but not so John Smith.

Mrs. Rutherford, true to her promise, regularly slipped provisions to the cabin through the instrumentality of a trusty servant who had loved Edna from babyhood, and Aunt Judy managed to make such "turns" in her dickering at the village grocery as enabled them to keep the larder comfortably supplied.

Mrs. Rutherford visited her daughter once during the winter, thereby raising such a domestic storm at home as prevented a repetition of the experiment. Her husband believed the custody of his wife was his paramount right, and it was not strange that he failed to consider her conscience or inclination in the matter. Had the wife been fully awakened to her own responsibility, she would have met the storm and conquered it, as many a woman has done in these latter years, thereby bringing peace to her own heart and comparative happiness to the soul of her husband.

Solon Rutherford was miserable, even in carrying out his own purposes. Every human being is endowed with the natural inception of tyranny. A proper distribution of frictions and forces brings a proper equilibrium of liberty. Supreme, or one-sided power, brings unhappiness even to its possessor. But, as we have said, spring came, and with it no visible change in the financial prospects of Edna and John.

"Have you made any plans for the future?" Edna asked one day, after having pored over Blackstone[1] until every page and paragraph was indelibly photographed upon her brain, while John, with a memory like a blurred sentitive plate, seemed to fail in all the finest points of comprehension.

"I don't know as I have," was the simple answer, while he kept his eyes riveted upon the printed page.

"When do you intend to have any plans?" asked Edna, impatiently. "At this rate you'll conquer your legal studies in a quarter of a century, after which, in another quarter, you'll be able to introduce yourself to practice. In the meantime—'a fool for luck and a poor man for children,' you know—you'll have a family to support and educate, and who's going to do it?"

John vouchsafed no reply.

"Do you think," continued Edna, "that we have a life lease on Aunt Judy? And would you be contented to accept this home and these surroundings for a lifetime, if we had?"

Still no reply.

Edna could have bitten him in her impatience.

"Did you intend that I should be compelled to live like this, a prisoner upon the bounty of a poverty-stricken grand-aunt, when you made such roseate promises for the future in the model love letters that captivated me, but which I find to be no more like you on close acquaintance than if you never had written them?"

John blushed. He did *hope* that Edna never would discover that those letters were copied ones.

"I expected, when I married you," he said, at length, "that I'd step into a great farm-house, with negroes and post horses, and a fine carriage and everything splendid around us. If you are disappointed, so am I."

"But, John, you had no right to expect these things. You did not prove yourself worthy of them. Do you know what I'd like for us to do?"

"No."

"Do you care?"

No answer.

"I'd like you to crop your hair short, tan yourself in oak tea, let your beard grow, and go to my father's as a hired man. You needn't tell them who you are, and they won't know you in this guise."

"Well?"

John was getting interested.

"Then, I'd have you go to work as a farm hand, and make yourself generally useful. In a little while my father would learn to like you. There's no use talking, John. It isn't in you to be a lawyer, any more than it's in me to be a washerwoman. You may become a farmer if you're willing to work. Then, when you've become a *factotum* about the farm, and father thinks he can't live without you, I'll come and claim you."

John laughed immoderately.

Edna was angry.

"I've read such things in novels," she pouted, "and I supposed I was marrying a hero instead of a fool!"

"Edna!"

It was Aunt Judy who spoke in tones of rebuke.

"How should you like it if John should talk to you like that?"

"I shouldn't care!" was the ungracious response.

John left the house, slamming the door as he went and muttering inaudible discontent.

"I don't doubt that you, in John's place, could carry out some such idea as you have laid before him. You are heroic and foolish and energetic and romantic enough for anything. But you and John are two persons, despite the fiction that a law has professed to make you one. And you can no more successfully lay plans for John to carry out than he can so lay them for you. Book life is one thing and real life another, as books go. So lay aside your romantic notions, and let us be sensible. Suppose you emigrate to a new country, like California, or Oregon, or Nevada, and begin your life out there?"

"You might as well say, 'Suppose you engage cabin passage to Jupiter,' auntie. The very idea is absurd. We have no money, no outfit, and John has no enterprise."

"Edna, I will not allow you to disparage your husband under my roof! You have no right to speak ill of him! A lady would not do it!"

Edna would have retorted, but she could not afford it. She had nowhere else to go, and could not risk being turned out of doors, so she hung her head and burst into tears.

"I am going away for a few days," continued Aunt Judy, "and I want you to promise me that you will not be unreasonable with John. He is not over strong in the upper story, but he means to be good, as far as he knows, and you must *encourage* him."

"How can I, auntie, when I am so utterly discouraged myself?"

"That's for you to learn, my child. Now keep a brave heart. When I return—now mind, you're not to whisper this to John—a way will open for you to go to California."

"O, auntie! Do you think so?"

"I know it, child. And now, remember! You must be considerate with John. He's just as much at sea as you are. A little adversity will do you both good. You mustn't reproach him. No man will bear reproaches from his wife. You must make the best of your bargain. That will insure harmony, without which you had better be dead."

"If *wishing* would kill me, I'd be dead this minute!" said Edna, impetuously.

"Which is very foolish and very, very wicked," said Aunt Judy, sadly. "You have a long life before you, and you have the talent and power to make it a very useful one. To want to die because you find yourself unprepared to live, is a thought wholly unworthy of a sensible woman."

[To be continued.]

from
*The New Northwest*
Friday, December 1, 1876.

# NO STORY THIS WEEK.

We regret to announce that Chapter VII of "Edna and John" did not come to hand this week. We cannot understand the cause of the delay, as a letter from Mrs. Duniway, under date of November 8, states that she started the story at the same time. All we can do is to ask our readers to wait and have patience.

from
*The New Northwest*
Friday, December 8, 1876.

# EDNA AND JOHN:
## A ROMANCE OF IDAHO FLAT.

### BY Mrs. A. J. DUNIWAY,
AUTHOR OF "JUDITH REID," "ELLEN DOWD," "AMIE AND HENRY LEE,"
" THE HAPPY HOME," "ONE WOMAN'S SPHERE," "MADGE MORRISON,"
ETC., ETC., ETC.

*Woman's degraded, helpless position is the weak point of our institutions today—a disturbing force everywhere, severing family ties, filling our asylums with the deaf, the dumb, the blind, our prisons with criminals, our cities with drunkenness and prostitution, our homes with disease and death.*—National Centennial Equal Rights Protest.

## CHAPTER VII.

**M**ARCH WAS ABROAD in the land. Accompanied by chilling winds and fitful snows, alternated by brief and brilliant sunshine that waked to life the early bloom of springtime, he searched through and through the rickety roof of Aunt Judy's humble home; blew ashes down the chimney; bit her tender chickens with frost nips, and played havoc with her ducklings; thawed the snow away from field and highway in great patches; brought mud and muck by day to alternate with icicles by night; and the prospect over all the landscape within Edna's range of vision was as dreary and hopeless and chill as the aching voice that slumbered within her desolate heart.

Her husband came in after Aunt Judy's departure, sullen and silent. When he had abruptly left her after her last cruel taunt, he felt that he would gladly remain away for all time, could he know where to go. But Aunt Judy's home, humble as it was, was better than no shelter, and he sauntered back at last resolved to make the best of it.

A kindly word or look or act of recognition or affection from Edna, and all had been temporarily healed that was well-nigh a rupture between them;

but Edna would not condescend. She merely stitched away, a trifle faster than before, upon a patch-work quilt, the material for which had been surreptitiously gathered from her mother's ample store and brought by the same trusty hands that had carried her wardrobe to Aunt Judy's dwelling, and she was resolved, as she formed patch after patch into shape, that, though she would always work for John, and as far as her conduct went, be true to him, he should never hereafter receive a word or look of love from her, unless he should himself inaugurate it.

What John thought she could not divine. He was as imperturbable as adamant, and it was long before she looked at the legal tome he was holding with sufficient scrutiny to observe that it was upside down. This discovery caused her to curl her lip contemptuously, but she would not speak.

At last John shut the book with a bang, and with a desperate effort so far conquered his pride that he threw himself upon a stool at her feet.

"It's no use, Edna; I can't live this way!" he exclaimed, impatiently. "I'm a poor dog, without home or master. I've no resources, no profession, and no trade. I've a wife that despises me, and I don't wonder at it. I'm going to California."

"O, John!"

"Are you willing, Edna?"

"*Willing,* John! I'm only too anxious! But you might just as well say you're going to Jupiter."

"I can work my way."

"I'd like to know how you'd work your way? You can't drive oxen; you've no horses or wagon, and no money nor energy."

Unwise Edna! How could you be so cruel? John needed encouragement and you failed to bestow it! Alas for Edna, and alas for John!

The husband was already suffering keenly from a humiliating sense of his own littleness, and needed kindness rather than censure. He buried his face in his hands and wept bitterly. Edna stitched spitefully at the patchwork quilt.

"I wish I were dead!" he said at last.

"There are two of us in that condition!" retorted the wife. "Anything to get out of this!"

"Would you be happier if you should never see me again, Edna?" asked John, his voice faltering.

Edna's expression of contempt changed to one of pity, and she left her needles in the cloth, and in spite of her resolution, laid her right hand caressingly upon his brow.

"Could you try to love me just a little, Edna?"

It was her turn to weep now.

"Get up and sit beside me, and be a man!" she said, through her tears. "As you have said, we're 'in for it,' and cannot help ourselves now. I want you to go to California, but I do not want you to go alone."

"Would you be willing to go with me, provided I could arrange for your comfort on the journey?"

"Yes, John. Anything to get away from the humiliation and discontent of this dreary existence. I feel like a prisoned eagle here. But what are we to do? You know that I and ours will need nursing and tenderness. I shall not be able to be of much help to you for months to come, and the Almighty Dollar is my constant dream."

"Is that your father riding through the lane?" asked John, suddenly.

"It's Solon Rutherford, Esq., sir," said Edna. "The man upon whose shoulders rests the responsibility of having trained me up in a conservatory, in order to fit me to grow on the bleak mountain top, and then left me on the mountain without any shelter, is no parent of mine. No, John, don't say he's my father. I disown him!"

Ah, Edna, what a discipline you are yet to have, ere all the woman in your nature shall assert itself and you shall come out of the crucible of a hard experience, tried, as by fire![1] What a pity the vast capabilities of your strong nature have been perverted by a false education! What a pity you were not trained aright from your infancy! And above all, how sad is the reflection that the worst mistakes of the parents are to be visited upon the children![2]

"I have an idea, Edna," said John.

"I'm astonished!" was the contemptuous answer. And then, as John only looked down his nose and made no further remark, she at length glanced up from her stitching and said:

"Well?"

"I'd only astonish you further by explaining, and my idea is of no consequence," was John's sullen reply.

Edna liked that. If John would only act with a little spirit of his own, even if directly opposed to her wishes in all things, she felt that she would like him better.

"Then you needn't explain your idea. I only suggest that you set upon it. Anything is better than this accursed stagnation."

"That's strong language for a lady, Edna."

"I look like setting myself up for a *lady,* truly, with these elegant surroundings and a wealthy husband!" was the unwomanly response.

John did not wait for further bandying of words. Leaving the house in a nervous, impatient way, he hurried across the fields toward the Rutherford farm-house, while Edna gazed after him with mingled curiosity and contempt.

"To be fettered for life to such a milk-and-waterish nonentity is an outrage on my common sense!" she exclaimed, involuntarily.

"She doesn't appreciate me, or depend upon me in the least, else I might have a little more ambition," thought John.

And so, while Edna went on with her stitching and John was hurrying across the fields, both were as thoroughly miserable as each had expected to be sincerely happy in the relation for which they were so poorly fitted that no state involving "cruelty to animals," over which philanthropists have distinguished themselves, could be compared to their condition.[3]

John found Mrs. Rutherford in the cheese-room, with her skirt turned up and fastened behind her waist with a pin, her sleeves rolled above her elbows, and a scrubbing-brush in her suds-wrinkled hands.

"I don't ask you to forgive me for marrying Edna, for I never can forgive myself," he exclaimed, stepping gingerly upon the wet flags and looking about him with a critical air.

"Why, John? What now?" and Mrs. Rutherford placed her arms akimbo and gazed at her son-in-law as though he had been a monkey.

"You didn't bring her up right, ma'am. She's as full of hoity-toity notions about her fancied superiority over me as I am full of determination to rule my own household."

"Yes, John Smith," said Mrs. Rutherford, excitedly, "and she has more sense in a minute than you'll ever have in your lifetime. If she were the man, and you the woman, as times go, she might lead you along and make a living; but with the power and the privilege all on your side, and the sense and ability to manage all on hers, you are both in a sorry predicament, John Smith—a sorry predicament."

Poor John! What could he do? Dependent, as this marriage had made him, upon the relations of his wife for his daily bread, he was compelled to accept the humiliation in silence.

"I want to go to California!" he said, at length. "And I want to know if you can assist me. I can't guarantee you any security against loss, but I will promise to do my best to repay you when I can."

"You know that married women have no right to their own earnings, John Smith. If they had, it would be easy enough for me to aid you. But I've toiled for a third of a century on this farm and there's nothing here that belongs to me. It's all Solon's. Why don't you see what you can do with him?"

"Because he won't even look at me. Edna might bring him to terms maybe, but she is so much like him that she won't bend an inch."

Mrs. Rutherford nodded satisfactorily.

"I'll break her in yet; see if I don't!" John added, *sotto voce*.

"What will you do with Edna while you are away?" asked the mother.

"She wants to accompany me," said John.

"And do you think you can take care of her?"

"That's a strange question to ask a man about his wife."

"But a very natural one for a mother to ask about her baby, John. You must remember that Edna is very dear to me."

"Of course; but it isn't to be expected that you will care for her as her husband does. A wife belongs to her husband, you know."

"I know," sighed Mrs. Rutherford, stooping to wipe her eyes with her wet apron; "but, husband or no husband, I can't forget the long years of her childhood, the sweet ways of her babyhood, the terrors of her birth, and the anticipations I have felt for her future. If a mother must yield up all claims to her child as soon as the child is married, there ought to be a provision in nature to uproot her fond affection at the same moment. But my scrubbing is done now. Let's go into the dining-room where the fire is. Solon won't be at home to-day, and we can have a chance to lay some plans."

The two had scarcely had time to be seated before Aunt Judy's rubi-cund face appeared at the door.

"Come and see what I have bought, Susan," she exclaimed, not know-ing John was by. "Four yoke o' cattle, a splendid wagon, provisions enough for six months, a tent and camp fixings, and I've made up my mind to go with 'em myself."

John shrank behind the door and his heart beat high with hope.

"Edna's strong willed, and isn't half disposed to be just to John. He's no Solomon, but he can be managed—"

Mrs. Rutherford put her fingers on her lips and the sentence was not finished. John wondered what it all could mean.

"What little household plunder I have doesn't amount to much, and I can give it away," continued Aunt Judy; "and you know I can control the team if it remains in my name, for I'm not married, whereas, if John knew it was Edna's—"

"John is here!" interrupted Mrs. Rutherford, turning deathly pale.

Aunt Judy saw the situation in a twinkling.

"I was just going to say," she said, extending her hand with a smile, "that if Solon knew the team and outfit I've been buying was for Edna, he could give us trouble."

"I don't see how he could give us trouble about anything that belonged of right to my wife!" said John.

Aunt Judy was nonplused. If Edna's husband did not comprehend her *ruse,* he was certainly informed as to his own legal prerogatives.

"At any rate," she continued, "the easier way is the better one. This team and outfit is mine, and, if you want to go to California, now is your time. Go home and tell Edna all about it. I'll be along presently, and we'll soon be on our way across the Continent. I'm going with you."

John obeyed Aunt Judy's suggestion with alacrity. He was not at heart a bad man. Indeed, his natural impulses were for good, and, had he been properly trained to rely upon himself, rather than depend upon an allow-ance that had, prior to his marriage, rendered personal effort for subsis-tence unnecessary, his case would have been by no means a hopeless one.

With a much lighter heart than he had carried an hour before, he re-traced his steps, and bounding into Aunt Judy's abode in a manner that frightened the dog and caused the cat to spit and grumble, he shouted:

"Eureka, Edna! We're off to-morrow for the setting sun! Aunt Judy's a *brick,* if she *is* old-fashioned and pokey."

"Much prospect *I* see for getting off!" said Edna, rising from the hearth with her face flushed from bending over the hot coals, where she had been baking "dodgers"[4] for the last ten minutes.

"The old woman's got the team and the outfit complete. I heard her say so. And Mrs. Rutherford put her finger on her lip and warned her to keep still, or I'd have gotten into the whole secret. Depend upon it, they're put-ting up some job on that refractory dad o' yours, and are trying to keep me in the dark, as well. I'll go to California, but I'll find out what they're up to."

"My mother and Aunt Judy will attempt nothing that is not honest, John, and you will show your good sense, if you have any, by holding your tongue over that which doesn't concern you. You know the team isn't yours, and if they give you and me the joint use of it, common courtesy, to say nothing of gratitude, will keep you from meddling in their private affairs."

"I heard Aunt Judy say the outfit was Edna's," said John, aside, "and if it's hers it's mine, and what's mine's my own. I'll have no wife o' mine owning property and holding it over me! That outfit's worth a cool thousand to start on. John Smith, you're a lucky dog."

A day or two of bustle and preparation, and all was ready for the journey.

At that time the Pacific Railroad was only a creature of ambitious imaginations.[5] Hundreds and thousands of adventurous pioneers accomplished the journey every summer, often leaving the buried remains of individual parties of their number as a tribute to the desert solitudes of the plains, and often enduring privations and fatigues which were only surpassed by the grief of sudden bereavement.

Mrs. Rutherford well knew that Edna's proposed journey would be no child's play. Her husband had not only forbidden Edna to enter his house, but had commanded his wife to see their daughter no more, and but for the fact of an unexpected call from home, which he, as owner of great possessions, was compelled to obey, Mrs. Rutherford would not have dared to bid her daughter farewell.

Edna's brothers and sisters, with their wives and children, had entirely cut her because of her new relation, and it was a sorry parting when her mother, alone, among all her many loved ones whom the sacred ties of affinity and consanguinity rendered dear, held her in a last embrace and mingled her tears with hers in a parting too grievous for mother and daughter to bear.

Aunt Judy alone was tearless. Her face beamed with a quiet pleasure, born of awakened purpose. The smallest preliminaries received her particular attention, and she could with difficulty restrain her curiosity when Mrs. Rutherford consigned a little fawn-skin covered trunk to Edna's keeping, with a few whispered words which caused the daughter to blush and reply, "I will, mother, and may God bless you."

[To be continued.]

from
*The New Northwest*
Friday, December 15, 1876.

# "NO STORY."

It is with extreme vexation that we again enter an apology under this head. Somebody or something is at fault, we know not whom or where. The story did not come, that annoying circumstance is certain, and our readers will please bottle their impatience, as we do our wrath, and wait with what composure they can assume for further insight into the journeyings of "Edna and John."

from
*The New Northwest*
Friday, December 22, 1876.

# EDNA AND JOHN:
## A ROMANCE OF IDAHO FLAT.

### BY Mrs. A. J. DUNIWAY,
AUTHOR OF "JUDITH REID," "ELLEN DOWD," "AMIE AND HENRY LEE,"
" THE HAPPY HOME," "ONE WOMAN'S SPHERE," "MADGE MORRISON,"
ETC., ETC., ETC.

*Woman's degraded, helpless position is the weak point of our institutions today—a disturbing force everywhere, severing family ties, filling our asylums with the deaf, the dumb, the blind, our prisons with criminals, our cities with drunkenness and prostitution, our homes with disease and death.*—National Centennial Equal Rights Protest.

## CHAPTER VIII.

**A**ND NOW THE LAST GOOD-BYE was spoken and the young couple who had made life's bitterest mistake were marching on in their weary way across the Continent.

Aunt Judy, strong in her will power, earnest and conscientious in purpose, and executive in all things, directed the incidents of the journey in her own peculiar way.

Edna had underrated John's ability as an ox-driver when she had taunted him with deficiency in that peculiar business; and she was compelled to admire the intuitive skill with which he managed the patient brutes under his care.

"My old notion that nothing was made in vain has received added strength since I discovered that John was really good for something," she said to Aunt Judy, as she watched her husband while he slowly trudged along, whip in hand, ever journeying westward and yet never getting nearer the setting sun.

"I never saw a man or woman yet who hadn't a useful niche in the world somewhere," was Aunt Judy's reply, "and I really believe that were it not for the abomination of the law, which gives the husband an undue advantage in all things, when he is disposed to accept and use it, that you and John might get along in the world first rate.

Edna curled her lip scornfully.

"If it hadn't been for me," continued Aunt Judy, "you would have been a *grass widow!* Think of it! And now you have so far conquered yourself—"

"That I am out here in the wide wilderness, fleeing from myself, from my mother, my home, and everything except John Smith, to whom this self-same law you speak of has bound me and from whom, rather than all else in the world, I would gladly flee!"

"*Hush, Edna!* Don't talk so loud. John will hear you and his feelings will be hurt. You have no right to think and talk and act as you do. You are very wicked. He's as good as you are, and is just as much disappointed in his marriage as you can be."

"Then why wasn't he willing to get out of it when I left him at the hotel? I'm sure I was ready to release him from all obligations on my part."

"Edna, could you give him back his heart?"

"I suppose not," was the meditative reply. "That is, supposing he had one, which I very much doubt. He loves himself and his own ease, I admit that, but it's moonshine to imagine that he loves me. You are welcome to all the glory which you arrogate to yourself for having prevented a rupture between us that would have made me that thing you so detest—a *grass widow;* but I loathe myself as I am, far more than I could if I were forty grass widows. For a whole month we have been journeying on. Day after day we toil and struggle, soaking our food in the mud and drizzle, or blistering our faces in the scorching sunshine; nothing to be seen but sage and sand hills; nothing at all to be enjoyed, not even the congenial company of a wise young man."

"Edna, you are morbid, and you disgust me!"

"I know it, and I don't care. I was brought up in a morbid condition. I detest John Smith. I abhor myself."

Here was a problem beyond the skill of Aunt Judy's brain to solve. She had through all her life, dreamed upon a beautiful conjugal theory, akin to that which Edna had imagined in the boarding school; and here was Edna, whom she had fondly looked upon as the embodiment of all things lovely, with a husband who was evidently striving to the utmost of whatever skill he had to make her paths pleasant, and she was as restive as a spirited, un-broken colt under the halter of its master.

But what could Aunt Judy do? To act as go-between the two such un-congenial yoke-fellows was to keep herself constantly between two fires.

And thus the days and weeks and months rolled on, bringing no satis-faction of soul to any one of the travelers who might, in other conditions and better moods, have viewed with a joy as unbounded as the atmosphere they breathed the diversity of hill and plain and mountain range and mighty cata-ract through which they slowly wandered.

"Behold me, Aunt Judy," said Edna one day, after they had wandered for a long time beside the waters of Great Salt Lake. "I am Edna Rutherford that was, but now Mrs. John Smith, wife of a man who can drive oxen. I was educated to fill an important station in the world of literature, science, and society. I am married now, and doomed to bear children, live among savages and drudge like a squaw. I'm sick to death of this tedious journey and I don't believe I'll budge another inch along this toilsome road."

"And what would you do here, Edna? Surely you would not turn Mormon?"[1]

"I don't see but I'd as well be a Mormon as what I am."

Aunt Judy turned away, mortified and sad. It was growing dark, and John Smith called a halt with his jaded team under the lee of a mighty spur of the Wahsatch Mountains and prepared to encamp for the night.

"Yonder comes a team," said Edna, seating herself with a painful effort upon the bare, hard ground, where, Turkish fashion, they were compelled to sit and eat their meals.

"As I live!" said Edna, "it's my old friend, Sue Randolph!"

"Why, *halloo!*" exclaimed John, rising to his feet to greet the new comers. "Glad indeed to see you. Been on the plains all summer?"

The man thus addressed looked a trifle older than John. He was more marked in feature, and evidently possessed more mental and physical stamina, as well.

"Yes; been jogging along since March," he said, cheerily. "Allow me to introduce my wife, Mrs. LaSelle, Mr. Smith."

"Ah!" said John, extending his hand. "Glad to meet you. Hal and I are friends since boyhood."

"Indeed? Then I know I shall like you, for I like everybody that Hal likes, don't I, dear?"

"Ay, ay, Sue. Let me tell you, John, she's a duck of a wife. Introduce me to Mrs. Smith, pray."

Poor Edna! Before her stood the man whom she had imagined was John Smith during the days of their clandestine, boarding school and letter courtship. She had often seen him from the fourth story window of the seminary for girls, and the one stolen and hurried interview she had held with John prior to their marriage in the shadow of the dark wall, where he had thrilled her with embraces, had always been associated in her mind, until the last interview dispelled the illusion, with the blissful shades of a departed dream.

"What's the matter, Edna?" asked Aunt Judy, turning from her new acquaintances to the wife of John Smith, who had fallen prostrate across a stack of ox-yokes beside the battered wagon.

For a long time Edna did not answer. Aunt Judy and Mrs. LaSelle held counsel for a moment, intelligent glances were exchanged between the two men, and preparations were speedily made for the coming night, which was one of solicitude, suffering, confusion, and patient watching, and the morning found Edna pale and peaceful, lying at ease upon the dingy pillows of her traveling couch and by her side a wee baby girl with raven hair and eyes like night.

"God has been very good to me, Aunt Judy," said the young mother, as she tenderly toyed with the tiny hands of her fragile babe. "I don't deserve this precious gift, for I've been rebellious and naughty, but I have something to live for now, something that is *mine*, and heaven helping me, I will try to prove worthy of the boon."

"Haven't you a kindly word for John, Edna? The poor fellow's heart is breaking for you. No matter what his motives may have been in marrying you, he certainly has done his duty toward you since he has been your husband, and has treated you with more devotion than you have bestowed upon him."

"Call Sue, Aunt Judy, please, and don't say anything more to me about John. I shall try hard, for the baby's sake, to fight my own battle; but anything and everything you say about him exasperates me. I believe I never should have hated him so thoroughly if you hadn't always been preaching him up."

"I've caught an idea and I'll use it," thought Aunt Judy, with a chuckle. "As soon as Edna's had a little time to forget that she has given me a cue to new tactics, I'll change my plans."

It cost Edna a great effort, weak as she was, and overcome by many contending emotions, to greet her old schoolmate and rival, Sue Randolph, with the unreserved affection of old days, yet she conquered herself and did it.

"Your baby is a beauty, Edna!" cried her friend, leaning over the pillow and crowing after the manner of a warm-hearted girl. "What name do you intend to give her?"

"I hadn't thought of a name, Sue. There isn't a name in the catalogue that will couple musically with Smith."

"Nonsense! I remember well, and it wasn't very long ago either, when you thought the name of Smith the most-to-be-desired of all cognomens."

"She little suspects that it was because I fancied it was worn by LaSelle," said Edna to herself. "She never shall suspect it, either, for I'll conquer my old fancy or die! For my baby's sake I'll endure this wicked farce to the bitter end."

"Call the babe Hallie, there's a dear," said Mrs. LaSelle. "Hallie Smith is a pretty name."

"But I like names that mean something. There's no significance in such a title as that."

"It means that you will name her for my husband."

"And that means a great deal too much," said Edna, with a laugh. "I'll call her Idaho."

"*Phoebus,*[2] what a name!" cried Sue. "What ever put such a thought in your silly pate?"

"I had a dream last night—a dream that means something, I know, though I'm not at all superstitious."

"I'd say not," said her friend, "seeing you do not believe in dreams, or anything of the kind."

"You needn't laugh, Sue. After the baby came, and you had all retired, and I was lying with my precious charge in my arms, afraid to fall asleep lest I should wake to find that she had vanished, I dreamed of Idaho. I hadn't thought of it before, but I'm going to persuade John and Aunt Judy to turn our oxens' heads in that direction tomorrow."

Mrs. LaSelle was disappointed.

"I thought, now we'd providentially fallen in each others' company, that we should, of course, remain together."

"No," said Edna, "it must not be. Sometime, when baby is quite a girl and we are all rich, you can visit me, you know. I may not tell you my dream, Sue, but it was prophetic and we must go to Idaho."

Mrs. LaSelle expostulated in vain, and after a time left Edna to her own reflections.

"I would not dare to go in the company of Hal LaSelle to California," she said to herself. "I know what I can and what I cannot bear better than anyone else can know, and if I cannot love John Smith, I will at least protect my honor, for his sake and my baby's."

In the meantime the two men had talked over their private affairs and had come to the conclusion to continue their journey together toward the Golden State. The thought of consulting the women had not occurred to them, and when the proposition was forced upon John, he treated it with supreme contempt.

"He was head in his own household and didn't propose to be ruled by any woman," he thought.

Poor Edna! How she longed to warn her husband! How gladly would she have unbosomed her whole sorrow, and sought to obtain his sympathy and forbearance, if she had only dared!

"I've only one alternative!" she said, as struggling with her tried affections she would press her innocent babe to her bosom and pray for strength and guidance in the paths of duty.

"This trial will kill me!" she sobbed in her helplessness. "At any rate, I must tell Aunt Judy all about it or I shall die!"

The opportunity for a private conversation with the dear old lady did not come till the day was far spent, and a score of miles over rocks and mountains had been laboriously overcome. By this time Edna was in a raging fever and her words were only half coherent.

"Prevail on John to go with me away from Hal LaSelle!" she cried, wringing her hands and clinging to her babe, as in a frenzy.

"Why, child, what harm will Hal LaSelle inflict upon you? He's a perfect gentleman and devotedly attached to his wife."

"I know it, auntie, dear. That is not the trouble. Will you try not to despise me if I tell you all?"

"Certainly, you precious simpleton! What is the matter?"

"O, auntie! I was weak and wicked and foolish and mistaken; but I thought Hal LaSelle was John Smith before I was married, and I really didn't know any better till it was too late."

Aunt Judy, woman like, needed no positive information expressed in indubitable language to enable her to comprehend.

"You know I never saw John but once, till I ran away to marry him, and then it was in the black shadow cast by the moonlight on the seminary wall that we met, and I could only half see him, and then for only a minute," said Edna. "It was his letters that bewitched me. Mr. LaSelle used to pass down the street and touch his hat to me, as I thought, from my perch in the window, but I now find that it wasn't me, but Sue Randolph, he was courting, and I—I—married the wrong man."

"You precious fool!" said Aunt Judy, bending low and kissing her tenderly.

"And you don't despise me, now you know all about it, auntie?"

"Despise *you,* you silly child? Of course not; but you must allow me to relieve my feelings by speaking my mind if you intend me to be able to be of any service to you in this matter."

"Now, auntie, you must prevail on John to go to Idaho. Hal has made his positive arrangements for California, and there is no danger that he will accompany us. Nobody but you and I need to know what I have told you. Do persuade John. I can't talk to him about it for fear he will suspect the truth."

"You'd better tell him all, Edna, and trust to his magnanimity. That's the best thing under the circumstances."

"Auntie, he has no magnanimity. He feels that I belong to him—am his property—and any revelation I make will only cause him to insult Hal and humiliate me. You don't know him as well as I do."

"Then let me talk to him, dear. I'll manage him."

The insane rage of the husband of Edna over Aunt Judy's cautious and necessary revelation could only be compared to the fierce dignity of a barnyard Bantam when he finds that the Dorking that he has proudly appropriated as his own has had the audacity to cherish a smothered preference for a superb Cochin China.

Instead of humbly blaming himself, inasmuch as he was blameworthy, for the clandestine manner of his marriage with a badly brought up child who had only known him under the false color of other people's love letters, he at once grew very tenacious of *his rights,* and fumed and cursed like a pirate.

Aunt Judy was frightened. Mr. LaSelle was astonished at his old friend's bad temper, for the cause of which he could discover no clue, and after a miserable night of wrangling that would have disgraced a Kanaka,[3] John Smith re-yoked his oxen and started in the morning with Aunt Judy and his feverish wife, whipping the cattle into a run over the rocky roads, and acting in all things as though it was his purpose to make Edna as thoroughly sick of her dearly bought bargain as it was possible for her to be and live.

[To be continued.]

from
*The New Northwest*
Friday, December 29, 1876.

# EDNA AND JOHN:
## A ROMANCE OF IDAHO FLAT.

### BY MRS. A. J. DUNIWAY,
AUTHOR OF "JUDITH REID," "ELLEN DOWD," "AMIE AND HENRY LEE,"
" THE HAPPY HOME," "ONE WOMAN'S SPHERE," "MADGE MORRISON,"
ETC., ETC., ETC.

*Woman's degraded, helpless position is the weak point of our institutions today—a disturbing force everywhere, severing family ties, filling our asylums with the deaf, the dumb, the blind, our prisons with criminals, our cities with drunkenness and prostitution, our homes with disease and death.*—National Centennial Equal Rights Protest.

## CHAPTER IX.

AUNT JUDY was so thoroughly annoyed over John Smith's rage and ranting that she was for a while completely cowed.

But when a woman is not the wife or mother of a man; when no special tie of affinity or consanguinity compels her to cringe and fawn through that overweening affection in which many generations of over stimulation has made the sex morbid, it is not possible for an unreasonable and unreasoning son or husband of some other woman to long hold her at a serious disadvantage.

After the first hour of John's revenge had been expended in inflicting tongue-lashes upon the spirit of poor weeping, sick, and wounded Edna, and equally unjustified and unjustifiable whip-lashes upon the bodies of the patient, toiling, suffering oxen, Aunt Judy took advantage of a lull in the tempest, sprang from the wagon to the ground—and for a woman of her avoirdupois the effort was not a slight one—and snatching the whip, exclaimed, in tones of defiant authority:

"John Smith, I discharge you from my service, sir! This wagon is mine, and the oxen, the bed, and everything else included."

"Maybe you'd like to claim the wife and baby!" said John, with a sneer.

"I do claim them, John Smith. You have outraged every law of God in your fury, and we are out of the reach of the laws of men, so I propose to protect this sick woman at all hazards."

John hung his head in silence.

"Give me the whip," continued Aunt Judy. "You are not fit to control a caterpillar."

John was astounded. Hadn't Aunt Judy always plead for him before? And now that she had turned against him, what was he to do? He had mortally offended Hal LaSelle, so he could not now go back to seek his assistance and advice. Indeed, that was the last thing he would have been willing to do, anyhow.

"Now, *travel!*" said Aunt Judy, looking him in the eye with a steady gaze, before which his countenance fell.

John did not know what to do, and as he stood before his fate, hesitating and helpless, his courage all oozed from his tongue and fingers' ends, what should Edna do but, woman-like, declare herself his sworn ally?

There are men, plenty of them, who will scold, ill-treat, and sometimes even whip their own wives, who become virtuously and instantaneously indignant if any other man offers them the slightest incivility; so there are women, plenty of them, who consider themselves fully licensed to speak evil of their own husbands, who will fight for them in an instant if anybody else attempts to coincide with them.

"Aunt Judy," cried Edna, "if you leave John by the roadside, you must leave me, too. Remember you have always told me that I accepted him for better or for worse, and if this isn't the 'worse' part of the bargain, I don't know how to find it."

Possibly this declaration, unexpected as it was, touched John's better nature. The look of innocent injury which he assumed as he said, in a despondent tone, "No, Edna; go with Aunt Judy; it makes no difference what becomes of me!" would have done credit to a star actor.

Edna was in a raging fever, and consequently in no condition to think or act with judgment; yet the hereditary disposition of woman asserted itself fully.

"Help me out of the wagon, John, and lay the baby by me on the sand," she said. "If Aunt Judy discards you, she must remember there are three of us."

Had Edna's wifely fealty but asserted itself yesterday, when Aunt Judy had been pleading for John, the dear old lady would have been thoroughly happy, but now she was entirely disgusted.

"Hear anything o' that, old woman?" cried the husband, exultantly. "Maybe you'd like, with all your boasted love for Edna Rutherford, to leave her to starve out here in the wilderness."

"I ought to," replied Aunt Judy. "It would serve her right for being such an idiot. But John, if I do allow you to go on with me, remember you are not to mistreat your wife. She has acted nobly in fleeing from the presence of Hal LaSelle. The trouble with you is that you are not capable of appreciating her motives."

"I can't for the life of me see where the nobility of the motives come in," said John doggedly. "If he had cared a straw for her, she wouldn't give a fig for her integrity. She's acted the fool about *him* when he didn't care the scratch of a pin for her feelings! It was Sue Randolph *he* was in love with, and she thought it was *herself,* the *silly goose!*"

"I guess you may help her out of the wagon, John! If you and she desire this cat and dog life, with starvation as an added inducement, I know no human law to restrain you. But *I* will not live in a wrangle, and we will not go a step further together till this thing is settled."

It was well for Edna that the bracing mountain air of Utah and Idaho surrounded her, supplying the fever in her veins with oxygen to keep her blood from consuming, else she would not have lived to continue her journey and fight her battle of existence longer.

She closed her eyes in an agony of humiliation and shame. Yes, it was true, too true; she had given her love, unsought and undesired, to Hal LaSelle. She did not stop to consider how much her own volition had or had not to do with the matter; she only felt the bitter, mortifying truth. And as she lay in helpless agony upon the way-worn, travel-soiled bed, and clasped her newborn infant to her breast, her bitter self-condemnation, whether it were wise or unwise, might well have made an angel weep.

John looked at the helpless young mother, as her tears watered the pillow, and a spasm of tenderness overcame his sordid, narrow soul.

"Aunt Judy, what say you? Suppose we bury the hatchet! Suppose we own up that we've all been too hasty and acted like idiots."

"I couldn't say it so far as Edna and I are concerned," was the calm reply.

"Then say it, so far as I'm concerned, and let it go! I don't see what we are to gain by continuing this quarrel."

"Then," said Aunt Judy, "will you let bygones be bygones? Will you forget your imaginary grievances and prize your wife all the more highly because you find that she is ready, even in the hour of her greatest weakness, to choose self-abnegation rather than possible dishonor?"

"I didn't think of that before, Aunt Judy. She is a jewel, and no mistake. Shall we stop quarreling and proceed to Idaho?"

"That seems to be the plan."

"Then take your seat in the wagon, auntie. We've up-hill work before us for many days and nights yet."

And up-hill work indeed they had. The country was new and the roads almost wholly unmade. The trails of Indians, though very good for Cayuse ponies, formed often a precarious footing for the oxen and a doubly dangerous bed for the wagon wheels. The mountains were high and the streams rapid; the plains were sandy, and to all appearances, sterile; and the wild and strange monotony of their journey was varied only by long trains of pack mules loaded with supplies for mountain miners.

Great phantom-like frameworks spread their skeleton arms high in the air, bearing aloft mighty streams of water for hydraulic mines, carrying the precious fluid across ravines and gulches and down into the fastnesses of the gloomy forests, where beds of golden sands lay hidden. The great desert-like valley stretching afar and anear in all directions with its ash-colored verdure of sage brush, through which wild rabbits roamed, the tortuous Snake and winding Boise Rivers, running like silver ribbon through the distant plain; the mountains, abounding in verdant grasses and gorgeous with floral beauty; the solitary stage making its daily journey through the arid plain, were all great helps to Edna as she lay in the wagon fighting her own battle, and resolving, with what heroism none who has not been the tried can know, that she would conquer her destiny and live according to her highest convictions of right, regardless of her own happiness.

The days and weeks wore on, and the long journey was near its close.

A recent mining excitement had broken out among the men who were digging for gold in myriads in another part of the Territory, and the crowd was now assembled at Idaho Flat.

Let no one who reads these pages ever act so insanely as to attempt to find the geographical locality which we have thus designated. Should he attempt it, he will surely fail, for the name is given thus on purpose to mislead him. The place was not a flat at all, but the exact reverse. It is a romance of real life that we are chronicling, however, and we expect you to studiously avoid being too inquisitive or critical about localities, identities, or even facts. Not that we would mislead you about these last. Indeed, the only object (aside from pecuniary reasons) that would induce us thus to write at all, is that we may lay facts before you; facts as parables; facts as lessons; facts as they are in the every-day life of more than one woman who pursues the allotted rounds of a life of heroic effort, combining the heroism of a general with the wisdom of a statesman, the toil of a bondwoman with the self-abnegation of a martyr, and the conscientiousness of a Christian with the lie-living existence of a hypocrite.

You may not be pleased at the picture, reader. We are not writing to please, but to instruct you; not to tickle your imagination, but to set you to thinking.

To prevent the unpleasant results of the possible identification of the real actors in this interesting drama, we purposely call places by fictitious names, and assign our characters to localities that do not exist. Now hearken:

Idaho Flat was a rocky gulch, upon whose precipitous sides a few men had discovered paying "prospects" in the early spring. A mountain stream which we shall call John's River after the fashion of the country, though it was not a river at all, being nothing but a rapid-running creek that lost itself in summer in a tributary to a larger stream that disgorged somewhere, five or six hundred miles below, into the current of the Columbia, and overflowed its banks in the early spring when the melting snows were seeking the sea level. John's River gave a very meager supply of water for mining purposes at the season of the advent of Edna and John, but men were working like beavers, in both effort and numbers, in getting the "pay dirt" excavated to make ready for the autumn rains. Cabins, of unique design and Lilliputian proportions, were perched here and there upon knolls; tents that had once been white, but had long reveled in the creamy color of the mountain dust, were planted here and there; pack mules, loaded with their burdens, stretched themselves lazily upon the hillsides; men in gum boots and gray flannel waded in the river bed; "saloons" and provision stores nestled together under the lee of some blasted pines, and a "faro bank"[1] stood ominously near the camp where Aunt Judy decided to pitch her tent.

Edna was now well and tolerably strong. The baby Idaho proved an obliging immigrant, who slept almost constantly, and there seemed nothing to hinder Edna, who, except Aunt Judy, was the only woman in the Flat, from building up a little fortune from the proceeds of her own labor.

Years after, when she had learned by bitter experience the folly of building fortunes over which she was allowed no control, she saw the folly of her young ambition, but the wisdom came too late to furnish her material aid.

John very soon struck a bargain with a logger and arranged to haul timber with the jaded team of Aunt Judy from the adjacent mountains.

A cabin had just been vacated on a knoll hard by, of which the women took possession, and they were soon domiciled therein in apparent comfort.

"I'll die here!" said Edna, after the first day of comparative inaction in the cabin. "I must do something to keep up the excitement. Suppose I turn pastry cook."

"Take my advice, Edna, and depend on John for a livelihood. He's not over ambitious, as you know, and whenever you begin to take other burdens on yourself than the care of your house and family, he'll begin to lop and lean, and you'll have the bag to hold."

"Nonsense, Aunt Judy! You're perfectly absurd. John will go on with his work and I with mine. He'll have his funds and I'll have mine. Times are good and gold is plenty. These miners are starving for a woman's cooking. Every one of 'em has been brought up by mothers and sisters, and when I display my pies and bread and doughnuts, they'll buy in quantities. We'll get rich after a year or two, and then won't I go home and show 'Squire Rutherford whether or not he can lord it over me?"

"I'd like to know what you are going to get to cook out here, and what arrangements you are going to make to cook it," said Aunt Judy.

"I'll build me a mud oven, and I'll make dried apple pies, auntie. Of course we wouldn't eat 'em at home, where we had everything else we wanted, but these miners will devour them by the wholesale."

To make the "mud oven" was anything but the romantic work that Edna had planned in the boarding school. The first attempt was a total failure. After a vast amount of mortar-mixing, that caused her hands to chap and bleed and her temper to exhibit none of the mildest of its phases, the mass of mud and rock was shaped into a sort of hollow dome, which was filled with combustibles and fired. The heat was too strong and too sudden, and the unwieldy mass cracked wide open, still further taxing Edna's temper, and causing several days' delay. Then the experiment of firing the oven was repeated, but with greater skill, and the first dozen of tempting, crispy pies that were exhibited upon a rough table covered with old newspapers brought a price that well repaid the tired caterer for all her trouble.

For a few weeks all went well. Then a drizzling rain made logging in the mountains difficult, and John Smith lounged for a day or two around the cabin, watching Edna's financial exploit with evident relish. Then he began to sell pies and pocket the change. Edna did not remonstrate. She had never intended to have interests separate from her husband, and was very glad to see him interested in her work.

After a while winter came and the oxen were pastured in a neighboring valley. Edna had brought her husband's law books from her former home, and one of the bitterest disappointments of her life lay in the fact that it was impossible to prevail upon him to pursue their study.

The saloon and faro table hard by possessed attractions which he fully appreciated, and often during that first trying winter of Edna's life in Idaho Flat, did the poor young mother listen in vain till the wee small hours of the morning for the return of her husband from the haunts of vice, where the fascination of gambling became his evil genius.

[To be continued.]

from
*The New Northwest*
Friday, January 5, 1877.

# EDNA AND JOHN:
## A ROMANCE OF IDAHO FLAT.

### BY Mrs. A. J. DUNIWAY,

AUTHOR OF "JUDITH REID," "ELLEN DOWD," "AMIE AND HENRY LEE,"
" THE HAPPY HOME," "ONE WOMAN'S SPHERE," "MADGE MORRISON,"
ETC., ETC., ETC.

*Woman's degraded, helpless position is the weak point of our institutions today—a disturbing force everywhere, severing family ties, filling our asylums with the deaf, the dumb, the blind, our prisons with criminals, our cities with drunkenness and prostitution, our homes with disease and death.*—National Centennial Equal Rights Protest.

## CHAPTER X.

EDNA HAD SO THOROUGHLY DISCIPLINED her mind to the idea that she must believe in her husband under all circumstances that it was long before she took real alarm from his idle habits.

John was not at heart a vicious man, and when half tipsy he was always supremely good natured. Edna's contempt for him in no way diminished as she saw him regularly appropriate her hard earnings to his own individual indulgences, but she only strove the harder to supply the fuel for the constant drain upon their resources, till at last she fell sick, and then the trouble came in earnest.

Aunt Judy, with whom the change in climate and surroundings had gone hard, was excessively rheumatic, and became utterly unable to supply the market with pastry, after Edna fell ill, and the family exchequer grew alarmingly empty.

"John," said Edna, one day, after a vain effort to arise from her bed to attend to the demands of her business had resulted in a relapse, "couldn't you learn to make the pies and doughnuts, and carry on the business till I get well again?"

"Do you take me for a woman?" John replied, with a maudlin laugh.

"Then what are we to do, John? I've worn out my strength in your service, and am no longer able to carry on the work. Do you intend to let us starve?"

John could not comprehend the situation. So long as there was a meal ahead he was as happy as the day.

"We'll be compelled to sell the team," said Aunt Judy, at last, though this conclusion was arrived at through many tears and misgivings, for the team was her only possession, and while she retained it she was not without hope that when the spring should come and the roads be again passable, she might get away from the mountain fastnesses and reach the settlements with Edna and the child. In her own mind John had been given up as lost from the first hour that his drinking habits became apparent.

"John," and Aunt Judy tried hard to speak cheerfully, "there was a miner here to-day who intends to engage extensively in flume[1] making in the spring. I agreed to sell him our wagon and oxen. It will be a great trial, for while we had the team we had the means of getting out of this, you know. But we'll starve unless we do something. Edna is like to be down for all time, for what I know—thanks to your kindly care for her comfort! I'm rheumatic and used up, and with the snow all around us, the mines frozen up for the winter, and the only able-bodied member of the firm so dignified that he isn't willing to work at making pies because he's of the sex that's able to plume itself upon dignity, I'll be compelled to close the bargain and part with the oxen right away. Now, I want you to go down to the bottom and get 'em up. Four hundred dollars will keep the wolf from the door till spring, if I have the handling of the cash."

But John did not go for the cattle that day, nor the next. He was always ready with some trivial excuse, and always promising to go to-morrow; but to-morrow never came, and at last the last loaf of bread was gone and the last mouthful of food of any description had disappeared.

John was not hungry. He was tolerably clever at draw poker, and the free lunches of the low groggery where he spent his hours of leisure, and they were not limited, seeing he was wholly without occupation, were regularly forthcoming; so, blunted as he was in his sensibilities by drink, he was incapable of an adequate conception of the real needs of his household.

If there is one place superior to all others in genuine liberality, that place is a mining camp. The little Idaho, the only child in the diggings, was an object of positive adoration among the bronzed and bearded men who had wandered far from the abodes of their loved ones, with whom was an ever-abiding and tender memory. Many of these men had left their homes to woo the fickle god of fortune, expecting soon to return; but with hopes long deferred by constant failure to secure the much-coveted wealth they had come in quest of, they yet lingered in Idaho Flat, eating and drinking, through the long winters necessarily spent in idleness in the mountains, the proceeds of every summer's toil.

Aunt Judy and John had had a fearful quarrel. After many seasons of importunity, in which the good woman had vainly plead with her idle ward to fetch the cattle that they might be sold to save the household from starvation, he said, one day, with provoking coolness, "I don't see why you need to worry. The miners won't see the women and children suffer."

"And, is it possible, John Smith, that you are so far dead to all sense of independent honor that you would willingly depend upon the efforts and charity of strangers for your family's support?"

John left the cabin, slamming the ponderous puncheon door with a clamor and bang that sent a thrill of nervous agony through poor Edna's temples and almost threw her into spasms.

"Aunt Judy," said she, speaking from a sudden impulse which a moment's reflection would have caused her to forego, "I'm afraid John has sold the team already."

"And what, pray, would he have done with the money?" cried Aunt Judy, the sudden start of surprise throwing her into a fresh tremor of rheumatic twinges.

"I don't know, auntie. Please forget that I said it. God knows I would not misjudge John. I have chosen my fate, and it is as little as I can do to honor it. This is your own teaching, you know."

"Yes, poor child! But I little thought, when I counseled you to make the best of a bad and foolish bargain, by sticking the closer to it, that you would ever be the means of bringing us all to the verge of both starvation and disgrace!"

It was a cruel taunt. Poor Edna, weak and helpless, and so full of her own miserable contempt for the weakling who was dragging himself and family to the lowest depths by drunkenness and profligacy, that she was paying the forfeit of her disgust by a lingering and painful illness, could only answer by silent tears.

Little by little the whole truth leaked out. John had sold the team and squandered the proceeds of the sale at the gambling board. At first he was penitent, but a consultation with his friends at the groggery put a new phase upon his affairs, and he became insolent and abusive.

There was little law, except of the Lynch[2] order, in Idaho Flat. Men were bound to each other by a code of unwritten honor, which the most of them instinctively respected, and woe to the transgressor who disregarded it.

But, if they knew how to deal with each other as men, they were signally at fault when differences of opinion concerning property rights grew up between husband and wife, hence they could not interfere with the rights of Edna and John, or even of John and Aunt Judy in property matters.

Could Aunt Judy have proved that the property in question was hers, instead of John's, or, rather, John's wife's, it would have aroused the indignation of every miner to its highest pitch to have known that he had thus appropriated it; but the accepted idea that a man cannot wrong a woman in person or property, if that woman be his wife, was orthodox law in Idaho

Flat, as it is in too many other localities in America where men are the sole arbiters of financial destiny.

"The team wasn't yours, but Edna's, and you needn't be putting on airs about it, Aunt Jude!" said John.

"I should like to know how you make that out!" was the old lady's help-less reply.

"I'm not always asleep when I'm supposed to be napping," continued John. "I heard you and old Mrs. Rutherford talking these things over to-gether before we left the States, and I know that you're infringing on my rights every time you interfere in my family affairs!"

This was a blow to Aunt Judy's pride, but how was she to help herself? She was absolutely without proof that she was other than a pensioner upon the bounty of John. It was not customary for women to own property in their own right when there was a man at hand to claim it. How was it that she had been so blind?

But it is useless to follow the miserable family through the sickening ordeals of that terrible winter. Over the humiliation of Edna, the wrath of Aunt Judy, and the dissipation of John, let us, in mercy to the reader, draw a veil.

Partly upon the charity of the miners, partly upon the precarious earn-ings of John's gambling, but chiefly upon such slight income as Edna was able to command by her pastry cooking on such days as she was able to creep around the cabin, the family subsisted.

Spring came at length, bringing balmy sunshine and gentle breezes to allay the rigorous cold that had held carnival through the long months pre-ceding her much-desired advent.

Work was resumed in the diggings as soon as the melting snows made water abundant, and soon the mines were literally black with searchers for the hidden ore.

With the return of pleasant weather came better health for Aunt Judy, whose rheumatic twinges gave way under the genial rays of the springtime sunshine.

The baby Idaho, or Ida, as the miners loved to call her, was the pet of the settlement, and her young life was a constant ovation in spite of her un-toward surroundings. Edna idolized the child.

"She came to me when I had nothing else," was her excuse to Aunt Judy for her deep attachment to the little waif, which was never allowed to be out of her sight for a moment, lest some harm might befall her. But John, poor demoralized and maudlin fellow, became an object of such utter in-ward loathing that her whole life was a hypocritical farce.

Things were in this unsettled condition when one day an old gentle-man with white hair and venerable mien approached the cabin, leading, and half bearing in his arms, the drunken head of the family, who, with silly smiles and voluble utterance, ordered Aunt Judy to prepare some food for the stranger.

The old lady was in the flour to her elbows, and so busy with the pastry cooking which Edna had long been unable to do that she was in no very amiable mood.

"I must say that I look like cooking food for strangers, don't I, now?" she asked, abruptly.

The stranger looked at her with a glance of surprise, and then, controlling his emotions with an effort of his will, said, pleasantly, "I beg your pardon, madam. I have no desire to intrude if my visit is not opportune. This man informed me that you accommodated travelers with food."

Where had Aunt Judy heard that voice? Had she ever heard it, except in her dreams? She turned deathly pale.

"O, sir," she faltered, "it's no trouble at all to get you a dinner."

And then, in spite of her ruffled temper, the good woman smiled like a sunbeam, as she flitted hither and thither about her work, and soon placed before him, on a snowy tablecloth, made of the bleached linen sacking of the flour used in the mines, carefully overseamed in the middle and as carefully fringed at the edges, one of the most savory meals ever gotten up from almost nothing, whether in the mines or out of them.

"Sir, will you be so kind as to tell me your name, and from whence you are come?"

The question was an abrupt one, and Aunt Judy was surprised at herself for having uttered it.

"I am known as 'The Stranger,'" was the abstract answer, "and I sometimes wonder if I am not the Wandering Jew."[3]

"I like that," said Edna, from her invalid's seat in the corner, formed of a dry goods box covered with gunny sacks, her head resting against the rough, unhewn wall of the cabin, and her feet ensconced upon a sack of beans, which a miner had given to Aunt Judy in exchange for a stipulated number of doughnuts and pies.

"And why do you like my title, if I may be pardoned for the question?" asked the stranger, turning from the repast before him and looking inquiringly into the eyes of the invalid, who regarded him with an interest bordering on fascination.

"I like it because there is mystery and excitement about it. I like anything better than this plodding, humdrum life that brings nothing with it but toil, pain, weakness, weariness, and disgust."

"You see, Mr. Stranger, that my wife's imbibed ever so many foolish notions," said John. "She's concluded that she's smarter than I am, that she lowered her dignity by marrying me, and all that. Just as if I'm not giving her as good a home as any poor man gives a wife in these diggings! She's been laid up for three months, too, and I have supported her through it all."

"Yes, John, you are a most exemplary husband! Anybody can see that!" thought Edna, turning her face toward the unhewn wall to hide the tears that would start in spite of her effort to subdue them.

"Never mind trouble," said the stranger. "When you've seen as much of life as I have, and have learned that in spite of the husks you get when depending on others for happiness that there is a perennial fountain within yourself, from which you can drink copious draughts of pure contentment, you will have found, not the philosopher's stone,[4] but the still waters of a quiet life. One must live one lifetime before he learns the art of living at all."

"And how, pray, can you learn to depend wholly upon yourself, and live for no one except yourself, when you have others depending upon you and hampering your life continually?"

"You do not understand me, madam. Husband and children are parts of your very self."

"Under some circumstances they are!" thought Edna. Then, aloud:

"I don't believe at all in living for one's self alone. I believe that the purest life is that which is given wholly for others; and of all selfish and unhappy mortals that I have ever met, the man or woman who has no domestic obligations is the most miserable."

"Then why are you unhappy, madam?"

"Because I am sick."

"And why are you sick?"

"Because of a good many things that do not suit me."

"Sir," said Aunt Judy, "you will find my poor charge to be the most inconsistent of mortals. She never talks in the same strain for two consecutive minutes."

"That is because she lives one life and dreams another," was the stranger's reply. "To be true to one's own inner consciousness is the secret way to the living waters of which I have spoken."

The stranger departed, leaving Edna in a maze of bewilderment.

"True to one's own inner consciousness!" she murmured, "ah, me!"

Aunt Judy sat down upon the pack-saddle just vacated by the stranger and closed her eyes in a dreamy reverie.

"But for you, my baby Ida, I would curse God and die!"[5] cried Edna, in her bitterness of spirit.

"Edna, you blaspheme! You make me shudder!" said Aunt Judy. "You must conquer such a spirit as that or you will have not rest here or hereafter."

"Auntie, did you ever see that man before?"

"Edna, what a question! Are you crazy?"

"I believe I am! Would to God I knew I were an idiot!"

"Idiots have very little sense of either pain or pleasure," said Aunt Judy. "It is very wrong of you to make such wishes. We are not always to live like this. If it were not for the legal hold John has upon you, which takes away your opportunity to control your own earnings, and renders me helpless also, we'd get along well enough. The trouble is not alone or chiefly that John is dissipated and improvident. The worst of it all is that the law, recognizing the husband and wife as one, and as that one the husband, you are not allowed to be the arbiter of your own destiny."

"There, auntie, you've said enough! When I take a notion to monopolize John's pantaloons, I'll let you know it."

"Poor child, if you could monopolize your own petticoats, I'd have a little more interest in life," was the sad reply.

[To be continued.]

[*Ed.:* Friday, January 12, 1877—"Edna and John" does not appear in the January 12, 1877 issue of *The New Northwest*, and there is no mention of its absence. Mrs. Duniway has, at this time, stopped off on her way home from New York to visit relatives in Illinois, and although we don't learn any particulars about this week's missing chapter, from her "Editorial Correspondence" we learn that she has been much aggrieved by the postal delays that have necessitated several previous missed installments. "We are so thoroughly vexed," she writes, "because you do not get the story fast enough for regular publication that we'd be tempted not to trust another chapter to the mails, only we'd fail to offend Uncle Sam and only insult our readers, who are already injured because the postal servants fail somewhere in the discharge of their duty."]

from
*The New Northwest*
Friday, January 19, 1877.

# EDNA AND JOHN:
## A ROMANCE OF IDAHO FLAT.

### BY Mrs. A. J. DUNIWAY,

AUTHOR OF "JUDITH REID," "ELLEN DOWD," "AMIE AND HENRY LEE,"
" THE HAPPY HOME," "ONE WOMAN'S SPHERE," "MADGE MORRISON,"
ETC., ETC., ETC.

*Woman's degraded, helpless position is the weak point of our institutions today—a disturbing force everywhere, severing family ties, filling our asylums with the deaf, the dumb, the blind, our prisons with criminals, our cities with drunkenness and prostitution, our homes with disease and death.*—National Centennial Equal Rights Protest.

## CHAPTER XI.

GRADUALLY, VERY GRADUALLY, did Edna's shattered health come back.

The spring passed far along toward its closing days; the chill breezes of the earlier months gave way to the balmy breath of May; the mountain snows, that lay fathoms deep upon the zigzag heights, melted under the genial action of the sun and air, making water plenty and gladdening the hearts and brightening the prospects of many a miner in Idaho Flat.

People flocked to the mines in droves. As yet, very few women had come to cast their lot with the two solitary ladies whose lives had been such a succession of hardships during the long winter months; and now that business was again active and the demand for Edna's pastry made it necessary that she should work to supply it, and as Aunt Judy's age and rheumatism both incapacitated her from doing active work, there were fearful drawbacks to be encountered.

"If John were only sober, or I were only well, or we were not bound to each other at all, I might see some ray of light for the future; but, auntie, I cannot live at this rate, and I must get rid of John!" said Edna, one day, in a sudden burst of angry defiance.

But to resolve, in her case, as in the case of many another woman thus situated, was one thing, and to execute another. Before she had had time, after having risen from her bed and again begun her pastry business with profit—a profit of which John availed himself daily by standing at the receipt of customs when sober enough—almost before she had had time to realize the ordeal that was before her, the mother of Ida, now a charming child of ten months, became the mother of a son, making what the miners call "two crops of children in a year," as the result of a hasty marriage and the wicked subjugation of the really responsible party to the contract.

Of course Edna was again prostrated, and now, with two babies and a sick mother on her hands and heart, dear Aunt Judy, outraged as she had been by John's conduct in robbing her of the team, as well as his drunkenness and want of thrift and foresight, may well be pardoned by the average reader, for we are compelled to chronicle the fact that she forbade John the house, and sought, infirm as she was, to set up an establishment wherein she would not be compelled to support him, although willing, as she expressed it, "to crawl on her hands and knees to get a living for Edna and the children."

But, as in the case of Edna, it was easier to resolve to get rid of John than it was to put the resolve into execution. John simply would not go.

"If Edna were to drink and lie around idle as you do, or, if she'd squander money as you do, it wouldn't take very long for you to *compel her* to go, my lord Smith!"

"But Edna *don't* drink nor gamble, as I do, and so the cases are not parallel! Though, as the *lying around* part, she's hardly earned her salt in the last six months."

"Auntie," said Edna, after she had so far recovered as to be able to wait a very little upon herself and a great deal upon the two babies, "I wish you'd get married!"

Aunt Judy gave a mellow laugh, as she settled herself with some difficulty upon a syrup keg that since the cabin had been able to boast such a luxury, served her, when covered with a gunny sack, as a seat.

"*Married, child!* Don't you think one fool in the family's enough?"

"Yes; but that isn't the idea. I can see that you consider your lot a hard one here, and I don't wonder that you do, I'm sure. The old gentleman who comes here every day for pies, and for whom I notice you invariably reserve the nicest ones, only wants a little encouragement—a very little. He doesn't drink or gamble, and as to the babies, I guess you needn't fear 'em at your time of life."

The old lady blushed and fidgeted, and Edna proceeded:

"If you had a home for me to flee to, Aunt Judy, I might get away from John."

"But suppose my—ahem! *he* would—would—*object?*"

"Who? *John?*"

"No, not John."

"Oh! how stupid I am! Suppose my uncle to be should object? Is that what you mean?"

"Yes, Edna."

"How *could* he object? Once I was clear of John, I might make my own living, you know. These babies won't be babies always; it's only the constant fear of bringing more along that makes me so miserable! And there is no law to protect any woman from the authority of a man to whom she's married, unless she leaves him for some other man, and I can't see how that would help her along any, for men are all alike, as times go."

"Edna, be ashamed of yourself! I hope you don't compare the gray-haired gentleman you want me to marry with John Smith!"

The ringing laugh that followed this indignant outburst was more like the Edna of old than any indication of her former self had been since her marriage.

"I guess you'll get well now," said Aunt Judy. "People never die so long as they can laugh like that."

"I don't propose to die, auntie. I've spent breath enough in idle, unavailing wishes to die. I am resolved to be free."

"Yes, you goose; and if I should say one word to you against your living with John, you would act the woman and stand by him through thick and thin. Do you remember how I tried to take possession of the wagon and team last summer, together with you and the baby, while I had everything in my own hands, and set John adrift to shift for himself?"

The memory of the humiliation through which Edna had passed when she had honestly striven to conquer an unwarranted attachment, overcame the poor victim of circumstances, and her tone of ringing laughter changed to one of half suppressed lamentation.

"I was imposing penance on myself, auntie. Hadn't I always been taught that self-sacrifice was woman's highest duty? How I wish the women of this so-called free country would rise in the majesty of their innate consciousness and overthrow the tyranny of custom that makes wifehood subservient in all things to the frailties of husbandhood!"

"Edna, you *shock* me!"

"I've been shocked with myself for nearly two years, good auntie. If I shock others, it is only the natural effect of a very unnatural cause. I tell you, auntie, that woman's degraded, helpless position is the weak point in our so-called free institutions to-day. It is a disturbing force everywhere, causing unequal, incompatible marriages, severing family ties, driving men and women to insanity, filling the world with paupers, criminals, drunkards, idiots, prostitutes, and monstrosities, and crowding our homes with disease and death!"

"Mercy, child! Where did you ever learn such talk?"

"Through the experience of the last two years, auntie. In the first place, had my mother been a free woman, she would never had consented that I, her precious child, as dear to her as her own heart strings, should have been sent away from her to spend my earlier days and dwarf my life through time and eternity through a false and wicked marriage, contracted in ignorance, yea, verily, conceived in sin and brought forth in iniquity! Had she had the power, she would have kept me near her, she would have given me responsibility and opportunity, and, instead of allowing me to dream my life away in a one-sexed *sham,* called a seminary, but more properly a cemetery, for the hopes of many a blighted life are buried in such vaults, I would have learned to estimate men, not through the roseate dreams of romantic girlhood, but through the avenues of sensible, practical acquaintance. Then, too, I would have learned that independence, or individuality, was not only my right, but my necessity, and instead of looking constantly for a matrimonial alliance with some ideal man, who proves to be no more like the real article than roses are like jimson weeds, I should have been laying plans for the future, as men do, that would have kept marriage out of my head till I should have been old enough to have chosen sensibly."

As Edna warmed with her theme, her countenance appeared as if glorified. Through mental and physical suffering she had become attenuated almost to a skeleton, and her great eyes beamed with an electric light that caused Aunt Judy to tremble for her sanity. "Edna, dear, you must not allow yourself to become so much excited," she said, soothingly.

"Auntie, I must have vent or I shall *die!"* was the earnest answer. "I have curbed 'excitement,' as you term it, till its inward fires are consuming me!"

"Then, Edna, why did you not consent for me to set John adrift on the plains, when I had the team and the power, and you only had one of these helpless babies to depend upon your weakness for a support?"

"Remember, auntie, I had a feeling that I had wronged John in having secretly loved Hal LaSelle. I was humiliated, too, beyond expression, over the whole affair. Though, now, as I look back upon my part in that awful drama—how awful none but me can ever know—I do not feel the self-condemnation that then possessed me, because I now know that I was in no wise responsible for the dream or its sad awakening."

"But did you not know it then?"

"Auntie, how could I? I had always been taught that affection was the creature of the will, and I believed that no pure girl had ever before allowed her heart to stray, even for an instant, where love had not been first expressed by the opposite party; and I, to do the penance that seemed my duty, in my self-abnegation, and in the abnegation imposed upon woman by precedent and custom, I resolved to die, if need be, to humiliate myself before John. Yet, auntie, what's the use? The more I am humiliated, the less he appreciates me, and the more I indulge him in his present course, the more deeply he degrades himself."

"Well, dear, I don't see what you are to do."

"Nor I, either, auntie. I'd rather die than be a grass widow, and if it were not for these children, I *would* die, by my own hand, to get free. But it *is* for these children, auntie, so I shall not die, but I'll get rid of John."

"When a sick mother, with two babies, and penniless withal, proposes to get rid of a drunken husband who *won't* leave, and *she can't,* I confess that I don't see through the mountain, Edna. If you were only back with your mother, now!"

"Ah, auntie, there's the rub![1] If my mother were as independent as So- lon Rutherford—and if she were allowed half as much control over her earnings as the laws of the United States protect him in, she would be as independent as he—she would write to me and say, 'Come home, my daughter! Your mother's arms *ache* to clasp your weary form to her grief- stricken heart. Come back to me! I have plenty for us both. Together we will rear your lambs. I will be happy when you are with me. Let bygones be by- gones, my darling.' I *know* she'd say this, auntie, for I dreamed it all out last night when John lay snoring beside me in a drunken stupor that made me breathe the stench-laden atmosphere he breathed. But yonder comes your stranger. I'd give a pie or two to know his name and history."

"It's a wonder you don't hate all men," said Aunt Judy, smoothing her collar and cap strings, and stealing a peep in the little cracked shaving glass that hung over the mud fireplace.

"I don't hate men, auntie. They'd be all right if women were free. Now, find out who he is this time, won't you? I know he's smitten."

"Nonsense, child! He's a married man, as likely as not."

But evidently Aunt Judy did not much believe this last surmise, for she stepped briskly, in spite of her rheumatism, and served the gentleman, as usual, to her choicest pie.

"Are you getting through the summer with comfort and profit, Mr.—, I beg pardon, I do not recollect your name?" she said, with a perceptible tremor in her voice.

"Profitably enough, thank you, madam. My mine proves to be a quartz lead, as we get further down, and the prospects are favorable, when the sur- face diggings are exhausted, for an immense business another year."[2]

"I rejoice in your good fortune for your family's sake, as well as your own," said Edna, archly. "It will certainly be grand news for your wife."

"There, Mrs. Smith, you are in error. I am sorry to say that I am yet a bachelor. And now, ladies, as we are alone, and I have eaten Mrs. Judy's pie and gotten in a communicative mood over her cup of tea, I don't mind tell- ing you something of my past life. I was once engaged to be married to a young girl who very much resembled you, Mrs. Smith."

"Indeed? She must have been handsome, and I congratulate you upon your taste," said Edna, sarcastically, as she strove, under cover of a faded shawl, to supply the needed lacteal nourishment for the vigorous and tyran- nical little Smith, who would never wait for company to retire before taking his meals.

"Beg pardon, madam. I don't pretend to say that you are handsome, since my saying so would displease you, evidently; but I reiterate my decla- ration that she very much resembled you."

"Why didn't you marry her?" asked Edna, abruptly.

"For the best reason in the world, madam. She jilted me."

"And why, pray?"

"For a richer man, madam. There was a young nabob came over from Boston to our part of the country, and he cut a swell and spent money, and the girls got wild; and he took a fancy to my *inamorita* and her father commanded her to marry him. She didn't love him, madam; at least, you would have thought, if you had seen that last parting, that she did care for me; and God knows I'd have broken my neck, as I did my heart, for her; but she had been taught that obedience to her father was heaven's first law, so she jilted me for the other fellow. I didn't stay for the wedding, but they were married, no doubt, and I've been a fugitive and a vagabond ever since. Not that I've been *wicked,* but I've been a wanderer, like a stray dog, without home or master."

"Maybe your lady love didn't marry, after all, sir. Maybe you misjudged her," said Aunt Judy.

"No, Mrs. Judy, I guess not. Women are for the most part fickle, and no wonder. They're trained to have no minds of their own. Do you know, madam, I would go further, and pay more to see a stanch, true woman, who would live or die for a principle, than for any other boon that could be given to the world."

"There are plenty of such women, sir, plenty of them," said Edna.

"I confess I have not found them."

"Because, sir, excuse me, you have not tried. You consider gold the most precious of metals. It is precious only because it is so hard to find. If it were as easy to procure as the bowlders on yonder mountain, would you strive to possess it as you do?"

The stranger had not thought of that.

"Now," continued Edna, "you say you are satisfied that you possessed your lady love's affections; yet it seems by your own confession, that when an obstacle came in the way, you helplessly abandoned the field. Suppose, after you have bored and blasted and striven as well as you know how to find your paying quartz you come suddenly to a great obstruction, previously unlooked for. Do you abandon the enterprise, or do you not, all the more earnestly work and wait?"

"Of course, madam, I should be compelled to remove the obstruction."

"But it seems that, when an obstruction came in your matrimonial way, you yielded the field, like a coward, to a rival who had no moral right in the premises, and then went your way, bemoaning the fickleness of woman. Why did you not say to her that if her heart was yours her hand was also, and no other claimant had a prior right? You didn't give her a chance to be true. You recognized her father's prior claim, and consoled yourself by finding fault with her. Sir, women will do more, and suffer more, and sacrifice more for a principle, a thousand to one, than men will ever think of submitting to. I know whereof I speak."

As Edna spoke, the thought of what she was now enduring for a principle, although that principle began to look to her awakening enlightenment as a false one, came before her in all its horror. And, as if to fill her cup of bitterness to overflowing, her husband came staggering in from the groggery hard by, as maudlin and silly as chain lightning elixir could make him.

"I was not aware that I was protracting my visit so much, good ladies; pray excuse me," said the stranger, as he placed the change for his lunch in Aunt Judy's hand and departed.

[To be continued.]

from
*The New Northwest*
Friday, January 26, 1877.

# NO STORY.

Again we are compelled to make the above announcement. *Why* the manuscript does not come to hand more promptly we do not know; but is perhaps not strange, when the distance which the author is from here is taken into consideration. We regret, but are unable to prevent, the break in the story.

from
*The New Northwest*
Friday, February 2, 1877.

# EDNA AND JOHN:
## A ROMANCE OF IDAHO FLAT.

### BY MRS. A. J. DUNIWAY,
AUTHOR OF "JUDITH REID," "ELLEN DOWD," "AMIE AND HENRY LEE,"
" THE HAPPY HOME," "ONE WOMAN'S SPHERE," "MADGE MORRISON,"
ETC., ETC., ETC.

*Woman's degraded, helpless position is the weak point of our institutions today—a disturb-
ing force everywhere, severing family ties, filling our asylums with the deaf, the dumb, the
blind, our prisons with criminals, our cities with drunkenness and prostitution, our homes
with disease and death.*—National Centennial Equal Rights Protest.

## CHAPTER XII.

"**A**NOTHER FAMILY HAS COME to Idaho Flat to live, and now you'll
have company," said John Smith one day, as he came staggering
into the cabin and deposited his rickety form upon Aunt Judy's customary
seat, leaving the good woman to balance her weight as best she might upon
the rheumatic foot that was less ailing than the other.

"A wife and children, did you mean, John?" asked Edna, with a show of
interest.

"A family generally means wife and children in my dictionary!" answered John.

"I wish the woman part of the family *joy!*" said Edna, with a sneer.

"None of your insinuations, Edna," exclaimed her husband. "I'll have
you know that your lawful husband is to be treated with respect in his own
house," he added, dropping his chin upon his bosom and falling into a
drunken sleep, while his mouth fell open and his tongue protruded, and a
crystal drop depended from the end of his nose, and two or three stray
beads of the same clear consistency trickled down his rum-flushed face.

"Treated with respect in his own house!" cried Edna, in scorn. "This house, shabby as it is, belongs temporarily to us only because of your industry and mine, Aunt Judy. And yet he taunts us with treating him *disrespectfully* in it, and lays claim to the virtue of *possession* and *ownership!*"

"In the eyes of men's law he is right, Edna."

"What do *I* care for men's law, auntie?"

"The law does not care what your cares may be, child. You are living under a government made by men and for men, and you must either obey those laws and take what comes, or break them and risk the consequences."

"Then I'll break them, auntie."

"Stop, child; you don't know what you are saying. Your husband never maltreats you; that is, I mean, he never whips or abuses your person, however much he may choose to bruise your spirit. There is no law upon the statutes of this formative territory to protect you from even an overt act of violence, provided your husband does not chastise you with a stick thicker than his thumb."[1]

"You have missed your vocation, auntie. You should have been a lawyer. Where did you get your information?"

"From John's law books. They constitute the only class of literature we have out here, except the Bible, and I'm getting disgusted with that."

"Why, pray?"

"Because woman is cursed within its pages for seeking after knowledge. The motive that possessed our maternal ancestor was a worthy one. She saw that the tree was good for food, and to be desired to make one wise; hence her determination to partake of its fruit."[2]

"What in the name of common sense are you driving at, auntie?"

"Just what I'm saying, child. The Bible says, 'Thy desire shall be to thy husband, and he shall rule over thee.'[3] One look at John Smith in connection with that command destroys all my respect for the Book."

"The conditions of penalty imposed upon man for the same transgression were just as arduous as that, auntie. Man was commanded, or, rather, he was foretold that he should eat the herb of the field; that thorns and thistles would be brought forth to him, and that he should till the ground in the sweat of his face."

"But comparatively few men obey their curse, Edna."

"Because, being the arbiters of their own destiny, they are enabled to conquer the conditions it imposes. If heaven had decreed these unhappy and insurmountable conditions, no man would ever have been able to rise above them."

"Then you don't believe in the justice or infallibility of the text any more than I."

"I'm sure, auntie, that I look upon man's curse, and woman's also, as simply the remarkable foretelling away back in the dawn of the Jewish era, of the very conditions that exist and have existed through the succeeding ages. Originally man was only a tiller of the soil. In the sweat of his face he ate his bread. The thorn and thistle, which it was predicted should grow for him, he has looked upon as his enemy—his legitimate prey. Woman, upon the other hand, has accepted the conditions of her curse as final. Man has so decreed, and she has blindly submitted. Now, I know that it is just as much the duty of woman to conquer and subdue this condition of evil and usurpation as it is the duty of every faithful husbandman to conquer the thorn and thistle, root and branch."

"But how are you going to begin, Edna?"

"First of all, auntie, dear, we must have woman just as free to follow the promptings of her own selfhood as man is."

"And how are you to bring all that about, when in all this broad America there is not the court of justice where she can have any prospect to figure except as a criminal?"

"Well, auntie, I can't see that we are to make anything by theorizing here. My sovereign lord and master, who will have me to know that he is head of the family that provides him with food and shelter, and who robs us daily of a considerable sum to keep himself boozy, will probably sleep for several hours, and if you will keep the babies, I will visit the new family of which his worship benignly consented to tell me."

"Why, *child!* You are not able to take such a walk! The road lays across the gulch, down one great hill and up another still larger, and you haven't been out of the house for weeks!"

"Never mind, auntie. Any sort of an adventure will be a change. I'll try it."

The wonderfully exhilarating air of Idaho Flat acted upon her being like an elixir of life. Instead of falling dead on her journey, as she had hoped and prayed to do, she grew suddenly strong in feeling and purpose. Walking with a firm step along the grade below the cabin, she paused, after a while, to watch the men at work. Some were walking waist deep in the yellow water of the rapid creek and upturning the gravel with long-handled spades, while with aching limbs they toiled from morning till night in preparing for the coming "clean up," when they hoped to reap golden rewards for the rheumatic twinges and the *tic douloureux*[1] contracted during the season's toil.

"If John would strive like that to earn his bread, I shouldn't mind my own toil and suffering," thought Edna; "and it is plain enough that all men are not idle or drunken. What a pity it is that a man who is idle or dissipated can ever be the sole arbiter of the destiny of woman whom he holds by virtue, not of his own good conduct and her desire, but through a fiction of the law which compels her, though not a party to the laws, to obey them in spite of her innate selfhood. Surely there is a great wrong somewhere."

Edna found the ascent of the opposite steep more difficult than she had supposed. Listening intently for sounds issuing from the house, she fancied that she could hear the low wail of her tiniest babe, and she hastened on, designing to complete her call and return ere Aunt Judy's patience should become exhausted.

In an erewhile abandoned cabin, seven feet by nine in area, and perched upon the very verge of an overhanging ledge of rocks under which the miners even now were burrowing, lay a woman in an evident state of intoxication.

"Well," thought Edna, "if this is the sort of recruits that come in the shape of families to Idaho Flat, I don't want to remain, even though gold abounded like bowlders. And yet, why has not this woman as good a right to drink as John?"

Edna had inherited from her mother all the feminine prejudices against evil in woman for which womanhood is everywhere commendable, and the sage reflection to which she gave utterance was born only of the force of example in her husband's home.

"I guess I won't rouse her. Guess I'll steal back and tell Aunt Judy that I've found a counterpart for John," she said, irresolutely.

Yet it had been so long since she had seen the face of any woman except Aunt Judy, that a curiosity to know more of this stranger possessed her.

The usual paraphernalia of a mining camp lay scattered about. There was no bed, except the roll of gray blankets upon which the woman lay, and no fire, or place for any, except upon the rocks outside.

As Edna stopped surveying the wretched scene, and pausing from the effect of her uphill walk, a rollicking yet sad-looking man, in sandy hair and plaid cassimeres,[5] approached the cabin, carrying a bag of beans and a flitch[6] of bacon.

A look of annoyance crossed his countenance as he met Edna, and his eyes fell.

"My name is Smith," said Edna, "and I came to make a formal call, after the custom in all villages."

"And my name is Young, madam. My—that is—Mrs. Young is not well to-day."

Edna breathed more freely. Perhaps she had mistaken the woman's indisposition for drunkenness.

"Have you been long in the West?" she asked, after a pause.

"Oh, yes; a year or two. It's up-hill work living in this country."

"I don't think there's any special need of its being such, sir. You look like a sober man. I think any man who is inclined to be sober, moral, and industrious can get along here all right."

"Would you be willing to live a lifetime in such a place as this?" and the man fidgeted uneasily as he saw a prospect that the sleeping woman might stir.

"Oh, no, sir; but I'd be willing to live almost any way for a few years, while we're young and while the children are little, if by so doing I could amass a competency for middle and declining life."

"Well, madam, if you can have any influence over my wife for good, I shall not regret coming to Idaho Flat."

The woman thus indicated rose suddenly to a half-sitting posture and began to upbraid her companion, not heeding Edna's presence.

"And so you've brought beans and pork, eh?" she said, speaking with a thick-tongued utterance that confirmed Edna's first impression.

"It was all I could afford," was the quiet answer.

"Yes, all you could afford, no doubt!" was the querulous reply. Then, turning suddenly, she encountered Edna's wondering eyes and dropped her own for an instant.

Where had Edna met that look before?

"You promised me, Jim Young, that if I'd become your wife you'd be fortunate in business and would always keep me in elegant style! You said I was too young, too fragile, and too handsome to keep boarders for a mining camp; and you managed to get a breath of suspicion against my good name and so induced my husband to believe your villainous lies, and he took all we had and abandoned me because he deemed me untrue. What can I do, Jim Young? My baby, even, was snatched from my arms because you made him believe I was guilty, and I became a discarded wife and a robbed mother. I'd kept boarders at Rocky Bar, Jim Young. I'd washed for the miners and toiled when I wasn't able, and my work more than *his*, had made the little we had; but you got me slandered, and I was turned out of home, disgraced, robbed, and yet innocent!"

"My wife is crazy, madam. It is a very unfortunate case," said the host.

*"Crazy, indeed!"* was the contemptuous reply. Would to Heaven I *was* crazy!"

"If you were an innocent woman, why did you live with this man, even when your husband had discarded you?" asked Edna.

"Why does any woman sell her soul or body?" was the fierce reply. "What else was left me that I *could* barter, except myself? There was no law in all the land to which I could appeal for protection in my property rights. Women shunned and starved, and men sought and tempted me, at least, this one did, and I fell for food and shelter. Fell, even while I loathed the man who wrought my ruin. Ah, madam, the men say that they protect us, and so they *do!* Just like they protect cattle! If we are their property, they'll house and feed and provide for us, but if we are nobody's property, they turn us out to starve, unless some of them take a contract to secure a certain amount of service from us for which we are in the end to pay with life and honor."

"Mr. Young," cried Edna, flashing her indignant eyes upon the man, "is this woman's story *true?*"

Something in the questioner's manner caused him to hesitate and blush.

"No," he at length replied, speaking with evident reluctance, "the woman is as crazy as a loon."

"And who drove me crazy, Jim Young? Who alienated a kind, hardworking husband from me by villainous lies? Who caused me to be robbed of my baby—my precious, precious baby? Who caused me to be driven into the world penniless and disgraced? Who, when the vile work of robbery had been accomplished, came to me when I was half sick, half famished, and half frozen and offered me, with honied words and promises as false as hell, a grand home in San Francisco? Who promised to see that I was legally and honorably divorced? Who promised, if I would but take the gold my perishing body needed, that he would treat me honorably till I was free, although an innocent outcast, to become his wife? Ah, Jim Young! Of course I'm crazy! Crazy with *gin!* And I intend to remain crazy every hour that I can find enough of gin to keep me so. When I'm dead drunk I can't see my white-faced Alma. When the stupor is on me I can't hear her cry for mamma. When I'm mad with whisky I can forget my sorrow in curses. But, oh, the sad awakening that comes! 'The wages of sin is death.'[7] If this is to go on through life, I'll never meet my darling in the land of souls. Eternal misery! Oh, God!"

The wretched creature fell prostrate on the roll of blankets, and Edna, who had found a case more heart-rending than her own, hastened to her home and poured the story into the wondering ears of her sympathetic relative.

"I am growing more and more strongly convinced," said Aunt Judy, "that the degraded position of woman is the weak point in our institutions today. I see more and more clearly that it is a disturbing force everywhere; that it severs family ties and peoples the world with knaves. The history of that woman's subjugation is like yours in kind, and differs from it only in degree. She evidently had a good husband, as men go, that is; he felt that he possessed personal ownership in her, and so long as she remained sound in his estimation she was entitled to food and shelter at his hands, if she would work for it! But he had only to be led to believe that his property was not the genuine article to cause him to cast it from him. Had he considered her as an individual, as well as a wife, her disgrace, whether merited or not, would have entitled her to her own earnings, and thus saved her from degradation. On the other hand, John Smith possesses the absolute power over your earnings that enables him to confiscate them for liquor, and gambling debts. He does not mean to discard you if he can help it, because he appreciates the fable about the golden egg."

"Aunt Judy, it's all wrong."

"I know it, child. Men would not be willing to endure the man power for a single day which they enforce upon womanhood continually without a thought that woman, whom they consider as property, can be wronged by their laws."

"Yonder comes your stranger, auntie. We'll see a perfect match when you and he are one."

"Nonsense!" replied the good woman, yet she did not scruple to smooth her glistening locks and steal an admiring glance in the little mirror as the gentleman ordered his customary pie.

[To be continued.]

from
*The New Northwest*
Friday, February 9, 1877.

# THE STORY.

Again are those who are interested in the fortunes and misfortunes of "Edna and John" compelled to wait the tardy movement of the mails for further enlightenment.

from
*The New Northwest*
Friday, February 16, 1877.

# NO STORY YET.

Either the mails, or the author, or both, are remiss in duty, and again we are compelled to go to press without further enlightenment concerning the adventures of "Edna and John." If this luckless couple could have foreseen not only their own vexations but ours in attempting to get theirs before the public, we are sure that there would have been one less elopement to chronicle, and baby "Idaho" and her baby brother would have been orphans—in advance.

from
*The New Northwest*
Friday, February 23, 1877.

# EDNA AND JOHN:
## A ROMANCE OF IDAHO FLAT.

### BY MRS. A. J. DUNIWAY,
AUTHOR OF "JUDITH REID," "ELLEN DOWD," "AMIE AND HENRY LEE,"
" THE HAPPY HOME," "ONE WOMAN'S SPHERE," "MADGE MORRISON,"
ETC., ETC., ETC.

*Woman's degraded, helpless position is the weak point of our institutions today—a disturbing force everywhere, severing family ties, filling our asylums with the deaf, the dumb, the blind, our prisons with criminals, our cities with drunkenness and prostitution, our homes with disease and death.*—National Centennial Equal Rights Protest.

## CHAPTER XIII.

"**AUNT JUDY, I REALLY BELIEVE** you are in love," said Edna, as soon as the old gentleman had departed.

"The idea!" replied the good woman, with a rosy blush. "Do you suppose I'd fall in love *at my time of life!*"

"You look and act a good deal as I did when I was in love," was the arch reply; and then a shade of sadness, not unmingled with mortification, passed over her face as she listened to the heavy breathing of John, while she sat down to quiet the cries of the year-old baby.

"People ought to marry, and they ought to be happy in the marriage relation," said Aunt Judy, musingly.

"I know they ought, auntie; but they should know what they are about before assuming the relation, and then, there should be no one-sided power, but a united head. I can imagine a perfect marriage, yet I confess I never saw one."

"O, Edna, *I* have seen happy matches—not perfect ones, because there is no perfection to be found in this world of imperfect conditions; but I have seen husbands and wives who are perfect counterparts to each other. I have seen them begin life without property, with no earthly possessions except loving hearts and willing hands, and being one in aim and effort, I have watched them growing more perfectly blessed as the years rolled on; have seen their children prove a blessing and a joy; and, though the years of toil and care that came and went left furrows on their faces and made them gray and old, there was still the same love light in their eyes as when, in the trusting and loving years of their youth, they stood before the altar and took upon themselves the solemn vows of conjugal fidelity."

"*Well,* Aunt Judy! Don't say to me that you are not in love! You are growing as poetic and dreamy and foolish as I was at boarding school."

The old lady blushed and worked vigorously at her rolling-pin and pastry, but did not look up or reply.

"Your picture may be a perfect one—at least, I know it ought to be," continued Edna, "but I confess that I have never seen such a couple as you have described."

"I am sure your father and mother love each other dearly, my child," said Aunt Judy.

"But my mother is not happy and the 'Squire is not satisfied," said Edna. "She is discontented because she endures so much unrequited toil and has no power to carry out some of her dearest ambitions in regard to her children; and he is unhappy because one-sided power brings no lasting happiness, even in its possessor. He has had his own way till even tyranny brings distaste, and now, when they ought to settle down to reap the happy and contented recompense of a united life, my mother goes sighing and toiling through her declining years, away from her child's companionship, and the 'Squire—I will not call him father—is morose and melancholy, and feels *abused* only because he has had his own way till he's dissatisfied with everybody, but most of all with himself. There might be many happy homes, auntie, if only there were perfect equality there. But you don't seem at all curious about our new neighbors. You have no idea of the strange suspicion that forced itself upon me as I heard that woman rave. I believe that she and Sue Randolph are one and the same person."

"Why, Edna! You shock me!"

"I am shocked myself, but I do believe it is she. True, she is blear-eyed and thick-tongued and an awful sinner, yet it seems to me that she is more sinned against than sinning, after all. Her story is a true one, I am sure, and that man Young is a dreadful reprobate."

"But what of her husband?"

"He only did what the laws of men justified, in order to protect his imaginary *honor.* Sue Randolph might have been imprudent; she was a young harum-scarum sort of body, with no more knowledge of real life to begin marriage than I had. She did not love Hal LaSelle as I did," and again Edna blushed as though confessing a crime. "No man is ever loved by more than one woman as I loved him; though doubtless I should have loved him less had I known him better. Sue married him without reflection, and you know they appeared to be happy enough when we saw them last. But hard times came, with toil and drudgery; and with her determination to make the best of circumstances was her equally strong proclivity to have what we girls called a good time. Her lord and master imagined that he could change her disposition and make her over to his own idea. Pity he had not foreseen the fact that a higher power than man's makes and rules woman. I see through it all perfectly. Sue's vivacity, which came from the depths of an innocent and exuberant heart, he looked upon as reprehensible. Then he grew jealous, and she became indignant because of his unjust suspicions and unjustifiable fault-findings. The tempter came. Good women are as scarce in one part of the mines as in another, and this villain, whom it would be base flattery to call a devil, poisoned her husband's mind against her and caused him to take advantage of cruel laws and rob her of her earnings and her child."

"But, Edna, you excuse her too much by far. Remember that, no matter what happens, no woman is ever excusable for deviating from the paths of rectitude."

"I grant it, auntie, and I do *not* excuse her. But I do say that it is awful for woman to bear all the consequences of evil deeds, or even evil surmises, while her companion in crime may go scot free. Or, what is worse, if she be innocent, her husband, through unjust suspicions, may rob her of home, shelter, food, children, and the fruits of all her toil."

John Smith aroused himself from his drunken stupor, sufficiently sober to begin an argument.

"If there's any one thing more to be despised in a woman than anything else that a man can think of," said he, rubbing his eyes and speaking in an angry tone, "it's this infernal fuss about rights. I thought I'd hear no more about it if I'd come to a new country; but you two women don't talk or think about anything else. A man'll hardly dare to say his soul's his own in a little while at this rate."

"Woman hasn't dared to say as much for *her* soul since the world began," said Edna.

"And she has no right to say it, either!" retorted John. "If a woman will mind her own business and take care of her house and young ones properly, she'll have enough to do."

"But how's she going to have a 'house' and the wherewithal to make her 'young ones' comfortable, if she has a husband who not only neglects to provide for her, but drinks and gambles away her earnings?"

"That's always the way! I can never have any peace of mind in my own house! Where's the half dollar you got for that old straggler's lunch? I'm going to raise on the price of these lunches. Might just as well have a dollar."

"And *we'll* not *allow* an advance on lunches!" said Aunt Judy, "and there's an end of that!"

"We'll see!" said John. "Give me a half dollar, Edna."

"I haven't a penny," was the quiet reply.

"The dickens you haven't! Now see here, Edna! I want you to understand, once for all, that I am to be the head of my own family! I've stood the interference of your infernal old aunt just as long as I propose to bear it. It's she that puts this mischief in your head. Old woman, you've got to get out o' this!"

"And what's to become of Edna if I do?" asked the old lady, with a scornful sneer that was wholly unlike her.

"That's *my* business," was the self-important answer. "I'll brook no more of your meddling in my family affairs. Edna would be easy enough to manage if it wasn't for *you!*"

The reader, who knows that but for good Aunt Judy's kindly care, John Smith would not have had home or shelter but a few weeks after his marriage, and who has followed her through all her seasons of forbearance while he was wasting the substance that had been entrusted to her keeping, leaving her destitute, and but for Edna and the helpless little ones, totally among strangers, John's conduct will appear dreadfully reprehensible. Yet, when he considers that in all he did the husband of Edna Rutherford kept himself rigorously within the pale of the law from which there was no court of appeals for woman; that Edna, being his wife, could not be robbed by him in such a manner as to make the offense criminal, and that Aunt Judy, having cast her lot with Edna, necessarily shared her fate and fortunes, he will, if a just reader, have less cause, after all, to blame the poor weak-minded, tyrannical, besotted husband, who, in spite of his weakness, there was no law to restrain, than he will have reason to find fault with the institutions of a so-called "free country" which, in direct violation of its Constitution, robs wifehood of its inalienable inheritance of equality before the law, and thereby excites domestic insurrection in ten thousand homes that might otherwise be both prosperous and endurable.

"I'll give him a half a dollar and let him go," said Aunt Judy. "He'll remain away till morning if he gets tight again to-day, and then we can have a little peace."

"O, auntie!" cried Edna, "*I* couldn't do that! I've given John the last dollar he'll ever get from me, unless he robs me, or steals it. He can't control his propensity to drink and gamble, and he ought to have a guardian."

But Edna's remonstrance came too late. The money was in John's possession and he was gone.

"I have wanted a little talk with you alone for several days, Edna," said Aunt Judy, apologetically. "I have wanted opportunity to tell you that you are right," and the good woman fidgeted uneasily. "I have learned all about the 'Stranger.' He and I are engaged."

"Well, auntie, I congratulate you, but I do not think your age has made you any more careful than my youth caused me to be in matrimonial matters. One thing is very clear to me, and that is, if I were out of this entanglement, I'd stay out."

"Till you got another chance to try again! That's the way with women," was the decisive rejoinder.

"Aunt Judy, you have not even learned the 'Stranger's' name."

"How came you to know so much, child?"

"He never would tell, you know."

"Have you heard all the conversations that have passed between us?"

"No, auntie; and I shouldn't want to, when the theme is of the very interesting nature that you have hinted."

"Edna, dear, I have a long story to tell you, which, until now, I have kept securely locked within my own bosom. Do you want to hear it?"

Edna was afraid to betray her interest, lest silence should again veil the good woman's lips.

"I have always thought you would tell me in your own good time, auntie, and so I could afford to wait," she replied, bending low over the new baby and cooing it to sleep with a gentle lullaby.

"I was a belle, and considered a beauty," said Aunt Judy, pausing to adjust her waving hair beneath a cap-frill, which she contrived to keep daintily white, in spite of her smoky and disagreeable surroundings. "I had no such opportunities for education as your young life afforded, Edna, and I grew up among slaves, with every want and whim anticipated, and was, as a matter of course, a spoiled child. My mother was fully imbued with all the old conservative ideas about a woman's sphere, and, though I know she found life sometimes very distasteful and oppressive, for she had an active brain and ambitious disposition, yet she so fully adhered to the chivalric notions that slavery fosters on the one hand, and military rule engenders on the other (my father was a military hero), that she would have suffered the martyrdom of death, and immolated us all upon the altar of social custom, rather than have foregone her pet proprieties. I think I never was any comfort to my lady mother. I was always breaking through and over some customary restriction. It was a custom, time-honored and sensible, to prevent young ladies from coming *out* until they had completed their eighteenth year. Doubtless this rule would have been satisfactory enough for me if I had had anything to occupy my hands or mind. But 'Satan finds some mischief still for idle hands to do.' There was a fine-looking young gentleman, a son of an aristocratic family who lived on a plantation a few miles from my father's home, who used frequently to meet me in my rambles in the woods. We had many pleasant chats together. I am sure the thought of the impropriety of our meetings never entered my brain, else I should not have indulged in them. His society was heaven itself. We would build such air castles as nobody but foolish young lovers can build, and the thought that they would ever topple and come down with a crash did not once oppress us. We were engaged. A beautiful sunset closed its eyes upon the scene of our betrothal. I was to be eighteen in another month, and, as I should then be free—what an idea! to make a girl of eighteen her own legal mistress, while a boy must wait till he is twenty-one—we were to elope, for we knew our parents would not consent to our marriage. It did not enter into my heart to doubt him. I made my preparations stealthily, and when I left my father's roof for the last time, to cast my fortunes in the lottery of matrimony, I reached the place of rendezvous and found, instead of my worshiped ideal, a black boy with a letter.

"'Massa says you will please excuse him, Miss. De letter will explain,' he said, and then he disappeared in the darkness.

"I have the letter yet," said Aunt Judy, as she tremblingly opened a little package and took therefrom an envelope, inside of which was a letter, rusty and worn, upon which were traced, in a boyish hand, the following lines:

"Too late. The governor knows all, and has spirited me away to West Point. My heart is breaking, but never mind. You'll find somebody else to take my place in your affections soon, for girls are never constant. I shall carve my own niche in the temple of glory, and while I carry a sad and aching heart, you will forget me and be happy.

Yours ever,

"HAL"

Edna started and turned pale.

"So you had a lover named Hal, too, did you, auntie?"

The good woman did not appear to heed the question.

"I could not bear to go home after that, Edna. The earth, the air, the sunshine breathed my darling's name. What a fool I was! I fondly imagined that he would prove as true to me as I felt that I would ever remain to him. But, alas for the vanity of foolish expectations, I heard from him once, and once only. That was twenty years ago, and he was married! I could not, and did not forget him, however, and the years and years rolled on. You know how I lived for many years on your father's farm. Solon was kind to me, child. You can now understand why I felt specially called upon to protect you when your time of trial came. My father and mother reproached me so bitterly for having dared to try to elope, and my old friends so persecuted me with ridicule because of my failure to secure my lover in marriage, that I pawned what jewelry I had and saw my home no more. I need not tell you all, or anything, about the events of that long and tedious journey. Suffice it to say that at last I reached your father's house, which was at that time, and for years after, a cabin on the banks of the Missouri River, where during the babyhood of your elder brothers and sisters I toiled as a menial, never asking or expecting remuneration."

"I don't see why you didn't ask or expect it, Auntie."

"Because I was brought up to believe it an awful thing for a woman to earn a livelihood. But I was better off than your mother, child; for when I made up my mind to adopt a style of living that would suit me better than to longer live as an unrequited servant in the home of wealthy Solon Rutherford, I had but to say so, and I became the acknowledged arbiter of my own destiny."

"But what about your approaching marriage, auntie? Are you not afraid to commit the folly which you so deprecate in other folks?"

"Circumstances alter cases, child."

"But who is this stranger who has fascinated you?"

"Don't you imagine what his name is?"

"Auntie, how should I know, when he has never told me anything about himself?"

"Edna, he is a widower now, but my old, old lover, and the brokenhearted father of Hal LaSelle!"

"O, Aunt Judy! Never let me look upon his face again," cried Edna; "I really could not bear it."

[To be continued.]

from
*The New Northwest*
Friday, March 2, 1877.

# NO STORY.

Again we are compelled to make this monotonous announcement concerning the fortunes of "Edna and John." We have made apologies and excuses until our stock is exhausted, and shall leave the reader to conjecture of its non arrival.

[*Ed.:* Friday, March 9, 1877—No story, and no mention of its absence.]

from
*The New Northwest*
Friday, March 16, 1877.

# EDNA AND JOHN:
## A ROMANCE OF IDAHO FLAT.

### BY Mrs. A. J. DUNIWAY,
AUTHOR OF "JUDITH REID," "ELLEN DOWD," "AMIE AND HENRY LEE,"
" THE HAPPY HOME," "ONE WOMAN'S SPHERE," "MADGE MORRISON,"
ETC., ETC., ETC.

*Woman's degraded, helpless position is the weak point of our institutions today—a disturbing force everywhere, severing family ties, filling our asylums with the deaf, the dumb, the blind, our prisons with criminals, our cities with drunkenness and prostitution, our homes with disease and death.*—National Centennial Equal Rights Protest.

## CHAPTER XIV.

"**WHY, CHILD!** I'm astonished at you!" exclaimed Aunt Judy. "Don't make a fool of yourself, I beg."

"But, auntie, Hal LaSelle has gone to destruction! I know he has! And he was once *so* good and noble! *I* might have saved him, but nobody else could do it."

"You precious simpleton," replied the good woman, allowing her hands to belie with a tender caress the words of reproof she uttered, "you needn't think it possible for any woman to save a man from ruin who proves himself unable to stand without her aid. I have no patience with the puling sentiment that time and custom have so long sanctioned which imagines it necessary for any woman to immolate her life upon the altar of any man's destiny to keep him in the paths of rectitude."

"But, auntie, if my memory is not largely at fault, this venerable lover of yours, this suitor with the snowy hair and glistening beard and brow, who has so deeply captivated you that you look young and beautiful again, is not himself a paragon by any means, for his different stories do not always tally.

You tell me that he is a widower, the father of Hal, and one of the best and most abused of men, and yet I remember that he told us once that he was still a bachelor, that he had remained true to the fancy of his boyhood, and all that. It seems that he can tell a story with two opposite interpretations as readily as any other man."

"He had an object in misleading us for the time being, Edna. He did not want me to imagine who he was unless he could first know that I had been true to his memory, so he spoke in parables."

"*Falsehoods,* I should call them, auntie, and so would you, if John Smith had uttered them."

"Well, I am satisfied, and I don't know as it's anybody else's business."

"Does he love you as devotedly as he would if you and he had married in your youth?"

"A great deal more devotedly, child. We have both erred and suffered, and have each grown broader and more charitable, as well as wiser, through life's mistakes."

"Well, auntie, I must say I consider your brain badly out of order. You forget that you have grown old."

"So has he grown old, Edna, and ours is a union of soul with soul."

Edna laughed outright.

"It's a languishing, lackadaisical outgush of vapid sentiment, that's as flat as dishwater to every one but the specially interested," she said, merrily.

"Poor child," replied Aunt Judy, patronizingly. "I do not wonder that your heart is steeled against the idea of possible happiness in matrimony."

"Auntie," exclaimed Edna, as if anxious to change the subject, "did you recognize Mr. LaSelle when he first came here to luncheon?"

"That's a leading question. You may draw your own inference."

Edna was puzzled. She could not draw a satisfactory inference, and whatever Aunt Judy's thoughts may have been, she kept their further expression in check, and indulged in an air of mystery that precluded further inquiry upon the part of Edna.

"There's something dark about the whole matter that I am wholly unable to solve," the young mother soliloquized, as she bridled her curiosity and busied herself in preparing needed garments to keep her babies comfortably clad, while the good old lady overhauled her own wardrobe and gave earnest heed to necessary preparation for her approaching nuptials. A wedding in Idaho Flat was an occurrence heretofore unheard of. There were no laws in the Territory requiring a would-be Benedict to procure a marriage license; there were no ministers or magistrates to pronounce the ceremony, and the prospect of a mule-back journey to the distant settlements was anything but an agreeable anticipation to a lady on the shady side of fifty, with a comfortable avoirdupois of over two hundred pounds with which to endure the strain and jolting of a ride to which she was wholly unaccustomed.

"If we only had my team and wagon, which John disposed of and left me in the lurch!" she said, speaking to Edna with emphasis, as she shrank from the prospect before her with a pardonable dread.

"Yes, auntie," replied Edna, with a ringing laugh that seemed in ill keeping with her desolate surroundings, "that ox team would furnish you a grand turn-out for a wedding excursion. Besides, it's always customary for the bride to furnish the means of conveyance to and from the parson's residence, you know."

"Quite as customary as for the bride's relatives to furnish an outfit for the groom, to keep himself and family from starving!" was the rather unkind retort.

Edna blushed painfully.

"Forgive me," said Aunt Judy, tenderly, "I did not mean to wound you, but it illy becomes you to be making sport of other people's matrimonial outfits."

"Is your husband-to-be a really rich man, auntie?"

"How should I know? Do you suppose I'm marrying him for his money?"

"From the lessons you have always given me, since my own marriage, about the necessity of business qualifications for such a union, I supposed I was excusable in looking after your affairs a little, seeing I so signally failed to look after my own."

"Yes, Edna, he is growing wealthy. The new flume is almost done; the new shaft has been yielding marvelous rock for a month or more; the new quartz mill is in full blast, and Mr. LaSelle is too busy to get married, by rights. We'll be able to give you and the children a home, my child, and that's one comfort."

"But, auntie, are you *certain* he is an eligible candidate for matrimony? You know there are so many men in this new, wild country who come here to get away from domestic unrest or infelicity. And when they get here they can pass for single men, when in reality they are married already."

"Child, do you mean to *insult* me? Mr. LaSelle would be incapable of such a thought. I wouldn't for the world *hint* such a possibility to him. He is the very soul of honor!"

"Auntie, for my life I cannot see but you are just as dreamy, just as foolish, and quite as impracticable as I was when I fell in love with one man and ran away in the night and married another by mistake. Women have no right to complain of the perfidy of men, since they trust them implicitly, as men would on no account dare to trust each other."

"I have not taken anything more for granted than he has, Edna. How does he know but I have a living husband? He'd scorn to ask me such a question!"

"Ah, auntie, if there had been the least shadow of a taint against your name, in any way, men would have told your paragon all about it long ago. John Smith would have known it, and then every man in the Flat would have been treated to it as a savory dish of scandal."

"And so, I take it, if there had been anything covered or hidden in the life of Mr. LaSelle, the scandal-mongers would have unearthed it, for men are not over fastidious concerning the reputation of their kind. But, Edna, look! As sure as you and I live there's a gentleman coming to Idaho Flat in a stovepipe hat and ministerial cloth. I won't be compelled to leave the Basin at all to get married."

"How a maiden in love does jump at conclusions," cried Edna, laughing. "I declare, auntie, that if this love-making and general gush goes on, I'll forget all my troubles—get 'em all drowned in a gulf of the ludicrous. How do you know that man's a preacher?"

"Can tell by his dress and manner, child. Do you suppose I never saw a clergyman before?"

"He's studying our *sign,* and will come here to lunch, and then we'll find out all about him," said Edna, contemplating the bit of shingle with the word "Pies" in grotesque letters in lampblack, nailed against the cabin wall upon the side nearest of the mule-path that led in a zigzag line up the narrow steeps.

The sequel proved that both ladies had been correct in their surmises. The stranger was a clergyman, in search of pies and piety, the latter being a scarce commodity in Idaho Flat, the former only attainable at the cabin of the Smiths. The minister's horse, a mottled Cayuse, somewhat the worse for wear, and noticeably hungry, was tethered to a bowlder hard by, and his owner was soon a guest at Edna's humble board, where he somewhat pompously said a grace before partaking of his lunch, after which his pie was liberally sandwiched between decisive layers of religious conversation.

"You could not have chosen a better place for the exercise of your skill as an evangelist, Mr.—, I beg pardon—your name?"

"Handel, ma'am; and I hope, by the grace and power of God, to be able to bring the harmonies of the spheres into the religious atmosphere of your life. You smile, but I never repeat my name to a stranger but some thought of the famous composer accompanies it. I fear I have said something decidedly absurd."

Edna smiled.

"It isn't every one who says an absurd thing that has sufficient critical acumen to perceive it, sir. But I beg leave to differ with your idea of that speech. Harmony is what we need most and seldom attain."

"It is what we should all strive for, madam. And, if we will live always according to the highest good that is in us, I think our existence will prove a blessing to ourselves and the human family."

"Do you purpose remaining in Idaho Flat?" asked Aunt Judy.

"Yes, if the Lord have need of me."

"Others may need you, if the Lord doesn't," said Edna. "I confess that the constant speaking as though mortals were necessary to the prosperity and happiness of the Lord vibrates in a sort of canting sound upon my ears."

The minister blushed. Evidently he hadn't thought of the subject in that light before.

"There is plenty of work for you in the mines," continued Edna. "Plenty of it. We have any amount of profanity and irreverence. We have drunkenness and gambling, and every vice that pertains to new countries where there is no equilibrium of restraints. There is much practical work for a preacher here, but I fear your ideal religion will not take much effect upon the miners."

"What do you know about the ideality of my religion, pray?"

"Nothing, except that your discourse upon harmonies was a little impracticable?"

The clergyman was much disconcerted. He was not accustomed to sparring upon technicalities with ladies, much less did he expect to encounter an original, independent, thinking woman in this miner's hut, so far from the comforts of civilization that he would have fancied her debarred from every opportunity to exercise an individual opinion, and every desire to express her own ideas.

"I have studied the mysteries of nature through the holes in the roof on cloudless, star-lit nights," said Edna. "I have contemplated the invisible universe and measured it by that which my limited sight could scan. I have never reached the beginning; I shall never reach the end. The microscope proves that the divisibility of matter is infinite; the telescope reveals the existence of myriads of solar systems far transcending this in which our lot is cast, and of which we know almost nothing."

"Madam, I hope you are not skeptical!" said the clergyman, speaking loftily. "I beg that you will not perjure your immortal soul by vague speculations. We have the written, revealed Word as a lamp to our feet and a light to our path. Be careful how you stray into the realms of unbelief through vague imaginings."

"If you think I talk like an unbeliever, you have widely missed my meaning, Mr. Handel."

"Beg your pardon. I am so anxious that your immortal soul may be saved from eternal condemnation that I tremble lest you lose sight of the Rock of Ages."

"I do not recognize your Rock, sir. My religion is the great ocean of Infinitude, into which my bark of thought has glided, with sails full rigged and banners flying. The waves of my ocean have risen so far above your Rock that, though I grope and grapple, I may not find it."

"Don't you believe in the divinity of Christ, madam?"

"Did I say I didn't, sir?"

Again Mr. Handel was puzzled.

"How anybody can doubt," continued Edna, "the divinity of the religion of Jesus, when we have the record that he left the Sermon on the Mount and the Golden Rule as a heritage to the barbaric people of two thousand years ago, is one of the mysteries of human absurdity. The divinity of the human and the humanity of the divine are the cardinal points in the doctrines of Jesus. His life was a crowning glory, his death a fiendish relic of the barbarism of the dark ages."

"Madam, I am astonished!" said the minister. "Shall we pray together?"

"No; you will excuse me."

"Edna, I beg that you will not be rude," exclaimed Aunt Judy, apologetically.

"I do not mean to be rude, auntie," was the quick reply. "I intend to obey the religious advice of Jesus till I can find something better. He tells us that when we pray we must enter our closets and shut the doors and pray in secret;[1] and if we violate this command, he says we are as the hypocrites who disfigure their faces that they may appear unto men to fast, and for pretense make long prayers, and so forth."

"If you have no objection, Mr. Handel, I should be pleased to unite with you in prayer," said Aunt Judy, meekly.

In spite of Edna's opposition, she felt a quiet calmness stealing over her senses as a simple hymn, sweet and plaintive, was wafted out upon the air and floated through the broken roof; and not more fully did Aunt Judy join in the audible breathing of "Our Father which art in heaven"[2] than did the intelligent wife of the drunken inebriate respond to the same sweet petition at the close of the impromptu call upon the Infinite that preceded it, filling her soul with sad, indefinable rejoicings.

The new minister became a welcome visitor from that hour, and the wedding at which he officiated a fortnight later in no way diminished his popularity.

To Aunt Judy's great relief it was no longer necessary to make a journey a mule-back to a distant settlement to consummate her connubial bliss, and her white-haired, beaming-faced suitor was all aglow with happiness.

"There is only one woman besides ourselves in Idaho Flat," said Aunt Judy, "and, Edna, shall we invite her to the wedding?"

"Of course we shall."

"But—but—you—know."

"Yes, yes, I know a good many things that I would to heaven were not true, but she was Hal's wife once, and her child is my new great-uncle's granddaughter. She shall come."

To see that John was duly sober for the wedding was Edna's next concern. Burdened as were her heart and hands by maternal and business cares, she had awakened to a clear perception of many of the miners' social needs, and was resolved upon a merry making which they should all have good cause to remember.

[To be continued.]

from
*The New Northwest*
Friday, March 23, 1877.

# EDNA AND JOHN:
## A ROMANCE OF IDAHO FLAT.

### BY Mrs. A. J. DUNIWAY,
AUTHOR OF "JUDITH REID," "ELLEN DOWD," "AMIE AND HENRY LEE,"
" THE HAPPY HOME," "ONE WOMAN'S SPHERE," "MADGE MORRISON,"
ETC., ETC., ETC.

[Entered, according to Act of Congress, in the
year 1876, by Mrs. A. J. Duniway, in the office of
the Librarian of Congress at Washington City.]

*Woman's degraded, helpless position is the weak point of our institutions today—a disturb-*
*ing force everywhere, severing family ties, filling our asylums with the deaf, the dumb, the*
*blind, our prisons with criminals, our cities with drunkenness and prostitution, our homes*
*with disease and death.*—National Centennial Equal Rights Protest.

## CHAPTER XV.

LUCKILY THE WEATHER WAS FINE. Mr. Handel, the new missionary, who had been looked upon with suspicion by some of the miners, with contempt by others, and by others with scorn, while not a few regarded his coming as a harbinger of better times among them morally and spiritually, proved an agreeable acquaintance to the colony of hardy delvers, inasmuch as he inaugurated the assembling of the men together on Sundays, after the primitive fashion of the earlier times, when men worshipped God under the fear of savage and wild beasts with their trusty guns beside them. It was difficult to procure seats for the many who attended upon the ministry of the evangelist in the open air, under the overhanging crags that formed the grand embattlements of Idaho Flat.

Lumber was too scarce and expensive a commodity, and too badly needed for flumes and sluice-boxes, to be spared by men in eager quest of gold for an hour or two of rest and sermonizing on Sundays. But Aunt Judy, whose heart was in the work of soul-saving, which she was not alone in believing God unable to perform without much human assistance, went assiduously to work to devise ways and means to overcome the difficulty.

With the aid of the minister, who, to do him justice, was only too glad of her assistance and advice, a square plat of ground was leveled and cleared of rubbish, and upon this, with infinite labor from the miners, a few hundred blocks, stumps, rocks, and logs were placed as seats. Over this uncouth arrangement a booth was erected, well covered with evergreen boughs to guard the worshipers alike against storm and sunshine.

It is comparatively easy to raise a religious excitement in a great city, where men, rushed alike with necessities and greed, get so little time to do their own thinking over spiritual affairs that they find it more economical, and vastly more to their liking, to hire somebody to work out salvation for them than to solve their own problem; but when you carry the blood of Jesus as an atonement to the miner, who communes with the Infinite beneath the stars, and place before him the plan of salvation according to the popular idea, he vexes you with all sorts of questions that would never have occurred to him had he remained in the old ways of thought and action.

Though the miners of Idaho Flat worked with a will in carrying out Aunt Judy's plans, it was not so easy, when the booth was ready for occupancy, to persuade them that they needed the administrations of Mr. Handel to save them from everlasting fire.

Curiosity brought them together, however, and the first Sunday's services were largely attended, the men having been astir from the earliest dawn, in order to get through with their cooking, patching, washing, and dishwashing. For Sunday to a miner who does his own domestic work is very much like the same day to the average mother of a large family—the busiest day in the week.

It is not our design to follow preacher and hearers through the drift of Mr. Handel's arguments. They can hear their duplicate at any Sunday morning service in all the land, and they are more deeply interested just now in Edna and John than in points of doctrine, and are probably wondering more and more about the romance of Idaho Flat.

Aunt Judy was particularly anxious that her husband-to-be should be regenerated before she should become his wife, which was one grand secret of her interest in the missionary and the meetings. But Mr. LaSelle was as unimpressible as the good lady was anxious. "I would to heaven you had as much faith in the Omnipotent One as I have, my dear," he ventured to say one day, after a very thrilling exhortation from the minister to all men to flee from the wrath to come had wrought her sensibilities to the highest pitch of concern for her darling's soul.

"Please explain," replied the good woman, not at all comprehending his meaning.

"I have sufficient faith in the Power that created me to believe He has the power and will to preserve and protect me, my dear. If there is not a sparrow falls to the ground without His care, surely we are of more value than many sparrows."[1]

"But that does not justify us in continuing in our sins and leading a life of unbelief, without God and without hope in the world."

"If I am such a sinner, darling, I advise you to be very cautious about casting your lot with mine. I certainly should fear to trust my life and happiness in your hands if you were such a sinner as you take me to be."

"Your sin is against yourself, dear, not against God and me."

"Are you in partnership with God?" he answered, smiling.

"I am heir of God, and joint heir of Jesus,"[2] was the enthusiastic reply.

"Then I congratulate you on your royal heritage," said Mr. LaSelle. "I prefer to believe that God is no respecter of persons;[3] that He has no favorites; and that *I* am not a favored child of royalty. If I were such I should be most miserable, for heaven would be to me a place of blackest torment, if I should go there, knowing that other human beings were irretrievably lost."

"Don't you believe in eternal punishment?" asked Aunt Judy, with a look of terror.

"As a father loveth and pityeth his children doth our Heavenly Father love and pity us.[4] Would you be willing to consign one of Edna's babies to eternal torment, no matter what its shortcomings?"

"No, I would not."

"Shall mortal man be more just than God, my dear?"

"But you know that's a dangerous doctrine to teach. Suppose, now, that the fears of endless torment were removed from the mind of John Smith? You know that is the only check he ever recognizes."

"There, my dear, is John's great trouble. He is feeling safe about the hereafter, for he believes he can repent at any time and be saved, no matter what may have been his misdeeds in the body. I would have all men know that the laws of God are unchangeable, that the atonement must come from within us, that restitution follows atonement, and that retribution is a natural law. I do not ask Jesus to be a scape-goat for my sins. When I stand in the Infinite Presence I want to feel that I have a right to stand there, with my head erect, not as a pardoned criminal, but as a redeemed and justified brother of the Lamb of God that taketh away the sin of the world."

"Don't you approve of Mr. Handel's preaching, then?"

"Oh, yes; as far as it goes. But I am sure he would do infinitely greater good by preaching the life of Jesus and holding forth His example for all to follow than he can ever accomplish by dwelling upon his death and the disgraceful details of his crucifixion."

"But, after all, suppose you are in error? Suppose you should find at last that the harvest was past and summer ended and your soul not saved?"[5]

"I should have the approbation of a good conscience, at least, for I should know that I never, for the sake of my personal safety, accepted a condition that my inner conscience rejected. To express faith and comply with conditions, merely through fear that, if I shouldn't, I might find myself in error when too late to remedy the evil, looks to me like putting up a sort of bankrupt job on Jesus—not sure ourselves that the note we accept is good, but afraid to reject it lest it *may* prove genuine, thinking in that case we'd be all right anyhow, for the other bank wouldn't fail if this one should."

Though this kind of logic silenced the good woman, it by no means convinced her that her suitor was on the safe track, and she took much to secret prayer, not, however, forgetting to rejuvenate her wardrobe and make her old clothes presentable for her approaching nuptials.

In the meantime, the meetings went regularly on. Men abandoned the faro table and forgot the game of poker in the interest awakened by the new sensation. The "saloon" hard by began to do a losing business, and there was strong talk of lynching the preacher, who was certainly no physical match for the brawny-armed men who upheaved the bowlders and burrowed out the earth in search of hidden treasures.

"I mean to get up a diversion that will take the men's minds off from the physical argument," said Edna, "for I shall issue tickets of invitation to your wedding to every miner in Idaho Flat."

"And how are we to feast and otherwise entertain them, I should like to know?" cried the good lady, in astonishment. "It would take me a week to make pies and doughnuts enough for dessert, to say nothing about the other things."

"I don't propose to feed their bodies, auntie, but I will try to prepare a diversion for their minds. I shall give them a sort of elocutionary entertainment."

"You?"

"Yes; why not?"

"A *woman,* to do such a thing! Brother Handel might preach them a sermon, but for *you,* a woman, to attempt such a feat would disgrace the whole lot of us."

"I'll risk the disgrace, auntie. You know I learned to declaim with skill while at school, and I have always been called a singer. I shall erect a temporary 'green room' behind the pulpit, and rig me up a few changes of toilet out of my unused States wardrobe, and give the miners spring, summer, autumn, and winter in character; and I'll sing 'Gentle Annie' and 'Lily Dale' and 'Sweet Home' and 'Annie Laurie,'[6] and it will be better than a wedding feast, besides saving us the toil and drudgery and expense."

"But, Edna, such conduct is unbecoming in a woman. I should feel disgraced to see you thus before the public."

Edna laughed long and merrily.

"What would John say?" continued Aunt Judy.

"I haven't asked him, and I don't mean to," was the firm reply. "What has he done for me that I should bow to his fiat? Haven't you counseled me to be my own arbiter, all along?"

Unable to cope with Edna in the argument that she saw just ready to assume formidable proportions, Aunt Judy changed the subject, and the preparations for the wedding on the following Sunday went briskly and regularly on.

A carpenter in Idaho Flat, who was a genius in his way, prepared wooden cards of invitation with a jack-plane, upon which Edna inscribed in bold letters the name of every miner in the neighborhood, requesting his attendance at the booth on the auspicious occasion.

"I shall invite Sue Randolph among the rest, auntie," she said, decidedly.

This announcement shocked Aunt Judy as much as did her determination to give the miners a benefit, but Edna was determined, and the good woman was obliged to yield, especially since Mr. LaSelle had decided in Edna's favor.

The wedding morning dawned with a delicious, mellow radiance, and the sun rode high in limpid, roseate splendor over the adjacent mountains.

The miners, one and all, seemed actuated by a desire to look their best. Old razors that had long lain away in rusty idleness, were rescued from their hiding-places and whetted on old leather boot tops. White shirts, or "b'iled" ones, as the miners call them, were unearthed from old valises, and many a pair of trowsers was treated to clean patches on basement and knees.

The services were to begin at ten A.M., Mr. Handel opening the exercises by singing,

"Joy to the world," etc., etc.,

In which a chorus of untrained voices joined lustily, and the very welkin[7] rang with rasping melody.

The sermon was a short one, the text, "It is not good for man to be alone,"[8] forming its appropriate heading.

"I hope he'll be short," said Aunt Judy, as, dressed in an antiquated and plum-colored garb of alpaca, her head adorned with a voluminous cap of well-starched lace, tied loosely beneath her double chin, she walked with a perceptible rheumatic limp beside the tall, straight, and supple groom, while both were as radiant as the rosy morning.

"I join you in the hope, darling," was the ardent reply, "for when the marriage ceremony is over you will be all my own."

Edna laid a blanket and pillows beneath the shadow of the booth, and placed her little ones there, surrounded with primitive playthings; and many a miner was more attracted by the chubby children than by the sermon or promised ceremony. All were in a mood to be pleased with everything they saw and heard. Mr. Handel had the good sense to be short in both sermon and ceremony, after which he announced that they were to be treated to some exercises which, although he did not absolutely approve, he had been compelled to assent to.

Saying this he left the platform, and Edna emerged from her "green room," personating spring. Her dress was of old-fashioned grenadine,[9] cut low in the neck and short in the sleeves, and was covered with grasses, ferns, and flowers gathered from the adjacent gulches, while her flowing hair was literally smothered in mountain ivies.

The silence was death-like. No one had looked for such a demonstration. Tears rolled down many a swarthy cheek.

> "I come! I come from the vernal lands
> Where the rivers of life are flowing;
> I come! I come from the golden sands
> That dazzle the eyes of the angel bands;
> And the seeds of summer I'm sowing,"

She said, as, scattering upon the earth a handful of grain, she proceeded to recite stanza after stanza, her declamation being as earnest as her sentiment, and all being beautiful.

Her presentation of summer and autumn, though good, was not as complete as spring, because of the absence of most of the fruits and cereals belonging to those seasons, but sentiments and rendition were alike faultless, while the simple, old-time ballads which she sandwiched between the acts were exquisite.

Gold and silver pieces were thrown at her feet like hail-stones, and as she stopped, blushing and radiant, to gather them up, it was little wonder she became infected with a stage mania, in which visions of possible future independence for herself and children played a prominent part.

The congratulations that poured upon her from all sides were far more hearty and profuse than those bestowed upon the blushing bride and tranquil groom. They were far more greatly needed, too, for those worthies were happy enough within themselves.

The crowd at length dispersed, and Edna, happier than she had been for years, was returning to her cabin, carrying one babe and leading another, when the wretched woman whom she had invited to the entertainment, and therefore could not blame for being there, came up to her with bloated face and babbling utterance and hissed:

"Enjoy your triumph while you may! You are living as the wife of a man you loathe, and you are no better than I, much as you may *despise* me. You pander to drunkenness and vice, and you will be rearing many sons to walk in the footsteps of their father! How do you like the prospect?"

Edna turned away, her heart sinking. Had not the woman spoken truly? And was not her self-hood of more value than the bonds she hated?

"I will consult Mr. Handel. Maybe he can advise me properly," she said, as she entered her cabin, to find John in a glee of maudlin hopefulness over her unlooked-for triumph.

"I've got a fortune in you, Ed, and no mistake," he said, chucking her patronizingly under the chin.

[To be continued.]

[*Ed.:* Friday, March 30, 1877—No story, and no mention of its absence.]

⋯⋯≡✦≡⋯⋯

from
*The New Northwest*
Friday, April 6, 1877.

# EDNA AND JOHN:
## A ROMANCE OF IDAHO FLAT.

### BY Mrs. A. J. DUNIWAY,

AUTHOR OF "JUDITH REID," "ELLEN DOWD," "AMIE AND HENRY LEE,"
"THE HAPPY HOME," "ONE WOMAN'S SPHERE," "MADGE MORRISON,"
ETC., ETC., ETC.

*Woman's degraded, helpless position is the weak point of our institutions today—a disturbing force everywhere, severing family ties, filling our asylums with the deaf, the dumb, the blind, our prisons with criminals, our cities with drunkenness and prostitution, our homes with disease and death.*—National Centennial Equal Rights Protest.

## CHAPTER XVI.

**E**DNA WAS MORE DEEPLY than ever disgusted with John. Not that his idea that she might make her newly awakened talent profitable was not in harmony with her own thoughts, but she had suddenly conceived the scheme, or a premonition of it, with a view of rendering herself independent of him, rather than with a thought of adding to his support.

Edna was not "strong-minded," that is, as men view strong-minded women. She was a timid, nervous thing, with no natural desire to protect herself or children, and she shrank, as sensitive women invariably do, from the contact with the world that rendered her life a routine of business and drudgery. How hard it was for her to face the abrasions of conflicting business interests, and grasping the nettles of her own timidity so tightly as not to allow them to pierce her shrinking spirit to the quick, go forth to life's earnest battles, no one may know who has not sometimes been in similar positions.

Had John opposed her new idea, she would have openly defied him. Had he feared that her rising popularity would result in his own humiliation, as many a weak-brained husband so situated has done, she might have scorned his puerile boasts of masculine superiority; but here was a dilemma for which she was not prepared. John was not only willing but anxious to place her before the world as a target alike for the vulgar witticisms of the rabble and the wise commendation of the thinking classes. To make money out of her toil or talents was his highest aim.

"I have a fortune in you, Edna!"

How the words rung in her ears! How their memory stung her with acute mortification! Yet how should she get rid of him and his newly aroused expectations? It seemed that her chains were growing tighter, and that continually they were festering deeper in her flesh and spirit.

The memory of poor Sue Randolph's words were like poisoned arrows to her soul.

"She is *right!*" she said to herself. "I am no better than she, and I am guilty of every charge in her indictment. But how am I to help it?"

Mr. and Mrs. LaSelle were so happy in each other that they seemed to forget poor Edna and everybody else. The bridegroom had arranged and furnished his miner's cabin with what skill and taste the rude region afforded, and thither they repaired after the ceremonies ended, leaving Edna so desolate and lonely that the poor creature was well-nigh distracted.

Her dream of independence had met a cruel stab, and more than ever did she ponder over the problem of getting rid of John. To cure him of dissolute habits was a hopeless task, with rum shops to the right and left of their lowly home, vile dens wherein every device to entrap him yet more deeply into sin was constantly in action, with no home for inebriates within thousands of miles, and no law to compel him to enter it for the cure of his disease if one were near. To leave her children to the tender mercies of an incapable father was not to be thought of; and to remain with them, and him, and run the certain risk of fulfilling Sue's prophecy was a fearful prospect. What was she to do?

It was the next day after the wedding. The bride and groom had gone to their own cabin, the miners had dispersed to their business, and the relaxation that naturally follows excessive mental and nervous effort was telling fearfully upon Edna's spirits, when Mr. Handel called. John was away at the gambling den, the baby Ida was asleep, and Edna was engaged to her elbows in her pastry cooking, while the younger babe was squalling vigorously for required maternal care.

"I am glad to see you," said Edna, "for I am sorely in need of a friend."

To make herself heard above the yelling baby's din was no small effort, yet Edna was blessed with excellent lungs and succeeded in raising her voice to the required pitch to make her utterances audible.

"Let your work go for a while and take care of the baby," suggested the minister, speaking at the top of his voice.

It was easy to say "let the work go," but it was quite a different thing to put in practice. The only revenue of the family was her pastry cooking, and they could not live without food, let the theory of letting her work go be ever so plausible. The pastry work had lagged during the preparation for the wedding, and now that Aunt Judy was away, the little one missed its accustomed attention, and was consequently "cross."

If, in the great hereafter, any mother of a family of exacting scions shall find that she did not in lifetime do sufficient penance for the peccadilloes of the body to insure her a home far more beautiful and attractive than the Fiddler's Green[1] can ever be to bachelors, it certainly will be because her sins of omission and commission far transcended the blackest crimes in masculine catalogues.

After a while the protected and supported subordinate of the Smith family was so far through her pressing work that by dint of hurrying till half distracted, her pies were in the clumsy oven and she was ready to ease the clamor of the incipient Smith by seating herself on the nail keg and supplying the bantling with feverish nourishment. Now she could talk and be heard.

"Any mother has work enough to do," she said, "who must take the sole responsibility of rearing and caring for children. I must not only do all this unaided, but I must do all the housework, laundrying, and sewing, and in addition attend to a business to support myself, the children, and my lawful master—a business that is in itself of sufficient magnitude to employ the entire time and energies of an able-bodied man."

"I am sorry to hear you complain of your lot," said Mr. Handel, solemnly. "The Lord loves a meek and uncomplaining spirit."[2]

"I believe the Lord loves justice,"[3] was Edna's decided reply, "else He is not a just God, and if you can make me believe He is not just, I will take no stock in Him, if I die for it!"

"*Mrs. Smith!* I wonder he does not strike you dead!" exclaimed the minister, with an unction that was sublimely awful.

"Why?"

Edna opened her eyes to their fullest extent, as she asked the question with a look of earnest eagerness.

"We are not to question the ways of Providence. They are past finding out, my dear madam."

"Then we are not to blame if, failing to find them out, we fail to obey them, are we?"

This question was asked with a genuine, irresistible frankness that made the missionary smile in spite of his horror.

"I don't look at these things as I once did," said Edna. "I have outgrown the old notion that many usages which our nature innately rebel against, because incompatible with our happiness, are at all necessary for our spiritual good. In short, I believe that the evils we labor under are the result of human imperfections rather than the will of God."

"What are you driving at, my sister?"

*"The truth,* Mr. Handel."

"Please explain."

"That is just what I am trying to do, sir. When I was a young, unsophisticated school-girl, with no more real knowledge of the ways of married life or the laws of the world for wives than baby Idaho possesses now, I yielded to the romantic nonsense of the atmosphere I breathed, and fancying myself a heroine, eloped and became a wife. I did wrong, foolishly, wickedly wrong, and I knew it before twenty-four hours had past. From that day to this I have repented, and have constantly tried to atone for my folly, acting, of course, according to the laws of men, and leaving the higher laws of my moral consciousness to take care of themselves. I have worked, as never woman worked before, to make a man of John. I simply *cannot do it.* There is no material in his make-up upon which to form the foundation to build manhood. He grows more and more addicted to vices, and I am but pandering to them by furnishing the means from my own labor to indulge his evil appetites. I cannot tell you how I shrink from the public contact of the world. I don't want the adulation of multitudes, nor do I care at all for fame. But I cannot go on in this way. I must do something to change the current of my life. As I live today I am no better than poor Sue Randolph, the only difference being that the law is on the side of my most loathsome subjugation, and custom is the chain that compels her to follow a life of no greater shame."

"The ornament of a meek and quiet spirit is in the sight of God of great price," said Mr. Handel.

*"Fiddlesticks,"* was the impatient rejoinder. "You might just as wisely ask the victim of the rack and thumb-screw to be calm and meek and cheerful and resigned, as to ask me to be meek and quiet in spirit under these bonds!"

"But you took your husband for better or for worse, you know."

"I did not know or think anything about 'better or worse' when I took him—or, rather, when he took me, sir. I was penned up away from the society of men, in a school for girls, where we were left to our own imaginings concerning the conjugal laws of nature. We saw life through distorted lenses and acted according to enforced ignorance, a condition for which we girls were not morally responsible, and should not be held to be legally so."

"But, remember your *vow,* Mrs. Smith.

"My vow was self-stultification, sir. In the eyes of God it is not binding, and under the laws of men it is a crying shame to recognize it. Do you know what I believe should be the law of marriage?"

The minister tried to smile, though in truth he was a little frightened.

"I should like to be enlightened," he said, falteringly.

"Well, I'd treat everybody who married as we did as outlaws till they'd come to their senses. I'd keep them in penitentiaries on bread and water at hard labor till they had had enough of each other, and then, if they wanted to continue the relation, I'd let it be sanctioned by law, and if either wanted it discontinued, I would grant them amnesty and send them forth, like other convicts whose time had expired, to begin their battle with life anew, feeling sure that the experience had made them wiser and tamer."

"Would you like to accept such a discipline, Mrs. Smith?"

"Indeed I would! I'd volunteer to live in the State prison as many years as I have lived with John, if by so doing I could get rid of him."

"Then, pardon me, but you are a very wicked woman."

"Do you *dare* to insult me, Mr. Handel?"

"I trust that I am brave enough to do my duty, madam. You sought my advice and confidence, you know."

"Why do you think I am wicked?"

"Because you are willing and anxious to revoke your vow."

Edna blushed. Poor child! How could she make the humiliating confession that she had married the wrong man? She could not, would not do it. He might think as ill of her as he liked, but he should not know the worst and most unfortunate part of her rash and foolish life-venture.

"'Thy desire shall be to thy husband, and he shall rule over thee,'"⁴ said Mr. Handel, solemnly.

"Pray, *don't!*" cried Edna, with supreme vexation. You'll make me hate the Bible, denounce all good, curse God and die, if you succeed in making me believe that divine inspiration authorizes my present trouble!"

"Then, my poor sister, what do you propose to do?"

"I shall be driven to the stage to earn my bread, sir."

"What!"

It is a pity that the printed page cannot produce the tones that burden a voice when betraying the most horrified astonishment. That *"what,"* as the missionary uttered it, was the acme of everything tragic that a human exclamation can express.

"You do not mean to be an *actress?"* he continued, gazing at her in a sorrowful, reproachful way.

"I *am* an actress of the worst pattern!" was the vehement reply. "There is nothing real in my life! I mean there is nothing *honest* in it. It is all sham!"

"You are trying to walk in your own strength, my poor sister. You should seek for wisdom from on high to guide you into ways of perfect peace."

"But, sir, the wisdom I receive from on high is balked and hindered at every turn by laws and usages of men. I cannot mock Almighty God by approaching the throne of grace with supplication when I know that I am daily leading a life of loathsome, cankering, festering sin."

"Are you not true to your marriage vows?"

Edna gave a gesture of impatience and disgust.

"My vows are in themselves an abomination, from which my better nature bids me flee with my children, while the laws of men give my legal lord the power to snatch both babes and earnings from me."

"But ruin awaits you if you go upon the stage."

"And respectability and competence and happiness await me now!" she said, with a bitter smile.

"What will you do with your babes, if you endeavor to put your rash resolve into execution, Mrs. Smith?"

"Take them with me and take care of them, sir."

"Alas, poor child, you are as ignorant of public life for women as you were of married life when you embraced it!"

"I know it. But there is one great advantage of which I am aware."

"What is it?"

"I shall not be legally compelled to remain in a hateful bondage if I find the stage to be unbearable. No slavery is absolute except it be matrimony."

It was all in vain that the good minister expostulated continually. Edna's mind was made up. Already the miners had tendered her a benefit, and she had agreed to give a second elocutionary entertainment on a stated evening a week hence, when her songs and recitations in character were to be well patronized and munificently rewarded.

Right here good Mr. Handel made a sad mistake. Had he encouraged the poor desperate wife, and directed her entertainments, choosing their tone and character, he could have prevented all the evils he dreaded by guiding a current he could not destroy. But he turned a deaf ear to Edna's further plans, and sought to conquer the natural desire of the men to be amused by solemn prayers and clerical exhortations.

[To be continued.]

from
*The New Northwest*
Friday, April 13, 1877.

# EDNA AND JOHN:
## A ROMANCE OF IDAHO FLAT.

### BY Mrs. A. J. DUNIWAY,
AUTHOR OF "JUDITH REID," "ELLEN DOWD," "AMIE AND HENRY LEE,"
" THE HAPPY HOME," "ONE WOMAN'S SPHERE," "MADGE MORRISON,"
ETC., ETC., ETC.

*Woman's degraded, helpless position is the weak point of our institutions today—a disturbing force everywhere, severing family ties, filling our asylums with the deaf, the dumb, the blind, our prisons with criminals, our cities with drunkenness and prostitution, our homes with disease and death.*—National Centennial Equal Rights Protest.

## CHAPTER XVII.

**E**DNA WAS DOING *EVERYTHING*. As she had said, her children required all her time and energy to enable her to properly care for them, and the extra toil of both brain and body were telling fearfully upon her nerves and temper. But her programme must be carried out. The miners were crazy for legitimate amusement, such as can only be enjoyed when there is honorable blending of the feminine element in the different phases of men's social life, and she had promised to supply it.

They were also in a mood to be highly pleased with anything in the way of entertainment which Edna could offer. But her ambition ran high. To so far perfect herself in her new calling that she might be satisfied with her own efforts was no slight endeavor. Meanwhile, to keep John placated and supplied with spending money, it was necessary that her pastry cooking should go on without interruption.

Mrs. LaSelle was too thoroughly happy as a bride to care, or seem to care, for Edna's further prospects.

There comes a time in the life of almost everybody when the concerns of others amount to nothing. When a man and woman are so deeply enamored of each other that they live only within themselves, they are in a state of ecstacy which ought to be pardoned, for certainly it is usually evanescent enough to only cause the concern of friends through fear of its instability.

Edna was in a great dilemma. To write her own declamations was a part of her programme. Not that she felt that she could not have chosen more wisely had collections from other sources been at her disposal from which to make literary selections; but books were a rarity in Idaho Flat—almost as scarce indeed as the women who desired to use them.

"John," said Edna, one day, as he came sauntering into the cabin with a maudlin grin upon his expressionless face, "I must have some help in the house, else I shall never be able to finish my literary work in time for the benefit."

"Let the work go!" retorted John, quite agreeing with Mr. Handel in giving advice, if in nothing else.

"But, John, you know I cannot do that. You and all hands must be fed and clothed. Suppose my new experiment should fail. We must then have something to fall back upon, as you know."

"But I don't see how we are to get any help. There are no women to be hired in Idaho Flat."

"There's Sue Randolph, John."

"*What?* Do you mean to say that you would bring that creature into the house, Edna?"

"She could cook and wait on miners, John. I guess she's as good as her companion, Jim Young, and you seem to think he is good enough to keep your company, and as an equal rather than a servant, at that."

Aunt Judy was fearfully shocked when she learned that Edna had concluded to accept the services of the disgraced and discarded wife of her husband's son, but Edna very soon settled that question by informing her that her own affairs were her own business, whereat the good lady waxed exceeding wroth, and betook herself to her new quarters in high dudgeon, where she lamented, for at least a minute over the reprehensible conduct of Edna in presuming to act upon her own convictions of expediency and right, and then forgot all about it in her new-found happiness.

"John makes Jim Young his prime associate at the gambling den, and I see no reason why it is not as well for me to give Sue employment as for John to give her companion in guilt the earnings of my toil," said Edna to herself.

And so it was that the blear-eyed woman became an inmate of Edna's hut, and was soon her sworn ally and friend.

"There is one condition upon which we may be a mutual help to each other in all things, Sue," she said, as soon as both were alone and busy.

"If there is anything that will help either of us, I should be only too glad to know what it is, and where to find it," was the sad reply.

*"You,* at least, can be true to yourself, Sue, for you are not the legal bondwoman of the man you detest. Now, I ask you, first of all, to begin now the ways of a better life by abstaining from intoxication and licentiousness. The first of these I am legally free from, thank God, and can therefore live above. The second sin I am bound, under the laws of men, to submit to, so I cannot be so good as you can become. Above all else you can be true to yourself. The rest of your redemption will come in time."

"But, Edna, I loved my husband. I meant to do my whole duty, and as far as I knew it I call God to witness that I did not shirk it. He wronged me as no man can ever be wronged. He took my earnings and used them to suit himself, and when a plot was laid to destroy me, he cast me off without my baby, without my earnings, without a character, and left me nothing but starvation or crime. I thought I could have chosen the former, Edna. It seems easy enough to starve when you are not hungry and there is no apparent prospect that you will ever want for food. But when you are homeless, hungry, crushed, and friendless, and some one comes with kindly sympathy to give you aid and comfort—whether you would fall if so situated, judge not till you are thus tempted."

"Well, Sue," said Edna, pausing in her labors, with her hands in the pie crust and flour flying in her hair, "I do not mean to reproach you. Hezekiah Bedott made a sage remark when he decided that we are all poor critters. I begin to feel as though Providence was leading me through my present trials to teach me an important lesson. Surely He can do the same for you as for me if we only take proper heed lest we continue to fail. Do you know how very near I came, in my own idea, to being Hal's wife?"

*"What?"* said Sue, pausing over the tub of steaming suds, wherein the greater part of the not over plethoric wardrobe of the infantile Smiths was being cleansed of its daily contact with the clayey mud of Idaho Flat.

"It is true," said Edna, blushing as she acknowledged the humiliating fact. "I knew just as much about men as a pig knows about Latin. Our interviews with men were all taken by stealth, and our curiosity was always all aflame through novel reading and other nonsense."

Then followed a long explanation with which the reader is already acquainted, and the result was that by the time the heavy work for the day was over the two unhappy victims of their own folly and the imperfections of human law and custom had decided that their fortunes should be as one henceforth.

"You have your children," cried Sue, "and oh, that I had mine!"

"I only get to keep them through my constant self-stultification, though," was Edna's sad reply.

John came in thoroughly indignant. His associates in vice had been afflicted with a spasm of virtue and had been venting their opinions freely in his presence over Edna's new departure from their idea of right in the matter of help in the house, and the protector of the family was determined to preserve the respectability of his establishment at all hazards.

Then Edna defied him. For once in her life her will became law, and the preparations for the approaching benefit went on.

"Yonder comes Mr. Handel with a letter," said Edna, after the domestic storm had cleared away and the two women were left alone with the children. "I haven't heard from home in ages, and I do *hope* it's from mother."

The letter was as follows:

"MY DARLING DAUGHTER:—How your sorrowing mother's lonely arms are aching for you to-night! Your father, Solon Rutherford, is dead. He had been complaining more than usual for several days, but we did not look for his death, and were wholly unprepared for it. It is very hard, my daughter, to part with the companion of all my life's weary years. He never spoke of you after your departure for the far, far West, yet I am sure he thought of you always, and would have been much happier had you never made the breach between you. But, my precious daughter, this is no time for reproaches. I know you are paying dearly for your thoughtless folly. Your brothers and sisters, nephews and nieces, were all here at the funeral, but you were missing, darling, and I miss you more than ever now that I know you are fatherless and penniless.

"It is very hard to turn from the clay-cold corpse of your father to confront the realities of a business upset by administrators and appraisers under a farce called law;[1] but O, Edna, he had hardly been settled in the tomb before the house was ransacked from top to bottom for the effects which I have gathered together with infinite labor during the last thirty years. The stock and farming implements, the bank account, the farming and timber lands, everything, went into account, and it was decided that I, as his wife, was entitled to the use of one-third of all the earnings of our united lifetime, so long as I should remain his widow. I was brooding over the humiliation of such a proviso and wondering that even the darkest ages had ever harbored such a law, when a will was found, giving the homestead to your eldest brother, and apportioning the other property among the other children, leaving me dependent upon your brother during my natural life, and cutting you off, as well as myself, without a shilling.

"Doubtless your father thought it was for the best. He never imagined that I was an individual, or thought it necessary to treat me as such. He fancied that he had provided for me well, but oh, it is so hard to be robbed in my old days of independence and selfhood. True, I have a right of dower and might contest the will, but then the lawyers would get the property, and it would bring reproach upon your father's name.

"My last hope is dead. I cannot do anything for you. My hands are tied and my heart is bleeding. Your brother Henry's wife and I never could harmonize, and yet I am doomed to live in her atmosphere till death shall take me away from the laws of men into the infinite paradise of God.

"I cannot weep. My sorrow is too deep for tears. Write to me, darling. Your lonely, stricken mother so longs for your dear presence! Kiss the poor babies for me, and give love to Judy and remembrances to John."

Edna was as one petrified.

"I have another duty to live for now," she said, as the lines of her face hardened and deep resolve stamped itself in her blazing eyes. "I must live for my mother as well as for my children and myself."

"Poor child! Your hands are tied, and you cannot even look out for your-self," thought Sue, as she wiped her swollen eyes and addressed herself to the care of the children.

"I have no time for the luxury of sorrow," said Edna, "and I must con-centrate my thoughts upon my work."

"Of course your entertainment cannot be given now!" said her friend.

"Of course it must be given now, and I will furnish the mental food for which the protectors and supporters of women will pay best."

"Then it will be a ballet dance or a minstrel show."[2]

Edna blushed with indignation.

"You know I did not mean that!" she said, emphatically. "I mean that I must be gay and cheerful and brilliant and witty, whether I possess the incli-nation and ability or not."

The evening for the entertainment found the meeting ground filled with an array of expectant miners. Candles sputtered in the moonlight air, and bonfires glowed here and there beside a massive bowlder.

John Smith was in his glory. He had decided from the beginning to be doorkeeper, if such a person there could be where door was not, and Edna decided otherwise to no purpose.

Was she not his lawful, wedded wife, and did not her earnings belong of right to the legal head of the family?

[To be continued.]

from
*The New Northwest*
Friday, April 20, 1877.

# EDNA AND JOHN:
## A ROMANCE OF IDAHO FLAT.

### BY Mrs. A. J. DUNIWAY,
AUTHOR OF "JUDITH REID," "ELLEN DOWD," "AMIE AND HENRY LEE,"
" THE HAPPY HOME," "ONE WOMAN'S SPHERE," "MADGE MORRISON,"
ETC., ETC., ETC.

*Woman's degraded, helpless position is the weak point of our institutions today—a disturbing force everywhere, severing family ties, filling our asylums with the deaf, the dumb, the blind, our prisons with criminals, our cities with drunkenness and prostitution, our homes with disease and death.*—National Centennial Equal Rights Protest.

## CHAPTER XVIII.

AUNT JUDY, OR MRS. LASELLE, as the reader is now requested to call her, no longer appeared to feel a shadow of interest in her ward.

Full of her own life, and that of her husband, who was as lover-like as a youth of twenty, the good woman laid plans for furthering her newly-awakened schemes for the increase of her liege lord's already ample worldly stores, and was as indifferent to Edna and her children as she had before been solicitous and motherly.

The world can laugh love and lovers to scorn as it may; men and women yoked in wedlock who have never been so deeply infatuated with each other as to destroy their better senses for a season, or while the fever of the honeymoon lasted, may deride it as they will; parents who have never been thus bewitched themselves, who see some member of their household of children who has erewhile been dutiful in all things suddenly transformed into the creature of some selfish and designing suitor's will, may groan and lament the loss of their jewels because they must, but all the scorn, derision, and groaning of all the ages has not altered the fact, nor will it till the couples thus afflicted run through with the disease, which, like small-pox, oftener destroys than restores those who are the blind victims of its ravages.

Sometimes love is like leprosy, fastening its virus in the veins of its victim and fettering the subject for life to the chains of a slow consumption of all that was sparkling and hopeful in the better nature previous to the attack. Rarely, and owing to human ignorance, very rarely, does it put forth buds that blossom and grow into a happy, healthy, and golden fruitage. And yet, despite the many mistakes that are made; despite the fact that not one married couple in twenty is mated; despite the fact that the appearance of harmony in nineteen out of twenty homes is a delusion painfully apparent to one or more of the parties most deeply interested, if not to all the nearest friends of the victims; despite the fact that men and women who gave fair promise of intellectual and physical progress of a high order prior to marriage are so often known to deteriorate when under the bond, there is, after all, an underlying principle of perfectness in the marriage relation which will in time resolve itself into something approximate to lasting endurance, even for women. But this will never be until it is the universal rule that the party most deeply interested in the marriage contract shall be the responsible arbiter, as she certainly is the responsible victim of conjugal circumstances.

Women of experience are the only mortals who should be entrusted with the making of marriage laws. Women when in love, and without the experience that love brings in its train of consequences, are no better qualified to rule the world of motherhood than are the present law-makers, who know no more of the needs of mothers than a goose can know of astronomical trigonometry.

Changed as Mrs. LaSelle had become through her new entanglement, she was, nevertheless, thoroughly grieved over the death of Solon Rutherford. It was a great pity that she could not see the propriety of Edna's sudden resolve to go on with her work at all hazards. That Edna had no time for and could not afford the luxury of grief was seemingly beyond her comprehension, and yet, judged by all that Edna had known of her in the years they had toiled together, it was passing strange that she had thus lost her senses. But this is the world's way, and we, as a chronicler of life as it is, who work only in the hope that in so working we may do our part, if an humble one, toward bringing life to what it ought to be, must be content to lay before the reader facts rather than fiction.

"I disown Edna, Mr. LaSelle! She is no relative of mine!" said the bride of a few days, pausing in the midst of her very light labors in the rustic cabin, where the two were living as cozily as newly-mated doves, and turning upon him an earnest look of righteous resolution, as though the fiat of ages lay within her power to wield, and she was ready, for once and all, to apply it in fullest force to everything concerning Edna and John.

"I am rejoiced, my dear, to hear you say so sensible a thing," replied her husband, seriously. "The greatest fear I had regarding our marriage lay in the fact that you thought so much of Edna and her children that you would be wanting to encumber me with their support. I always did detest the idea of marrying a whole family!"

Had Mrs. LaSelle been a wife of older experience, or had she as a bride been less infatuated with her husband, she would not have permitted her ideas of self-dependence to lay dormant under this covert thrust, for she well knew that her own labors as wife and housekeeper possessed an intrinsic value far in excess of any remuneration she was likely to receive for them.

But women have thought through all the stages of historic human development that they must lay aside all selfhood and merge existence and aspiration into the embodiment of their idea of the husband they love, and it was too much to expect of Aunt Judy that she should prove a marked exception to the general rule.

Heroines, like heroes, are born and not made, and we may theorize to the end of life's chapter, but we will always fail to find our fullest expectations realized in anybody.

When the evening for the promised entertainment had come, John Smith, the legal arbiter of Edna Rutherford's destiny, was in the zenith of his glory. To be "door-keeper" at his wife's "benefit" was his highest ambition, and when the miners, some of them, demurred, he had but to exercise a husband's authority to make everything bend to his wishes.

It is a noted fact in human ethics that men and women are much more readily inclined to act honorably when rules for their regulation of business affairs are necessarily voluntary than when laws and bars and bolts are everywhere employed to hold them in abeyance.

Three-fourths of the miners in Idaho Flat could have availed themselves of the use of the benches in the open air, under the star-lit skies, where they could have listened without let or hindrance to the evening's exercises, but there was not a man in the mines who would thus have dishonored his self-respect.

All paid the admission fee promptly, John Smith accepting the silver as it dropped into his hands, and from thence into his many pockets, with a relish that would have been pardonable under the circumstances had he not needed a guardian to keep him straight while holding it in possession.

The entertainment, coined as it had been from Edna's brain, under her dire necessities, and amid a harassing perplexity of conflicting interests that would have appalled the strongest man, was a success in every way. True, it would hardly have succeeded at Wallack's, and might not have been *encored* at Maguire's, but it was thoroughly appreciated in Idaho Flat, and Edna became so deeply absorbed in her work that for once since her marriage she was oblivious to John.

Two hours passed in alternate songs and recitations, in which "the grave and gay, the lively and severe," were alike intermingled. The miners were half wild with varying emotions. One had lost a little daughter in the far-off flats of Jersey, and the plaintive strains of "Under the Willow Sue's Sleeping," awakened a resolve in his soul to return at once to the bereaved and lonely mother of the "Fair, fair, and golden haired" darling that had lain for years beneath the flowers and grasses. Another shed tears of melting tenderness over the plaintive minor of "Thou has learned to love another," as he remembered a rustic maiden of the days gone by and the fact that she had jilted him and set him adrift, a delver, unloved and alone, who no longer sought home or happiness, but instead was in constant quest of means wherewith to go back to the old haunts and set up a bachelor establishment that should make both his old-time flame and successful rival half frenzied with envy.

Still another, and scores of yet others, were convulsed with laughter over her quaint witticisms of the Betsey Bobbitt order, and when, at last, the imaginary curtain fell upon the last act, and the crowd was at liberty to retire from the unusual feast, and Edna remembered her children and Sue, and turned to seek for John, she found the former safely housed with her infant charges and the latter missing.

John was nowhere to be found. Search was made for him in all the burrows round about, the general suspicion being that he had met with foul play. But Edna knew better.

"Let them hunt for him to their heart's content," she said to Sue. "My only dread is that he will find himself sooner than we desire. I have no doubt but he ran away to see what he could do toward building up his shattered fortunes by gambling in a new quarter. He must have collected five hundred dollars at my 'benefit.' A pretty fair beginning for a faro table at Boise or Lewiston, you know."

"But I'd pursue him with the law. I'd have my money if I were you, and I'd put him in the penitentiary for embezzlement."

"You forget, poor child, that a man cannot commit a crime against his wife! He may kill her, and thereby commit a crime against the commonwealth, but he may rob her of her earnings, of her liberty, of her children, of everything that life is worth, and she can only help herself through death or divorce, and then the remedy may, for aught we know, become as bad as the disease. For my part, I think I'm cheaply rid of him, if I am rid at all. The only thing I fear is his return, which will be almost sure to occur if I make another public effort to earn money."

There was another man in Idaho Flat who disappeared immediately after John, and that was no other than Jim Young, the lawless tool of Hal LaSelle and the prime destroyer of Sue Randolph's innocence and peace.

The mountains between Idaho Flat and the great basin were, in the time of this narrative, as well as now, an almost interminable wilderness. The moon was at her full, and riding high over the forest-embattled heights, cast a shadow of purple blackness into the gloomy gorges and made the ominous croak of the tree frog seem more dismally lonesome to John Smith than any other sound he had ever heard. He had decided to run away.

While Edna was in the midst of her entertainment, he had retired to the cabin, unobserved by her, where he counted over the proceeds of the evening's venture, and would doubtless have disbursed the same among his convivial chums before morning, if it had not been for the suggestion of his chum, the poor creature before alluded to, who thought it would be a capital thing for both if they should pocket the prize and disappear.

"You take the swag and go," said John. "I will come on in a day or two."

"Indeed, you don't catch me on that layout," was the quick reply.

"Why, man? Are you a *coward?*"

"No, but I'm not a fool! Don't I know that if I take the swag[1] and *vamose,* the minions of the law will be after me, and I'll fetch up at the end of a rope? Life's cheap in the diggings, and I wouldn't give much for a woman's legal feller who couldn't run off with his own booty and save the liberties and neck of both himself and friend."

"What would you advise, then?"

"Why, *you* go. Nobody can hurt you if they do find you, for you can tell 'em you're going to a different locality to look up something bright for your family's future. And so you *are,* you know."

"And what then?"

"When?"

"When you've got away, what would you do?"

"I'd make tracks for Lewiston. After you get into the mountains, where deer's thick, you can bag one easy enough with your old yager,[2] and you can just stop for a day or two in Wild Horse Gulch, and when they won't think of looking for me, I'll slip off and hunt you up, and we'll tramp and decamp together, and have a bank of our own. 'Smith & Young, bankers,' ain't bad, by golly."

"But, Jim, this money is Edna's. If I take it she'll snatch me bald-headed."

His companion laughed long and heartily.

"Before I'd be hen-pecked by any woman I'd get into petticoats," he cried, speaking with that peculiar contempt with which ignorant men are apt to regard all women.

The result of the interview is already known to the reader.

By the time that Edna's entertainment was well over, John was making a beeline for the Gulch, and Jim Young was snoozing under his blankets on the lee side of a ledge of rocks, and both were alike unconscious of having wronged the helpless mother of John Smith's helpless progeny.

After the excitement over the entertainment was past and the usual gossip about the disappearance of the two men had subsided, Edna fell sick. The mental and physical strain had proved too severe for her strength, and the reaction brought her very near the grave.

Then Sue Randolph's natural goodness of heart asserted itself. Edna had befriended her and she was resolved to protect her friend in her affliction. The miners, seeing her determination to reform was genuine, became her deferential allies. True, there were men in the Flat who were inflamed by liquor and all the base accompaniments that further degrade a human being, and these were clamorous for her further debasement, but they were few in number, and the wronged woman, when one of her sex had the courage to set the example, found no difficulty in securing all the respectful patronage necessary to keep the wolf from the door of Edna during her protracted indisposition.

Wearily the weeks and months wore on. Summer gave place to autumn, autumn to winter, and the rigor of a winter in the mountains, unprotected as they were from the snow and wind, was anything but pleasant for the lone women and children to contemplate. But it was better than when John was at home, for now they could use their entire earnings for the family's benefit, or lay by the surplus for future needs.

Mr. LaSelle moved to the settlements when winter set in, his amiable wife making a farewell call upon Edna as a plainly expressed duty, but offering her none of the personal or pecuniary assistance which she had prior to her nuptials expressed her determination to marry merely to be able to bestow.

[To be continued.]

from
*The New Northwest*
Friday, April 27, 1877.

# EDNA AND JOHN:
## A ROMANCE OF IDAHO FLAT.

### BY Mrs. A. J. DUNIWAY,

AUTHOR OF "JUDITH REID," "ELLEN DOWD," "AMIE AND HENRY LEE,"
" THE HAPPY HOME," "ONE WOMAN'S SPHERE," "MADGE MORRISON,"
ETC., ETC., ETC.

*Woman's degraded, helpless position is the weak point of our institutions today—a disturbing force everywhere, severing family ties, filling our asylums with the deaf, the dumb, the blind, our prisons with criminals, our cities with drunkenness and prostitution, our homes with disease and death.*—National Centennial Equal Rights Protest.

## CHAPTER XIX.

TEN DAYS OF WEARY MARCHING over the sandy sage plains, swimming across the rapid streams, and climbing precipitous acclivities, and John Smith and Jim Young, "bankers," had reached Lewiston and settled themselves at "business."

Critical reader, we will spare you. Should we undertake to initiate you into the mysteries of any of the tricks of the sporting fraternity, we should fail, for we could give no detail from personal knowledge, and some of you would be sure to detect the counterfeit. Again, did we know exactly what these men were doing, and precisely how they did it, we should not sully these pages with a repetition, for no good would come of it so long as women are not law-makers.

If your neighbor gets the small-pox, you, as a physician, do not shake his infected garments in the air and under the nostrils of your friends; so, when alluring crimes of any kind are committed, unless by publishing the fact you are enabled to warn others to keep away from the scene of danger, you should not scatter the details broadcast, lest by so doing you make the contagion general. Suffice it to say that for six or seven months, during the entire cold season after their departure from Idaho Flat, the two adventurers eked out a precarious existence as professional gamblers.

Nobody knew that John Smith had a wife and children, and, in truth, nobody cared.

Why, indeed, should the public mind be interested in such a subject? Were not women supported and protected by men? And wasn't that enough to content the entire sisterhood with their divinely appointed sphere? Then, too, do not many women who happen to be fortunately situated in spite of the laws and usages, that consign many others to lives of poverty and uncongenial toil—others who, but for such laws and usages, could rise to comfortable circumstances themselves—do not many independent or wealthy women forge the chains of the oppressed through their own selfishness?

There is little guessing what the outcome with our adventurers might have been had not a vigilance committee appeared upon the scene and checked the gambling laws for a season.

John Smith was not sufficiently adept in low cunning to evade the rigor of border vigilance. Besides, his "luck" had turned, and he was hungry and penniless.

"I'd go back to my wife if I were you," counseled his friend.

"But she will not receive me," answered John.

"The dickens she won't!" exclaimed the other, angrily. "I'd like to know how she'd help herself! All you've got to do is to go there and stay, and if she kicks up a muss, you can give her a taste o' jaw bone!"

"What'll *you* do if I go back?" asked John, as he began to comprehend his advantage over Edna in the new light in which his associate had placed it.

"I don't know," was the hesitating answer. "If Sue LaSelle were only *my wife* I'd be perfectly independent. But, bless you, man, as it is the law would protect her in turning me out o' doors."

"Then why the mischief didn't you marry her in the first place? You don't catch me letting the law get such a power over me that a woman I keep can turn me out if I've a mind to stay."

With Edna and Sue the winter had been tolerably successful, as far as business went. The children throve and grew, and Edna's health gradually improved, until, with the return of pleasant weather, she had great hope of resuming her public labors to better their worldly prospects still further.

"Only let us keep our heads above water till the weather gets warm," she would say to her companion. "We'll renew our entertainments then, and we'll soon have money enough to enable you to go after your child."

"Alas, Edna, you little heed what you are saying! Recollect, I am, in the eyes of men, an awful sinner. In the eyes of God and in my own estimation I am far from being what I ought to be, but I know I'm as worthy to possess my baby as Hal is, and certainly as her mother I have a far better right to her than he has."

"Well, my dear, there is no kind of use in our talking about *right*. We have no rights that men are bound to respect."

"But, Edna, I have known many women who have been so petted and shielded in comfortable homes that they have never seemed to know a care. My mother lives like that. You know my father is a just man. And I am sure my mother never felt any keen sorrow till I ran away and left her desolate. Ah, me! I thought I was abused in my father's home! My brothers were thoughtless and selfish, and sometimes teased me dreadfully. They never cared whether I had company, when I wanted to go anywhere, or not, and, being a girl, I could not go alone."

"Why couldn't your father accompany you?"

"Oh, he never seemed to want to go anywhere unless mother went along, and she couldn't go much because she always had a baby. It was fearfully lonesome for me at home after my boarding school days were over."

"And so it was for me," said Edna, with a bitter laugh. "And yet, when we got married to escape the home duties, didn't we jump from the frying pan into the fire, though?"

"What a pity girls cannot be made to see the evil consequences of those rash acts before it becomes irretrievably too late," replied her friend, sadly.

"The trouble is," said Edna, "their advisers, or the only ones, at least, to whom they will listen, are girls as silly as themselves and suitors who are thoroughly selfish. These last are backed and urged to take legal advantage of the verdancy, inexperience, and affections of girls by 'smart Alecks' around town who couldn't pay for a darkie's breakfast, who are barely out of pinafores into pantaloons, and who think it a capital joke on the 'old woman' to get somebody who is wholly unable to care for the daughter, who has always been shielded and protected in her mother's home, to spirit away the child according to law and leave her to repent ever afterwards."

"Girls ought to know better!" cried Sue, with a shrug of impatience.

"The laws of the land ought to be better, and the law-makers ought to know better than to recognize as valid any marriage which contains a flaw, whether that flaw be in law or ethics," added Edna, with a spiteful stamp of her tired foot.

"Who is responsible for law, I wonder?" said Sue, following the interrogation with a far-away look over the adjacent mountain-tops.

"Men alone are responsible," was the sad reply. "If women helped to make the laws there are a thousand ways in which both men and women could make them better."

"Well, there's no kind of use in our longer theorizing here," said Sue. "We must begin to lay our plans for a summer campaign. If we would give a couple of entertainments we could get a thousand dollars ahead, and then we might get away from Idaho Flat."

"And where would we go, pray?" asked Edna, quickly.

"Back *home!*" was the sad reply.

"Back to poverty on my side and to disgrace on yours, you'd better say, my dear."

Poor Sue burst into tears. For the nonce this fact had failed to intrude, and now Edna had forgotten to let it sleep.

"Beg pardon, my poor darling; I did not mean to wound you," said Edna, soothingly.

"No harm is done," replied her friend. "You spoke truly. Strange that I did not remember. But what would you advise me to do, and what course do you intend to pursue?"

"I don't see that we can do better than to remain in Idaho Flat. We are well acquainted here. The mines hold out reasonably well. Improvements are going on around us constantly, and we can soon hire quite commodious rooms on the other side of the gulch. We can work together and grow up with the town if we will. I cannot go back to my mother, much as I long to do so, for though I know she is waiting anxiously to receive me, she is left a widowed, penniless pensioner upon the bounty of my eldest brother, and her hands are tied. I am determined to build myself a home, and surround it with every comfort, and bring my mother out to live with me."

"Then what will *I* do?"

"Live with us, of course! What else should you do?"

"And never see my baby?"

"Poor girl! I know it's hard," said Edna, feelingly. "But I do not see how we are to make things any better. When you get plenty of money you can do as you please, you know."

A few weeks later and the two women were ensconced in their new and comparatively commodious quarters, which were furnished after the prevailing frontier fashion for eating-houses, with long tables in a large dining-room, a mammoth stove at each end, and a few dozen roughly-made stools as seats. The bedroom furniture overhead was of the same primitive pattern, and the bedding of gray blankets represented equally primitive civilization. A stout and stupid Mongolian[1] was placed in the kitchen as cook, another as scullion, and Edna soon found herself with a growing income and was proportionately independent.

"How lucky that first public benefit was for me," she exclaimed to Mr. Handel during one of his regular pastoral visits, after that gentleman had partaken of a hearty meal.

"But, my dear Mrs. Smith," was the deeply-intonated rejoinder, "if you had not given those entertainments, he would not have had the means to leave you, and would not have been tempted to do so. It is a grave responsibility for a woman to step out of her sphere and take upon herself the responsibilities that rightfully belong to man!"

"And how is a woman to help it, pray, when the man ignores his responsibility and leaves her to bear the burdens outside the home, as well as within, or starve?"

"She should trust in the Lord, madam, who has never seen the righteous forsaken or his seed begging for bread."[2]

"But John is not overly righteous, as you are well aware, and I fail to comprehend the manner of getting bread for *his* 'seed,' unless somebody else earns it, for he won't."

"This is very unwomanly, my dear madam, very much so indeed. I sometimes fear that you are growing skeptical."

"I am not growing but *grown* skeptical concerning many old notions that I once thought infallible, Mr. Handel. I know that if I should fold my hands and pray for food till doomsday I should fail to get it except I was ready and willing to use these hands to earn it. I want a little less *cant* and a little more *righteousness* and common sense in my religion."

"You are bitter, Mrs. Smith."

"Never was sweeter in my life, sir. I revere the Infinite Presence more than I can tell you. I revel often in the realm of the Unseen, and am led by ways that I know not. But that does not convince me that all my prayerful importunities can alter the eternal fiat of Omnipotence."

"Well, we needn't argue that question, Mrs. Smith, as it is quite plain we never should agree. A woman's first duty is to her husband, always."

"But suppose he deserts her?"

"Then, madam, pardon me, but I cannot help thinking it is mainly her own fault. Let women live at the feet of Jesus, as they ought, and their husbands will never desert them."

"Then you consider me wholly to blame about the misconduct of John?"

"I do, madam. If you had curbed your ambition and been content with your lot, John would have done passably well, I think."

"You remind me," said Edna, wiping the suspicious moisture from her eyes as she spoke in a voice husky from wounded feeling, "of a man who was born blind. Much effort had been made to teach him the difference between the various primal colors. Finally his tutor asked him to explain his idea of scarlet, and he said it resembled a *cart wheel.* Now, sir, with all becoming deference to your superior piety, allow me to tell you candidly that you know as much, practically speaking, about the necessities that drove me into a sphere you call unwomanly for the maintenance of my family as the blind man, who had never seen colors, could know of the difference between color and diameter. Heaven knows it's hard enough to bear a woman's trials when she is encouraged in her endeavors to gain a livelihood by the intelligent and better meaning classes of men. But when, added to her sensitive nature, her pain and weariness and anxiety and toil, we hear her reproached and maligned by her best friends for doing the only things left her to do, we may well wonder what the world is coming to."

"Edna," cried Mrs. LaSelle, as she burst into the room with blanched countenance and fluttering heart, "I do believe I see John Smith!"

"I shouldn't wonder," said Edna, compressing her lips tightly for an instant and then relapsing them into a ghastly smile, "for I dreamed of vermin last night, and I felt sure I was going to see trouble."

John was as ragged and dirty as a Digger Indian.[3] Since his food and money had disappeared he had been compelled to depend during his journey from Lewiston upon such provender as he could steal, which was very little, owing to the scarcity of settlements in the mountainous region over which his route lay.

"I don't believe you're half as glad to see me as you ought to be," he said, dropping upon a stool and surveying his surroundings impudently.

"Where have you spent the winter?" was Edna's reply, in a tone several degrees below the freezing point."

"That's *my* business, Mrs. Smith! It's enough for you to know that I'm deuced hungry and am ready to go foraging for grub."

Edna bustled about and rearranged one end of one of the long dining tables, trembling in every limb as she did so.

"Where's the cubs?" he exclaimed, authoritatively.

Edna made no answer, and he repeated the question in a louder key.

"Sue has gone out with them, if you mean the children when you speak of cubs," said Edna, quietly. "You know you insulted her by your rudeness when you were here last, and she has gone out to avoid you. She was here a few minutes ago."

"And do you keep that disreputable woman in the house yet?" asked John, fastening his watery blue eyes upon her with an air of stern rebuke.

"Sue is not a disreputable but a reformed woman, Mr. Smith. When did you cease to associate with her companion in guilt? And has *he* ever showed symptoms of reform?"

"A man's business is his own affair, madam! I associate with whom I please."

"There is one person with whom you will associate no more, John Smith, and that person is Edna Rutherford, your former wife!"

John raved and swore furiously for a while and then begged like a child to be forgiven and reinstated.

"This comes of women imbibing independent notions," said Mr. Handel, solemnly. "No woman would have thought of taking such a stand as this when I was a boy. I knew a dear mother in Israel[4] in my childhood who endured privation, suffering, and even *stripes* from a drunken husband for the Lord's sake. But, bless you, she was none of your strong-minded sort."

"And I knew slaves in my childhood," retorted Edna, "who endured toil without recompense and stripes without stint, without a thought but that they must endure. Their children ran away and otherwise resisted the injustice, though, and so will the daughters of your model, if they should marry badly."

"And so you intend to turn your lawful husband out o' doors, do you?" asked John Smith, doggedly.

"I have no husband!" was the decided reply.

"We'll see about that!" cried John, with an air of extreme importance, as he posted off to see a lawyer and Edna hurriedly resumed her work.

[To be continued.]

from
*The New Northwest*
Friday, May 4, 1877.

# EDNA AND JOHN:
## A ROMANCE OF IDAHO FLAT.

### BY Mrs. A. J. DUNIWAY,
AUTHOR OF "JUDITH REID," "ELLEN DOWD," "AMIE AND HENRY LEE,"
" THE HAPPY HOME," "ONE WOMAN'S SPHERE," "MADGE MORRISON,"
ETC., ETC., ETC.

*Woman's degraded, helpless position is the weak point of our institutions today—a disturbing force everywhere, severing family ties, filling our asylums with the deaf, the dumb, the blind, our prisons with criminals, our cities with drunkenness and prostitution, our homes with disease and death.*—National Centennial Equal Rights Protest.

## CHAPTER XX.

**E**DNA PASSED A SLEEPLESS NIGHT. Both babies were unusually unwell and fretful, and what with her own troubled thoughts and their continued restlessness, the morning dawned ere she had closed her eyes in slumber. To rise with the peep of dawn was one of the necessary contingencies of her business, and it was with heavy heart and heavy eyelids that she appeared at breakfast to wait upon a long line of hungry boarders, all of whom had learned of her determination to try to live without further interference from a drunken gambler, no matter what the law might demand.

And, in truth, the better class of men in Idaho Flat were in open sympathy with the struggling bond-woman. More than once had numbers of them held private indignation meetings wherein they had half resolved to lynch the vagabond who ruled over her, but the feeling of respect for the lawful rights of a husband, let that husband be never so worthless, was as deep rooted as the prejudice against a separation for other than nameless causes was firm.

Edna moved nervously about the breakfast tables, serving each in turn with her accustomed alacrity, pausing now and then to give a word of advice to Sue, who was minding the children in a room adjoining, when John Smith, the legal head of the family, and consequent lawful owner of the premises, came sauntering in beside a young limb of the law who had recently displayed his shingle in the Flat, and was solicitous of securing legal business to counteract his board bill.

"A half-dozen eggs, well done! I say, wife!" exclaimed John Smith, in a loud, commanding key, "I propose to see whether or not I can rule my own household!"

"Eggs are a dollar and a half per dozen," suggested Edna falteringly.

"I didn't ask the price of eggs!" was the loud rejoinder; "I want 'em well done!"

"Then *buy* them!" replied Edna, turning to the lawyer for his order, and further ignoring John.

"A nice breakfast, please. I am not over particular," said Mr. Brief, complacently.

"My rule is *money in advance,* as you are aware, Mr. Smith," quietly remarked the trembling wife, while her soul seemed to flash through her great, rabbit-like eyes.

"See here!" cried John, in a sort of sibilant whisper. "You just hurry up that provender, and do as I bid you, or I'll break every dish on this cussed table!"

"And get fined for your pains," said Edna, quietly.

"Is *that* it!" he exclaimed, giving the table a kick that made the dishes clatter.

"I say, Brief!" he added, after Edna had left them to enjoy their breakfast minus the eggs, "isn't it a jolly joke for a man's wife to talk about *fining him,* no matter what he does?"

"I should say it was," said Mr. Brief. "The fact is, women are getting a great deal too saucy, and they need a check upon their growing spirit of independence. If I were you I'd go over to the saloon and run the biggest kind of a bill. Debts of honor, you know. That is, I wouldn't call them that, exactly, for they've got a new Territorial Judge over at Boise, and he's playing sad havoc with many of our pet projects. He's one o' your white-cravated kind of sticklers for morals and all that sort o' thing, and he's working to keep divorces out of the Legislature and before the courts. That part of it is well enough for the lawyers, and I'm not complaining at all, but he rules out all debts for monte[1] or faro, or anything else of the kind, so we must call it something else. Now, I have it, by jingo! She refuses to give you board and lodging. Of course that's moonshine, for she can't help herself, seeing she's your lawful wife, but you can make it a pretext, and you can board and lodge in the Eureka and get your drinks and amusements in the bargain. Of course I'll have a good round fee against you, though I'll be reasonable, 'pon my word. But this legal business always costs like sin, you know."

"Yes, I know; but what next?"

John was so deeply interested in this profound "legal advice" that he almost forgot his food.

"Well, I was going to say that I'll board along with you at the Eureka, and that'll make the bill bigger."

"What then?"

"You can come onto your wife for the pay, my boy."

"But I just don't see what good that would do me, or Edna, or the cubs. You'd have had your board, and I mine, but old Sol of the saloon would get Edna's business. You can't quite come that over me, if I am a wronged and outraged man."

"But don't you see the beauty of the thing? The woman needs to feel your *power,* as you know. She needs to be taught her place. When she finds, after cooking hard all summer in the hotel business that a suit will be brought in the District Court and judgment rendered in favor of old Sol against everything she possesses, she'll come to her senses deuced quick."

"But I can't see that what you advise would be right."

"The dickens take the right of the matter! We weren't considering *right,* but *expediency* and *power,* my boy. She refuses to live with you, that is certain. Can't say that I blame her so dogged much, for you're a sad scamp, and no mistake; but women must learn to obey the laws and must be compelled to respect them, too."

"That's a fact," said John Smith, decidedly.

"After you've run a bill for, say six months," continued Mr. Brief, "you can give your note, payable on demand, and then you'll be sued on the note, the hotel property will be attached, and your wounded dignity and honor will be avenged."

"But, hang it, Brief, I don't just like to do such a thing as that. There's the cubs, you know. She'll have to keep something to raise them on."

"Oh, *drown* the cubs! Ten to one they're not yours, you know."

John Smith did not know anything of the kind. Indeed, such a thought had never before crossed his brain.

"She's a plaguey sight more intimate with that jackanapes[2] of a preacher than I'd allow a wife of *mine* to be!" said Mr. Brief, speaking low and looking extremely wise.

John Smith was suddenly struck with a new sensation. The idea of doubting Edna's honor, or of pretending to do so, was affecting him strangely. Rising from the table, where he had gorged to repletion off the proceeds of his wife's labor, he spent the day in discussing her and the minister among his conferees at the Eureka, and when night came and he and his legal adviser had abandoned Edna's temperance house[3] and transferred their patronage to the "opposition" establishment, where there was a bar, a faro bank, and a billiard table, the sense of relief the tired and perplexed woman experienced was the merciful result of total ignorance concerning the real designs of her protector and head.

When Mr. Handel again called in his pastoral rounds, he found her in good spirits and remarkably prosperous.

"Of course, Mrs. Smith, you are responsible for your own conduct, and you alone must bear its consequences," he said, solemnly. "But if I were you I should never have gone to such extreme measures."

"You have no idea what you would do if you were me, sir. But I know that if you were in my place you would do even worse than you think I have done. I am struck with intense admiration over the sublime fortitude with which you bear my burdens."

"Well, my dear madam, a woman is never justified in leaving her husband for other than Scriptural reasons. You have perjured your immortal soul."

"I have obeyed the Golden Rule, sir, and if in so doing I have perjured my salvation I am ready to bear the ordeal. I have done by John Smith exactly as I should want him to do by me under the same circumstances."

"Then, madam, I suppose our next dereliction will be the disgrace of a divorce court."

"And what do I want of a divorce, pray? All I ask of John is that he leave me in possession of my children and earnings. I have had enough of *marrying,* God knows."

"Madam, I am much relieved. I feared that you were on the downward track."

"Then, if getting a divorce from a man whose marriage was a moral fraud in the beginning is what you call the 'downward track,' you may possess your soul in unconcern. I shall not want a divorce. Yet I confess I fail to see the 'upward' tendency of a 'track' that keeps me on the legal treadmill, subject to the whims of a drunken idiot."

"You ought not to have married him in the first place," said Mr. Handel, looking extremely wise.

"I know it, sir; but having done myself an injury, and made a fearful mistake in so doing, do you think it my duty as a Christian to continue in the evil way? I thought it was the part of a Christian to repent of and forsake all evil. It seems to me that lack of common sense is your besetting sin."

"There!" said Mr. Brief, exultantly, as he and John Smith stood on the walk outside, peering eagerly through the partly opened door. "Didn't I tell you that she and that preacher were entirely too friendly?"

"I believe it, 'pon my soul!" replied the injured (?) husband, as he repaired to the Eureka and indulged more freely than ever in potations and play.

One day a miner, ragged and way-worn, called at the hotel, bringing with him a little child of tender years, as ragged and unkempt as himself. He was pale and care-worn, and a hacking cough betokened the presence of a fell disease.[4]

Edna was busy with the chamber work at the time, and Sue was left in charge of the dining-room.

At first Sue did not recognize the newcomers; but ever since her babe had been wrested from her embrace she had peered eagerly into the face of every stranger she met in the hope that she might see some person she might recognize who could give her tidings of her long-lost child. Children she had not seen at all, except Edna's, and now the unexpected appearance of this forsaken little one awakened all her motherly solicitude. Taking the child in her arms, she retreated to a chamber, where she proceeded at once to bathe the attenuated body, which was literally covered with a cutaneous eruption, the result of a neglect that had well-nigh disfigured it utterly.

"O, my God!" she exclaimed, as, disrobing the child, she began a thorough cleansing process with deft and careful hands, "what if my poor baby were to come to this!"

After long and gentle application of much-needed soap and water, and a careful and successful effort to rid the matted hair of tangles and vermin, the little girl revealed so much of her natural semblance to a human being that a sudden wild, ardent and yet shuddering hope seized the bereaved and childless mother, and she hugged the waif in an ecstacy of mingled expectation and dread.

"Where is your mamma, little darling?" she said, passionately.

"I ain't dot any," was the artless answer.

"Is your mamma dead?" and Sue Randolph trembled in every nerve.

"She's *stoled!*" replied the child. "She's stoled by a bad man, and my papa goed away and never comed back."

"What was your papa's name, darling?"

Sue could hardly wait for a reply.

"My mamma called him Hal, and he called me Blossom," was the artless answer.

"Would you know your mamma if you should see her, Blossom?"

"I dess so. Her had boo eyes and her didn't whip me, but Jim does."

"Who's Jim?"

"The man I comed with."

"Where's your papa?"

"Stoled too, and poor little Blossom's all alone."

Again and again did the poor woman caress the little hideous-looking waif, while tears of mingled joy and sorrow streamed down her pain-furrowed face and a tumult of contending emotions well-nigh overpowered her. Meanwhile, the hungry applicant for dinner was impatiently awaiting her tardy movements, and expressing his impatience by oft-repeated thumps upon the table.

Edna, hearing the commotion, hastened to the rescue and served the customer without demanding the usual fee in advance.

"I'll give him one meal and let him go," she soliloquized, "for I know he has no money."

"You seem to be prospering, Mrs. Smith. Where's John?" he asked, helping himself to the late dinner of warmed-over meats and vegetables like one to the manner born.

"I am not advised as to the present whereabouts of Mr. Smith, but I think you will find him at the Eureka," was the dignified reply.

"You don't seem to know me," continued the guest.

"I have not the honor," was the freezing rejoinder.

"Well, madam, I'm what's left of Jim Young, Sue's old flame, you know. John and I spent last winter in Lewiston together, and when our luck turned we had deuced hard times getting hash. I lost my way in coming back and found myself at last away over yonder at the foot of Alturas, where there are lots of new diggings. I should have gone to work there and been contented, only Hal LaSelle took a notion to die."

"What?"

Edna was fearfully pale.

"Hal took a notion to die, and there was nobody but me to care for the kitten, and I thought, as I'd caused the old boy a good deal of trouble, it was nothing more than fair that I should do him a good turn, so I took charge of the young one and brought it over to Sue."

"And where's the child?"

"Off somewhere with its mother. I don't think she knows the kit. It's had an awful hard time of it."

Edna fairly flew to join her friend upstairs, and the two held a long consultation over their future plans, while laughing and crying by turns over the recovery of the little storm-tossed waif they had so long mourned as dead.

"From his home in the skies poor Hal will be able to see things as they are, I hope, and then he will realize how deeply he has wronged me and our darling," sobbed the half-distracted mother.

"Sue, do you know who it was that brought her to us?" asked Edna, after the agitated mother had grown somewhat calmer.

"Oh, no; but I must go and thank him. He must have money, too. Evidently the fellow needs it."

Taking the child in her arms, she proceeded to the dining-room, and there, much to her astonishment and consternation, confronted the only man who had ever had remotest cause to look upon her with dishonor.

"Your amend in bringing my poor child to me has covered a multitude of sins," she said, offering a purse, and bowing with dignified politeness. "Take this money, get you some clothes, and equip yourself like a man and go to work. I am a reformed woman, and when you prove yourself as strong to do right as you have been foremost to do wrong, you shall not fail to find a friend in me. But you must do right, and prove yourself able to sustain yourself, ere I shall again attempt to assist you."

[To be continued.]

from
*The New Northwest*
Friday, May 11, 1877.

# EDNA AND JOHN:
## A ROMANCE OF IDAHO FLAT.

### BY Mrs. A. J. DUNIWAY,
AUTHOR OF "JUDITH REID," "ELLEN DOWD," "AMIE AND HENRY LEE,"
" THE HAPPY HOME," "ONE WOMAN'S SPHERE," "MADGE MORRISON,"
ETC., ETC., ETC.

*Woman's degraded, helpless position is the weak point of our institutions today—a disturbing force everywhere, severing family ties, filling our asylums with the deaf, the dumb, the blind, our prisons with criminals, our cities with drunkenness and prostitution, our homes with disease and death.*—National Centennial Equal Rights Protest.

## CHAPTER XXI.

**M**RS. RUTHERFORD found the home of her daughter-in-law so unlike the home she had so long presided over as the wife of Solon Rutherford that her life in that atmosphere became unendurable.

There was scarcely a nook or corner of the great farm-house to which she could retreat and feel herself free from the prying eyes of her son's wife and the mischievous fingers of her many grandchildren.

When mothers are young, and have the charge of their own little ones, nature prepares them for the burden; and the work being a labor of nature, glides along in some way till almost before the mother knows it she finds her children grown and herself arrived at mature womanhood. But there comes a sad experience to many mothers when a second growth of yet younger scions comes to them, when already worn out in the battle and toil of life, they must again take up the treadmill round of responsibility and care for their many grandchildren. The power of exercising their own authority is also gone in such a case, thus giving them additional perplexities that, but for the refining influence of long suffering and bodily endurance, would crush out the life of many a mother-in-law ere the time should come for her hair to be frosted with silvery gray.

Men have ridiculed mothers-in-law from time out of mind. Women have snubbed and abused them. The press and even the pulpit has habitually slandered them; and now the time cometh for the average mother-in-law to have her side of the story unfolded.

Behold the young mother with her babe on her bosom. The year of anxiety, suffering, anticipation, love, apprehension, and solicitude that preceded its existence is looked upon like the passing of a pleasant and yet horrible dream. She did not expect to survive the terrible ordeal. But now, as the tender bud of promise looks with wondering eyes into her love-lit face, what dreams she weaves for her darling's future! How her thoughts flash forth to span the coming years, and how she longs to lift the curtain that mercifully veils the decades that must come!

A year or two, and then other birdlings come; added years, and yet others take their places, increasing the mother's suffering, care and toil; but through it all there is an unwavering solicitude for the eldest born, as though the first fledgling had touched a tender chord in the mother-heart which none other had been able to reach.

Almost before the care-torn and toil-worn mother has been able to think of the possibility of such an experience for her tender child as she has herself struggled with through all her weary years of "sowing for others to reap," she finds her straying away from her love and confidence.

A stranger, one who has no thought or anticipation for her beloved birdling except a selfish and sordid desire to own and possess her, steps between the mother and the child. He fascinates her; he carries her away captive; he stands ever after between the two who were one hitherto, and with law and custom upon his side, speaks of the mother-in-law with unfeeling coarseness and sarcastic ribaldry. The mother has no alternative but to suffer and endure. One thing, thank heaven, she is used to suffering, having experienced little else since the honeymoon of her own marriage was over; but she had hoped and prayed, oh, so earnestly, that a better and happier lot might be in store for *her* child, that the awakening comes to her like the living consciousness of ever-abiding birth pangs. The husband *owns* the wife, according to men's laws and gospels. Ever after the mother-in-law is an interloper, a supernumerary, a melancholy infringement upon the husband's rights.

Sometimes, as in the case of Mrs. Rutherford, the mother-in-law is the husband's mother, and the bone of hidden contention. Then the trouble is aggravated, especially if the mother-in-law be pecuniarily dependent, as is almost invariably the case; for she has toiled without recompense for half a lifetime; the fruits of her labors have gone into the family fund; her earnings have been appropriated by her children. The long years that she might otherwise have spent in laying up an independence for her declining years have been devoted to the work of rearing the children for whose sake she is now beggared and ridiculed and wounded continually. If the husband is called away by death—and being almost invariably the older by a term of

years, he is apt to die soonest—he may will away the accumulations of a lifetime to his sons or sons-in-law, and the mother-heart and purse are alike left
unto her desolate, while her hard-earned home becomes another's. Her
step is no longer elastic; her strength and vigor of youth are gone; her children are no longer hers, but somebody's else, and she is left to the alternative of a life of dependence and unwelcome impecuniosity as a cumbersome
mother-in-law whom "nobody wants around," or to become the second wife
of some elderly man with obstreperous children, who takes her into a family
whither she would not have thought of going had she not been robbed by the
laws of men of the rightful earnings of her long life of suffering and labor.

Mrs. Rutherford had borne the odium of being a mother-in-law for
years, and had almost become accustomed to it, just as people will get accustomed to living with the heart broken; but until her husband's death she
had not known what it was to be dependent in any way upon her married
children. Where to go to better her condition she knew not. Her children
were all married, and in the home of every one of them she would be a
mother-in-law.

But, as we have said, her old home was unendurable.

Now, it is strange, but true, that no matter what your trouble may be,
there is always some palliating circumstance, or unexpected ray of hope,
that beams in upon you when your hours are darkest, to light your pathway
through the densest places in your way of gloom.

It was a scorching summer day. The fervent sun beamed down upon
the fervid earth, and harvest time, in all its oppressive, heated glory, hurried the farming force of the old Rutherford homestead and gathered in the
neighbors to assist in the many fields.

Mrs. Rutherford junior was an invalid with a new baby that was, in
time, to grow up and make a despised and unwelcome mother-in-law herself; but mercifully for her, the young mother did not consider that. The
kitchen labor of the farm depended wholly upon Mrs. Rutherford senior,
who, now that the home was in no sense hers, not even so much as belonging to her by the fiction of possession as a wife, had as little heart as
strength for her labors. Her step was languid and her health poor. There
was work enough about the house for three strong women, yet the thought
of help for her entered not into the calculations of her son.

But a letter from Edna settled the question.

"Dear mother, I am free," she wrote. "I have a home large enough for
you, and I am rid of John. Come over to Idaho Flat. You can get in with
teams almost any day from Omaha, or what is better, you can come by
stage. If you have no money, let me know, and I will forward the necessary
amount."

"How should I have money, when I've never been allowed to control a
cent of my own earnings?" queried Mrs. Rutherford, pausing to think the
situation over calmly.

"You will not be a mother-in-law here, dear mother; for John is gone,
and only I and the children and Sue Randolph are together," wrote Edna. "I

*pine* for you; I *long* for you! *Do come,* and we will make you happy, for you shall have a daughter's love."

The words of Edna's letter settled themselves like a song of gladness in the weary mother's heart. But she had no time now to fold her hands and think. It would soon be dinner time, and the household must be fed.

The children were cross and ungovernable. The baby was fretful and sick. The house, where for so many years comparative quiet had reigned, was in a continuous uproar, and "grandma" was in constant requisition to settle childish quarrels, as best she could without authority, to give bread and butter here, mend a whip there, tie up a wounded finger in another direction, or feed the fretful baby on catnip tea.

"I have a letter from Edna inviting me to join her in Idaho Flat, and I'm going next week," Mrs. Rutherford said to her son, the lawful possessor of her hard-earned domain, as he came sauntering into the long dining-room to see if dinner was ready.

"You must be crazy!" was the quick reply.

"If it will console you any to think I've lost my senses, you are welcome to the delusion, my son. But I am resolved to go, and I want money enough to meet the expenses of the journey."

"Do you think I'm made of money?" asked the injured son. "You couldn't get there short o' three hundred dollars, economical as you are, and I don't propose to take that much cash out of my business for anybody's whims."

"My son," replied the mother, shaking her head and speaking falteringly, while a tear stole down her furrowed cheek, "do you think I am a pensioner upon your bounty?"

"Not exactly that, mother; but everything about this place belongs to me, as you know, though you shall have a home as long as I have it. Now, I'm perfectly willing to grant you every needed comfort. You have a good home—just as good as my father provided. You have plenty to eat and wear, and you ought to be contented. I'm just about buying the farm in the next township that old man Rankin won't stay on since his wife died. I'll get it at a bargain, too, and I've no money for pleasuring."

"Well, my boy, suppose you had lived on this place and toiled on it as I have for thirty years. Suppose you had come here, as I did; when the land was wild, without a comfort or convenience for a home. Suppose you had made butter and cheese for market, and that butter and cheese had not belonged to you but to your wife. Suppose that in addition to bearing and rearing a large family you had done all the work for a house like this. Then when you came to be old and infirm, how would you like for your wife to have the power to will the entire property that you had earned to one of your children, leaving you a pauper in your old days, or, at most, a pensioner upon the bounty which your child might see fit to bestow upon you, leaving you no choice but submission?"

"I can't see that the cases are at all parallel, mother."

"And I confess I fail to see why they are not so."

"Well, mother, there is no use in arguing the point, for it is plain we never shall agree. You'd just as well make up your mind to be contented."

"My son," said Mrs. Rutherford, choking back her tears with a great effort, "if you will give me five hundred dollars, I will never trouble you again."

"And what would you do with five hundred dollars, pray? The very idea is absurd."

"I could rent Aunt Judy's old cabin, if you would let me have it, and be a great deal more independent there than I am here."

"What the mischief do you want to be independent for?"

"For the same reason that you like it, my son. I have earned my independence, and I propose to enjoy it."

Further conversation was interrupted by the appearance of the hired men at dinner, and Mrs. Rutherford buried her tears by an effort of will and resumed her place for the nonce as a protected and supported subordinate.

It was three in the afternoon before her work was so far completed that she could get away from the sick-room and kitchen and steal for a little while to the one little, low, unfinished room in the attic that had been left as her realm, and even here she was not safe from intrusion.

The sun beamed upon the roof till the room was like an oven; but Mrs. Rutherford was fully aware that it was "better to dwell in the corner of a house-top than with a brawling woman in a wide house."[1]

Throwing herself upon the bed, she indulged for a long time in an agony of tears that at last soothed her ruffled feelings. She was away from the noise of children, too.

Rising, at length, and opening a little quaint old trunk that bespoke, in its antique style and diminutive size, of the times long ago, she searched among old keepsakes till she came to an old-fashioned brooch and ear rings of considerable value.

"I intended to keep them till my change should come," she muttered, "but fate has willed it otherwise. I took a journey to St. Louis once, and I will go again. Ah, me!"

Then for a long time she lived over the memory of that never-to-be-forgotten time when she had dared to claim some money from the bank wherewith to assist her daughter to remove to the far, far West.

"I felt like a culprit then," she soliloquized. "And yet why did I? I had earned the money. By every moral right it belonged to me without my having to steal it. Yet what could I do? I had no right to my own earnings which my husband was bound to respect. Every dollar I had ever earned belonged to him, and now, through his will, to his son. Luckily my father gave me these jewels before I became a wife or mother, else I would not have them now. Eben says it will cost three hundred dollars to get me to Edna's. The jewels are worth twice that, but I don't care. It's all they'll fetch. I'll sell them and have it over."

"You must get somebody else to do this work to-morrow, my son," she said, when he and the men came in to supper. "I am going to St. Louis to transact a little business on my own account. And while you are getting help you'd just as well make a permanent arrangement, for I am going to Idaho."

It was all in vain that the son demurred. It was all in vain that the daughter-in-law expostulated. It was equally in vain that the children cried.

When they all discovered the futility of their efforts to retain her as housekeeper, she heard her daughter-in-law say, petulantly:

"Well, I'm glad we're going to get rid of her! I never did fancy such an incumbrance as a mother-in-law!"

The good woman might have retorted, but did not. She knew that in the event of a family disturbance the mother-in-law would surely get the worst of it, and it was bad enough to be robbed and insulted, without bearing the blame of an open outbreak.

[To be continued.]

from
*The New Northwest*
Friday, May 18, 1877.

# EDNA AND JOHN:
## A ROMANCE OF IDAHO FLAT.

### BY Mrs. A. J. DUNIWAY,

AUTHOR OF "JUDITH REID," "ELLEN DOWD," "AMIE AND HENRY LEE,"
" THE HAPPY HOME," "ONE WOMAN'S SPHERE," "MADGE MORRISON,"
ETC., ETC., ETC.

*Woman's degraded, helpless position is the weak point of our institutions today—a disturbing force everywhere, severing family ties, filling our asylums with the deaf, the dumb, the blind, our prisons with criminals, our cities with drunkenness and prostitution, our homes with disease and death.*—National Centennial Equal Rights Protest.

## CHAPTER XXII.

**M**RS. RUTHERFORD was as badly at a loss about pawning her old-fashioned jewels in St. Louis as she had once been about securing a thousand dollars from the bank.

As before, the bustle and roar of the busy city bewildered her. As before, she longed for Solon's aid and confidence, but she had not the feeling of insecurity akin to guilt which had before possessed her. Unconsciously to herself she was sustained as she had not before been in any of her many resolutions. A quiet determination to overcome every obstacle, and a positive feeling that she must succeed, nerved her with unwonted strength.

It was as though a ministering angel guided her.

The sum realized from the sale of the only relics of her life of toil that she could call her own was far too meager to meet the necessities of her journey as they should have been met, but she was resolved to attempt it at all hazards.

When she went to purchase her ticket she was not surprised to find that men, in business, do not take woman's impecuniosity into consideration when they deal with them. She was not surprised to find that in traveling as in everything else, it costs a woman just as much to meet expenses as it costs a man; but she was grieved over the fact as she never before had been, and was astonished that the injustice of compelling women to spend their lives as servants without wages had not before given her more indignant concern.

Had Mrs. Rutherford been left to the choice of forty lashes or a return to her old home, before starting West, for her few personal effects in the way of wearing apparel and little keepsakes, she would have chosen the former as the lesser evil. But her means were too limited to enable her to do without the very scanty wardrobe that the laws of men called hers, and there was no alternative but to go and get it.

Very cool was her reception as she again ventured to cross the threshold that was once her own. But Mrs. Rutherford took no heed of glowering looks or contemptuous words. Her daughter-in-law was not treading a path strewn with roses, and she felt for her a pity strongly akin to pain, as she saw her struggling with loads of labor and care while walking wearily in the same hard road of life through which she had toiled in bringing up her own family.

"Why don't you keep help, my child? You are not strong enough to perform so many duties. The care of your family is enough without your making butter and cheese and doing cooking and washing for hired men," she said, earnestly.

Mrs. Rutherford junior was astonished. Such an expostulation from her own mother would not have surprised her, but coming from a mother-in-law made it simply wonderful.

"Take my advice and never earn a dollar outside of your household labor, which must be performed, of course, to satisfy the bodily demands of your children. I have toiled all my life for that which was nothing to me when I came to need it worst. Women's work does not belong to them but their husbands, or whosoever their husbands may choose to will it."

"But Eben says he can't get help, mother. He is very angry because you are determined to leave us."

"Did you get right up out of your bed, after I started to St. Louis, and go into the kitchen to shoulder all this load?"

"Of course I did. How could I help myself? Eben wouldn't get me any help, and the work had to be done."

"Well, child, you just go to bed and stay there till you get well. You have not been so kind to me, heaven knows, as to place me under any obligations to you; but I will give my advice gratis. He'll be compelled to employ somebody to do the work for good and all if you keep on at this rate. The average man knows nothing whatever about taking care of a woman."

"If you had only stayed!" sobbed the poor weak mother.

"And why should I stay, I'd like to know? You didn't appreciate anything I was doing, and nobody paid me for my labor. I've resolved to spend my little remaining strength in working for myself, since the toil of a lifetime has been willed to my husband's children. You know that a

mother isn't supposed to have any children of her own!" and Mrs. Rutherford gave a bitter laugh.

"Well, I'm sure there is no use in worrying over that," replied the
daughter-in-law, "for everything would go to the children anyhow as soon
as you'd die. It's just as well to let them have it a little while beforehand."

"You'll chant in a different key by the time you've reached my age,"
said Mrs. Rutherford. "But I don't blame you overmuch for taking sides
with Eben. Women always did go against themselves to please their husbands, and I guess they always will."

"I should say that Edna Smith was a marked exception, and it's little
wonder her husband left her, seeing the bringing up she's had!" retorted
the junior, and Mrs. Rutherford answered her not a word further.

"I might have known better than to say anything to her as her mother-
in-law," she soliloquized, as she left the kitchen and continued her packing.

The journey by steamer to Omaha, and thence by stage to Idaho Flat,
was very different both in duration and manner from the journey in an ox
wagon that Edna had taken years before.

For a few days her bones were bruised and sore, and then she became
accustomed to the jolting. After this she journeyed comfortably, the won-
ders of the prairie and desert opening up to her a constant theme for reflection and conjecture.

But more than all, she was shortening the distance between herself
and Edna every hour. What cared she for dusty roads and tedious rides?
Had she not endured a thousand times greater trials that she might be near
her children? And yet, what had it all availed her? Had not her deepest
mother love proved her keenest anguish? Had it not always failed her when
she needed it most?

Then she would muse and wonder much about how Edna would appear when she should meet her. She could remember her vividly as a
dimple-faced baby darling, the light of her home and the joy of her heart.
Again, she could recall her as a blithe and joyous schoolgirl, graceful,
bright, and beautiful. She could follow her through the dreary days and
weeks and months of loneliness spent by the young girl in a boarding
school—a period of probation that ended at last in years of almost total
estrangement on the part of Edna from the mother who would have died
for her.

The days and nights of travel continued, and now they were in Idaho,
traversing the great plains and greater mountains that intervened between
herself and the lone toiler in Idaho Flat.

Now they were getting very near the wild, weird home of her daughter
in the wilderness, and Mrs. Rutherford could think of nothing else but the
fearful shock she had felt when the news of Edna's marriage had burst
upon her like a thunderbolt. Alas, she had cared nothing for life since then.
Indeed, she had only lived at all because she knew that the time would
come when Edna, repentant and sorrowing, would yearn for the mother
love that in her blindness she had cast from her for the bauble of a professed affection that had transformed her from a dutiful and affectionate

daughter to the creature of a stranger's will. She knew the time would come when her daughter would be glad to come back to the mother love she had thus ruthlessly cast from her; and she had felt all along that she *must* live to comfort her then, else she would have given up her last hold on life on Edna's wedding day.

And now the last mountain height between herself and child was reached, and the great coach was already rumbling down its side, revealing Idaho Flat, which, as the reader knows, was not a flat at all, but a succession of rocky ridges and gulches, through which a noisy, muddy, tortuous river ran, bearing in its busy current the stirred up ore from the adjacent and distant burrows that, with their Erebus-like[1] openings, gaped everywhere.

Edna was expecting her. Out upon a knoll, hard by the spot where Aunt Judy and Mr. Handel had once arranged a place for holding meetings in the open air, and where now a church stood, she had taken her position an hour before to watch.

The stage halted when near her, and Edna's heart beat painfully, while Mrs. Rutherford was fairly stupefied with overpowering sensations.

"Can you show me the residence of Mrs. Edna Smith?" asked the mother, addressing her without the faintest idea that she had found her child.

*"Mother,* don't you *know* me?"

That was enough. Mrs. Rutherford could never afterward remember how she had climbed from the high seat above the stage-coach boot to the rise where Edna stood. In an instant they were locked in a mute embrace. Both were overcome by unutterable thoughts.

Ah, reader, there is a love that hath no tinge of selfishness. A love that never dieth; that clingeth when hope is dead and joy hath fled; a love that never faileth, but is always burning brightest when you need it most. But it is not conjugal love; it is not paternal affection; it is mother love, and it sustaineth you when all else fails. Cherish it tenderly, nourish it constantly, consider it well.

Other loves will fail you, but this will not. Other loves have selfish motives, this has none. Let your right hand forget its cunning and your tongue cleave to the roof of your mouth ere you trample upon or in any way wound this holy passion that hath naught of self in it.

Your mother will crucify her own motherly affection and lay it weltering at your feet in her own heart's gore, rather than see you suffer the deserved results of your own ingratitude. She will gladly allow you to despise her, and will permit herself to be unjustified forever in your eyes, rather than you shall feel the wounds recoil upon yourself that you inflict upon her. If you are a daughter who has been unfilial, your atonement will come when your own children trample upon your heartstrings. If a son, your trouble will come in some other way, for retribution is a law of nature, and like all immutable laws, refuses to be violated with impunity.

Mrs. Rutherford quivered in every nerve. Could it be possible that this faded, jaded, care-worn woman was the delicate, blooming girl that John Smith had stolen from her mother's home and lured with false pretenses from the paths of filial duty a few short years ago?

O, human law, where is thy vaunted justice? where thy great protection? where thy sovereign wisdom?

Echo only answers, where?

A man may get your land by false pretenses and you can send him to the State prison. He may get your hog by theft and you can commit him to the county jail; and you may recover your goods in either case. But when he makes false pretenses that lure your child to a ruin that he can legalize by marriage laws, you can only welter in your own agony. On his side lies the might, and might is right with him and law.

"I know I'm faded, mother, dear. But don't look at me so pleadingly, please. I am your Edna, your own darling. I wronged you and I am ready to atone. You must be tired. Come with me to the hotel. I want you to see my babies."

Mrs. Rutherford could not speak. Edna led the way down to the house and up the narrow stairs to a primitively furnished room, which she assigned to her as her own.

The children were not Rutherfords, but Smiths. The grandmother saw this at a glance, and a new disappointment awaited her; but she choked down the expression of regret that well-nigh found utterance and tearfully asked for Sue.

Little by little the great gaps that the passing years had made between them all were spanned and bridged.

Aunt Judy came over in a few days and made a visit, though her manner was constrained and distant, as though she feared that any great show of interest or sympathy would open the channels of her husband's purse to those who might become pensioners upon her bounty.

"Let her go," said Mrs. Rutherford. "I was her friend when she needed me. She was a friend to you in your darkest hours, Edna. Let us love her for the good she has done and lay the blame of her present conduct to her husband, to whom she is indebted for her present prosperity."

"If I could see a man whose soul was large enough to rise above his own personal consideration and enable him to look upon woman as an individual with selfhood equal to his own, I could fairly bow down to him and worship him," cried Edna, her eyes beaming.

"A phenomenon that you can hardly look or hope for, since every man is born of a woman who is herself a serf," said Mrs. Rutherford. "Men are good enough, considering the circumstances under which they are generated and raised. They are what their mothers make them."

"Then I'll train one boy in such a way that he shall know how to treat a woman," replied Edna, looking fondly upon her baby son.

"Alas, he's a Smith, and the born image of John," sighed the grandmother, averting her tear-stained face and gazing abroad into vacancy.

[To be continued.]

from
*The New Northwest*
Friday, May 25, 1877.

# EDNA AND JOHN:
## A ROMANCE OF IDAHO FLAT.

### BY Mrs. A. J. DUNIWAY,
AUTHOR OF "JUDITH REID," "ELLEN DOWD," "AMIE AND HENRY LEE,"
" THE HAPPY HOME," "ONE WOMAN'S SPHERE," "MADGE MORRISON,"
ETC., ETC., ETC.

*Woman's degraded, helpless position is the weak point of our institutions today—a disturbing force everywhere, severing family ties, filling our asylums with the deaf, the dumb, the blind, our prisons with criminals, our cities with drunkenness and prostitution, our homes with disease and death.*—National Centennial Equal Rights Protest.

## CHAPTER XXIII.

**T**HE TERRITORY OF IDAHO had recently been judicially districted, and Circuit Court was now to hold its opening session in Idaho Flat.

Several young lawyers who had struggled long with legal technicalities in their, at last, successful endeavor to be admitted to the bar in the States, and who had struggled longer with less successful effort to obtain clients in their native haunts, had recently come to dispute possession with Mr. Brief, while older lawyers, broken-down politicians, ex-judges badly out of date, governmental employees, and not a few men of more than ordinary ability, as brains go, but badly deficient in purse and public appreciation, flocked hither and thither in the Territory to prey upon the cupidity and credulity of those who might have needed justice, but they seldom got it when appealing to the law.

"Be composed," said a lawyer once to a client on trial for grand larceny. "No doubt you will be treated justly."

"Faith, sir, and justice is the very thing I'm afraid of," returned the Hibernian, who, had he been a native American, would have felt little fear on that score.

Several of the new Territorial officials brought their families to Idaho Flat, and society began to assume some of the phases of older civilization, though there was yet one sad drawback to morality among the majority of men, and that was nothing less than the scarcity of good women.

Nature always seeks an equilibrium. When humanity interferes with the equalization of masculine and feminine forces by removing the restraining influence of one sex from the other in any of the departments of life, from the domestic to the educational, social, or religious, to the legal and governmental, the channels of life become vitiated, and nature, in the only effort left her to restore the equilibrium thus disturbed, will send bad women where the good are not plenty, and the feet of her whose "steps take hold on hell"[1] will too often lead the unwary into pitfalls of his own creating, to hold him captive ever after at her will.

Idaho Flat became the rendezvous of abandoned women who were bent upon spoils. Money was plenty, for gold abounded in the river beds, and gold and silver was in the gorges and on the very mountain tops.

Mrs. Rutherford, wholly unaccustomed to the vice and immorality that flourished before her eyes, was thoroughly horrified with what transpired daily. Women whom older and more settled society would have sent to jail for lewdness, flaunted their silks and jewels before her face and seated themselves at table to be fed like queens.

"I wouldn't stand it, Edna!" she exclaimed in indignation, as these people multiplied in their midst.

"I make the bread and clothing and shelter for all of us by feeding the men who support them, mother. They are just as good as any man who visits them."

"But I will order the very next bad woman out of doors who comes here to get her dinner—I'll have no such baggage around."

"Then I will order every man away who is seen in their company, mother. Did you notice the costly diamond ring that one of them sported this morning? That was presented her by a government official who pays me a round price for board—his board and hers. That man is feasted and *feted* in the best Washington society every winter. He has a big salary with perquisites, and leaves his poor dupe of a wife at some obscure country village every summer, while he comes home to his constituents, to lobby for re-appointment and run with fast women, who are as good as himself, bad as they are. You turn the woman out and I will dismiss the man, and then, if this thing is carried out, we'll see where our bread and butter comes from."

But mother and daughter were spared the necessity of putting their designs into execution.

It was autumn now, and the Circuit Court was in session, giving many a lawyer an opportunity to turn an honest hundred or two by attending to the disputed claims, real and imaginary, of opposing miners, who, now that chances for going to law abounded, were not slow in taking legal steps to overreach or underreach their neighbors in any way that was legally possible.

Edna was busy to her very eyes in the kitchen, dining-room, and everywhere. Her Mongolian help had found the work too hard for him when Court met, and, when increasing crowds of men materially increased the kitchen efforts, had taken French leave and no other help was to be had.

The harvest that Circuit Court brings is never to be despised by the inn or boarding-house keeper of a country town, and those engaged in that business in Idaho Flat were no exception to the general rule.

"We have heavy bills to meet, mother, and I am depending upon this harvest season to pay for our winter's wood and lights, and many other necessaries that must come. I want to build an addition to the house, also, and I can't afford to turn away a single boarder, so we must make hay while the sun shines. Everybody's money will help us along, so don't be squeamish, but just help me out this month and we'll get several hundreds ahead."

Mrs. Rutherford and Sue Randolph each heeded the advice thus freely given, and the hotel became a place of gaiety and noise and money changing, which Edna would never have consented for it to become had she been permitted by her legal head, or even advised by her minister, to keep up legitimate and wholesome amusements of the intellectual character that she had at first inaugurated.

But, as we have said, she was busy to her eyes in work. In all the married years of her life she had not felt so free and happy. Business was unusually brisk, even for a mining town. There were many intellectual legal gentlemen in attendance at the court, and though her time was all taken up with her culinary cares, she managed to keep herself and children tidy and apparently comfortable, so that she was ready at any moment for a brilliant sally of wit or a brief dissertation upon legal technicalities, mining stocks, theology, philosophy, or recipes for cooking.

The county sheriff was a very important personage in Idaho Flat. He was short and obese, with a thick neck and fleshy jaws set squarely upon shoulders slightly rounded, and he carried a pair of flabby fat hands with the digits in his pantaloons pockets and the stubby thumbs protruding awkwardly. From the day that Edna had first met him he had been her pet aversion. True, his habits were more correct and his conduct more circumspect than that of her boarders in general, but there was an air of selfishness, and a want of fine sensibility about him that was particularly offensive to her feelings.

He had a habit of making broad assertions that were generally as wide of the truth as they were broad in utterance, and clinching the same by a coarse guffaw that would silence, though it always failed to convince, those holding a different opinion.

"I have a document in my possession that particularly concerns you, Mrs. Smith," he exclaimed, as, thrusting his burly figure inside the kitchen, he broke into a loud ha! ha! ha!

"A document concerning *me!*" cried Edna, rubbing the flour from her hands, and reaching to take the paper from his pudgy digits and pudgier thumb.

"I wonder if John isn't applying for a divorce?" she asked herself, and then came the pleasing reflection that divorces were easy to obtain in Idaho Flat.

But Edna did not comprehend the import of the mysterious document. It was loaded down with the ambiguous technicalities that usually overshadow papers of its ilk, and after a moment's reflection, she looked enquiringly at the officer for an explanation, while a dark foreboding, as undefined as dismal, crept into her heart.

"It's a writ of ejection from these premises by old Sol, the saloonkeeper. Ha! ha! ha!" said the legal protector of women.

"I don't see how that can be," replied Edna, turning deathly pale. "I never owed him a dime in my life."

"But, madam, John Smith and Mr. Brief have been boarding at his *chebang* all summer on the strength of John's claim upon this business. You'll have to liquidate. Ha! ha! ha!"

"But, I *shan't!*" exclaimed Edna. "So *there!*"

The guffaw that followed was so exasperating that Edna refrained with difficulty from belaying the officer with her rolling-pin. But she felt instinctively that she was at the mercy of the law, and wisely held herself in restraint.

"You see," he continued, "John had to have some place to stay, and when you turned him out he went over to Sol's, and as he had no money, he gave his note. Mr. Brief has been his counselor all along, and John gave him his note of hand also. Ha! ha! ha!"

"Stop that guffawing, or I'll dash your brains out!" cried Edna, in a frenzy of indignation that made the sheriff fairly tremble.

"Brief sold the note to Sol," he continued, sobering down, "and Sol got judgment on this property, and the cheapest thing you can do is to get out."

"But John has never raised a finger to earn a dollar here. Everything in the house and about it belongs to me."

"That's the very reason you don't own it, madam. If you weren't a wife now! But you *are,* you see, and everything you own isn't yours at all, but your husband's. If you'd been sharp, you'd have let everything be held in the name of Sue Randolph, or your mother, for both of them are without husbands, and they can hold property, you see. Ha! ha! ha!"

"My mother has often said that woman's degraded, helpless position is the weak point in our institutions to-day. She says it is a disturbing force everywhere, severing family ties, filling our asylums with victims, our prisons with criminals, our towns and cities with prostitution, our homes with disease and death. I never saw the force of this abominable truth as I see it now. I have toiled like a galley slave to build up and sustain this business and maintain myself and children. It has not occurred to me once this summer that my being a wife by a fiction of law, under which I have found no protection, would render it necessary for me to put my earnings into other hands than my own for safe keeping, else I would have done it and defied the law. As it is, I am powerless. But what am I to do?"

"Just what this writ advises, madam. You are to vacate the premises at once, to satisfy the judgment."

"Leave my house this minute, sir!" said Edna, folding the paper and resuming her rolling-pin. "You can't put me out under a writ of ejectment under thirty days after having given ten days' notice. I know a few things about law when I stop to think of them, if I am a woman."

"Sol'll be madder'n thunder!" soliloquized the sheriff, as he waddled away to carry the news to him and Mr. Brief and John.

"How strange that I should have been so blind!" thought Edna. "I knew, or might have known, that John Smith, as my husband, could commit no recognized or punishable crime by robbing me of my earnings; but here I have been toiling and accumulating for months as though unconscious of existing facts. Luckily I have a few hundred dollars hidden away. I intended to use that money toward liquidating bills, but Sol, or whoever gets the house, may do that. I'll save all I can during the next thirty days."

Her resolve thus taken was followed for a week, and then came a legal injunction forbidding the boarders to pay their bills to Edna, and there was no alternative but to lose the result of her summer's toil and begin preparing anew in the autumn for the near approach of a rigorous winter.

"Whom the Lord loveth He chasteneth,"[2] said Mr. Handel, with a sanctimonious air, as soon as he learned the facts.

"I should say that whom the devil despiseth he destroyeth," was Edna's prompt rejoinder.

"I am sorry, my dear madam, that you do not accept your trials in a meek and quiet spirit,"[3] observed the preacher.

"And I am surprised that you are such a consummate fool!" was the impulsive retort.

"What?"

Mr. Handel would have been scarcely less surprised had the heavens fallen. He had long felt it his pastoral duty to call upon Edna once or twice in every week, and had never failed to share her hospitable board. She had always before been passably courteous, despite some of her heterodox vagaries, of which he constantly warned her.

"I've done what I could to keep you in the straight and narrow path,[4] Mrs. Smith, but I find you constantly drifting upon the breakers. You know what the Scripture saith. 'He that, being often reproved, hardeneth his neck, shall suddenly be destroyed, and that without mercy.'"[5]

"Leave the house this minute with your mocking cant!" exclaimed Edna. Indeed, she was nearly crazed, and no wonder.

Let any reader of these pages who would chide her put himself in her place and see if his human nature would not instantly rebel. It is very easy, always, to bear other people's troubles with fortitude. It is our own that come to us to stay.

"Awful as a divorce is, Edna, you will be compelled to get one, or starve," said Mrs. Rutherford, while the thought that her beloved daughter, in whom she had so long indulged more pride and anticipation than in all else in the world, would be that loathsome thing, a "grass widow," was enough of itself to prostrate her on a bed of sickness.

Another week elapsed, and Edna, with her mother, Sue Randolph, and three little children, was again ensconced in the diminutive cabin where she had begun her struggle for bread when she had first settled with Aunt Judy in Idaho Flat.

"Men are constantly placing a premium upon crime," said Edna, bitterly. "See how much better off a fallen woman is than the wife of a bad man. Those courtesans you were complaining of, mother, are safely housed and fed in the very hotel from which I, though toiling sixteen hours out of twenty-four to keep it going, have been driven as a criminal. Do you wonder that I despise men?"

"That's wicked, daughter. Pray do not talk like that. Your father was a man, and you have brothers and a son."

"Don't quote my father to me, mother. You know I would not own him for years before he died."

"Which was very unfilial of you, my child. The girl that fails to honor her father or mother need not expect prosperity or happiness. Your father did what the laws and customs of men empowered him to do, and he thought it was all right. True, it was not right, but his intentions were good. I cannot bear to have you blame him."

"Well, mother, one thing is certain, and that is that I shall sue for a divorce at this sitting of the court. If I wait till spring, John will have another chance to rob me, for no man can be punished for impoverishing his wife."

"And so you are to be a *grass widow!* O, Edna!"

"Don't reproach me, mother. I cannot bear it. I would rather be a dead carcass than a grass widow, if I could have my choice, but men do my choosing, and I cannot help myself."

Edna's application for a divorce upon the ground of the habitual drunkenness of her husband was followed the next day by an application for a like decree from John, the alleged cause being improper association with Mr. Handel, the conscientious Christian missionary. Each complainant prayed for the custody of the children, and the lawyers looked for a good harvest, and the public, for an attractive and disgraceful scene in court.

[To be continued.]

from
*The New Northwest*
Friday, June 1, 1877.

# EDNA AND JOHN:
## A ROMANCE OF IDAHO FLAT.

### BY Mrs. A. J. DUNIWAY,

AUTHOR OF "JUDITH REID," "ELLEN DOWD," "AMIE AND HENRY LEE,"
" THE HAPPY HOME," "ONE WOMAN'S SPHERE," "MADGE MORRISON,"
ETC., ETC., ETC.

*Woman's degraded, helpless position is the weak point of our institutions today—a disturbing force everywhere, severing family ties, filling our asylums with the deaf, the dumb, the blind, our prisons with criminals, our cities with drunkenness and prostitution, our homes with disease and death.*—National Centennial Equal Rights Protest.

## CHAPTER XXIV.

**M**ANY OF THE DISGRACEFUL SCENES of a divorce court must again be passed in silence by. Would to heaven it were possible, under the existing order of one-sexed laws, to expunge from the law practice every vestige of the cross questionings that bring blushes to the cheeks of suffering modesty, and outrage the sense of decency in every quivering nerve of every martyred woman who may be a victim of the disturbing force of inequality that severs family ties, and fills so many human hearts with a lingering misery that can only be assuaged by death.

"Don't appear against John, daughter," wisely advised her mother. "His unjust accusations will not injure you in the eyes of God, and it makes no difference to you as to what man may say when you have a clear conscience."

"But, mother, my silence will be a virtual admission that John Smith's charges are true," said Edna, weeping bitterly. "It will disgrace our minister and destroy his usefulness, and will brand me as a bad woman. I really cannot bear it."

"Let your daily walk and conversation be your refutation of the charge, my dear. As to Mr. Handel—don't worry about him. He's a man, and can take care of himself. I have never considered him a favorite of yours in any sense. If he can't stay here and hold his head up and continue in the ways of usefulness because a drunken sot has slandered him, he hasn't the complete elements of a reformer. Let him try new fields of missionary labor and we can get another preacher."

Well had it been for Edna had she taken her mother's advice. But several lawyers were idle in Idaho Flat, and a firm was found which was not slow in enforcing the thought upon her brain that she must vindicate herself before the bar of justice. As though a slandered character was ever vindicated by appealing to the law!

When the day of trial came, Edna appeared in opposition to the plea of John upon the ground that he had accused her falsely. She did not want a divorce at all, she said, except upon the ground of her husband's drunkenness.

Then followed a long research into the early history of John, the object being to discover whether or not Edna had known, prior to her marriage, that he had been addicted to dissipation.

Edna was overcome with humiliation at the remembrance of their meager acquaintance in the days before the law had professedly made them one. That the Court might not guess the secret fact that she had mistaken John for another, under the darkness that covered their clandestine elopement, and had married him without understanding herself at all, seemed so silly to her maturer senses that she felt that she would have died willingly to conceal the fact from the public in general and His Honor, the Court, in particular. But, under the skillful cross fire of a barricade of counsel that Mr. Brief had summoned to the cause of John, the whole mortifying truth came out, and the Court settled himself into the belief that John was an abused husband of a designing woman.

Yet Edna had many friends in Idaho Flat. Honest, sober, sensible men there were in plenty, who remembered their own wives, sisters, mothers, and daughters, and some of them were just enough to see that a marriage which was clearly a fraud in ethics ought to be considered a fraud in equity. But such was not the opinion of the Court.

His Honor was a small, spare man, with kindly blue eyes and lanky yellow hair, a very Ascetic in abstinence from everything sensual, and thoroughly just, as far as he was able to comprehend justice. Yet, in his eyes, justice to woman was one thing and justice to man entirely another. He believed devoutly in the infinitude of human law; and the farther back the law that seemed to suit a case in point began, the more was the law entitled to his respect, as precedent.

Clearly, as he saw it, the law had united this couple. Clearly both had given unqualified consent. License had been procured after a legal form, and a certificate of marriage was exhibited by John.

Now, the question was not upon the legality of the union, but upon the alleged causes for its annulment. There was no proof that John Smith had deceived his wife in regard to his personal habits prior to marriage. Evidently Mrs. Smith had acted wholly upon her own volition in assenting to the copartnership. The deception, if any, was her own fault. It was not shown that her husband had mistreated her. On the contrary, his extreme good nature when intoxicated had been amply proven. There was evidence, however, that she had forbidden him the house and premises, and that, in exercising a husband's right to his own home, he had gone no farther than the majesty of the law permitted.

"See 'Blackstone on Marriage,' paragraph so-and-so, page such-and-such; 'Story on Divorces,' page this-and-this, paragraph that-and-that; 'Kent on Marriage Contracts,' chapter such-and-such; 'Greenleaf on Married Women's Disabilities,' book second, and-so-forth, and-so-forth.[1]

"The Scriptures of the New Testament and the Common Law of England[2] are alike explicit upon the causes for divorce. If John Smith can prove his wife guilty of marital infidelity the case will rest in his favor and the marriage will be dissolved, in which case the custody of the minor children will be given into his keeping, together with all the property accumulated by both.

"Men have heretofore been known to turn their wives away from home for some real or fancied misdemeanor; but in all the practice of all the courts we are unable to find a precedent for the unnatural conduct of a wife who turns her lawful husband away from his own doorstep, as in this instance. Such conduct is worthy of a Xanthippe,[3] but was hardly to be expected in a woman of the present era.

"In summing up the testimony for the plaintiff, the Court holds to the opinion that marital infidelity, though not proven, is to be suspected on the part of the party of the second part. That the husband is an injured man, there is little room for doubt. That the wife has grievances, both real and imaginary, is probable. Women are subject to these. There is, however, a legal barrier to a divorce in this case, which the attorneys have strangely overlooked. I allude to the fact that each party desires the dissolution of the copartnership. Had the husband alone desired the divorce, upon the ground set forth in the complaint, the protest of the wife would have availed her nothing, unless his case had been proven. Had the wife, alone, put in *her* plea for a dissolution of the holy bonds of matrimony, upon the ground of desertion for the space of three years, or for bodily maltreatment, or for failure, as far as able to fulfill his agreement, to support and provide for her, the plea would have been granted. But, as there is neither law nor precedent for granting a divorce to either party upon the grounds alleged, the Court will dismiss the case and proceed to the next business upon the docket."

"Your Honor," said Mr. Brief, rising with some agitation and considerable hurry, "pardon me, but you have forgotten to assess the costs of suit."

"Oh! ah! yes! The husband will pay all costs, of course."

"But, beg pardon—allow me to whisper in your ear."

His Honor bowed to listen.

"John Smith has no property whatever, and you must hold the defendant liable for costs."

"And get my labor for my pains," whispered the Judge in reply. "Don't you know that the property of a wife belongs to her husband, and whatever's his is his own?"

The perturbation of Mr. Brief was quieted, and the two legal protectors of the rights of married women enjoyed a quiet laugh together, of which none but themselves knew the purport.

"If this is human law and human justice, I decline to take any stock in it!" cried Sue Randolph, indignantly starting up from her seat beside Edna and Mrs. Rutherford, and facing the Judge defiantly, while Edna wept in silence and Mrs. Rutherford groaned aloud.

"I fine this woman twenty dollars for contempt of Court!" said His Honor, with a smile that was child-like and bland.

"I'd like to see you get your money!" was the pert reply.

"Conduct this woman to jail!" said His Honor, waving his hand in the direction of the sheriff.

"Stay, your Honor," cried Edna. "I will pay her fine."

"In the name of her husband, I object!" said Mr. Brief.

"You have enough to do to look after your own affairs, Mrs. Smith," replied the Judge, severely. "My advice to you is to pray without ceasing.[4] Keep yourself close to the feet of Jesus, and remember that piety, sobriety, meekness and obedience are the crowning glory of a wife. You are to return to your wifely duties and observe them, looking well to the ways of your household and eating not the bread of idleness."[5]

Edna glanced mutely at her toil-battered hands and then appealingly into the Judge's eyes, but answered him never a word.

"You have done yourself a great injury," continued His Honor, "by shielding and harboring the unhappy woman who is now being remanded to prison. She is not a person with whom I would like my wife to associate."

Edna bit her lips till the purple blood in them fairly curdled. Alas, she could not reply without being compelled to follow the fate of poor Sue, and then who would assist her heart-broken mother in caring for the children and keeping the wolf from the door?

"Please, sir, may we be excused—my mother and I?"

The question was asked as a timid child might ask it of a tyrannical, rod-applying schoolmaster. The Judge looked at her enquiringly.

"I must go to my work," continued Edna, "or I shall have no means to support the husband you have to-day decided that I must protect."

His Honor was puzzled. Was the woman impudent or crazy, that she should thus pretend to occupy a position which God and nature had assigned to man?

"I am afraid that some of the strong-minded fallacies that are disturbing the elements of domestic life in the East have made their appearance in Idaho Flat!" he said, solemnly.

"May I be excused?" repeated Edna, her voice husky with smothered indignation and sorrow.

"Yes, madam. Go home and get your husband's dinner and make his home happy. That is the duty of every married woman. Your whole duty is in the home, his out of it. He is to provide the comforts of life, you are to take care of them. I trust that I shall hear no more of your unreasonable repining. The Court has been lenient with you, and you have not been proven guilty as charged in your husband's indictment. Always meet your husband with a smile and a word of encouragement, and never let him see your brow clouded. Nothing drives a man to ruin like smothered tempests in his home. You have time in plenty to atone for your errors of the past, for you are young yet. Do your duty, and many sons and daughters shall yet arise to call you blessed. Nothing else in nature is so beautiful as a well-ordered, comfortable home, with a dutiful wife and smiling children to welcome the husband and father from his labors at nightfall. A contented mind is a continual feast. I further advise you to request your pastor to discontinue his visits, seeing they give your husband trouble. I am aware that Mr. Smith has some unfortunate habits, but I am unable to learn that they have ever caused him to commit personal violence upon you. And for the rest, I feel assured that it lies in your power to cure him of drunkenness by wifely obedience and womanly thrift. Good-day, madam."

How Edna reached the open air she really never knew. It seemed to her that her heart was frozen.

Walking with a firm step toward the door, and staring with stony eyes into vacancy, she heeded not the eager gazes of the gaping crowd, nor paused an instant to contemplate the changes in her situation. Everything seemed covered as with an impenetrable pall of blackness. It was as though a great gulf yawned before her, upon the very brink of which she paused, while behind her stood a bland-faced oracle, armed with tomes of sheepskin, with which he was driving her forward to destruction.

The eye of many a bronzed miner was filled with tears, while murmurs of indignation filled the crowded room.

In one corner of the rude building, and inside the bar, sat a young lawyer with medium proportions, broad forehead, clear brown eyes, dark chestnut hair, and firm-set mouth. Nobody had noticed him, as he was a new arrival who had that day presented his credentials and taken his seat among his fellows without clients, and likely to remain so.

The stranger watched Edna till she passed out of the house, and again caught sight of her through the window, as she toiled up the hill to her wretched abode.

"May it please your Honor," he at length exclaimed, rising to his feet and breathing heavily, as though under the impetus of some strange excitement, "I have a request to make."

"Proceed," replied the Judge, as he settled himself to look over the columns of a stale newspaper.

"I should be pleased to get the use of this hall of justice for this evening, as I wish to deliver a lecture."

"Certainly," said His Honor. "We shall be pleased to hear from you."

"Then, gentlemen, allow me to announce that I shall be most happy to give you an address this evening upon the 'Rights of Women.' I shall not ask a door fee. My object is not to make money, but to consider the claims that

mothers, wives, and daughters ought to have under the laws of our so-
called free country for their protection. This evening at eight o'clock I shall
be here, and I hope to see you all as eager to listen to my humble speech
as you have been willing to pay deferential heed to Judge White's decision
to-day."

His Honor called the next case, and Edna and John were soon forgotten in the consideration of the rights of some disputants over a mining
claim, who had managed to get themselves entangled in a legal broil.

Court took recess at four P. M., and Mr. Shields, the strange young lawyer, passed on his way to the hotel to speak a kindly word to poor Sue
Randolph, who was weeping in the jail, whither she had been conveyed as a
prisoner.

"We'll show you that the good men are not dead by great odds," he
said, cheerily. "Sometimes the darkest hour of the night is just before the
morning."

[To be continued.]

from
*The New Northwest*
Friday, June 8, 1877.

# EDNA AND JOHN:
## A ROMANCE OF IDAHO FLAT.

### BY Mrs. A. J. DUNIWAY,
AUTHOR OF "JUDITH REID," "ELLEN DOWD," "AMIE AND HENRY LEE,"
"THE HAPPY HOME," "ONE WOMAN'S SPHERE," "MADGE MORRISON,"
ETC., ETC., ETC.

*Woman's degraded, helpless position is the weak point of our institutions today—a disturbing force everywhere, severing family ties, filling our asylums with the deaf, the dumb, the blind, our prisons with criminals, our cities with drunkenness and prostitution, our homes with disease and death.*—National Centennial Equal Rights Protest.

## CHAPTER XXV.

**T**HE NEWS OF THE FORTHCOMING LECTURE upon "Woman's Rights" spread through the mines like a conflagration.

With the exception of Mrs. Rutherford and Edna and Sue, there were but two or three women residing in the place at the time who were not known to be Magdalenes.[1] And, while the few who conducted themselves with womanly propriety were known to be more than self-supporting, the *demi-monde* were always idle, always elegantly clad, and always visible.

The majority of people of both sexes fail to look upon the everyday occurrences of life with the least atom of philosophy. Whatever appeals directly to their careless observation is taken for granted, as a rule, and as such is applied by them to all the conditions and circumstances of human existence, whether the rule is in any way applicable or otherwise.

Most men in Idaho Flat judged all women of all localities according to the standard set up at the hotels, where only those of the class whose steps take hold on hell were to be seen, and the idea that any woman or set of women should desire or need more rights than those possessed already, was, to their minds, as hideous as ridiculous.

But all were anxious to attend the meeting, as they anticipated a great deal of merriment.

"Shall *we* attend and hear what our friend has to say about our rights?" asked Mrs. Rutherford, addressing Edna, who was bending low over her children and trying to soothe Sue's lonely babe to sleep by a coaxing lullaby.

"Yes, mother, of course we'll go, as soon as we get the children to sleep. I want to see if women in America have any rights that any man feels himself bound to respect."

"But there will be no other ladies present," faltered Mrs. Rutherford.

"No other ladies were present during the trial to-day, mother, and yet the men did not devour us. I'm not afraid of any man, unless the law compels me to be under subjugation to him as his wife. For the rest, I can take care of myself."

"O, Edna! I cannot bear to have you talk that way," said the mother, pleadingly. "You outrage every sense of propriety by such speeches."

"I can't help it, mother dear. The only trouble I have ever had in my life was on account of bad marriage laws."

"But marriage is a holy institution, my dear."

"I know it ought to be, mother. Aunt Judy and I have talked all these *pros* and *cons* over many a time. But example is much more striking than theory, and experience much more powerful than ethics. No amount of moralizing will ever convince me that John Smith's legal power over me is a good thing, or that it ever by any stretch of human imagination can be construed into a blessing."

"O, Edna! What shall we do tonight if there are fast women at the lecture?" and Mrs. Rutherford paled with apprehension.

"We'll let them alone, mother dear. There'll be plenty of fast *men* in attendance, and they won't dare to hurt us, either. That is, none of 'em except John Smith, and I shall go armed to protect myself from him."

"Don't you intend to live with him any more, Edna?"

Edna did not answer, but slipped a revolver from a pocket beneath the folds of her dress and showed it with a significant nod.

Mrs. Rutherford uttered a little scream.

"Don't be a fool, mother!" cried the daughter, returning the weapon to its hiding-place. "I'm not intending to take the life of John. I will defend myself, however, for I am desperate."

Soon the children were asleep and the cabin double-barred, and the mother and daughter were on the way to the lecture-room.

When near the door they met Mr. Handel, who paused a moment for a kindly word with Mrs. Rutherford. Edna would not recognize him.

"I'll teach any man to waver when he's needed to stand by his friends," she thought. "If he were half a man he'd horsewhip John."

But, in truth, Mr. Handel was not deserving Edna's unqualified displeasure. As a minister, he felt it his duty to be non-combative, and as far as possible non-committal. And he had shrunk from any contact with the vicious element that bandied his name and Edna's about the gambling dens as a pure and sensitive nature will naturally dread such contact, be he man or woman.

"Will you attend the lecture, Mr. Handel?" asked Mrs. Rutherford.

"No, madam," was the quick reply. "I have agreed to meet the Judge and a few other friends for a season of prayer to-night, and I must always attend to the most important duties first."

"But God is with you all the time, if you are only willing to acknowledge and accept Him!" said Edna, with scorn in her voice. "If I couldn't trust God any further than you can, I wouldn't think Him worth serving."

"Daughter, how *could* you?" asked her mother reprovingly, as the pastor passed on and they entered the crowded hall.

Edna had no opportunity to reply. The orator was already upon the stand, and the derision with which the crowd had met him at first gave way to curiosity after a while, and gradually, as he proceeded, to the deepest interest.

"The laws by which men govern women," he said, "have descended to them from the dead ages. Away back in the history of humanity, when man was little else than a brute, he acquired supremacy over woman through superior physical power, or mere animal force. Woman, as ignorant of the higher laws of intellect as himself, yielded to the animal law of might. The ascendancy thus gained was kept by man, and as his intellect expanded, she was yet more strictly guarded, for in order to keep the weaker sex in subjugation, they must be kept in ignorance. After the lapse of ages, maybe, men crystallized their oral laws into statutes, always recognizing women as property, always regarding them as serfs.

"Then came the age of chivalry. Gallant knights outvied each other in the homage they delighted to pay to woman, because such homage placed them before their limited world in the light of benefactors to the weaker sex.

"Understand me, gentlemen. I am an ardent advocate of the holy law of monogamic marriage. The God of Nature designed that men and women should live in pairs; that they together should rear their children and surround themselves with happy, genial hearts and pleasant, beautiful homes.

"All human laws should be framed in keeping with this design. There is a palpable violation of divine law in the state of society we find in all new localities where the wives and mothers of men are not yet plenty.

"I am sorry the learned Judge, who rendered the decision to-day in the divorce case with which this community is interested, is not here to-night. It is to be regretted that the good minister is absent also. Those who take upon themselves the responsibility to judge or teach the people should be the last persons to absent themselves from opportunity to hear what the representatives of the people say.

"I should like to ask Judge White to inform us how it is possible for a woman to remain in her husband's home and render it beautiful and happy when the husband utterly fails to provide her any comfortable home to keep? I should like to ask him if he thinks *he* would possess sufficient Christian fortitude to enter the home of the victorious plaintiff in the case just cited and take upon himself the drunken companionship, the unrequited toil, the burdens and penalties of every kind which such a wife as the plaintiff claims must necessarily endure at the hands of such a man?

"Seriously, we have all had enough of this kind of mawkish theory. But the worst of it all is that in all this land of vaunted freedom there is not a single court where women can be their own judges or jurors; not one where their individual interests can be personally represented."

A large man with well-cultivated whiskers and elegant clothes, that looked in strange keeping with their surroundings in Idaho Flat, arose to his feet and said:

"Beg pardon, but I have a question to ask. I hope I don't intrude."

The speaker bowed and said "certainly," but whether in response to the first or second observation, Edna could not tell.

"You say," said the questioner, "that women are not permitted to enjoy their rights. Now, I contend that right here in Idaho Flat the women have all the rights and the men none. Look at the hotel over yonder. There are a dozen women in it, and not one of them lifts her finger even to cook her own mutton; yet they dress like queens. Who supports them, sir? I call on you to answer me."

The questioner was by this time wrought into a frenzy of indignation. His voice was pitched to its highest key and his manner was that of one thoroughly in earnest. Having asked the question, he had no notion of allowing the speaker to answer it, but proceeded to make his own reply.

"I say that *men* support the women, sir! Yes, sir!! The *men!!!* They earn the money! They dig in the mines for it! They keep saloons, carry on mercantile business, they—"

*"Drink whisky!"* interrupted Edna, who, surprised at her temerity in having thus spoken, shrank back into her seat in fright and mortification, while a murmur of subdued applause filled the air.

Edna had many an honest friend among the men present, and her opinion of the sex would have been vastly improved could she have known the respect the working and sober masses entertained for her. But, alas, she did not know; and judging men on the one hand by John Smith, who represented one and the lowest class, and on the other by the zealous and honest but impractical missionary, and later by the learned Judge who had dealt out his stereotyped advice to her without the least regard to its adaptability to her case or circumstances, the reader need not wonder that in spite of her naturally warm heart and affectionate nature, she had deluded herself into the belief that she hated men.

The lecturer smiled.

"The lady has struck the proper chord," he said, in a modulated voice that had a tone of tenderness in it that, in spite of her efforts to repress it, caused her to fall into an uncontrollable fit of weeping.

"Evidently my interlocutor has been thinking only of women as outlaws," the speaker continued, turning his attention to the questioner, who was breathing heavily. "And he seems also to forget that God never ordained two codes of laws, one for men and one for women, but that all that we see today that is wrong in human society is the direct result of a one-sided state of law and ethics. Bad women, who toil not, neither do they spin,[2] abound in your midst only because there is a demand for them; and that demand exists because the moral atmosphere is vitiated through the absence of the equilibrium that the feminine element only can supply. Gentlemen, I have been a resident of this village for only a fortnight, yet I have learned lessons here that never can be forgotten. Every man of you who is here without his family should see to it that his loved ones are brought to him at once. And, if any of you cannot bring them here, I advise you to go to them."

"Have you a family in Idaho Flat?" asked the champion questioner, amid a general titter.

"Not yet, nor anywhere else, but please God I intend to have some day, and I shall not support bad women, either! I am not here to consider the rights of women as outlaws, but as wives, mothers, sisters, daughters, sweethearts, and friends."

Edna listened with deeper and yet deeper interest, and when the conversational tone was abandoned, and the speaker went into a logical dissertation upon the status of American representation, he fired up with an illumination of inspiring thoughts that led the multitude into complete sympathy with his theme and purpose.

Many a man that came to ridicule went back to his couch to meditate; and many a husband who had almost forgotten the duties and obligations of his far-off home resolved that, come what might in the line of fortune, he would not remain much longer away from his family.

Edna listened to the entire discourse as one in a dream. The looks, voice, gestures, and intonation of the speaker were perfectly familiar to her senses, yet where and when had she ever met anyone like him? To save her life she could not tell.

"Mother," she said, at the close of the lecture, "let us stay and speak to Mr. Shields. I am determined to become acquainted with the woman's friend."

"But John will talk," replied her mother, falteringly, though, in truth, she wanted much to address the stranger herself.

"That will be something new for John, certainly!" exclaimed Edna, bitterly.

In a moment they were conversing with their champion, while his eyes beamed and his countenance radiated with happy exultation.

"How much I thank you for your golden words," said Edna, feelingly.

"Oh, that's nothing! I'm not a speaker! This was my first attempt at oratory. I only tried to do my duty. That was all. This morning I had not thought of making an address. It was the trial to-day and the Judge's decision that prompted it. Have you anyone to accompany you home?"

"My mother, thank you. I would not dare to accept the escort of anyone else, for the lord who holds the chains of a legal bondage upon me is watching constantly for an opportunity to accuse me, that he may rob me of my children."

They bade the lecturer good-night, and reached their lowly home to find John Smith installed therein with a bevy of boon companions, who had helped themselves to Edna's pies till satisfied, and were now engaged in playing cards upon the dining table.

"You thought you'd lock your husband out, didn't you?" cried John with a ribald laugh. "Remember that a man has a perfect right to his own home hereafter. Everything I do is under legal advice. Eh, Mr. Brief?"

That dignitary bowed.

Edna sat down in a stupor of bewilderment. She had seen daylight through the blackness of her trouble a few minutes ago. Now she saw the very gall of bitterness.

"O, my God! The God of the destitute and desperate, is there not in all America a Canada for fugitive wives?" she wailed at length, while Mrs. Rutherford wept in helpless agony.

The other men soon left the cabin and John Smith was alone with his wife and mother-in-law.

Luckily for them, his libations had been so copious that he was very soon in a drunken stupor, and Edna and her mother awakened the children and conveyed them to the county jail, where they spent the night as vagrants might, upon the cold, hard floor. The jailor was merciful, else they would have had no shelter whatever.

"The law may hound me to the death if it will, but I will not yield to its demands," said Edna, savagely. "I know it is not right for me to sin against myself by stultifying my own womanhood to live as the wife of a man who has outraged every sense of womanhood by his downward career of dissipation and idleness. If he were not my legal master I would put him in the penitentiary for breaking open my house and helping himself to its contents. And what binds us, mother? Only think! When I was very young and wholly inexperienced, the victim of a vitiated education and cheap novels, I allowed a country 'squire to say a few words to which I assented; and though I loathed the bonds as soon as I understood them, straightway men called them *holy!* They said God had ordained them. But yourself and Aunt Judy commanded me to stand by them. I have done all I could. I have immolated myself upon the altar of abomination for years. Now my eyes are opened and I know good from evil. Men may kill me, or they may compel me to kill them, or myself, but they cannot compel me to longer outrage the laws of God by living a life with my body to which my soul is not true."

Sue Randolph, who was incarcerated in the prison for contempt of court, overheard the earnest words of Edna, and rising from her uneasy prison couch, came to the little room to join them.

"What was the purport of the lecture this evening?" she asked, after she had heard a detailed statement of Edna's grievances at home.

"O, Sue, it was perfectly splendid! I don't mean that it was flowery, or finished, or eloquent, but it was *true*. After he had finished, we waited to introduce ourselves, and when he shook my hand and spoke so deferentially, I felt that I never could say again that I hated men, for it was as though God Himself had spoken."

In spite of their gloomy surroundings, Sue could not restrain a silent laugh.

"Be careful that you don't get into another matrimonial entanglement before you get fairly out of the one you are groaning under," she said, archly, as she hugged her sleeping child to her bosom, and the three women tried, as best they could, to dispose of their tired bodies upon the hard stone floor.

"Don't talk to me about any more entanglements of that sort, if you don't want to say your last prayer," said Edna, indignantly. "All I ask is to get out of this snare, and then, you may depend, I'll stay out."

"We shall see!" said Sue. "The women are all alike."

"Then they're all fools!" was Edna's bitter rejoinder.

[To be continued.]

from
*The New Northwest*
Friday, June 15, 1877.

# EDNA AND JOHN:
## A ROMANCE OF IDAHO FLAT.

### BY Mrs. A. J. DUNIWAY,
AUTHOR OF "JUDITH REID," "ELLEN DOWD," "AMIE AND HENRY LEE,"
" THE HAPPY HOME," "ONE WOMAN'S SPHERE," "MADGE MORRISON,"
ETC., ETC., ETC.

*Woman's degraded, helpless position is the weak point of our institutions today—a disturbing force everywhere, severing family ties, filling our asylums with the deaf, the dumb, the blind, our prisons with criminals, our cities with drunkenness and prostitution, our homes with disease and death.*—National Centennial Equal Rights Protest.

## CHAPTER XXVI.

**M**ORNING CAME, bringing with it bodily hunger and renewed mental anxiety upon all sides.

The jail where the women had slept was cold, bare, and comfortless, and they had had all they could do during the night to keep the children warm.

Edna looked longingly at the hotel that she had toiled so faithfully to build up and sustain.

"Mother," she said, brightening up with sudden animation, as she turned from the barred window through which she had been gazing. "I have caught an idea. John Smith has no longer any claim upon that house, and I'm going over there to offer my services as cook. I will work no harder than I did as proprietor, and we'll get our board, if nothing more, till I can get legal release from my protector and head."

"But, daughter, think of the degradation of being scullion in a hotel. What will your brothers and sisters say?"

"What in the name of human reason do *I* care? What they say or think won't bring us bread and butter! Would you have me go back to my legal head and accept the situation in all due humility? Would *you* do it if you were *me?*"

"Well, my child, it's useless to fight against the inevitable. You have got us into this pickle, and you will be obliged to help us out."

Edna blushed, but had no time for tears or indignation.

"There are better days in store for us, mother; see if I'm not a prophet," she exclaimed, as, hurrying across the rocky common, she entered the hotel and asked to see the proprietor. That dignitary sat at the receipt of customs and looked at Edna searchingly as she advanced to meet him.

"Mr. Sol, I want employment," she said, abruptly.

"My name, madam, is not Sol, but Solomon," he answered, puffing a black volume of smoke into her face, regardless of its effect upon her nerves or his own manners.

Edna coughed and strangled, but rallied easily. She was almost used to tobacco smoke, she thought.

"I want to take the place of your head cook in the kitchen, Mr. Solomon," she added, falteringly, for somehow her courage seemed oozing from her very fingers' ends.

The dignitary was delighted. Everybody in Idaho Flat was well aware that Edna was a famous cook.

"I want a private room," continued Edna, "large enough for my mother, myself, and two children, and I will cook for you to pay our board till such time as the law may declare me free from my legal incubus."[1]

The bargain was concluded, and Edna was speedily installed as a servant in the house where she had long been proprietor.

"What we are to do for clothes I do not know, mother, but I trust there will be some way provided. If everything else fails, you can make dresses for the bad women that the men support, you know."

"O, Edna! Don't ask me to work for fallen women! Indeed I cannot do it!" said the mother, piteously.

"We'd starve if I'd refuse to work for fallen men!" was Edna's bitter rejoinder.

When John Smith had sufficiently recovered from his drunken stupor to realize that the morning was far advanced toward noon, with no prospect of Edna's return, he began, for the first time, to fancy that, after all, his bird had flown. He was miserably, sickeningly hungry. And yet, his appetite was gone. He had a blinding headache, and longed for a morning dram as none but drunkards can long for anything. He opened his blurred eyes and gazed vacantly around the cabin. The sun was shining in brilliant streamers through its many crevices. Evidences of his night's debauch were visible here and there. Edna's clothing hung against the wall, and various articles of baby apparel lay scattered about.

He arose with difficulty and staggered feebly around the little room. The bright sunlight blinded him. Dizziness overcame him. He returned to the bed, and the bitterness of remorse overtook him. He cried like a child.

Good reader, have mercy upon him. Drunkenness is a disease. The victim to its ravages is unfit to run at large. Habitual, or even periodical drunkenness, is a malignant form of insanity. Its victims should not run at large, and there should be asylums all over the land for their proper treatment until cured.

John Smith remembered his mother, whom his drunken father had long since worried to her grave. He meditated upon his past life and thought bitterly of Edna.

"If she would only care for me!" he sobbed.

"But why should she care?" said remorse. "What have I ever done for her that she should care for me?"

Then the gnawings of his diseased appetite overcame remorse and resolution. With difficulty he rose again and staggered out into the street. Slowly and totteringly he sought the saloon. But, poor fellow, he had neither money nor credit. With the fiery liquid all around him he could not secure a single drop to cool his parched tongue.

He wandered back to the cabin in his despair. How his brain reeled! How his stomach gnawed! A pen with ink and paper occupied a conspicuous place upon the rude mantel. He helped himself to the writing materials and sat down, quaking like an aspen.

"Life is a failure," he wrote, in a trembling, almost illegible hand. "The drunkard's hell gapes to receive me," he added, with more power. "May God have mercy, for man has none," he wrote again. "Forgive me, Edna, mother, and my poor thwarted children," was his next sentence. And then, "I die by my own hand. May God for—"

There was nothing further added.

A huge knife lay upon the table, a knife that Edna had used in her cooking. John raised it with surprising strength of nerve and flashed it back and forth in the streaming sunlight.

An instant and all was over. His head was half severed from his quivering body, and when, an hour later, Mr. Brief and a bevy of boon companions went to call at the cabin to apprise him of Edna's change of base, they found the lifeless body of the poor inebriate weltering in a dismal sea of clotted blood. There was horror depicted in every countenance as the news spread through the mines and mountains of Idaho Flat.

Edna was as one turned to adamant. Much as she had detested the bonds that had held her as an unwilling sacrifice to the legal power of the man she loathed, she possessed a depth of womanly sympathy for which none gave her credit. She did not weep, or scream, or swoon. Under her directions the remains of the poor victim of his own excesses were decently prepared for burial. The ghastly wound in his throat was concealed by her own hands under a snowy shawl that had been one of Sue Randolph's bridal treasures.

The fine of Sue had been paid an hour before by a subscription fund raised at the hotel by Edna's effort, and she temporarily took her benefactor's place as cook at the hotel, thus giving Edna a chance to bury her dead.

The funeral obsequies were largely attended. Mr. and Mrs. LaSelle came over in their carriage from Boise, and volunteered to adopt Edna's baby girl. This offer was indignantly spurned.

"I kept my children together, and fed and clothed them while the laws of men robbed me, through my unhappy husband, of almost everything I could earn, and I have no notion now of giving them up, since death has removed my shackles!" she said, haughtily.

They made a grave for poor John Smith's body hard by the overhanging cliffs that crowned the summit of the gulch beyond Edna's humble cabin.

Good Mr. Handel did not know what to do. He feared that the evil tongues that had been all too busy in circulating damaging reports concerning himself and Edna would speedily interpret any attempt at officiating on his part as a tacit acknowledgment of wrong; and he also feared that a failure to do so would be an indirect refusal to give the body Christian burial.

In his dilemma he called upon Mr. Shields, who counseled him to do his whole duty without fear or favor of men.

"But, beg your pardon, sir. Mrs. Smith has not invited me to officiate. There's another difficulty."

"Then act according to the dictates of your own judgment," replied Mr. Shields, testily.

In his heart he despised the cowardice that would for an instant hesitate about anything that was conceived to be duty.

"If I thought praying over John Smith's dead body would be of any special benefit to the dead or the living, I'd do it, though the heavens fell," he exclaimed, decidedly.

"Then you think I ought not to stand upon ceremony?"

"I think you ought always to act in truth to your own inner consciousness, by doing whatsoever you believe to be right, no matter what others may think."

"But I would not intrude where I might not be welcome," said the clergyman.

"Truth is seldom welcomed anywhere till it has pushed its own way to respectful consideration," replied Mr. Shields.

"Then you will not advise me?"

"No. Be your own counsellor."

"Then I will offer my services. Mrs. Smith may be as sensitive as I am. I didn't think of the possibility of that before."

The resolve thus taken was easily executed. Mr. Handel spoke as one inspired. His prayer was a direct appeal for mercy to the power of the Infinite that Edna could not but wonder at, seeing the pastor did not believe restoration after death to be possible. Yet, somehow, the simple and sublime truth of the words of love, forgiveness, and tender mercy that he uttered sank into her heart like a balm of healing.

"John is in the hands of God, Edna. Let us leave him with the Author of all existence," said Mrs. Rutherford, gently drawing her daughter away from the open grave, and leading her back to the wretched cabin, which the kind-hearted miners had by this time cleansed of every vestige of the awful tragedy its silent walls had witnessed.

"I guess I needn't work at the hotel now, mother," said Edna, "for there will no longer be any need that I shall hide from John. Some ministering angel must have prompted him to thwart his own designs by suicide, else he would live to plague me yet. But, mother, do you think I did my whole duty?"

"Dear child, I have no reproaches to offer. After the marriage, which was the first great misguided step, the other wrongs came naturally. Human laws, at best, are human imperfections, and only God can fully interpret the divine. There is nothing left for us now but to look to the future. The past is irrevocable. Let it bury its dead, though the phantoms of its memory will ever haunt us."[2]

A year passed, and Edna and her mother were again inmates of the hotel, but this time as owners. Strict attention to business in the flush times, with no idle, dissipated overseer, or legal owner, to spend her money, had made the bondwoman whom suicide had rescued an independent owner of her own income. Everybody in Idaho Flat was pleased at her success. Her children grew and thrived, and everything she handled seemed to turn to gold.

Jim Young, the unfortunate consumptive, who had once lured poor Sue Randolph to the very depths of infamy—poor Sue, who had only been rescued at the eleventh awful hour by Edna's kindly assistance—became a coughing, helpless, irritable, and impecunious invalid, to whom Sue became a veritable good Samaritan. She ministered to his many wants, often serving him menially, in the capacity of nurse, even while her lip curled with scorn as she remembered the advantage he had once taken of her dire necessities to lure her to degradation.

"He was kind to me once, for he brought me my child, when but for him I should never have found her," she would say, by way of explanation, when any one presumed to question her conduct, and she cared for him till death relieved her.

Mrs. Rutherford and Edna improved the hotel property till it became a marvel of cleanliness and convenience, for the inn of a pioneer mining town is not always the excess of cleanliness.

Edna was as brilliant as energetic. Everybody courted and flattered her, but to all entreaties for another matrimonial alliance she was strictly deaf.

The grave of John became a very bower of beauty.

"I have a notion that angels visit earth sometimes," she would say, "and I feel sure that God inspires me to surround the remains of John with pure and beautiful devices, that only the good and pure may be attracted thereto. My conduct may or may not assist the departed. Nobody knows any more about that than I do; but one thing is certain; the living may profit by a visit to this spot if they will but heed its teachings."

Quaint devices were formed around the grave with rocks and pebbles, into which various kinds of plants were placed, forming mottoes and quotations, every one containing a warning or expostulation which none could pass by unheeded.

Busy as Edna was with all her other cares, she found time to visit the town daily, always calling at the post office on her return, and almost always receiving a mysterious package which she carried to her own private room to read and answer.

But, as we have said, a year had passed since the awful tragedy that had removed the bondage from her life, and all was prospering, save only that Sue Randolph's charge would linger on and could not die. Yet six months later, and with the roseate return of spring the life of the invalid waned and flickered and then died out. A quiet funeral and all was over.

Three women who were widowed indeed,[3] took up their daily burdens and carried them, and the world believed as before that women were supported and protected by men.

Aunt Judy, who visited them occasionally, "had all the rights she wanted," so long as her husband lived. In fact, her marriage seemed to have turned her head, as well as her heart, from the first. She lived and breathed and had her being only in the atmosphere of the man she loved. It made no difference to her that there were discrepancies in his account of himself in former years that no amount of ignoring could justify. He was her idol, her ideal, her all. Happy indeed are they who are thus intoxicated with love when there is no legal barrier to the union. Had there been a barrier—but Aunt Judy did not stop to think of *ifs*. It was enough for her that she was happy. Surely other women should be contented, too.

But death came, one day, and laid her idol low. Mr. LaSelle had come over from Boise to look after the interests of his famous mine, and in descending the shaft, the machinery broke, precipitating him to the bottom, whence his body was rescued—stark, mangled, and lifeless.

The widow was inconsolable. Of what use to her were costly equipage and elegant surrounds now?

But the realities of business must be met. As a wealthy widow, still fair, though far from being young, she did not lack for friends. But there came a day when she looked upon her husband's death as the very least of her tribulations. And that was when a legal wife, with prior claims, came over to Idaho Flat, and, with her children, inherited the property, a very small fraction of which, while it was in Aunt Judy's power to bestow, would have rendered Mrs. Rutherford and her daughter comfortable in the darkest hour of their destitution.

The woman who had been deceived had no redress, the legal wife no mercy. Aunt Judy's only alternative was to return to the home of Edna and her mother, heart-broken and desolate.

"Have women all the rights they need? Have you all the rights you want now?" asked Edna, as she smoothed her troubled brow and regulated the folds of her widow's cap.

"Oh, don't, Edna! Don't reproach me, darling! I was kind to you once. Won't you love me now?"

"Certainly, auntie. And you shall have a home as long as there is one for me. And, auntie, do you remember Mr. Shields? I mean the young lawyer who made his logic felt in Idaho Flat a good while ago."

"Yes, Edna; but why? What of him?"

"Oh, he's been away for a year or more, occupying an important Federal position in another part of the Territory, and now he's coming back, and I'm going to marry him."

"*What,* child? After all our hard experience?"

"Yes, auntie, dear. I've been corresponding with his mother for the past six months, and lately with his father and sisters. I'm well acquainted with his antecedents, and I love him, as my life. He was disappointed in love once. So was I, you know. He was married once, and his wife died by suicide."

Edna shuddered at the mention of the word.

"How did you get so well acquainted with him?" asked Aunt Judy. "He's been in Boise for a year."

"He went at my request, auntie. We became acquainted by letter."

"But, after my experience, I'd never dare to trust another man, and I should think you wouldn't either."

"So I thought once, but after all, there's no sensible way to live except in marriage. People should belong to each other—should live in pairs. But there should be a legal and honorable way to settle all matrimonial, as well as all other differences. Your husband was not a bad man at heart, yet, under the imperfections of human law, he was tempted, and he deceived you cruelly to become your husband. The worst adultery on earth is that which is the result of inharmonious marriage; for the weaker party to the contract must live forever in subjection unless human law is broken. We are going to be happy—Mr. Shields and I; yet had either John Smith or Mrs. Shields failed to commit suicide, each of us would have been in legal bonds, and would have been compelled to observe and obey them, despite the fact that God had united us. Thus does one person's crime conduce to another's supposed superior virtue. Man looks upon outward appearances, but God looks at the heart.[4] Verily we have no moral right to judge others lest we ourselves be severely judged."[5]

There was another wedding in Idaho Flat. The church that occupied the site where Edna had first assisted to prepare a bower for public worship and literary entertainment, was liberally festooned with evergreens and flowers.

Mr. Handel, who had been called away from Idaho Flat a year before to another field, came over the mountains by special invitation to officiate, bringing his bride with him.

Edna arranged herself for her nuptials in somber gray, relieved by sprays of pale forget-me-nots in her hair and bosom, and, as she stood beside the man to whom she felt that God had united her, and spoke the fitting vows that men should recognize as binding, a tear or two of quiet gladness stole down her cheeks, and a silent prayer was wafted heavenward from many a sympathizing heart, invoking the blessing of God upon those whom he, through tribulation, had joined till death should part them for a season.

That Edna was saved, was not because of the protection of human law, but in spite of it; that she became a true and glorious woman, foremost in good words and works, who, as the new Territory gained in population and wealth and civilization, grew more and more earnest in her zeal for woman's emancipation from her degraded and helpless political and financial condition, we are proud to chronicle; that her good husband is today a shining light in the political firmament, where he uses the powerful influence he possesses on the side of freedom, justice and equality, we rejoice to tell you.

Sons and daughters have been born to them, and the two children of Edna and John are being educated under their mother's personal supervision. That the sins of the father may not be visited upon the son is her ardent hope—a hope in which we prayerfully join her.

Sue Randolph is also happily married. Mrs. Rutherford is visiting her children in the States, whither her mother heart has called her for a season; for now that she has control of her own earnings through virtue of widowhood, she is as free to do as she likes as though she were a man.

Dear, patient, loving, but delightful Aunt Judy is dead. To the last she clung to the conviction that her *pseudo* husband had been her genuine counterpart. Edna laid her away in the quiet retreat where John was buried, and the little children strew her grave with flowers.

THE END

# NOTES TO
# EDNA AND JOHN

## CHAPTER I, PAGES 1-7

1. In November 1876 Duniway made the decision to go by the name Abigail Scott Duniway, rather than Abigail Jane Duniway or Mrs. A. J. Duniway as formerly. This decision was made based on feminist concerns about retaining her individual identity and was reported to readers in her "Editorial Correspondence" (*NNW* December 15, 1876). In May 1879 she began identifying herself as "Abigail Scott Duniway" or "ASD" in notices appearing in the *New Northwest*. The first novel to bear this byline at the time of original publication was *Mrs. Hardine's Will* (*NNW* November 1879–August 1880).
2. The name Solon was chosen by the author with facetious intent. The original Solon (638–558 B.C.E.) was an Athenian statesman, considered to be the founder of Athenian democracy. In common usage, the term "Solon" has come to mean "wise lawgiver." Duniway often referred to the members of America's all-male electorate as "Solons" with bitter irony, because although they did in fact make the laws, as in ancient Greece the process was by no means democratic—one-half of the people (women) were excluded from participation.
3. Letter writing guides, including samples which could be copied nearly verbatim to suit a variety of situations, were commonly used in the nineteenth century.
4. *Billet doux:* a love letter. Literally a "sweet little letter."
5. From Proverbs 31:30–31, "Favour is deceitful, and beauty is vain: but a woman that feareth the Lord, she shall be praised. *Give her of the fruit of her hands; and let her own works praise her in the gates.*" This chapter in Proverbs is said to describe the "virtuous" woman. However, it should be noted that "virtuous" is a dubitable translation of a Hebrew word that connotes a soldier-like quality and can best be translated as "valorous."
6. Firkin: a small wooden vessel or tub, originally a British unit of measure usually equal to a quarter of a barrel.

## CHAPTER II, PAGES 8-14

1. Suffragists and other women who advocated woman's rights were contemptuously referred to as "strong-minded." A woman said to be "strong-minded" was deemed to be unnatural or masculine, because according to popular presumptions women were supposed to be weak and submissive rather than assertive. "Short-haired" was another insult. Newly liberated women often showed their independence by cutting their hair, which also was thought to be unfeminine.

2. Another Biblical reference, of which there are many in this novel. *Edna and John* is more heavily strewn with Biblical allusions than many of Duniway's other works. This is partially due to thematic content, particularly the debates between Edna and Mr. Handel (in later chapters) about the interpretation of Christian doctrine as it relates to women's subjugation. In Duniway's time (and still in our own), many attempted to justify women's subordinate position by quoting scripture verses that seemed to support their views. Developing appropriate refutations was an important task of the early woman's movement. All quotations that follow are from the King James translation of the Bible. Mark 10:6–8. "But from the beginning of the creation God made them male and female. For this cause shall a man *leave his father and mother, and cleave to his wife;* and they twain shall be one flesh: so then they are no more twain, but one flesh."

3. Benedict: a newly married man, especially one who long has been a bachelor. Named after "Benedick," a character in Shakespeare's play *Much Ado About Nothing*, who courts and finally marries the witty Beatrice.

4. Nine days' scandal (or wonder): an event that causes a great temporary sensation.

5. Sodom apple: a fruit said to grow on or near the site of Biblical Sodom, described by Josephus and other ancient writers as externally of fair appearance, but turning to smoke and ashes when picked. Figuratively, some fruitless thing, which disappoints one's hopes or frustrates one's desires.

6. In this instance, and in John's case (in the preceding lines), "friends" is assumed to mean relatives, a common usage of the word at that time.

7. At this time, a "grass widow" meant either a woman whose husband had left her or was absent for an extended length of time, or a divorced woman. In earlier usage, the term referred to an unmarried woman who had cohabited with one or more men; in other words, a discarded mistress or someone who pretended to have been married when, in fact, she was not. While some believe the word grass is used because it refers to a woman who has been put "out at grass" or sent to the country while her husband was away, other sources claim that the word grass is used much like the word straw in "straw man" (scarecrow), i.e., a fake man set up to fool the inquisitive (in this case, a fake widow).

8. Dives: the name associated with the rich man of the parable in Luke 16:19–31 who repented too late to do himself any good.

## CHAPTER III, PAGES 16-22

1. Psalm 51 (called "the *miserere*"); an appeal for mercy.
2. Distaff: an attachment to a spinning wheel; a staff with a clef end for holding wool, flax, etc., from which the thread is drawn.

## CHAPTER IV, PAGES 23-29

1. Puncheon: a heavy slab of timber, roughly dressed.
2. Avoirdupois: taken to mean excess weigh. Originally the weight of anything according to the avoirdupois system in which 1 lb. = 16 oz. Synonymous with "weight."

3. I Corinthians 13:9–12. "For we know in part, and we prophesy in part. But when that which is perfect is come, then that which is in part shall be done away. When I was a child, I spake as a child, I understood as a child, I thought as a child: but when I became a man, I put away childish things. For now we *see through a glass, darkly;* but then face to face: now I know in part; but then shall I know even as also I am known."

## CHAPTER V, PAGES 31-37

1. Columbia: the land "discovered" by Columbus, more specifically, the United States.

## CHAPTER VI, PAGES 38-44

1. Blackstone's *Commentaries on the Laws of England* (1765–69), the basic textbook for law students. Sir William Blackstone (1723–80) was an English jurist and writer.

## CHAPTER VII, PAGES 46-51

1. Isaiah 48:4–10. "Because I knew that thou art obstinate, and thy neck is an iron sinew, and thy brow brass; . . . Behold, I have refined thee, but not with silver; I have chosen thee in the *furnace of affliction.*"
2. Deuteronomy 5:9–10. "Thou shalt not bow down thyself unto them [graven images, or false gods], nor serve them: for I the Lord thy God am a jealous God, visiting *the iniquity of the fathers upon the children* unto the third and fourth generation of them that hate me, and shewing mercy unto thousands of them that love me and keep my commandments."
3. In truth, philanthropists banded together to protect animals against abuse before there were organized efforts to prevent humans from similar abuses. The Association for Prevention of Cruelty to Animals (ASPCA) was founded in 1866. The Society for the Prevention of Cruelty to Children (SPCC), which sought to protect children who were the subjects of abuse, was founded afterwards, as an offshoot of the ASPCA.
4. Dodgers (more commonly, "corn dodgers"): a hard bread made of cornmeal.
5. The Union Pacific and Central Pacific railroads were chartered in 1862 and 1864, and the first transcontinental route was completed in 1869.

## CHAPTER VIII, PAGES 53-58

1. Aunt Judy is aghast at the idea of Edna turning Mormon because of the Mormon practice of polygamy, which she finds distasteful.
2. "Phoebus," used here as a substitutionary oath (in place of "God!"), refers to the Greek deity, Apollo, appearing in the role of sun god.

3. Native Hawaiian or South Sea Islander, from Hawaiian for "man." Many Hawaiians took part in the various gold rushes in the western states and territories.

## CHAPTER IX, Pages 59-64

1. Faro is a gambling game in which players place bets on a special board, betting on each series of two cards as they are drawn from a box containing the dealer's or banker's pack. It was popular in the mining regions of the American West.

## CHAPTER X, Pages 65-71

1. Flume: a trough used for conducting water. Hundreds of miles of flumes were constructed in arid or seasonally arid mining areas.
2. Punishment, usually death ("lynching"), inflicted by a group of persons acting without authority of law. Named for a Virginia justice of the peace, Charles Lynch (1736–96), who ordered extralegal punishment against Tories during the American Revolution.
3. Wandering Jew: a character who, in an anti-semitic legend, was condemned to roam without rest because he struck Christ on the day of the crucifixion. It should be noted that Duniway had strong ties to the Jewish community in Portland, Oregon, and was by no means anti-semitic herself.
4. Philosopher's stone: a term from the pseudo-science of alchemy. An imaginary chemical substance or preparation believed capable of transmuting baser metals into gold or silver, and of prolonging life.
5. Job 2:9–10. After Job (considered by God to be "a perfect and an upright man") had been afflicted by Satan to test if he would remain loyal to God, Job's wife said to him, "Dost thou still retain thine integrity? *curse God, and die.*" However, Job remained true. His reply was, "What? shall we receive good at the hand of God, and shall we not receive evil?"

## CHAPTER XI, Pages 73-79

1. From Hamlet's "To be or not to be" soliloquy: he longs to commit suicide "To sleep, perchance to dream," but is hindered by the thought of what may follow, "ay, there's the rub/For in that sleep of death what dreams may come,/When we have shuffled off this mortal coil,/Must give us pause" (III.i.64–67).
2. In most gold mining regions, operations usually underwent two distinct phases. Initial discoveries were of placer gold found on or near the surface, often in stream beds. These deposits were the result of erosion acting on exposed outcroppings of gold-bearing quartz veins or lodes. The weathering action of water upon the rock ground it down, thereby freeing the gold which sank into stream gravels. After prospectors had worked over these easy pickings, they (or others more skilled in mineralogy) traced the gold deposits back to their source in quartz veins farther up the streams. This led to a second round of discoveries of the veins buried in solid rock extending deep into the earth—resulting in the

establishment of quartz, lode, or hard-rock mines. The Stranger's mine evidently is a placer deposit overlying a quartz vein. The Boise Basin area, where *Edna and John* is set, experienced mostly placer mining; few quartz discoveries took place in the region, although lode mining was quite extensive in other parts of Idaho.

## CHAPTER XII, PAGES 81-86

1. From this practice, which originated in British common law, the expression "rule of thumb" is derived, now taken to mean a general or approximate procedure or rule based on practice and experience.
2. Genesis 3:6. "And when the woman *saw that the tree was good for food,* and that it was pleasant to the eyes, *and a tree to be desired to make one wise,* she took of the fruit thereof, and did eat, and gave also unto her husband with her; and he did eat."
3. Genesis 3:16–19. The consequences meted out by God for Adam and Eve's rebellion (their eating of the fruit): "Unto the woman he said, I will greatly multiply thy sorrow and thy conception; in sorrow thou shalt bring forth children; and *thy desire shall be to thy husband, and he shall rule over thee.* And unto Adam he said, Because thou hast hearkened unto the voice of thy wife, and hast eaten of the tree, of which I commanded thee, saying, Thou shalt not eat of it: cursed is the ground for thy sake; in sorrow shalt thou eat of it all the days of thy life: *Thorns also and thistles shall it bring forth to thee; and thou shalt eat the herb of the field; In the sweat of thy face shalt thou eat bread,* till thou return unto the ground; for out of it wast thou taken: for dust thou art, and unto dust shalt thou return."
4. *Tic douloureux:* a darting pain and muscular twitching in the face, also called facial neuralgia. Literally a "painful tic."
5. Cassimere: a twill-weave, worsted suiting fabric, often with a striped pattern.
6. Flitch: a side of a hog, salted and cured, or a board-like piece or strip.
7. Romans 6:23. "For *the wages of sin is death*; but the gift of God is eternal life through Jesus Christ our Lord."

## CHAPTER XIV, PAGES 96-101

1. From the "Sermon on the Mount," Matthew 6:5–6. "And when thou prayest, *thou shalt not be as the hypocrites are:* for they love to pray standing in the synagogues and in the corners of the streets, that they may be seen of men. Verily I say unto you, they have their reward. But thou, *when thou prayest, enter into thy closet,* and when thou hast shut thy door, pray to thy Father which is in secret; and thy Father which seeth in secret shall reward thee openly."
2. The "Lord's Prayer," Matthew 6:9–13. "After this manner therefore pray ye: *Our Father which art in heaven,* Hallowed be thy name. Thy kingdom come. Thy will be done in earth, as it is in heaven. Give us this day our daily bread. And forgive us our debts, as we forgive our debtors. And lead us not into temptation, but deliver us from evil: For thine is the kingdom, and the power, and the glory, for ever. Amen."

## CHAPTER XV, Pages 102-107

1. Jesus to his disciples (Matthew 10:29–31): "Are not two sparrows sold for a farthing? *and one of them shall not fall on the ground without your Father.* But the very hairs of your head are all numbered. Fear ye not therefore, *ye are of more value than many sparrows.*"

2. Romans 8:16–17. "The Spirit itself beareth witness with our spirit, that we are the children of God: And if children, then heirs; *heirs of God, and joint-heirs with Christ;* if so be that we suffer with him, that we may be also glorified together."

3. As stated by the apostle Peter: "Of a truth *I perceive that God is no respecter of persons:* But in every nation he that feareth him, and worketh righteousness, is accepted with him" (Acts 10:34–35).

4. Psalm 103:13. *"Like as a father pitieth his children, so the Lord pitieth them that fear him."*

5. Jeremiah 8:20. *"The harvest is past, the summer is ended, and we are not saved."*

6. Sentimental ballads popular at this time.

7. Welkin: the sky, the vault of heaven.

8. Genesis 2:18. "And the Lord God said, *It is not good that the man* [Adam] *should be alone;* I will make him an help meet for him."

9. Grenadine: a thin fabric of leno weave in which paired warp yarns are intertwined in a series of figures eights, and with filling yarns passed through each of the interstices so formed.

## CHAPTER XVI, Pages 108-113

1. Fiddler's Green: a paradise to which sailors are thought to go after death.
2. 1 Peter 3:1–4. "Likewise ye wives, be in subjection to your own husbands; that, if any obey not the word, they also may without the word be won by the conversation of the wives; While they behold your chaste conversation coupled with fear. Whose adorning let it not be that outward adorning of plaiting the hair, and of wearing of gold, or of putting on of apparel; But let it be the hidden man of the heart, in that which is not corruptible, even the ornament of a *meek and quiet spirit,* which is in the sight of God of great price."
3. Proverbs 21:3. "To do justice and judgment is more acceptable to the Lord than sacrifice."
4. Genesis 3:16–19. See Ch. XII, note 3.

## CHAPTER XVII, Pages 114-118

1. The inheritance laws then in force were very unfavorable to widows, a subject often addressed by woman's movement leaders.

2. "Ballet dances" (not necessarily classical ballet) were favored by male patrons because of the brief, thin costumes often worn by the performers. Minstrel shows featured comedy (much of which was extremely racist in nature) and other performances. The banter could be quite lewd.

## CHAPTER XVIII, PAGES 119-124

1. Swag: slang for plunder or booty, i.e., the money.
2. Yager: a hunting gun. Also *jaeger* or *jager* (hunter).

## CHAPTER XIX, PAGES 125-130

1. There was a large Chinese population in Idaho during the gold rush years, subjected to virulent prejudice and discrimination. After coming to America to work on the railroads, many Chinese then went on to the mines to seek their fortunes.
2. Psalm 37:25. "I have been young, and now am old; yet have I *not seen the righteous forsaken, nor his seed begging bread.*"
3. The characterization of so-called Digger Indians expressed in this simile is, of course, racist and erroneous.
4. Deborah, the Judge who ruled Israel at one time, referred to herself as "a mother in Israel" (Judges 5:7). In II Samuel 20:19, another wise woman also refers to herself as "a mother in Israel." Interestingly, when she characterizes herself by this term, she is complaining that she has unnecessarily been put at risk because an army has her city under siege although they are seeking just one man, and she bargains with the soldiers to obtain the safety of the populace of her city (herself included). She was *not* one to suffer quietly.

## CHAPTER XX, PAGES 131-136

1. Monte: a gambling game played with a 40-card pack in which players bet that one of two layouts, each consisting of two cards drawn from either the top or bottom of the deck and turned face up, will be matched in suit by the next card turned up.
2. Jackanapes: an impertinent, presumptuous young man; whippersnapper; impudent, mischievous child.
3. During this period many temperance houses, or restaurants-hotels where strong alcoholic beverages were not allowed, provided an alternative for those wishing a sober atmosphere. Sometimes temperance houses served light alcoholic beverages, such as cider, but not hard liquor; sometimes their policy was total abstinence. When the Scotts first came to Oregon, Abigail's father, John Tucker Scott, managed a temperance house where Abigail worked before taking a teaching job.
4. The cough indicates that the "fell disease" was tuberculosis, a major killer in the nineteenth century.

## CHAPTER XXI, Pages 137-142

1. Proverbs 21:9 and 25:24. *"It is better to dwell in a corner of the house top, than with a brawling woman in a wide house."*

## CHAPTER XXII, Pages 143-147

1. Erebus: from Greek mythology, the darkness under the earth imagined as the abode of the dead.

## CHAPTER XXIII, Pages 148-153

1. Proverbs 5:3–5. "For the lips of a strange woman drop as an honeycomb, and her mouth is smoother than oil; But her end is bitter as wormwood, sharp as a two-edged sword. Her feet go down to death; her *steps take hold on hell."*
2. Hebrews 12:5–6. "Despise not thou the chastening of the Lord nor faint when thou art rebuked of him: For *whom the Lord loveth he chasteneth,* and scourgeth every son whom he receiveth."
3. I Peter 3:1–4. See Ch. XVI, note 2 above.
4. Matthew 7:13–14. "Enter ye in at the strait gate: for wide is the gate, and broad is the way, that leadeth to destruction, and many there be which go in thereat: *Because strait is the gate, and narrow is the way,* which leadeth unto life, and few there be that find it."
5. Proverbs 29:1. *"He that being often reproved hardeneth his neck, shall suddenly be destroyed, and that without remedy."*

## CHAPTER XXIV, Pages 154-159

1. Refers to various legal authorities. See Ch. VI, note 1 above on Blackstone.
2. American law was based on the Common Law of England, taking Common Law as its authority when no legislation had been enacted pertaining to the subject at hand.
3. Xanthippe: wife of Socrates, known as a scolding, ill-tempered, or shrewish woman.
4. I Thessalonians 5:17. *"Pray without ceasing."* An exhortation given to the Thessalonians by the apostle Paul in his epistle.
5. Proverbs 31:27. *"She looketh well to the ways of her household, and eateth not the bread of idleness."* See also Ch. I, note 5 above.

## CHAPTER XXV, Pages 160-166

1. Magdalene: a prostitute (or sometimes, reformed prostitute). Named so after Mary Magdalene, traditionally identified as the repentant woman whom Jesus forgave in Luke 7:37–50.

2. Matthew 6:28. "And why take ye thought for raiment? Consider the lilies of the field, how they grow; *they toil not, neither do they spin.*"

## Chapter XXVI, Pages 167-174

1. Incubus: a demon or evil spirit supposed to descend on sleeping persons; especially one in male form fabled to have sexual intercourse with women in their sleep. Something that weighs upon one as a nightmare.
2. Matthew 8:21–22. "And another of his disciples said unto him [Jesus] Lord, suffer me first [before following Jesus to another locale] to go and bury my father. But Jesus said unto him, Follow me; and *let the dead bury their dead.*"
3. I Timothy 5:3–5, 16. "Honor widows that are *widows indeed.* But if any widow have children or nephews, let them learn first to shew piety at home, and to requite their parents: for that is good and acceptable before God. Now she that is a *widow indeed,* and desolate, trusteth in God, and continueth in supplications and prayers night and day. . . . If any man or woman that believeth have widows, let them relieve them, and let not the church be charged; that it may relieve them that are *widows indeed.*"
4. 1 Samuel 16:7. "But the Lord said unto Samuel, Look not on his countenance, or on the height of his stature; because I have refused him: for the Lord seeth not as man seeth; for *man looketh on the outward appearance, but the Lord looketh on the heart.*"
5. Matthew 7:1. "*Judge not, that ye be not judged.*"

# AFTERWORD

## WHEN WIVES WERE SLAVES

*Marriage is the only actual bondage known to our law.*
*There remain no legal slaves, except the mistress of every house.*
—John Stuart Mill, *The Subjection of Women*[1]

*O, my God! The God of the destitute and desperate,*
*is there not in all America a Canada for fugitive wives?*
—Edna Rutherford Smith in *Edna and John* (165)[2]

IN 1876, AS ABIGAIL SCOTT DUNIWAY began to write her eighth novel, *Edna and John*, the land of the free was celebrating its Centennial Anniversary amidst hoopla and pageantry. But all were not in agreement that this was truly an occasion for celebration. On July 4, that day held most sacred to the memory of liberty by national tradition, angry protesters rallied to impeach the government on the grounds that, over a decade after "negro" emancipation, "one-half the people"[3] were still enslaved. The stories of this Centennial Protest and *Edna and John* are intertwined. At the time Duniway's narrative was written, single and married women alike were denied suffrage, which alone could be said to represent a form of slavery by placing all women under the political domination of men. But, with few exceptions, marriage brought an end to a woman's legal identity altogether—a state of civil death—a thoroughly subjugating type of enslavement. Married women had no right to property nor any legal existence apart from their husbands; the twain had been made one, and that one the *male* "partner" in the enterprise.

Under English common law, the basis for American law, the woman thus blessed became a *femme coverte* (a female who, for legal purposes is covered, or overshadowed by her husband's presence). Married women could not sign contracts, had no title to their own earnings, no right to property (even when it was theirs by bequest), nor any claim to their children in case of separation or divorce.[4] Because the beginnings of the woman's movement are shrouded by the suffrage issue, however, the fact that women's civil disabilities were ever this extensive is obscured. Thus, the enormity of the struggle that leaders in the vanguard of the movement undertook has not been properly appreciated.

By 1876, due to the efforts of dedicated male and female activists, legislation had been passed in many states to begin alleviating such conditions; but the former status of most wives was little altered. The first Married Woman's Property Act was passed in 1839 in New York, and other states began to follow suit. Such laws commonly entitled women to possessions received by bequest or inheritance, or to those which were theirs before marriage. But early legislation generally did not entitle women to the proceeds of their own labor after marriage . . . or even to ownership of their own wardrobes.[5]

In Oregon, Duniway's first victory came in the form of a Married Woman's Sole Trader bill passed by the Senate in 1872, enabling "any woman engaged in business on her own account to register the fact in the office of the county clerk, and thereby secure her tools, furniture, or stock in trade against the liability of seizure by her husband's creditors."[6] The rights thus gained were quite limited and contingent on a woman's registering her business. This could be problematic if the husband objected, or if a woman did not consider it important to register *before* marital or financial conflicts involving her husband ensued.

Not until 1878 was a Married Woman's Property Act finally passed in Duniway's home state, allowing wives to possess real estate and other goods in their own names, keep their own wages, and manage, sell and will their own property. By 1900, after three decades of effort, Duniway could report that in Oregon "All laws have been repealed that recognize civil disabilities of the wife which are not recognized as existing against the husband, except as to voting and holding office."[7] Voting rights would not come until 1912.[8]

In popular nomenclature, the leaders of the first wave of the woman's movement are referred to as "suffragists,"[9] but this designation is misleading in that it deals only with the voting issue. The struggle for woman's rights *devolved* merely into a campaign for the vote in the late nineteenth century, *after* most states had already passed legislation removing the worst of women's civil disabilities. But from the outset, movement leaders, particularly those of the radical wing of the movement to which Duniway belonged,[10] saw the necessity of working to secure equal rights in all areas of life, e.g., the right to engage in any and all occupations, equal pay for equal work, issues surrounding the abuse of women, including marital and extra-marital rape, etc. In retrospect, it is apparent that concentrating efforts only on securing the vote, to the exclusion of other equally important concerns, falsely lulled women into believing that their goal had been accomplished with the ratification of the Nineteenth Amendment in 1920. Hence, nearly a century later, women are still hampered by many of the same lingering inequities.

The gross injustices perpetrated by nineteenth-century marriage laws are well illustrated in the *New Northwest*. Wives, a form of chattel property, had little recourse. In a blurb under "Home [Portland area] News" on April

27, 1877, Duniway's paper relates the incident of a 20-year-old woman who chose to enter "a house of ill-fame . . . to escape from the brutalities of a drunken husband. This monster, she alleges, had at one time dragged her half a mile by the hair of her head, and was in the habit of abusing her inhumanly." Because of unjust laws, many of the most well educated and intelligent women of the age refused to marry, or hesitated to do so—with good reason. Voting rights, in such an equation, could even be said to be a null issue. Married or unmarried, a woman could not go to the polls, but if married she couldn't even elect to retain her own rightful property or personal dignity.

Thus was the situation in the U.S. Centennial year, 1876, when Abigail Scott Duniway began composing *Edna and John*. Although the main events of this novel can be dated to the early 1860s (see *Preface*), the experiences suffered by Edna Rutherford Smith, her mother Susan Rutherford, her Aunt Judy "LaSelle," and her bosom friend and boon companion in misery, Sue Randolph, could just as easily have plagued any woman in Idaho territory (or most places in the land of the free) a decade later. In the rhetoric of the early woman's movement, marriage was often likened to slavery, and with good cause. In *Edna and John*, Duniway set out to showcase this condition and illustrate the reason for all Americans to mourn rather than boast at the occasion of their nation's hundredth birthday.

From its inception the movement had been strongly associated with the activities of abolitionists; many of its principal workers labored assiduously in both fields and hoped that releasing African-Americans from bondage would free all women from their captive state as well. However, when the Fifteenth Amendment was passed in 1870, it guaranteed voting rights to black males without specifically allocating them to black or white females. When the courts maintained the nonvoting status of women, the bleak irony that many women had fought for and secured the freedom of others while they themselves remained virtually enslaved caused a tremendous upsurge in women's activism.

In the process, the woman's movement had split into two rival factions, the National Woman Suffrage Association (NWSA) and American Woman Suffrage Association (AWSA). The members of the NWSA, headed by Stanton and Anthony, had wanted to press for women's rights to be included in the Fifteenth Amendment. The AWSA, representing the more conservative element that did not want to rock the boat, went along with the Republican Party in asserting that the rights of black males should be secured *before* women's issues were addressed.[11]

By the time the country began to plan the grand Centennial Celebration that would take place in Philadelphia during the summer of 1876, the women of the NWSA were very angry. It was their firm conviction that they had been deceived and cheated, and they were deeply affronted that the vain promises of the men in power had led them to expend such tremendous amounts of effort in vain. Susan B. Anthony, one of the principal figures of the abolitionist movement, had labored tirelessly, along with other dedicated women activists, for twenty years and more to secure freedom for all, regardless of race or gender. For these devotees of liberty, the abolition-ist and woman's rights movements had been one and the same. They be-lieved, and were led to believe by their political associates, that when free-dom was secured for the "negro" slaves, and efforts were made to gain enfranchisement, then every effort would be made to bring about the en-franchisement of women as well. As recorded by Ida Husted Harper in her biography of Susan B. Anthony, "All the Abolitionists and prominent Repub-licans had upheld the principle of equal rights to all, and now, when the test came, they refused to recognize the claims of woman!"[12] They were be-trayed, and everywhere "met by the cry, 'This is the negro's hour!'"[13]

The Centennial Celebration in Philadelphia was a truly spectacular event, and included a "grand exposition," a notable forerunner of the great Columbian Exhibition of 1893. Not so strangely, in capitalist America, "cen-tennial fever" spread throughout the land long in advance of the actual holi-day, and "centennial buncombe" was "retailed on every street corner" (*NNW* 4/7/76).[14] In November, after the exhibition had closed, it was re-ported that total receipts from May 10 to November 10 included admission fees of $3,813,724, income from concessions of $290,000, and percentages and royalties of $205,010, for a grand total of $4,308,735 (*NNW* 11/24/76). On one September day alone, there were 110,588 cash admissions by one o'clock (*NNW* 9/29/76). Although few women as yet were voters, the changing position of women in society would not be altogether forgotten; a Woman's Congress and Woman's Exposition were scheduled to be held in Philadelphia in conjunction with the Centennial in October. But for the out-raged women of the NWSA this presence would not be enough. They began to plan a massive protest that would disrupt the keynote event of the entire celebration—the reading of the Declaration of Independence on July Fourth.

In June a convention was held to formalize plans formulated by move-ment leaders months earlier.[15] Resolutions were passed, drawing on the rhetoric of the Declaration, asserting that women had been denied the right of self-government and therefore owed no allegiance to, nor were they bound to obey the government that had deprived them of their liberties.[16] A press release was issued, signed by Anthony and Gage, stating that "On July 4, while the men of this nation and the world are rejoicing that 'all men are free and equal' in the United States, a Declaration of Rights for woman will be issued . . . and a grand protest against calling this Centennial a cel-ebration of the independence of the people, while one-half of the people are still subjects—*still political slaves*" (*NNW* 6/23/76). They also issued a call "for the friends of Woman Suffrage in every state, county, and township, to gather together as best they can, on the same day and hour" to voice their dissatisfaction (*NNW* 6/2/76). The National Centennial Equal Rights Pro-test had been conceived.

Stanton, Anthony, and Gage drafted a document in the form of articles of impeachment, arraigning the United States government for violating its own fundamental principles.[17] This *Centennial Protest*, or *Declaration of*

*Rights,* as it has been called, is a masterful piece of writing that makes its more widely known antecedent, the *Declaration of Sentiments*,[18] blanch by comparison. In this document, the government is impeached for: introducing the word "male" into state constitutions, denying suffrage to women and thereby making sex a crime; holding the writ of habeas corpus inoperative by allowing the rights of the husband to subsume the rights of the wife; denying a right of trial by a jury of one's peers; taxation without representation; allowing unequal codes for men and women (the double standard); enacting special legislation for women; denying woman's right of self-government; establishing an aristocracy of sex more despotic than monarchy; and failure to render judicial decisions consonant with the spirit and letter of the constitution.

Stanton asked permission to present the women's protest officially to the President of the United States, Ulysses S. Grant, at the conclusion of the formal reading of the Declaration on July Fourth. Permission was denied. The places of honor on the speakers' platform in Independence Square were filled with foreign dignitaries (all male), including monarchs and the representatives of monarchies, and only after the "utmost effort" several leaders of the NWSA were seated at the rear.[19] These women—Susan B. Anthony, Matilda Joslyn Gage, Sara Andrews Spencer, Lillie Devereux Blake and Phoebe W. Couzins—determined to submit their complaints despite the lack of official consent.[20] After the reading of the Declaration, the NWSA leaders walked to the front of the platform, and Anthony presented the Centennial Protest. The group of five then left the platform, distributing printed copies of their complaint along the way, and made their way to a stage that had been erected for musicians on the other side of Independence Hall, where they read their own Declaration of Independence to an applauding crowd which had been gathered in advance by movement organizers. Somewhat later, a meeting of the association was convened at the Unitarian Church, and orations continued for five hours. This brave act was a monumental event in American history.

The epigraph to *Edna and John*, found in the original serialized version at the beginning of each chapter, reads:

> Woman's degraded, helpless position is the weak point of our institutions today—a disturbing force everywhere, severing family ties, filling our asylums with the deaf, the dumb, the blind, our prisons with criminals, our cities with drunkenness and prostitution, our homes with disease and death.

This statement is drawn from the Centennial Protest's penultimate paragraph, where it is preceded by the allegation that such conditions pose a grave threat to national security and stability. Knowing the circumstances under which that document was authored accords the epigraph greater weight, and reveals that the events of the novel are designed not just to demonstrate its claims (although important in itself), but to argue for a radical break from the status quo, in fact, an impeachment of the entire United States government. When Duniway's own role in the Centennial

Protest is examined, the intent of the author and the truths of woman's sub-jugation are more fully elucidated.

In April of 1876 Susan Anthony extended an invitation to Duniway to come to Philadelphia and be one of the principal orators on the afternoon of the Fourth. "We depend upon you, and you must come," she wrote. "This protest *must* be uttered on historic grounds in this Centennial year of men's independence, and its echo will be repeated over and over among the tax-paying and unrepresented women of America, till its reverberations are heard and heeded from Maine to farthest Oregon" (*NNW* 4/7/76). Abigail accepted the invitation, and set out on June 8 with every intention of arriv-ing by the Fourth of July, but she was delayed en route because of insuffi-cient funds, and didn't reach her destination until later in the summer. Alto-gether she would be gone ten months—lecturing, attending woman's congresses held in the ensuing seasons, visiting friends and family, hob-nobbing with eastern intellectuals—and would even find a New York pub-lisher for her epic poem, *David and Anna Matson*. Along the way, she would conceive and write most of *Edna and John*, sending the chapters home for publication as she completed them. Her experiences and the development of her thought are reflected in its pages.

In May, not having received a definitive answer to her earlier letter, Anthony sent another plea to Duniway, begging her presence on the day of the protest, and punning with her name:

> Now, Mrs. Abigail Duniway, *you* must *forge the thunder* for us that shall roll its echoes through the past and present centuries! As the namesake of Abigail Adams, wife of one President and mother of another, and the first woman who asked suffrage for her sex at the hands of the First Federal Congress, we look to *you,* planted as you are upon the furthest slope of the American Occident, to *come over and help us* until taxation without representation shall be Done-away. (*NNW* 6/2/76)

Abigail was very short on funds at this time, and left Oregon by stagecoach, with plans to raise the extra financial backing she needed for such a trip by stopping to lecture as she went, and then travelling east by train. She left her associate editor and sister, Catherine Scott Coburn,[21] in charge of the *New Northwest*, and headed on her way. On June 9, we find Coburn pleading with readers to contribute to the project and help send Duniway to the Centennial:

> Hearken for a moment, friends! Suppose some man, half as well and favor-ably known in this State as is Mrs. Duniway, had received the appoint-ment to deliver a centennial address upon historic grounds on the one-hundredth anniversary of our nation's birth—would he have been compelled to have made his toilsome way, staging by day and lecturing and canvassing of evenings, to earn his way across the continent, arriving at last, tired, worn, and travel-soiled, at his destination? . . . Or is it only a woman—a member of the unrepresented and *protected* class—who is left thus to work and struggle and fight her way, overcoming difficulties at which the strongest man would stand appalled?

Unluckily for Duniway and the Centennial Protest, but fortuitously for future readers of *Edna and John*, the necessary funds did not materialize, and its author was forced to make her way eastward at a much slower pace. She decided to make a number of lecture stops in the mining districts of Idaho, which had already passed their goldrush heyday but still contained sizeable populations from which she hoped to draw support. These towns included Idaho City—at one time, as noted in Leonard J. Arrington's *History of Idaho*, "the largest city in the Northwest, even greater than Portland"[22]—and Placerville, both in the Boise Basin area forty miles northeast of present-day Boise.

In these boom towns of the Boise Basin, and in Silver City in Idaho's Owyhee district, some miles further south along her route to Nevada, Duniway would conceive her idea for *Edna and John*.[23] In the summer of 1876, on approaching Idaho City she found "a collection of sun-bleached shingle roofs . . . nestled together in friendly intimacy, right under the lee of a mighty mountain," and a town that was "compact, but not large," an apparition that a decade earlier would have borne some resemblance to the Idaho Flat found in the novel. She reports that although the "exigencies of mining trade" had built it up, "with the decay of mines, the town suffers. But there is yet much business" (*NNW* 7/21/76). The scene would have been much more frenetic in 1863, the probable year of Edna and John Smith's arrival in Idaho (please refer to the *Preface* of this volume for a detailed discussion of the dating of the novel). As noted by Arrington, by 1864,

> Within a year of its founding, Idaho City (still called West Bannack with the Montana spelling) had 6,167 people, including 360 women and 224 children, and 250 businesses. These included a printing office, eight bakeries, nine restaurants, twenty-five saloons, forty variety stores, fifteen doctors, twenty-five attorneys, seven blacksmith shops, four sawmills, two dentists, three express offices, five auctioneers, three drugstores, four butcher shops, three billiard tables, two bowling alleys, three painters, one photographer, three livery stables, four breweries, one harness shop, one mattress factory, and two jewelers.[24]

And many more thousands swarmed to other newly established towns and fly-by-night camps. Boise City (now simply Boise), farther south, at this time had a much smaller population of only about 1,000. It began as a trading, not a mining, town and soon metamorphosed into the state capital.[25]

Duniway describes a terrain much like the approach to Idaho Flat found in *Edna and John* (62–63). On July 8, she reports in her "Editorial Correspondence" that:

> about noon we gained the summit overlooking Boise valley upon one hand, and the great basin, as they term it, on the other. What a picture! No pen can do it justice. Boise River, and the Payette and Weiser, sparkled like threads of silver among the cloud-mottled shades of the great valley through which they run; and Snake River, like a monster anaconda, wound its tortuous lengths among the far-away foothills as it crawled and surged toward the distant Columbia. Ahead of us lay in grandeur

inimitable the mighty mountain fastnesses, decked here and there with forests, and here and there marred by worked-out mines. Below us lay, for miles and miles, the winding stage road, unrolling its dusty lengths like a great silver ribbon, as it seemed to unwind itself in coming to meet us.

On July 13, bound for Placerville, she writes:

Our road lay through, or rather over, the great Idaho basin for twelve miles. We have never in our life seen but one thoroughfare that equaled it in crookedness, and that is the tidal river Skipanon, which lies like raveled crochet loops between Astoria and Clatsop beach. All the afternoon we rode through the interminable mountain gorges, now gazing high upon the surrounding and distant peaks, bald here and there in mighty patches, and again clothed in primeval forests of pine and fir, and now peering from our precarious perch beside the driver into awful abysses, so deep and dark and solemn in their silent dignity that we would hold our breath and ask, as did the Psalmist of old, "Lord, what is man, that thou are mindful of him, or the son of man, that thou visitest him?" Oftentimes the road lay alongside of purling, crystal streams that laughed at the feet of vernal groves of stinted cottonwood, wild cherry, willow, and alder, flanked by syringas in snowy bloom, and currants loaded with yellow fruit. Again, we would ascend a sidelong ridge where mother nature had carpeted the parched earth with variegated hues, too beautiful to be allowed to "Waste their sweetness on the desert air."

And again, on July 24, telling of her journey from Placerville to Silver City, she adds:

The scenery upon our road to Silver City, after leaving the plain and striking the mountains which formed an ancient sea-rim, was much like that before described in going from Boise to Idaho and Placerville. Mountains, wild and weird and mighty, lifted their ghostly crests into the blue ether of heaven; chasms, so deep and so near you that a single misstep of your horses would plunge you into the literal bottomless pit; abandoned gold fields, all burrowed out by miners in the days gone by; trees, "massy and tall and dark," lifted their blue-green crests in the air; rivulets laughed at the foothills; and far, far away rose other mountain ranges, till it seemed as though the magnificent vastness of creation was indeed immeasurable, even with observation confined to this terrestrial ball.

The author had found the setting for her latest tale. Here, on the margins of modern society, she could portray how truly degraded and helpless a woman's position could be, and what a "disturbing force" this degradation in fact was, in *all* cases—threatening to national security and stability— even in non-frontier settings where, by tacit assumption (or myth) women were said to be members of a "protected" class.

In *Edna and John*, as in all her novels, Duniway describes a "worst case scenario," one that could take place given current laws and in many recorded instances had—particularly in the rougher environs of the more scantily settled West—even though in practice most women did not suffer as greatly. This serves the purpose of heightening the readers' awareness, and allows them to observe how bad the current situation actually is, and how urgently action is required. As John Stuart Mill describes his task in writing *The Subjection of Women,*

> I have described the wife's legal position, not her actual treatment. The laws of most countries are far worse than the people who execute them, and many of them are only able to remain laws by being seldom or never carried into effect. If married life were all that it might be expected to be, looking to the laws alone, society would be a hell upon earth. . . . In domestic as in political tyranny the case of absolute monsters chiefly illustrates the institution by showing that there is scarcely any horror which may not occur under it if the despots please, and thus setting in a strong light what must be the terrible frequency of things only a little less atrocious.[26]

In *Edna and John,* and in her other narratives, Duniway does the same, and makes us think, "If an 'absolute monster' such as John Smith becomes can exist, how many other men can then be found who serve their wives only a little less malignantly?"

And so, in the fall of 1876 as she began to craft the chapters of her novel, the author set the concerns of the Centennial Protest, meticulously worded and drawn up in New York parlors, against the backdrop of frontier Idaho, where the least expected could become reality, and where the true atrocity of existing law would appear in highest relief. Certain conditions in the remote areas of the West tended to create more opportunity for women. For example, Edna was readily able to go into the pie business and later stage an "elocutionary entertainment" that raised enough money to serve John's illegitimate dealings as well as her own legitimate goal of becoming proprietor of her own restaurant and hotel. On the other hand, women could be taken advantage of in ways not as likely in the East. For example, a woman like Aunt Judy could fall prey to a man such as Hal LaSelle Sr., who left a wife and family elsewhere and, assuming a new identity as "the Stranger" could woo and wed another unbeknownst. Men such as his son, Hal LaSelle Jr., also taking advantage of anonymity provided by the frontier, could freely abandon their wives on scant pretexts, when in longer-established communities restraining influences might have prevailed. And men like John Smith could be so seduced by an environment dominated by 24-hour-a-day casinos and freely flowing alcohol (there were twenty-five saloons and four breweries in Idaho City alone) that their better natures could not stand a chance.

After her stay in Idaho, Duniway travelled eastward, through Nevada and Utah, where she met with Mormon women—including some of Brigham Young's wives—then stopped in Illinois to visit relatives before finally arriving at her destinations of Philadelphia and New York. Since her 1852 migration to Oregon, she had been east of the old Oregon territory only once, in 1872 when she attended the national Woman's Congress held in New York. At that time she traveled by steamship to San Francisco and continued by rail (just three years after the opening of the Transcontinental

Railroad in 1869), arriving swiftly at the convention where "she was immediately invited to a platform seat."[27] Her lengthier trip in 1876–77, involving exposure to a wider variety of influences, seems to have had a more profound effect on her work as a writer than the journey in 1872.

In the articles written during this journey and in her work from this point on (until a notable decline in her later years), Abigail entered her literary maturity. Her prose took on a stronger luster, particularly in the novels, which were more carefully and eloquently worded even in her perpetual haste. *Edna and John* displays this more fully adept composition style: the ironic tone set in the introductory chapter is reminiscent of Dickens, whom she greatly admired; often-powerful wording in descriptive and narrative passages rises to the level of the Centennial Protest from which the novel derives its theme. Edna's speeches, particularly in her arguments with the Reverend Mr. Handel, are not merely didactic interludes, but points at which the author engages in urgent philosophic debates. The right of woman to be self-governing and self-supporting had *not* been established in most sectors of society, hence the continued struggle by Duniway and other equal rights leaders to overthrow the old order. Reports in the *New Northwest* during the period of *Edna and John*'s publication reveal that quite commonly local clubs and literary societies held public or private debates on "the woman question," with much celebrating by activists when the outcome favored equal rights. Hotly contested issues were woman's right to speak and preach in church and in other venues, and her right to stand up for herself rather than continue to submit in Pauline meekness. An entire belief system was at stake.

Although she had missed the Woman's Fourth of July (or Woman's Independence Day, as some sources report it), Abigail was a principal speaker at the Woman's Congress held in Philadelphia in early October. Of her experience, she reports:

> When we think of the persecution and obloquy we have borne in days gone by because we saw the right and humbly dared to espouse it, and realize that we now have opportunity to meet and mingle with other women who have also dared and done, we feel that some of the sharpest stings of our present exile from home and the dear ones there are being somewhat compensated. (*NNW* 10/27/76)

She was clearly inspired, even a little overwhelmed. At this time, the author was busy overseeing the publication of her poem, *David and Anna Matson*, a beautifully illustrated souvenir volume. The prosody was then, and has more recently been sharply critiqued, but the marvel is that she dared to pen an epic poem at all, being thoroughly familiar with her own rough habits of composition.

One must imagine her, travelling around the countryside canvassing for suffrage, hurriedly scratching notes at odd intervals, which she describes as "numerous waifs in our traveling basket, many of which are destined to be strangled in their incipiency, and many more to be remodeled before the world shall witness them" (*NNW* 3/10/76). Her travelling sometimes forced her to continue working on her novels without any record of the chapters she had already written. On November 10, she candidly related of *Edna and John,* "That story worries us *awfully.* We have no copy of it, can't get the back papers, don't remember the names of the characters, and are going it blind to keep the boys in copy; so we are making bricks without straw."

At home in Oregon, a suffrage bill was introduced to the state legislature by Oregon State Woman Suffrage Association (OSWSA) president Hattie Loughary. Although it was later tabled, the *New Northwest* urged its supporters not to be discouraged, progress was being made—the bill was not treated with the contempt it would have been ten years ago (*NNW* 10/27/76). The content and editorials of the *New Northwest* tended to be less strident and acerbic in Duniway's absence. There was more filler, short inspirational sayings and anecdotes, and humorous quips and jottings unrelated to—or only marginally related to—equal rights concerns, than when the paper's owner was at the helm. Nevertheless, the associate editor fed the press the better part of its usual diet, continued to praise legislators and other public figures when they supported suffrage and related women's issues, and to hold them up to scorn when they did otherwise. Women's successes in unusual occupations were reported with relish in the journal's customary fashion—the proprietor of a real estate agency, a watchmaker, an apiarist, a photographer, women ministers, doctors and lawyers, and women clerks in British railway stations—all received commendations. The independence that widowhood could bring (if not impeded by unjust dower laws) was frequently extolled, and we read of those who appeared to be more blessed in that state than in matrimony, such as the "Cattle Queen of Texas," who owned 75,000 acres of land "on which 15,000 beeves per annum are fattened" (*NNW* 2/23/77).

Yet, as Duniway prolonged her journey, sister Kate Coburn became increasingly exasperated. After reaching the East Coast, Abigail wrote that the book needed her attention and was taking longer than planned. Unfortunately, after completing her business, she became ill and underwent lengthy periods of convalescence, first in the East at a friend's home and later with relatives in Illinois. Repeatedly, chapters of *Edna and John* failed to arrive on schedule, and the associate editor had to scrounge for other copy to take their place. Because the serialized novel was the most prominent feature of the publication—given the slot normally occupied by a headline story on page one—this created difficulties.

As absences continued Coburn's vexation escalated, and her comments grew increasingly satiric, in the sharply pointed style of Western journalism.

11/17/76  We have received no word from Mrs. Duniway since our last issue. . . . to the best of our knowledge and belief she is either in New York City or at some other city or point between that city and San Francisco. . . . If she is not home in time to take Thanksgiving turkey, she perhaps will be in time to dispose of her annual allowance of chicken-pie on Christmas.

12/1/76    Everywhere . . . we were interrogated as to the probable time of Mrs.
           Duniway's return. . . . Our answers to these questions were as lucid and
           conclusive as uncertainty could make them.
12/15/76   There is nothing later from Mrs. Duniway than the "Editorial Corre-
           spondence" published in this issue. It will be seen that she talks 'home'
           and we still expect her by Christmas.
1/5/76     Mrs. Duniway, much to our regret, still tarries. . .
1/19/77    No news from Mrs. Duniway since our last issue. She is no doubt sigh-
           ing for the balmy breezes and humid skies of webfoot, as she sits
           shivering on a snow-bound train or plunges through drifts in her efforts
           to fill lecture engagements. Serves her right.
1/26/77    A letter from Mrs. Duniway . . . states . . . that she was coming West as
           fast as the weather and the state of her health would permit. So she will
           evidently be home sometime, if not sooner.

Although few comments on the novels were printed in the paper, they indi-
cate that the occasional absence of *Edna and John* was bemoaned. A letter
from J.L. York in California complained that:

> it's not just the thing to work our feelings up to the highest pitch of inter-
> est in the well being of "Edna and John" and then leave them to cool off by
> degrees in suspense. The last we heard of that worthy couple, they were
> just entering upon a little episode of a thrilling character, such as to break
> the monotony of steady going married life.
>
> I had forgotten, but wife, . . . tells me that "Edna," the better half of this
> unfortunate family, with "Aunt Judy," were being driven off in an ox
> wagon at a fearful rate over rocks and mounds on the wild desert plains
> by the lawful husband of the former, who seemed to be goaded to des-
> peration by a startling discovery made the night previous. . . . Did they
> reach any place worth mentioning, or are the oxen still traveling toward
> the setting sun? Are they living together yet in misery, or did they apply to
> the law for legal separation?
>
> The above questions answered in a satisfactory manner will bring
> peace again with its healing balm to our troubled household.
> (*NNW* 2/2/77)

In York's case, the paper hadn't arrived at all for several weeks, and he was
afraid his subscription had been stopped. His was probably typical of the ex-
asperation felt by subscribers when promised episodes were delayed from
week to week.

The winter of Duniway's absence was an interesting one on the national political scene. It was the year of the disputed Hayes vs. Tilden presidential election. Although Tilden, the Democrat, led in the popular and
electoral vote, he was one vote short of a majority in the electoral college,
with some votes disputed. Months later, after a great deal of furor and scandal, the election was awarded to Republican Hayes. On January 12, the *New
Northwest* reprinted an excerpt from the Lincoln, Illinois *Herald*, which
quoted Abigail lecturing that "it is quite time women discuss constitutional
affairs when men have got political matters so badly muddled that they cannot tell who is President."

On the suffrage front, after the Centennial Protest the next move of the NWSA was to renew the appeal for a Sixteenth Amendment—not the one approved in 1913 providing for an income tax, but a proposed amendment prohibiting states from disenfranchising any of their citizens on account of sex. As envisioned, it would have served much the same purpose as the Equal Rights Amendment proposed, but not adopted, a century later. An appeal to circulate petitions, signed by Stanton, Anthony and Gage, was published nationwide, and queried "Is not a civil rights bill, that shall open the college doors, the trades, and professions, and secure to woman her personal and property rights, as necessary for her protection as for the colored man?" It went on to proclaim that:

> all the evils of society center in woman's degradation and demoralization, and until her equality is recognized, the spiritual, the aesthetic, the moral elements in humanity will be forever subjugated to brute force. All attempts at reform are fragmentary and hopeless, until woman, in freedom and independence, understands the true science of life. As political equality is the door to civil, religious, and social liberty, here must our work begin. You who are laboring for social purity, temperance, peace, the rights of labor, if you would take the speediest way to accomplish what you propose, demand the ballot in your own hand—a voice in the government. (*NNW* 11/24/76)

Although the vote was the principal focus, some of the allegations of the Centennial Protest were reiterated, particularly those cited in the epigraph of *Edna and John* attributing "all the evils of society" to woman's degradation.

Yet, despite Duniway's novel coming to completion many months after the Sixteenth Amendment became the top item on the NWSA's agenda, suffrage *per se* never became one of the story's major concerns. This might partially be attributed to the storyline already being set, but could also reflect the author's ongoing preoccupation with the many conditions surrounding women's disabilities. The book's epilogue explains that the need to work for a more broadly formulated "emancipation" (not limited to the suffrage issue) was to be Edna's future work (174). The most significant theme of *Edna and John* is that of women's *freedom* and the steps necessary to liberate this "half of the American people" from both actual and figurative slavery. Because Duniway and other suffragists were currently engaged in campaigning to procure the vote for women, we must realize that the novel argues implicitly, even if secondarily, that the vote is necessary to securing women's freedom.

Duniway's ten-month sojourn to the East and Midwest concluded with a heartbreaking irony. After her arrival home she learned that her twenty-three-year-old only daughter, Clara, had secretly married Don Stearns. Abigail heartily disapproved of him,[28] and felt as betrayed as Edna's mother Susan Rutherford. The eventual outcome of the match seems to have justified her concern: Don Stearns' business disappointments; Clara's early death in 1886 from what was apparently tuberculosis, but according to the wisdom of the more limited medical knowledge of that era appeared to have been contracted from the swampy surroundings where Stearns took her to live; and his neglect of their only child, Earl, after Clara's death (subsequently raised by Abigail and Ben).

In this atmosphere of disappointed hopes Duniway completed *Edna and John*. With five sons, each with his own more masculine concerns, she had fondly dreamed that her only daughter, her eldest child, would follow in her footsteps and dedicate her life to the cause. Duniway's biographer, Ruth Moynihan, reflects that the bitter comment made in Chapter XVIII, that "love is like leprosy, fastening its virus in the veins of its victim and fettering the subject for life to the chains of a slow consumption of all that was sparkling and hopeful in the better nature previous to the attack," reveals the anguish she must have felt.[29] At this point, however, reality parts with fiction. Clara endured her less-than-perfect marriage to Don until *her* death, and Abigail suffered with Ben until *his* death, after which she felt herself to be too old for a second time around. But the saga of *Edna and John* drew to a close on June 15, 1877, with Edna (nee Rutherford, then Smith, and now Shields) fortuitously freed from her first unhappy connection, and blissfully married to another. It proves again that romances revel in the types of denouements people long for but seldom realize in everyday life.

In exemplary narratives (stories written to teach lessons by example) such as *Edna and John* and other Duniway novels, happy endings serve a purpose—they offer a vision of hope. Making that hope as tantalizing as possible, and thereby inducing her readers to work ever more fervently for its fulfillment, was one of the author's principal goals. She accomplished this by sharpening contrast, likening the afflictions of her female characters to slavery and elucidating how every woman, suffering these same afflictions to some degree, must share their plight. It is not by accident that *Edna and John* opens in Missouri. Because Duniway is intent on showing that woman's position is as "degraded" and "helpless" as that of the slave, it is suitable to begin her story in a slave-holding locale. This allows her to draw an unmistakable parallel between wives-as-slaves and unliberated African-Americans.

In *Edna and John*, the author juxtaposes the character of the typical slave against the character of the typical married woman, not only to show that she is a veritable slave because she labors for her husband without wages, but also to disclose the full extent of her subjugation along with all its degrading effects. The simile that married women are like servants without wages is completed by extending the comparison to note that they are like servants without wages because "they'll appropriate whatever they can gather surreptitiously if they can't do any better" (28). This theme, that woman's legal position forced her to act deceitfully—and illegally—for her own protection, was one which Duniway often repeated. On April 20, 1877, the *New Northwest* carried the report that she had recently lectured in San Jose on the "Subjugated Classes," and had said that:

> [a] subjugated or alien class of people like women, were of necessity, an intriguing class; forced to practice deceit, resort to questionable subterfuges, and even to what the law denotes as petty crimes, in order to obtain that

which rightfully belongs to them, but which under the one-sex government is denied to them, and declared to be vested in man alone. . . . It was a common saying years ago, that 'the negro will steal.' Nothing strange about that. Why shouldn't they steal when they saw their masters appropriating the money earned by their labor, and giving them comparatively nothing? This was true of any subjugated class, and was practiced by the women of America to an alarming extent. The women themselves know this to be so, though the husbands and fathers rest in blissful ignorance of the fact.

Without condoning immorality, Duniway recognized that it might be necessary to employ guerrilla tactics to survive the conditions created by a despotic government and to foment a rebellion. She also recognized that women had developed a slave mentality, and that this mentality, as well as the laws restricting women's freedom, must be changed if their position were to be permanently improved.

Referring again to John Stuart Mill's *The Subjection of Women*—not merely because this was an extremely influential essay in its time, but because Duniway was a known disciple of his philosophies (leading her to name her utopian community "Utilitaria" in her later work, *Margaret Rudson*)—we find that helping readers to recognize that women's civil disabilities were equivalent to political slavery was an important project for feminist writers of that time period. Mill admits that he is "far from pretending that wives are in general not better treated than slaves," but argues that:

> no slave is a slave to the same lengths, and in so full a sense of the words, as a wife is. Hardly any slave, except one immediately attached to the master's person, is a slave at all hours and minutes; in general he has, like a soldier, his fixed task, and when it is done, or when he is off duty, he disposes, within certain limits of his own time. . . . But it cannot be so with the wife. . . .[30]
>
> It is the sole case, now that negro slavery has been abolished, in which a human being in the plenitude of every faculty is delivered up to the tender mercies of another human being, in the hope forsooth that this other will use the power solely for the good of the person subjected to it. Marriage is the only actual bondage known to our law. There remain no legal slaves, except the mistress of every house.[31]

In Duniway's era it was generally harder to generate sympathy for a fugitive wife, when conditions forced her to flee her master-husband, than for a fugitive African-American slave. This condition lent credence to Abigail's illustration of woman as slave.

Custody cases were particularly difficult, because a man did not need to establish his ability or desire to care properly for his children; they were automatically awarded to the father on the basis that they were his "property." Often, in cases of separation or divorce, a man would demand possession of his offspring to exercise vengeance against his wife, leaving many women in positions similar to that of Sue Randolph. Susan B. Anthony's biographer relates the story of abolitionist William Lloyd Garrison pleading with a woman to give up possession of her child to her negligent husband, who had legal custody:

> "Don't you know the law of Massachusetts gives the father the entire guardianship and control of the children?" he said. "Yes, I know it," she replied, "and does not the law of the United States give the slaveholder the ownership of the slave? And don't you break it every time you help a slave to Canada?" "Yes, I do." he replied. "Well," she said, "the law which gives the father the sole ownership of the children is just as wicked and I'll break it just as quickly. You would die before you would deliver a slave to his master, and I will die before I will give up that child to its father." [32]

Anthony helped the woman to go into hiding with her child, despite Garrison's objection, and her Quaker father offered her his support in that matter, saying, "I think you have done absolutely right, but don't put a word on paper or make a statement to any one that you are not prepared to face in court. Legally you are wrong, but morally you are right, and I will stand by you."[33] Thus, it is no wonder that Edna, after being denied a divorce, and remanded by His Honor the Judge to "return to your wifely duties and observe them" (157), and to "Go home and get your husband's dinner and make his home happy" (157), is driven to desperation by her entrapment. She becomes desperate enough to start carrying a revolver, and poignantly cries out, "O, my God! The God of the destitute and desperate, is there not in all America a Canada for fugitive wives?" (165).

When Edna finally begins to realize her actual position as a slave, she begins to rebel. "No slavery is absolute except it be matrimony," she declares when, sick of John's insolvency and dissipation, she determines to start a career on the stage. When Mr. Handel adjures her that it is her womanly duty to endure further privation, she retorts, "I knew slaves in my childhood . . . who endured toil without recompense and stripes without stint, without a thought but that they must endure. Their children ran away and otherwise resisted the injustice, though, and so will the daughters of your model [the long-suffering 'mother in Israel'], if they should marry badly" (130). The more thoroughly she realizes the conditions of her own slavery, which she has denied previously (and which denial has caused her to take insufficient heed of her own interests), the more radicalized she becomes. A new Eve, no longer blinded by the patriarchal interpretation of feminine experience, no longer satisfied to live under a biblical curse that the ruling class decrees will have a greater effect on women than on men,[34] Edna proclaims "Now my eyes are opened and I know good from evil. Men may kill me, or they may compel me to kill them, or myself, but they cannot compel me to longer outrage the laws of God by living a life with my body to which my soul is not true" (165). Duniway's passionate rhetoric in the mouth of Edna aims to stir in the reader a similar epiphany.

Edna determines to act as an outlaw if necessary, because as a wife the legal system declares she has no individual existence, and so by rights, because she is not represented, she should not be subject to its constraints. "The only trouble I have ever had in my life was on account of bad marriage

laws," she tells her mother (161), and "The law may hound me to the death
if it will," she declares savagely, "but I will not yield to its demands" (165).
Here we find that *all* the laws and customs governing women's status, not
voting laws alone, are defective and must be revolutionized—and must be
disobeyed, if circumstances require.

Like Thoreau, in his essay "Resistance to Civil Government," Edna discovers that a person "cannot without disgrace be associated" with the
American government as constructed at present, and must regard unjust
laws as null and void.[35] Forced by law to accept John into her home, the only
safe place she can pass the night with her children is in jail with the unjustly
imprisoned Sue Randolph. She finds, again like Thoreau, that "Under a government which imprisons any unjustly, the true place for a just man is also
a prison."[36] In the end, after John's gruesome but convenient suicide, we
find that "Edna was saved, . . . not because of the protection of human law,
but in spite of it" (174). And this is the lesson Duniway's earliest readers
were to learn, if they were to know how to act—that the law as it was then
enslaved women and did not protect them.

In *Edna and John*, Duniway acts as the magician's antipode—one who
must dispel, rather than create illusions. Expectations are turned upside
down. Although the story begins like a classic seduction narrative, the plot
is inverted. In the typical story of a girl duped into marriage or pseudo-mar-
riage with a man who is not worthy of her, her downfall comes when her
lover later abandons her; here she is ruined because he refuses to leave!
Likewise, the author labors to convince her audience that all the stories
they have been told and have believed about the nature of woman's condition are false, reversals of the truth, illusions wrought to perpetuate women's
bondage. If there is any chance that a reader still imagines that, despite certain flaws, marriage laws ultimately serve women's best interests, *Edna and
John* will set them straight. Each female character in the narrative is held up
as an example of how a woman may suffer under the status quo. Each represents one or more major issues central to women's enslavement, and the collective evidence of the injustices thus perpetrated works to eliminate any lingering misconceptions concerning their subjugated state.

Susan Rutherford represents the important issues of a wife's impecuniosity, and the even more profound impoverishment widowhood brings. Presided over by her Solon, who, like his prototype, lays down the law, she con-
tributes substantially to the family income, not just by attending to the
expected housekeeping tasks, but also by running a creamery, producing
large quantities of butter and cheese for sale. Nevertheless, as her lord believes her unentitled to any part of their joint earnings, she's forced to admit
that "I've never had control of a dollar in all my married life!" and is held in
such complete thralldom she must say to Edna, "I cannot harbor you as a
fugitive wife, daughter; not even if my heartstrings break with a longing to
do it" (10).[37] But as the narrative progresses, we find that such conditions
are not even the worst part of what Susan must endure. The ultimate indig-
nity comes when, after her husband dies, the entire estate is willed to their

eldest son, and Susan is left a pensioner on his charity, without a penny to call her own. Despite its cruelty, such a situation was common and well within the bounds of acceptable legal practice.[38] Susan could have fared worse. No wonder her dreams were filled with images of liberty in bondage.

In Sue Randolph we find, interestingly, another Susan, and another "S.R.," a ploy often used by Duniway in choosing names, to show the interchangeability of fates, particularly for all women subject to men's laws. Her situation represents not only the problems associated with a father's exclusive right to the custody of his children, but also the concern with the double standard expressed in the Centennial Protest. Edna was quick to support Sue after the latter's "fall," as soon as she was willing to sober up and reform, by which action the rest of the community was induced to accept her, despite its earlier reservations. Duniway adamantly demanded that women not suffer for moral lapses any more severely than men. In 1872, a prominent clergyman rose at an Oregon State Temperance Alliance meeting, objecting to an equal rights initiative, and charged "the sins of the world upon the mothers of men." He claimed that there were "twenty thousand fallen women in New York—two millions of them in America," and that decent citizens could not "afford to let this element vote." Enraged, Abigail countered:

> How *dare* you make such charges against the mothers of men? You tell us of two millions of fallen women who, you say, would vote for drunkenness; but what say you, sir, to the twenty millions of fallen men—all voters—whose patronage alone enables fallen women to live? Would you disfranchise them, sir? I pronounce your charge a libel upon womanhood, and I know that if we were voters you would not *dare* to utter it.[39]

These sentiments are echoed by Edna who, rebuking her mother who has complained about serving prostitutes and the mistresses of statesmen at the hotel, states plainly that "I make the bread and clothing and shelter for all of us by feeding the men who support them, mother. They are just as good as any man who visits them" (149).

Aunt Judy, of course, gets her comeuppance by being left "heartbroken and desolate," as well as destitute after her supposed husband dies, when she discovers that he was a bigamist and she's been the victim of a fraud. Nevertheless, even though she turned her back on Edna and woman's rights when her supposed honorable marriage brought her wealth and comfort, she is still somewhat of a sympathetic character in light of the aid she rendered at the story's outset, when even Edna's own mother was afraid to help. And yet, this doesn't present a conundrum. Judy can be seen to represent the inconstancy and lack of selflessness displayed by various erstwhile "supporters" of the woman's movement, or sometimes friends who flee when the going gets too rough. She also models the ability of each individual to affect outcomes for better or for worse, and the necessity of realizing that one cannot be too smug or secure, because under the current practice every woman is a potential victim and must act accordingly.

In Edna we find, of course, the whole issue of wifehood's equivalence to slavery. But we also find the problem of what to do about divorce, and the unfair laws regulating it, especially given the prevailing moral climate that allowed for divorce and remarriage only under certain very circumscribed conditions. There are many signs that Duniway herself was very unhappily married, particularly from the comments made in her personal letters—despite her public commendation of Ben's role in her work. During the later years of his life, before his final illness forced her to resume care of him, Ben lived in the Lost River area of Idaho while Abigail resided in Portland. They were virtually separated, but the need to maintain appearances was vital; her detractors would be eager to claim her case as an example of how extending rights to women would surely lead to the breakup of family life. In addition, Duniway was a woman of her age, despite her radicalism, and there is every indication that she was loath to see divorce except when suffering was so great that it became absolutely necessary. She would rather see bad marriages prevented, as she explained in an editorial published in the *New Northwest* January 5, 1876:

> We are not an advocate for "divorce made easy;" neither do we believe that separation between husband and wife should occur but for the gravest causes. . . . The only remedy, if there is a remedy for frequent divorce, and, far more frequent married misery, is in laws that will prohibit immature marriages, and careful training that will prevent precipitate action in a matter of such grave import. We would think it much more to the purpose if ministers should solemnly declare that they would not officiate at the marriage of persons under the age of twenty-five years, if the prevention of divorce is what they are aiming at.

Such views are reflected, not only in Edna's realization shortly after her marriage that boys and girls ought to be educated together on "the ethics of matrimony" (13), but also in her subsequent scheme to treat all people who elope "as outlaws till they'd come to their senses," feeding them bread and water in penitentiaries "till they had enough of each other, and then, if they wanted to continue the relation," allowing it, or otherwise granting amnesty (111). As Edna later states, "there should be a legal and honorable way to settle all matrimonial, as well as all other differences" (173), although the form that will take is as yet undetermined. What is clear, however, after the disastrous outcome of Edna's trial, is that present laws do not suffice, and matrimony that ought to be holy is more often a moral outrage.

The male characters in the story, even though for the most part less of a focus than their female counterparts, are also important, and representative as well. Mr. Handel materializes the whole heated debate on women from a Christian perspective, and LaSelle senior along with LaSelle junior, Solon Rutherford, John Smith and Jim Young all actualize the various ways in which women can be persecuted. Yet none are portrayed in a wholly negative light, and Mr. Shields is a veritable hero, bringing the armor of his rhetoric to woman's defense, showing that the only real protection a man can offer a woman is the granting of her rights. Duniway's readership was partly constituted by men, who also took active and prominent roles in the movement, and she knew full well that any changes in laws could only come as the result of actions taken by an all-male electorate. The happy endings most prevalent in her novels, showing that marriage could be a blessed state (although generally the second time around), effectively display that when men and women both change, conditions can improve for all.

John Smith is, by his name, the generic male, and as much of a type as Sambo. His fate displays the symbolic outcome that must take place if women, having become aware of the extent of their subjugation, begin to fight back and, illusions dispelled, assert their real power. Hence, when the old-fashioned female is no more, the old-fashioned male will self-destruct. The solution in this case might seem to be accidental, but by nearly decapitating himself it is truly a "far, far better thing"[40] that John does for Edna.

It is certain that Duniway did not blame John for his drunkenness. In all her writing, she is insistent in the belief that alcoholism is a disease that must be treated medically, and as she says in this case, "The victim to its ravages is unfit to run at large . . . there should be asylums all over the land for their proper treatment until cured" (169). Yet the fact remained that because present laws did not recognize this, but instead gave him absolute authority over Edna because "his extreme good nature when intoxicated had been amply proven" (156), Smith—the old Adam—had to go, and make way for a new prototype in the guise of Shields. Edna is not saved because of the law, but in spite of it, and because she fought back, which deprived John of life as he knew it and created circumstances under which he could not survive. When Edna, as a fugitive wife, could find sanctuary only in jail, she found that for American women "Canada" must be of their own creation. Because Edna could transcend the mentality imposed by enslavement to the point of willingness to break the law, she could claim her freedom.

## NOTES

1. John Stuart Mill, *The Subjection of Women,* 2d ed. (London: Longmans, 1869), 217.

2. In this Afterword, page references for quotations or specific sections of text in *Edna and John* are cited parenthetically.

3. This phrase is derived from the penultimate paragraph of the "Centennial Protest" authored by Susan B. Anthony, Matilda Joslyn Gage, and Elizabeth Cady Stanton, the same portion of the document from which the epigraph to *Edna and John* is drawn. For the complete text, see the following Appendix.

4. Eleanor Flexner, *Century of Struggle: The Woman's Rights Movement in the United States* (Cambridge: Belknap, 1959), 7–8.

5. In a move quite advanced for the day, the state of Connecticut passed a law in 1876 providing:

> husband and wife shall not by marriage acquire any right to the property of the other; that the husband shall be liable for all debts

incurred for the *joint* maintenance of husband, wife, and children; that the separate earnings of the wife shall be her own property; that the wife may make contracts or sell her real or personal property; that all her property shall be liable for debts; that the husband shall be liable for none of her debts contracted before marriage, nor for those contracted after, except for articles for the support of the family, or for the joint benefit of both, and that the husband and wife respectively, upon the death of the other, shall inherit during the remainder of life the use of one-third of the other's property. (*New Northwest* 4/13/77)

Such amelioration of the status quo was hailed as a major triumph.

6. Abigail Scott Duniway, "The Pacific Northwest" in *History of Woman Suffrage,* Vol. III, 1876–1885, eds. Susan B. Anthony, Elizabeth Cady Stanton, and Matilda Joslyn Gage (Rochester: Mann, 1886), 771. This chapter is Duniway's most extensive contribution to the compendious, six-volume *History of Woman Suffrage* that chronicles the movement from its beginnings until the passage of the Nineteenth Amendment.

7. Susan B. Anthony and Ida Husted Harper, eds., *The History of Woman Suffrage,* Vol. IV, 1883–1900 (Indianapolis: Hollenbeck, 1902), 896.

8. Oregon women had secured the right to vote in school-related elections in 1878 (widows with school-aged children were so entitled even earlier), but they would not win full voting privileges until 1914, six years in advance of the enactment of the Nineteenth Amendment providing for woman's suffrage on a national scale.

9. Although "suffragist" was used extensively, "suffragette" is a misnomer when applied to American women; they were never called this in their own era.

10. In 1869, the woman's movement split into two camps. The more radical wing (which advocated more widespread societal changes) was led by Susan B. Anthony and Elizabeth Cady Stanton and became the National Woman Suffrage Association (NWSA). The more conservative, headed by Lucy Stone and Henry Blackwell, became the American Woman Suffrage Association (AWSA). These groups were reunited in 1890 as the National American Woman Suffrage Association, although after unification the focus became increasingly geared towards suffrage alone and surrounding issues were in the background. For a complete discussion, see Eleanor Flexner's *Century of Struggle.*

11. However, "politics makes strange bedfellows." Despite the fact that Anthony and her associates were dedicated to the principle of equal rights for all, while quarreling with the leaders of the Republican party they accepted support from some others who had held proslavery sentiments and worked to deny African-American rights during the Reconstruction era.

12. Ida Husted Harper, *The Life and Work of Susan B. Anthony,* 2 vols. (Indianapolis: Hollenbeck, 1898), 265.

13. Ibid., 267.

14. The *New Northwest,* 1871–87. For the sake of convenience, most references from the *New Northwest* are cited in the text parenthetically as *NNW,* along with the publication date.

15. The minutes of the convention in June report:

> Mrs. Gage said that during the past hundred years man had had his share of the advantages of the Declaration of Independence, but woman at the outset of the second century of the Republic stood just where she had in 1776, not having the advantages which the declaration professed to give. There were, she continued, 20,000,000 women in America who were unable to say who shall rule them; they were governed solely by a sex not their own; they were taxed without representation, and were tried by those who were not their peers. In the Revolutionary day women looked forward to the rights of their posterity. Mrs. John Adams [Abigail Adams], the woman whose name had come down through years, wrote to her husband that she longed to hear that the men had declared a Declaration of Independence, but hoped that in a new code of laws the ladies would be remembered, and the injustice of their forefathers no longer perpetuated by the granting of absolute power to the husbands to the subjugation of the wives. The speaker, in concluding, said that if Woman Suffrage was not recognized by one of the great political parties before July 1876, its advocates proposed to celebrate the Fourth of July by issuing to the world their own Declaration of Independence, and added that if the political powers failed so to recognize their claim, the coming national celebration would not be a celebration of the independence of the whole, but only half, of the American people. (*NNW* 6/9/76)

16. The resolutions passed at the meeting are as follows:

> Whereas, The right of self-government inheres in the individual before governments are founded, constitutions framed, or courts created; and,
> Whereas, Governments exist to protect people in the enjoyment of their natural rights, and when any government becomes destructive of this end, it is the right of the people to resist and abolish it; and,
> Whereas, The women of the United States, for one hundred years have been denied the exercise of their natural right of self-government and self-protection; therefore,
> *Resolved,* That it is the natural right and most sacred duty of the women citizens of these United States to rebel against the injustice, usurpation, and tyranny of our present government.
> . . .
> Whereas, The men of 1776 rebelled against a government which did not claim to be of the people, but, on the contrary, upheld the "divine right of kings;" and,
> Whereas, The women of this nation to-day, under a government which claims to be based upon individual rights, to be "of the people, by the people, and for the people," in an infinitely greater degree are suffering all the wrongs which led to the war of the Revolution; and,
> Whereas, The oppression is all the more keenly felt because our masters, instead of dwelling in a foreign land, are our husbands, our fathers, our brothers, and our sons; therefore,
> *Resolved,* That the women of this nation, in 1876, have greater cause for discontent, rebellion, and revolution than our fathers of 1776.

...
*Resolved,* That with Abigail Adams in 1776, we believe that "the
passion for liberty cannot be strong in the breast of those who are
accustomed to deprive their fellow creatures of liberty; that, as
Abigail Adams predicted, "We are determined to foment a rebellion, and will not hold ourselves bound by laws in which we have
no voice or representation."

17. An account of the events that transpired along with a copy of the protest is
found in *History of Woman Suffrage,* Vol. III. Further details are supplied by
Harper in *The Life and Work of Susan B. Anthony.*

18. The *Declaration of Sentiments* was presented in 1848, at the convention held in
Seneca Falls, New York, which officially heralded the beginning of the woman's
movement.

19. See J.S. Ingram, *The Centennial Exposition,* (1876; Reprint, New York: Arno,
1976), 656–57. According to Ingram's account,

In front of Independence Hall a platform was erected.... The ceremonies in Independence Square began soon after ten a.m. There were
probably 50,000 people on that historic ground; even the trees were
filled with men and boys who were determined to see what was going
on. The stand upon which the exercises took place was a wooden
structure upon which workmen had been engaged for about a week.
It extended across the whole width of the north side of Independence
Square, in the rear of the State House, projecting from the building to
a distance of about seventy-five feet, the rear portion, against the
walls of the old State House, being at the height of the second floor
windows, from which access to the platform was obtained. The platform sloped gently down toward the front so that at the rail, where the
speaker's stand occupied the center, it was only a few feet from the
ground. Seats for 4,000 were provided upon it for invited guests, and
it is needless to say that every one was filled.

20. Harper, *The Life and Work of Susan B. Anthony,* 477.

21. Catherine Scott Coburn (1839–1913), Abigail's younger sister, served as associate editor of the *New Northwest* in 1874–79 (See Ruth Barnes Moynihan, *Rebel
for Rights: Abigail Scott Duniway* [New Haven: Yale University Press, 1983],
175). She later served as one of the editors of the Portland *Oregonian,* while
brother Harvey Scott was editor-in-chief.

22. Leonard J. Arrington, *History of Idaho* (Moscow: University of Idaho Press,
1994), 196.

23. On July 28 the *New Northwest* carried an announcement that "A New Serial
Story" would commence shortly, "the principal incidents of which she [Duniway]
doubtless collected during her recent visit to Idaho."

24. Arrington, *History of Idaho,* 195–96.

25. Ibid., 197.

26. Mill, *The Subjection of Women,* 161–65.

27. Moynihan, *Rebel for Rights,* 92, 173.

28. Ibid., 124–25.

29. Ibid., 120.

30. Mill, *The Subjection of Women,* 159.

31. Ibid., 32.

32. Harper, *The Life and Work of Susan B. Anthony,* 204.

33. Ibid.

34. Women's supposed duty to be submissive to their husbands because of Eve's curse and subsequent Pauline injunctions was one of the most difficult points to tackle for nineteenth-century feminists; any effective argument demanded reinterpreting the Bible in a more liberal fashion than most mainstream Christian denominations allowed. Mill countered the standard claim that women must display unconditional meekness of spirit by asserting:

> We shall be told, perhaps, that religion imposes the duty of obedience . . . it would be difficult to derive any such injunction from Christianity. We are told that St. Paul said, "Wives, obey your husbands:" but he also said, "Slaves, obey your masters." It was not St. Paul's business, nor was it consistent with his object, the propagation of Christianity, to incite any one to rebellion against existing laws. The apostle's acceptance of all social institutions as he found them, is no more to be construed as a disapproval of attempts to improve them at the proper time, than his declaration, "The powers that be are ordained of God," gives his sanction to military despotism, and to that alone, as the Christian form of political government, or commands passive obedience to it. (*The Subjection of Women,* 176–77)

Other arguments maintained that if Eve was cursed with pain in childbirth and the rule of her husband, then Adam was equally cursed to toil by the sweat of his brow (Genesis 3:16–19) and that it seemed to be allowable for men to alleviate the effects of the "curse" by lightening their toil, and so by the same reasoning women ought also to be able to work towards putting an end to such punishment instead of enduring it everlastingly.

35. Henry D. Thoreau, "Resistance to Civil Government," in *Walden and Resistance to Civil Government,* ed. William Rossi, 2d ed. (1849; Reprint, New York: Norton, 1922), 226–45.

36. Ibid., 235.

37. An article published in the *New Northwest* on September 1, 1876, and most likely authored by Duniway, entitled "The Reason Why," shows that Susan's plight is hardly unique:

> It is a fact too well established to provoke denial or excite controversy, that women are, as a rule, paupers. And this not because they are inefficient or indolent, for the reverse is easily provable. Now, when we see an effect, we know certainly that there is a cause, and, as women laborers who are wives and mothers—and their name is legion—are almost universally economical even to parsimony, and industrious

even to slavishness, and yet impecunious even to beggary, we know there must be a cause that produces so universal a result. We must thank our masculine friends for occasional, albeit unwitting, admissions that throw light upon the subject. For instance: We find in a recent exchange an account of the editor's visit to a large fruit farm, and he grows eloquent over the profusion and variety of fruits there grown, supplementing this with the information that the wife of the owner of the farm—not the joint owner, mind you—was busily employed in preserving, canning, and drying fruits; that she had several Chinamen and one Indian employed in gathering the fruits, and aiding her in preparing them for the market, and the belief was expressed that the *husband* would certainly make money out of it. Now comes the question, why not the *wife* "make money out of it?" If she were in the condition of the Chinamen or Indian, she would be sure of her wages. So much, at least, as there is. But for *her* toil and thrift and good management, her husband receives the reward. Think of a woman working like this and never owning a dollar. . . .

The husband himself will not probably claim that he has worked harder through the harvest just past than has his wife, yet the proceeds of the same are in his pocket, and she has "no money." Make the circuit of a thriving neighborhood, and see if this is not a true picture. Now, we ask in all candor, what incentive have women to industry, thrift and economy, when they are so defrauded during their wifehood by custom, and their widowhood by law of the control of even a portion of their own earnings? And what reason can possibly or plausibly be urged in favor of the continuance of such injustice? The custom itself was founded upon physical force, and is pampered by selfishness, and would, in many instances, be easily vanquished if man would only stop and think about it.

38. An editorial entitled "Women and the Law" (also probably written by Duniway) appearing in the *New Northwest* on January 14, 1876, described the law as it existed in Oregon and discussed, quite satirically but in all seriousness, its possible application:

Most women have an idea, somewhat undefined, it is true, that the laws regarding their property rights discriminate very unjustly against them in the disposal of property acquired during the continuance of the marriage contract. True, they have heard of "widow's thirds," "widow's jointure and dower," etc., etc., and may have vaguely wondered if the laws are so beneficent to women, why they never hear anything about "widower's thirds," or disposal of property after the death of a wife.

Let us consult the general laws of Oregon, and see what light they will throw upon this subject. We find in Chap. XVII., I., "that the widow of every deceased person shall be entitled to dower, or the use, during her natural life, of one-third part of all the lands whereof her husband was seized of an estate of inheritance, at any time during the marriage, *unless she is lawfully barred thereof*"—not even one-third, mind you, that shall be her own, to dispose of in any manner that she shall see fit, as a widower might do with the whole estate, but simply one-third to *use* during her natural life, unless *lawfully barred thereof.* But this is not all, for we find in par. 13 of the same chapter that "when a widow is entitled to dower in the lands of which her husband died seized, she may continue to occupy the same with the children or other heirs of the deceased, or may receive one-third of the rents, issues, and profits thereof"—mark now—"so long as the heirs or others interested do not object." In other words, a widow may continue to occupy a home she has helped to earn, until some one is seized with a desire to turn her out of doors. Isn't this a strong incentive, women, toward living a life of economy, toil, and self-denial, that thereby you may have a shelter for your age? Don't it make you feel like saving and scrimping, doing without things yourselves, and sitting up nights to turn clothes for heirs that in turn may, if they choose, turn you from the home earned by such pitiful economy?

But do not despair, for we find in par. 23 the following cheering provision, to wit: "A widow may remain in the dwelling-house of her husband one year after his death, without being chargeable for rent therefor, and shall have her reasonable sustenance out of the estate for one year."

Just pause, we beseech you, and contemplate the munificence of this most munificent proviso. One whole year free of rent in your own house, and somebody who knows perhaps nothing of your needs to decide what shall be *reasonable* sustenance for the same period! Surely women should sit forever in abject thankfulness at the feet of their law-givers, speaking only to extol their bounty.

39. Duniway, "The Pacific Northwest," 772.

40. Charles Dickens, *A Tale of Two Cities* (1859; Bungay, Suffolk, Great Britain: Penguin, 1971), 404. In the conclusion, ne'er-do-well Sydney Carton heroically takes the place of a more worthy friend on the guillotine, saying, "It is a far, far better thing that I do, than I have ever done; it is a far, far better rest that I go to than I have ever known."

# APPENDIX

## THE NATIONAL CENTENNIAL
## EQUAL RIGHTS PROTEST

by Susan B. Anthony, Matilda Joslyn Gage & Elizabeth Cady Stanton
presented to the President of the United States, Ulysses S. Grant,
at the United States Centennial Celebration
in Philadelphia, Pennsylvania
July 4, 1876

**W**HILE THE NATION IS BUOYANT with patriotism, and all hearts are attuned to praise, it is with sorrow we come to strike the one discordant note, on this one-hundredth anniversary of our country's birth. When subjects of kings, emperors, and czars, from the old world join in our national jubilee, shall the women of the republic refuse to lay their hands with benedictions on the nation's head? Surveying America's exposition, surpassing in magnificence those of London, Paris, and Vienna, shall we not rejoice at the success of the youngest rival among the nations of the earth? May not our hearts, in unison with all, swell with pride at our great achievements as a people; our free speech, free press, free schools, free church, and the rapid progress we have made in material wealth, trade, commerce and the inventive arts? And we do rejoice in the success, thus far, of our experiment of self-government. Our faith is firm and unwavering in the broad principles of human rights proclaimed in 1776, not only as abstract truths, but as the cornerstones of a republic. Yet we cannot forget, even in this glad hour, that while all men of every race, and clime, and condition, have been invested with the full rights of citizenship under our hospitable flag, all women still suffer the degradation of disfranchisement.

The history of our country the past hundred years has been a series of assumptions and usurpations of power over woman, in direct opposition to the principles of just government, acknowledged by the United States as its foundation, which are:

*First*—The natural rights of each individual.
*Second*—The equality of these rights.
*Third*—That rights not delegated are retained by the individual.

212 Edna and John

*Fourth*—That no person can exercise the rights of others without delegated authority.

*Fifth*—That the non-use of rights does not destroy them.

And for the violation of these fundamental principles of our government, we arraign our rulers on this Fourth day of July, 1876—and these are our articles of impeachment:

*Bills of attainder* have been passed by the introduction of the word "male" into all the State constitutions, denying to women the right of suffrage, and thereby making sex a crime—an exercise of power clearly forbidden in article I, sections 9, 10, of the United States constitution.

*The writ of habeas corpus*, the only protection against *lettres de cachet* and all forms of unjust imprisonment, which the constitution declares "shall not be suspended, except when in cases of rebellion or invasion the public safety demands it," is held inoperative in every State of the Union, in the case of a married woman against her husband—the marital rights of the husband being in all cases primary, and the rights of the wife secondary.

*The right of trial by a jury of one's peers* was so jealously guarded that States refused to ratify the original constitution until it was guaranteed by the sixth amendment. And yet the women of this nation have never been allowed a jury of their peers—being tried in all cases by men, native and foreign, educated and ignorant, virtuous and vicious. Young girls have been arraigned in our courts for the crime of infanticide; tried, convicted, hanged—victims, perchance, of judge, jurors, advocates—while no woman's voice could be heard in their defense. And not only are women denied a jury of their peers, but in some cases, jury trial altogether. During the war, a woman was tried and hanged by military law, in defiance of the fifth amendment, which specifically declares: "No person shall be held to answer for a capital or otherwise infamous crime, unless on a presentment or indictment of a grand jury, except in cases . . . of persons in actual service in time of war." During the last presidential campaign, a woman, arrested for voting, was denied the protection of a jury, tried, convicted, and sentenced to a fine and costs of prosecution, by the absolute power of a judge of the Supreme Court of the United States.

*Taxation without representation*, the immediate cause of the rebellion of the colonies against Great Britain, is one of the grievous wrongs the women of this country have suffered during the century. Deploring war, with all the demoralization that follows in its train, we have been taxed to support standing armies, with their waste of life and wealth. Believing in temperance, we have been taxed to support the vice, crime and pauperism of the liquor traffic. While we suffer its wrongs and abuses infinitely more than man, we have no power to protect our sons against this giant evil. During the temperance crusade, mothers were arrested, fined, imprisoned, for even praying and singing in the streets, while men blockade the sidewalks with impunity, even on Sunday, with their military parades and political processions. Believing in honesty, we are taxed to support a dangerous army of civilians, buying and selling the offices of government and sacrificing the best interests of the people. And, moreover, we are taxed to support the very legislators and judges who make laws, and render decisions adverse to woman. And for refusing to pay such unjust taxation, the houses, lands, bonds, and stock of women have been seized and sold within the present year, thus proving Lord Coke's assertion, that "The very act of taxing a man's property without his consent is, in effect, disfranchising him of every civil right."

*Unequal codes for men and women.* Held by law a perpetual minor, deemed incapable of self-protection, even in the industries of the world, woman is denied equality of rights. The fact of sex, not the quantity or quality of work, in most cases, decides the pay and position; and because of this injustice thousands of fatherless girls are compelled to choose between a life of shame and starvation. Laws catering to man's vices have created two codes of morals in which laws, women are fined and imprisoned if found alone in the streets, or in public places of resorts, at certain hours. Under the pretense of regulating public morals, police officers seizing the occupants of disreputable houses, march the women in platoons to prison, while the men, partners in their guilt, go free. While making a show of virtue in forbidding the importation of Chinese women on the Pacific coast for immoral purposes, our rulers, in many states, and even under the shadow of the national capitol, are now proposing to legalize the sale of American womanhood for the same vile purposes.

*Special legislation for woman* has placed us in a most anomalous position. Women invested with the rights of citizens in one section—voters, jurors, office-holders—crossing an imaginary line, are subjects in the next. In some States, a married woman may hold property and transact business in her own name; in others, her earnings belong to her husband. In some States, a woman may testify against her husband, sue and be sued in the courts; in others, she has no redress in case of damage to person, property, or character. In case of divorce on account of adultery in the husband, the innocent wife is held to possess no right to children or property, unless by special decree of the court. But in no State of the Union has the wife the right to her own person, or to any part of the joint earnings of the co-partnership during the life of her husband. In some States women may enter the law schools and practice in the courts; in others they are forbidden. In some universities girls enjoy equal educational advantages with boys, while many of the proudest institutions in the land deny them admittance, though the sons of China, Japan and Africa are welcomed there. But the privileges already granted in the several States are by no means secure. The right of suffrage once exercised by women in certain States and territories has been denied by subsequent legislation. A bill is now pending in congress to disfranchise the women of Utah, thus interfering to deprive United States citizens of the same rights which the Supreme Court has declared the national government powerless to protect anywhere. Laws passed after years of untiring effort, guaranteeing married women certain rights of property, and mothers the custody of their children, have been repealed in States where we supposed all was safe. Thus have our most sacred rights been made the football of legislative caprice, proving that a power which grants as a privilege what by nature is a right, may withhold the same as a penalty when deeming it necessary for its own perpetuation.

*Representation of woman* has had no place in the nation's thought. Since the incorporation of the thirteen original States, twenty-four have been admitted to the Union, not one of which has recognized woman's right of self-government. On this birthday of our national liberties, July Fourth, 1876, Colorado, like all her elder sisters, comes into the Union with the invidious word "male" in her constitution.

*Universal manhood suffrage*, by establishing an aristocracy of sex, imposes upon the women of this nation a more absolute and cruel despotism than monarchy; in that, woman finds a political master in her father, husband, brother, son. The aristocracies of the old world are based upon birth, wealth, refinement, education, nobility, brave deeds of chivalry; in this nation, on sex alone; exalting brute force above moral power, vice above virtue, ignorance above education, and the son above the mother who bore him.

*The judiciary above the nation* has proved itself out the echo of the party in power, by upholding and enforcing laws that are opposed to the spirit and letter of the constitution. When the slave power was dominant, the Supreme Court decided that a black man was not a citizen, because he had not the right to vote; and when the constitution was so amended as to make all persons citizens, the same high tribunal decided that a woman, though a citizen, had not the right to vote. Such vacillating interpretations of constitutional law unsettle our faith in judicial authority, and undermine the liberties of the whole people.

These articles of impeachment against our rulers we now submit to the impartial judgment of the people. To all these wrongs and oppressions woman has not submitted in silence and resignation. From the beginning of the century, when Abigail Adams, the wife of one president and mother of another, said, "We will not hold ourselves bound to obey laws in which we have no voice or representation," until now, woman's discontent has been steadily increasing, culminating nearly thirty years ago in a simultaneous movement among the women of the nation, demanding the right of suffrage. In making our just demands, a higher motive than the pride of sex inspires us; we feel that national safety and stability depend on the complete recognition of the broad principles of our government. *Woman's degraded, helpless position is the weak point in our institutions to-day; a disturbing force everywhere, severing family ties, filling our asylums with the deaf, the dumb, the blind; our prisons with criminals, our cities with drunkenness and prostitution; our homes with disease and death.* It was the boast of the founders of the republic, that the rights for which they contended were the rights of human nature. If these rights are ignored in the case of one-half the people, the nation is surely preparing for its downfall. Governments try themselves. The recognition of a governing and a governed class is incompatible with the first principles of freedom. Woman has not been a heedless spectator of the events of this century, nor a dull listener to the grand arguments for the equal rights of humanity. From the earliest history of our country woman has shown equal devotion with man to the cause of freedom, and has stood firmly by his side in its defense. Together, they have made this country what it is. Woman's wealth, thought and labor have cemented the stones at every monument man has reared to liberty.

And now, at the close of a hundred years, as the hour-hand of the great clock that marks the centuries points to 1876, we declare our faith in the principles of self-government; our full equality with man in natural rights; that woman was made first for her own happiness, with the absolute right to herself—to all the opportunities and advantages life affords for her complete development; and we deny that dogma of the centuries, incorporated in the codes of all nations—that woman was made for man—her best interests, in all cases, to be sacrificed to his will. We ask of our rulers, at this hour, no special favors, no special privileges, no special legislation. We ask justice, we ask equality, we ask that all the civil and political rights that belong to citizens of the United States, be guaranteed to us and our daughters forever.

# SELECTED BIBLIOGRAPHY

## PUBLISHED WORKS BY
## ABIGAIL SCOTT DUNIWAY

*Captain Gray's Company, or Crossing the Plains and Living in Oregon.* Portland, Oregon: S.J. McCormick, 1859.
*David and Anna Matson.* New York: S.R. Wells, 1876.
*From the West to the West: Across the Plains to Oregon.* Chicago: A.C. McClurg, 1905.
"Journal of a Trip to Oregon." Ed. Kenneth L. Holmes and David C. Duniway. *Covered Wagon Women: Diaries and Letters from the Western Trails, 1840–1890.* Vol. 5. Glendale, California: Arthur H. Clark, 1986. 39–135. *Also* reprint, Lincoln: University of Nebraska Press, 1997.
*Path Breaking: An Autobiographical History of the Equal Suffrage Movement in Pacific Coast States.* 2d ed. Portland, Oregon: James, Kerns, & Abbot, 1914. Reprint, New York: Shocken, 1971.
Newspapers edited by Duniway:
    The *Coming Century* (Portland). 1891. [Oregon Collection, University of Oregon Library, Eugene].
    The *New Northwest* (Portland). 1871–87. [Oregon Historical Society, Portland. University of Oregon Library, Eugene. Microfilm.]
    The *Pacific Empire* (Portland). 1895–98. [Multnomah County Library, Portland. Bound volumes contain: 16 August 1895; 3 October 1895 to 11 February 1897; 10 March 1898 to 23 June 1898. Oregon Historical Society, Portland. Unbound issues include: 3 October 1895 to 11 February 1897; 2 September 1987 to 7 July 1898.]
Serialized novels in the *New Northwest:*
    *Judith Reid, A Plain Story of a Plain Woman.* 12 May 1871–22 Dec. 1871.
    *Ellen Dowd, The Farmers Wife.* Part one, 5 Jan. 1872–26 April 1872. Part two, 1 July 1873–26 Sept. 1873.
    *Amie and Henry Lee; or, The Spheres of the Sexes.* 29 May 1874–13 Nov. 1874.
    *The Happy Home; or, The Husband's Triumph.* 20 Nov. 1874–14 May 1875.
    *Captain Gray's Company; or, Crossing the Plains and Living in Oregon.* 21 May 1875–29 Oct. 1875.
    *One Woman's Sphere; or, The Mystery of Eagle Cove.* 4 June 1875–3 Dec. 1875.
    *Madge Morrison, The Molalla Maid and Matron.* 10 Dec. 1875–28 July 1876.
    *Edna and John, A Romance of Idaho Flat.* 29 Sept. 1875–15 June 1877.
    *Martha Marblehead, The Maid and Matron of Chehalem.* 29 June 1877–8 Feb. 1878.
    *Her Lot; or, How She was Protected.* 1 Feb. 1878–19 Sept. 1878.
    *Fact, Fact and Fancy; or, More Ways of Living than One.* 26 Sept. 1878–15 May 1879.

*Mrs. Hardine's Will.* 20 Nov. 1879–26 Aug. 1880.
*The Mystery of Castle Rock, A Story of the Pacific Northwest.* 2 March 1882–7 Sept. 1882.
*Judge Dunson's Secret, An Oregon Story.* 15 March 1883–6 Sept. 1883.
*Laban McShane, A Frontier Story.* 13 Sept. 1883–6 March 1884.
*Dux, A Maiden Who Dared.* 11 Sept. 1884–5 March 1885.
*The De Launcy Curse; or, The Law of Heredity—A Tale of Three Generations.* 10 Sept. 1885–4 March 1886.
*Blanche Le Clerq, A Tale of the Mountain Mines.* 2 Sept. 1886–24 Feb. 1887.
Serialized novels in the *Pacific Empire*:
*Shack-Locks: A Story of the Times.* 3 Oct. 1895–26 March 1896.
*'Bijah's Surprises, An Up To Date Story* (a.k.a. *Margaret Rudson: A Pioneer Story.).* Book one, 2 April 1896–26 Sept. 1896. Book two, 1 Oct. 1896–31 Dec. 1896.
*The Old and the New.* 7 Jan. 1897–30 Dec. 1897.

# SOURCES ON ABIGAIL SCOTT DUNIWAY

"Abigail Scott Duniway Addresses the Idaho Constitutional Convention." *Idaho Yesterdays* 34 (1990): 21–27.

Anthony, Susan B., Elizabeth Cady Stanton, and Matilda Joslyn Gage, eds. *History of Woman Suffrage.* Vol. III, 1876–1885. Rochester: Mann, 1886.

Anthony, Susan B., and Ida Husted Harper, eds. *The History of Woman Suffrage.* Vol. IV, 1883–1900. Indianapolis: Hollenbeck, 1902.

Bennion, Sherilyn Cox. "The *New Northwest* and *Woman's Exponent:* Early Voices for Suffrage." *Journalism Quarterly* 54 (1977): 286–92.

Clark, Malcolm H., Jr. "The War on the Webfoot Saloon." *Oregon Historical Quarterly* 58 (1957): 48–62.

Douthit, Mary Osborn. "Abigail Scott Duniway, Mother and Home Builder." *The Souvenir of Western Women.* Portland, Oregon: Anderson & Duniway, 1905. 43.

Duniway, David D. Introduction. "Journal of a Trip to Oregon." *Covered Wagon Women: Diaries and Letters from the Western Trails, 1840–1890.* Vol. 5. Ed. Kenneth L. Holmes and David C. Duniway. Glendale, California: Arthur H. Clark, 1986. 21–38.

Flexner, Eleanor. *Century of Struggle: The Woman's Rights Movement in the United States.* Cambridge: Belknap, 1959.

_____. Introduction. *Path Breaking: An Autobiographical History of the Equal Suffrage Movement in Pacific Coast States* [Abigail Scott Duniway. 1914] New York: Schocken, 1971.vii–xviii.

Gaston, Joseph. *Portland Oregon: Its History and Builders.* 4 vols. Chicago: S.J. Clarke, 1911.

Horner, John B. *Oregon Literature.* Corvallis: n.p., 1899.

Kessler, Lauren. "The Fight for Woman Suffrage and the Oregon Press." *Women in Pacific Northwest History: An Anthology.* Ed. Karen J. Blair. Seattle: University of Washington Press, 1988. 43–58.

_____. "A Siege of the Citadels: The Search for a Public Forum for the Ideas of Oregon Woman Suffrage." *Oregon Historical Quarterly* 84 (1983): 117–50.

Larson, T.A. "Dolls, Vassals, and Drudges—Pioneer Women in the West." *Western Historical Quarterly* 3 (1972): 1–16.

_____. "Idaho's Role in America's Woman Suffrage Crusade. *Idaho Yesterdays* 18 (1974): 2–15.

_____. "Woman's Rights in Idaho." *Idaho Yesterdays* 16 (1972): 2–19.

Morrison, Dorothy Nafus. *Ladies Were Not Expected: Abigail Scott Duniway and Women's Rights.* New York: Atheneum, 1977. Reprint, Portland: Oregon Historical Society Press, 1997.

Moynihan, Ruth Barnes. Introduction. *Covered Wagon Women: Diaries and Letters from the Western Trails, 1852.* Vol. 5. Ed. Kenneth L. Holmes and David C. Duniway. Bison Books ed. Lincoln: University of Nebraska Press, 1997. vii–xiii.

_____. "Of Women's Rights and Freedom: Abigail Scott Duniway." *Women in Pacific Northwest History: An Anthology.* Ed. Karen J. Blair. Seattle: University of Washington Press, 1988. 9–24.

_____. *Rebel for Rights: Abigail Scott Duniway.* New Haven: Yale University Press, 1983.

Nelson, Herbert B. *The Literary Impulse in Pioneer Oregon.* Corvallis: Oregon State College Press, 1948.

Powers, Alfred. *History of Oregon Literature.* Portland: Metropolitan Press, 1935.

Ross, Nancy Wilson. *Westward the Women.* New York: Knopf, 1944.

Scott, Harvey. *History of the Oregon Country.* 6 vols. New York: Cambridge, 1924.

Solomon, Martha M., ed. *A Voice of Their Own: The Woman Suffrage Press, 1840–1910.* Tuscaloosa: University of Alabama Press, 1991.

Victor, Frances Fuller. "Literature." *History of Oregon. Vol II. 1848–1888. The Works of Hubert Howe Bancroft.* 39 vols. San Francisco: History Co., 1883–90.

Ward, Jean M. "Abigail Scott Duniway: Oregon's Pioneer Feminist." *Portland Scribe* 5 (1976): 1. Reprint, *Old Stuff* [Portland] 2 (1977): 1.

_____. "Women's Responses to Systems of Male Authority: Communications Strategies in the Novels of Abigail Scott Duniway." Diss., University of Oregon, 1989.

Ward, Jean M., and Elaine A. Maveety, eds. *Pacific Northwest Women 1815–1925: Lives, Memories, and Writings.* Corvallis: Oregon State University Press, 1995.

Willard, Frances E., and Mary A. Livermore, eds. *A Woman of the Century: Fourteen Hundred-Seventy Biographical Sketches Accompanied by Portraits of Leading American Women in All Walks of Life* [1893]. Reprint, Detroit: Gale Research, 1967.

# ABOUT THE EDITOR

## DEBRA SHEIN

Debra Shein lives near Pocatello, in southeast Idaho, where she teaches English at Idaho State University. She received her Ph.D. with an emphasis on nineteenth-century American literature and studies of the American West from the University of Oregon in Eugene. She became interested in the life and work of Abigail Scott Duniway as a graduate student, while working at the University of Oregon library, readying the Duniway papers for public view. Captivated by Duniway's charisma, she devoted herself to the project of recovering the serialized novels published in the 1870s through 1890s in Duniway's newspapers, the *New Northwest* and the *Pacific Empire,* but not produced in book form in their own time. The research on the Duniway novels has been assisted by a grant from the Center for the Study of Women in Society.

Shein, who was born in New York and grew up in southern California, has also lived on an Israeli kibbutz, and in remote areas of Alaska and British Columbia. "As a young mother," she reminisces, "I lived for nearly five years in the Canadian bush, 60 miles from the nearest town, where I gave birth at home, hauled water by hand from a dug well, boiled water on a wood stove to wash cloth diapers, and trimmed the wicks on kerosene lamps. Although my life in the 1970s and 80s was far, far easier than the sort of life experienced by frontierswomen such as Duniway, her contemporaries, and her fictional heroines in the 1850s through 1890s, I believe that my own experiences have given me a profound appreciation for the nearly miraculous determination that transformed a generation of pioneer farm wives into the vanguard of the woman's movement. The stupendous efforts and trials endured by Duniway and the other female political activists of that era, particularly those of the West who would lead the nation to equal suffrage, are exemplified in fiction by Edna of her 1876 novel, *Edna and John.* Their accomplishment cannot be overrated, and should not be forgotten."